Allison Dickson has been writing novels and short stories for over a decade. After having a small hit with an independently published novel, she found her home in the world of dark thrillers and psychological suspense. When she isn't writing, she's usually overdosing on true crime shows, crocheting something cute and/or creepy, or wandering the urban sprawl of Dayton, Ohio with her husband and two teenagers.

Allison keeps a semi-regular blog full of ramblings at www.allisonmdickson.com, and you can also find her on Twitter (@MsAllieD) and Facebook (AuthorAllisonMDickson).

The
Other
Mrs
Miller

ALLISON DICKSON

SPHERE

First published in the United States in 2019 by G.P. Putnam's Sons,
a division of Penguin Random House US
First published in Great Britain in 2019 by Sphere
This paperback edition published by Sphere in 2020

13 5 7 9 10 8 6 4 2

A CIP catalogue record for this book
is available from the British Library.

ISBN 978-0-7515-7479-1

Printed and bound in Great Britain by Clays Ltd, Elcograf S.p.A.

Papers used by Sphere are from well-managed forests
and other responsible sources.

For Ken,
who has seen and
loved every version of me

The
Other
Mrs
Miller

PART 1

MRS MILLER

CHAPTER 1

THE BLUE CAR is there again this morning. It's parked just down the block, never in the same spot twice, but always within easy view of Phoebe's peering eyes. The older Ford Focus, with its rusted fenders and a cracked windshield that makes seeing the driver almost impossible, even with powerful binoculars, would go unnoticed almost anywhere else in Chicago. But on a quiet Lake Forest street, where a three-year-old Land Rover seems ancient, it sticks out like a rotting incisor in a set of bleached teeth. The only clue to the driver's identity is a magnet on the front passenger door that reads *Executive Courier Services*, but she has yet to see any delivery take place.

Phoebe isn't exactly sure when the car first started showing up, but once she noticed its repeat visits, she began keeping a log like the sort of busybody neighborhood watch captain who would ordinarily annoy her. In the little notebook are three columns: when the car arrives, where it parks, when it leaves. The appearances seemed more sporadic at first, maybe two or three times a week, for an hour at most. But for the last week, the car has been there daily and staying for at least three hours, sometimes as many as five, well beyond any normal break in a workday. If the occupant has exited to so much as stretch their legs, Phoebe hasn't noticed. She has considered asking the neighbors what they think about this interloper, but in the years she's lived in this house, she hasn't gone out of her way to make friends with any of them.

It's not that she doesn't like people. She just . . . well, maybe that isn't too far from the truth. People are burdensome beasts, always prepared to lump their expectations onto you. This is especially true if your name lends you a little status, however dubious that status may now be.

She's tried expressing these concerns to her husband, but Wyatt thinks she's being paranoid, about both the recurring car and what the neighbors probably think of her. He insists it's just stress, that the media frenzy will pass when someone else either dies or says something stupid approximately three seconds from now. Because he's a therapist, his smugness when he says these things is thick enough to gag her. The subtext, of course, is that she has far too little to do with her day if parked cars and imagined gossip are the sorts of things that occupy her mind. He may be right, but it still makes her grit her teeth.

Calling the police is an option she's mulled over a few times, but what exactly would she say? This isn't a gated community. People can come and go as they please. A lifetime ago, a less reclusive Phoebe wasn't interested in a walled-off fortress like so many of the other places here, or especially like her father's oppressive lakefront estate in Glencoe. She was taken by this house's relative normalcy, how openly the modest-by-comparison Tudor-style home at the end of the lush cul-de-sac presented itself to the world, with only a couple of neighboring houses in decent but not overly intimate proximity. That accessibility is biting her in the ass now with this car in the picture, but then again, she's received no threats or strange phone calls. All she has is exhaustion-fueled speculation, and not even a description of the driver, who she's about 90 percent positive is either a woman or a very slight man, based mostly on the petite silhouette. The only other details she can note with any confidence are the light blue shirt and baseball cap, an apparent uniform. *Because she's probably just a flipping delivery driver,* she thinks in her husband's calmly exasperated voice. So no, she won't call the cops. Not until she has a real reason.

Of course, Phoebe could put all these questions to rest right now. Just step outside, walk up to the car, knock on the window, and kindly ask what they want. But with everything else going on, she can't handle the thought of being even a little humiliated. What if this really is just some lowly courier who likes to sit there for breaks and catch up on paperwork? Or a friend of one of the neighbors Phoebe has spent years ignoring? She can already hear them gossiping. *Oh, her? That's Phoebe Miller. Haven't you heard of her? Well, surely you know about her father . . .*

Then there's the worst-case scenario, that this courier could actually be a reporter scoping her out, waiting to catch some unflattering footage of a disheveled heiress at the height of her paranoid desperation. The public would cease to function without its regular dose of schadenfreude, after all. Why shouldn't she have her time in the limelight?

But she's also begun to consider a likelier reason for her

inaction: watching this car has become a game for her, a blip in her otherwise flat line of a day. The truth of this person is probably so mundane, it would only add to her depression if she learned it, so why bother? Let her enjoy this one odd thing. It won't last forever. Nothing does.

After making note of today's appearance, she returns to the kitchen to refill her coffee and focus on other things, like what Wyatt wants for dinner tonight, and whether he's going to watch the remaining episodes of *Game of Thrones* with her or if she should go ahead and knock them out herself. Ah, the glamorous life. He's currently slurping down a bowl of cereal, and the sound immediately grates on her nerves. Has he always done that, or is she just now starting to notice it after ten years?

She's discovered several other micro-habits of his lately that make her fantasize about bludgeoning him with an iron skillet like an old-fashioned cartoon wife. For instance, when he pretends he's about to laugh right after he says something passive-aggressive, which seems to be every other sentence that leaves his mouth these days. Or the way he licks his finger every time he turns a page in a magazine; Phoebe is certain she can now hear the rubbing of his tongue against the ridges of his fingertips, and she has to leave the room as soon as she sees him going for his *Newsweek* or *Rolling Stone*. In a more cliché man move, he has also started leaving his hair in their bathroom sink after he cleans out his electric razor. But of all the ways her husband has found to grind her gears, she's sure it's the disgusting racket of his slurping, crunching, and tearing into his every meal that will finally send her over the edge. She recently read about a study linking a sensitivity to eating sounds to a higher IQ. Phoebe is sure she now qualifies for a Mensa membership.

She soothes herself with a simple thought. In just a few minutes, he will be off to work. Blessed silence will soon wrap around her like a fuzzy blanket, at which point she'll lock all the doors, arm the security system, and return to bed, spreading her arms and legs wide across both sides like a starfish. Sometime around noon, she will get up, put on her bathing suit, and bring a book and a bottle of wine poolside. Two hours before Wyatt comes home from work, she will put on actual clothes and brush her hair, trying to ignore the outgrown roots and the split ends that have cropped up over the months since she last visited a salon. She'll dab on a little makeup, hoping to hide the deepening lines around her eyes and brighten her increasingly sallow complexion. She will put on clothes that have a bit of extra stretch in them to accommodate her ever-widening rear end.

She can't recall suddenly letting herself go. It feels like more of a gradual surrender. Even two years ago, she wouldn't have thought twice about spending hours in the salon, or covering herself in dozens of expensive serums and creams designed to make women think they can roll back the miles on the odometer. She vividly recalls spending two or three hours a day in the gym, while partaking in whatever fad diet promised to keep the dreaded muffin top at bay if she just avoided this One Newly Reviled Ingredient. That pampered cream-puff version of herself hadn't yet succumbed to several failed fertility treatments. She also hadn't watched the father she'd spent most of her life fearing, hating, and loving in painfully equal measure die so rapidly of pancreatic cancer that he'd had no time to leave her with any of the closure or apologies he'd surely spent his whole life hoping to gift her.

Now, in the aftermath of Daniel's death, she more closely resembles an *actual* cream puff—pale, a bit round, only a whole lot less sweet. That's mostly thanks to the fertility hormones that wreaked havoc on her system, but the daily ice cream and booze regimen isn't helping. Some good has come from this transition, however. For instance, she's rediscovered the grace in being childless, and how it affords limitless opportunities for poolside reading and day drinking. She has also found nirvana in wearing yoga pants with no intention of doing poses, peace in ignoring ingredient lists, calories, and macro counts. Her favorite synonym for serenity is French: cabernet sauvignon.

She also embraces the quiet ease of a shut-in lifestyle, where all incoming calls are sent to the oubliette of an overflowing voicemail box, where her father's misdeeds are just a headline she scrolls by in search of another mindless quiz that promises to tell her what kind of cheese she is (gouda) or which country she should have been born in (Switzerland, neutrally). Daniel Noble may be the source of the trust fund that affords her this life, but she isn't responsible for the man himself. She considers the family fortune a well-earned restitution for having to grow up with the bastard.

Wyatt doesn't seem to have noticed this quiet evolution of his wife, or if he has, he's choosing to ignore it. Despite knowing she's given up the fertility treatments, he's still asking her if she's ovulating before sex, a question that would hobble any normal person's libido at the starting line.

After he finishes his breakfast, he rinses his bowl and places it in the dishwasher. At least he still has a few good habits. But he doesn't pick up his keys. Instead, he comes back to the table. "My first appointment isn't until ten. Want to sit out back for a bit?"

She hesitates. This is aberrant. Even when he has extra time in the morning, he usually spends it at the office catching up on paperwork. He must want to discuss something, which is a guarantee they'll end up in a petty argument of some sort. But the faster they get through whatever is on his mind, the sooner she can have her blessed solitude. She nods and follows him outside, where she sits on one of the long couches.

Their covered porch has nicer furniture than most people's houses, complete with a full kitchen, bar, and integrated stereo system. Propane heaters placed around the perimeter ensure they can use the space late into autumn if they want, but usually she covers everything back here in October. This would have made her sad once, but now she's looking forward to winter, when Chicago's famously miserable cold and snow will provide a much more natural barricade to going out into the world.

Wyatt has his briefcase with him, which makes him look more like a trial lawyer than someone who relays platitudes and affirmations to menopausal divorcées and stressed-out bankers who can't get it up anymore. Upon closer inspection, his shirt looks new and pressed, and she's never seen that tie before. Phoebe also notices his neatly groomed hair, combed and carefully smoothed with one of the many tubes of product she's bought him over the years that mostly go unused. His baby-smooth face hints that he shaved with a blade rather than an electric razor. For some reason, he wants to look good this morning, and Phoebe doesn't like it.

He's handsome in the classic sense. Strong jaw, dark hair, and eyes with lashes so thick he almost looks like he's wearing eyeliner. Those eyes attracted her in the very beginning when they locked drunken gazes at a mutual friend's Super Bowl party back in their Northwestern years. In those days—nearly fifteen years ago now, she shudders to think—good looks were all it took to get her heart pumping for just about any guy. But it was Wyatt's combination of brains, sense of humor, and taste for mischief that made her come back for a second date and countless others after that. So long ago now are those days of clandestine sex in public places, crashing parties, and racing his old Mitsubishi Eclipse along Lower Wacker in the middle of the night while passing a small joint between them, that sometimes it's only those eyes that remind her he's the same rebellion against all of Daniel Noble's prerequisites for a son-in-law. A middle-class guy who had enough smarts and ambition to get into a prestigious school like Northwestern but never got all the way to his PhD.

"I think it's time for us to consider next steps," he says, sitting next to her. His tone is hard to read, but there's the barest quaver in his voice, like he's nervous. She feels a bit of that in her own gut too, but it's time they acknowledge this deep chill between them, which dates back to long before Daniel's death and the drama that's followed on its heels.

She thinks immediately of their four failed attempts with in vitro, but she knows it goes back even further, to the reason they got married in the first place: an unexpected plus sign in the result window of a drugstore pregnancy test. Heavily under the influence of romance and freshly surging pregnancy hormones, Phoebe considered an abortion for all of thirty seconds before swiping away the idea for something much shinier: a chance at respectability befitting her family name. A handsome husband, a beautiful home in the suburbs, and a brand-new baby to tie it all together. They decided on a spontaneous civil ceremony at the courthouse. It would have horrified her mother had she still been alive, but Daniel seemed happy to avoid the expense, especially given his ambivalent-at-best feelings about the groom. He accepted the news about a coming grandchild with little reaction but did seem to warm a bit when he learned it was going to be a boy.

Unfortunately, the attempt at living the domestic bliss her mother had dreamed of for her never got off the launchpad. Their son, Xavier Thomas Miller, was stillborn at twenty-eight weeks. He has a tiny grave she hasn't mustered the steam to visit since the day of the short, quiet ceremony that only she and Wyatt attended.

Despite the loss, they went on okay for a few years after that. Wyatt got his counselor's license and started up his therapy practice. Phoebe dabbled in work with her father's company. They also did the sorts of things couples untethered by kids and financial stress do: travel, concerts, trying on temporary new hobbies before ultimately discarding them, like Wyatt's obsession with brewing his own beer, and Phoebe's more expensive forays into modern-art collecting and photography. But as they approached their thirties, the unspoken question of whether they should try again to start a family began to grow louder, and Wyatt finally asked about it over carpaccio and cocktails while celebrating their eighth anniversary at Francesca's, their favorite local Italian haunt. Maybe it was the wine warming her blood or the flicker of candlelight in his eyes, but she felt open enough to at least stop taking her birth control pills and see where nature took them. Eventually, nature failed, and thus came the in vitro and four resulting miscarriages.

Her father's falling ill made it easy for her to finally put on the brakes. Not that his palliative care had become her responsibility—he had a team of nurses around the clock—but she was able to at least claim emotional exhaustion, and Wyatt acquiesced. Running interference on the baby-making debacle ended up being one of the few kindnesses Daniel ever offered her, even if it was unintentional.

But she has sensed a transition point looming ever since she told Wyatt she was done trying for kids, and this must be it, the moment where they both acknowledge they've had a good run but it's time to get off this merry-go-round altogether. Nearly fifteen years together, ten of them married, is a respectable achievement. Especially in her family.

She sighs. "Okay. How should we go about this?"

He looks a little relieved as he unclasps his briefcase. "I'm glad you're feeling open-minded. I just have a few papers here."

Wow. He already has papers? While she's feeling cooperative, she can't deny being a little irked over how far ahead he's planned. Shouldn't there be a talking phase first?

Her heart stops when she sees the stack of colorful pamphlets he pulls out and places on the table. These aren't divorce papers, not this glossy array of sheets featuring smiling children against a backdrop of sunshine, rainbows, and words like "hope" and "chance" and "family." This is about adoption, the ace-in-the-hole for rich people with uncooperative wombs. Wyatt's demeanor morphs from solemn to giddy while Phoebe's stomach begins to burn. She was so convinced this door was not only closed but locked tight. But here he is telling her in very explicit terms that he never got past it and doesn't intend to. How could they be so out of sync?

"This is perfect for us, babe. I already spoke with the woman who runs Heart Source, and she can't wait to meet you. With our backgrounds, we could probably have a newborn by next week." He notices Phoebe's lack of expression and keeps going. "Or, you know, we can bypass the whole newborn thing and adopt an older child. Skip the diaper-and-midnight-feeding phase altogether. That sounds like a bonus, doesn't it?"

Phoebe wants to darken the beaming glare of his smile permanently. "When you say *our* backgrounds, you mean my background. My name. They would practically sell a kid to someone from the Noble family. Isn't that what you're getting at?"

"Honey, these places are all legal and ethical. There would be no selling. But yes, let's be honest, your name helps. I see no shame in that. We should use whatever works to our advantage."

"Jesus! Have you not been paying attention to the news? The Noble name is in the trash right now."

Wyatt eyes her patiently. "That doesn't matter. The Noble name is more than your father. It's also you, and whoever the next generation will be. If you think about it, this could actually be a way to take the wind out of that whole nasty business."

Her anger is near boiling. He isn't hearing her now, and clearly wasn't hearing her before, when she told him she couldn't do this anymore. Maybe she hadn't been concise enough, which had left him room to believe this was a viable alternative. That there were any alternatives at all. She has to be brutal now. He needs to see there is no life down this path, that she's already burned it and salted the earth.

"I don't want this," she says.

He doesn't look fazed. It's as if he anticipated this response during his rehearsal of this conversation, because of course he rehearsed, probably while picking out his pretty new tie. "Look, I know it's a big step," he argues. "We've been through a lot, over the last few years especially, and I know all this Daniel stuff has thrown you for a loop too. You're afraid of another heartbreak, but our odds are excellent here. Far better than they were with in vitro. This is a chance for a new start, not only for us but for a child who needs a home too. I don't know why we didn't think of this first, but we should have."

She sighs and pinches the bridge of her nose. "Enough with the goddamn sales pitch. I already told you my answer. I do not want this. I couldn't love one of these children."

Here come his pitiful lamb's eyes, which only make her heart stonier, because they're so condescending. They say he knows her feelings better than she does. Her father looked at her that way almost by default, even when Phoebe would say she wanted chicken for dinner instead of steak. "Of course you can, honey. Bonding is always a process, even for parents and their biological children, but you'll do great. *We'll* do great. We're in this together."

It's hard to maintain eye contact as she prepares to nail her final words home. Despite her anger, she still cares for him enough that she doesn't want to be cruel for the sake of it. But pain is all that works sometimes. It's the only sensation that forces humans to focus on what's right in front of them. She's about to be that hot grease splatter, the hammer on the thumbnail, the slippery rung on the ladder. "Having kids was always more your dream than mine. I thought I could learn to want it like you did, but it never took, and . . ." *Come on, Phoebe, get it out there.* "I'm relieved it didn't. I'm not one of those women who always dreamed of being a mother."

He's trying so hard to be stoic, but the color has drained from his face, and he doesn't appear to be breathing. Nevertheless, she's glad the truth she's been nursing in secret all these years, like an abomination no one else could love, is finally out.

"What about Xavier?" he asks. The words are clipped into shards, and they're the only ones capable of getting through her bubble.

She swallows, tamping down those memories and covering them with a thick layer of stone for good measure. "He's dead, Wyatt. What else is there to say?"

"That's enough. I'm not letting you dismiss him like that." He haphazardly gathers the pamphlets and stands up. Then he stops and looks at her with a deep frown. "What did you think we were going to talk about when we first came out here?"

She looks at her lap now. "It doesn't matter."

"You thought I was going to ask for a divorce, didn't you?"

She shrugs, her capacity for brutal honesty exhausted. It's answer enough, anyway.

He walks off without another word. But instead of going for the door to the house, he goes down the steps leading to the pool. After a moment's contemplation, he throws the sheaf of papers into it.

CHAPTER 2

PHOEBE REMAINS IN her spot on the porch long after Wyatt's departure, examining the pile of smoldering shrapnel that is now her marriage. Why couldn't he have brought home information on dog breeders? She would have been more open-minded about a puppy, though she probably would have tried talking him into a cat instead, a far less needy option. But Phoebe is pretty sure this wreck couldn't be mended with even a hundred puppies and kittens, let alone a baby, even if she called him back right now to say she's changed her mind. It's tempting to at least try, just to bring back the tiny sparks of hope she extinguished in Wyatt's eyes this morning. She's worried about what she might see in their place when he comes home tonight. Anger? Sadness? Or worse, nothing at all?

But she won't call him, and she won't change her mind. She's done the right thing by being honest for a change. Hasn't she? If her mother were here, she would quietly shake her head and tell Phoebe this is not what a Good Wife would have done.

The phrase "Good Wife" always felt like a proper noun when

Carol spoke it. Phoebe spent most of her formative years listening to her mother espouse dubious nuggets of wisdom about love and marriage rather than ever question them, but they all boiled down to a simple philosophy. To be a Good Wife, a woman must nurture and love her husband more than she nurtures and loves herself.

This, of course, does not mean neglecting her physical appearance. There is a very long list of beauty rituals required to keep a Good Wife up to her husband's high standards. Perfect hair, makeup, and wardrobe are a must. In Carol's case, this also included daily laxatives and strict portion control to maintain her trim figure. If she could see the extra ten pounds on Phoebe's petite frame, her daily wardrobe of yoga pants and T-shirts, the lack of makeup on her face, and the length of her roots, her scream would rival that of a B-movie horror queen.

The Good Wife always knows her place in the family hierarchy. It's at the very bottom, the perfect spot from which to hoist her husband and requisite offspring high over her head without ever showing a hint of strain. If she finds herself sinking into the muck beneath her feet, she celebrates the warmth and protection it provides from the dangerous world above. A Good Wife wouldn't have dreamed of rebuffing her husband's wishes to adopt a child after their attempts to conceive one of their own failed. She would have sought out those adoption pamphlets herself first and surprised him with them instead. She wouldn't engage in enough navel-gazing to conclude she isn't mother material. First of all, Good Wives never navel-gaze. Second, Good Wives are always Good Mothers.

Phoebe considers how this Good Wife business ended up

working out for Carol. The woman was always impeccable, both in style and in the way she ran the house. Nothing was ever out of place. Neither Phoebe nor her father had to think about any desire for more than a second before Carol took care of it.

So Carol was on it when it came to looking after her family, no doubt about it, and Phoebe never felt a lack of motherly love and attention. But she also remembers the woman's fragility, the faintest tremor in her hands that only seemed to crop up when she didn't think anyone was watching, how she smoked almost endlessly, probably as another effort to keep herself away from extra calories. She did her fair share of drinking too. And despite all her best efforts, she was only able to produce one child before heart disease, probably from all the cigarettes, the crash diets, and the stress she kept locked tight inside her, dug her an early grave. So no. Being a Good Wife didn't pay off for Carol. If anything, it killed her. And she wasn't the only one.

Her father married three more times after Carol. Not an evil stepmother in the bunch. They were all kind and pretty, respectful of Phoebe, and eager to make her father happy, at least in the beginning. Unfortunately, the first post-Carol wife, Helena, died within six months. Daniel told her it was a stroke, but he'd wrongly assumed Phoebe was in the dark about Helena's tendency to pop amphetamines and chase them with vodka. Ava came along a year later, and she died in a car crash right before their second anniversary. Kirstin, the final wife, didn't die, but she did get an annulment after three months, never to be heard from again, though when Phoebe plugged the name into Facebook a few years ago, she found her working as a tour guide in Italy and looking absolutely radiant. Phoebe had liked Kristin best. Her spunk made her immune to the deadly lullaby of the Good Wife. Phoebe wonders what she must have thought about her ex-husband's posthumous scandal, whether she felt the latent breeze of a bullet dodged years before.

Phoebe was determined when she got married to do things differently, refusing to believe that if she sacrificed pieces of herself to a big, powerful man, she would somehow gain the world. They made independence a priority, both financial and personal. Thanks to Wyatt's humbler upbringing, he was accustomed to working for his bread, and he was good at managing his small therapy practice, never coming to her once for a bailout. Phoebe was happy to pay for all the fun stuff with her money. Vacations, cars, shopping sprees, the house, nice clothes. It was a marriage, after all, not a business arrangement. Her father had never thought it would last, especially after they lost Xavier, but she'd been thrilled to find another way to defy the old man's expectations.

Wyatt had made it easy, though. It was his core of sweetness that set him apart from all the other alpha males in her social circles, and even Phoebe had been surprised to find that this was enough to tame her. His sweetness, but also enough confidence that he never seemed desperate to prove himself to her, either. It made his companionship comfortable, like a pair of beloved, well-worn slippers. Unfortunately, that sweetness also made her too docile to heed her inner voice when the question of kids started cropping back up. It made her like Carol.

She goes into the kitchen for a bottle of wine and carries it, along with a glass, back outside. It's far earlier than her usual cork-popping time, but the circumstances warrant the bending of an already arbitrary rule. The papers are still floating in the pool, a mess he obviously expects her to clean up. She will, only because she wants to swim later. From a backyard on another block, she can hear kids splashing around in their own watering hole, playing Marco Polo. The monotony of their little voices repeating the same words ad nauseam reinforces her sense of righteousness.

She doesn't get up and go inside to escape the racket. It's freeing enough just to know she can escape it whenever she wants. Unlike the person who has to mind the little tax deductions over there, she's able to move at will. She could go right now and get a pedicure, or a full-body massage. She could take herself to the movies and see something R-rated, hogging the popcorn and armrests for herself. She could even pack her bags and take an impromptu monthlong trip to any destination in the world without having to do anything more than put a hold on her mail.

Of course, she won't do any of those things. Freedom is as much choosing not to do something as it is choosing to do it. All her necessary comforts are right here. Besides, if she leaves for any extended period, the person in the blue car might do something, like break in and steal something or maybe plant a bunch of cameras and microphones around the place.

Phoebe lingers on that thought and its implications about her freedom before taking a long drink of her wine.

■ ■ ■

E VERY MORNING, NOT long before your husband leaves for
work, I wait for the blinds beside your front door to twitch as
you peek through them. You never disappoint. It's like Morse code,
communicating the start of our daily dance, telling me you know
I'm not really a delivery driver, that you're curious, but maybe not
so curious you're ready to come out here and talk to me, or send a
cop over to check my credentials instead. If you're wondering
whether the other people on this street have looked in on me, the
answer is no. Not only is my little disguise probably doing its job,
but they're likely all assuming someone else checked me out by
now. What's that called again? That thing where you can basically
murder someone in front of a bunch of witnesses, and no one calls
the cops? Bystander apathy, I think. This isn't quite as extreme as a
murder in the park, but you get my point.

Something tells me you aren't apathetic at all. I think you might
actually be enjoying this. Of course, considering the news about the
recently departed Daniel Noble, you probably have good reason to
think someone might be watching you. Who would have guessed

that over a career spanning forty years, with interests in real estate, venture capital, and exotic cars, he would have also had his greedy hands up the skirts of countless non-consenting women, all of whom are now eager to share the gritty details? With that kind of bombshell, you're lucky you don't have reporters camping on the front lawn. Maybe they only do that with the entertainment moguls. At any rate, I'm glad it's quiet around here. It serves my purposes better.

As much as I enjoy that ritual of communication between us every morning, I've noticed our little tango doesn't really begin until after your husband is gone. Then I watch those blinds twitch sporadically throughout the morning as you go about whatever routine you have for the day, a routine that rarely takes you outside where I can see you, though I know for a fact you get out once or twice a week. Even a shut-in has to get her groceries, I guess. You could just have them delivered, but maybe you're old-school. Maybe getting out of the house a few times a week to buy that cookie dough ice cream and cab sav you love so much is your one opportunity to feel normal. Yes, I know what you buy. How I know isn't as alarming as you think. What is alarming is your level of consumption. You may need to tone it down a bit, actually. I've seen older pictures of you online, and you're looking a bit puffier these days. Not judging. Just concerned. Watching your back.

CHAPTER 3

PHOEBE IS WOKEN by the sound of the doorbell. She fell asleep sitting up with a full wineglass, judging by the purple puddle soaking into her lap and the reek of cabernet wafting up from it. She's in no condition to answer the door, but it could be a package delivery, or maybe even a florist. It wouldn't be the first time Wyatt sent flowers after a spat. She grabs one of the bathing suit wraps draped over a nearby chair and covers the stain on her shorts, but there isn't much she can do for the smell.

One thought chills her spine as she approaches the door. What if it's the person from the blue car? The prospect nearly stops her in her tracks, but she shoves it away. She may be gradually sacrificing herself to the hermit life, but the day she stops answering her door like a functional member of society is the day she asks Wyatt for a referral to one of his colleagues.

She looks through the peephole and sees not a woman in a blue Executive Courier Services shirt—in fact, the car appears to be gone for the morning—but a young man in a green tank top and board shorts. When she opens the door and sees him fully, her first reaction is to gape. He's the sort of hot that's cliché. Shaggy hair the color of dark sand, blue eyes, lean body, tan skin, light stubble on his face that looks almost airbrushed on. Considering the flip-flops on his feet and the paracord bracelet on his wrist, the only thing he's missing is an acoustic guitar and a beach bonfire where he can serenade her with Jack Johnson cover tunes. She feels a bit breathless, like she's dashed too quickly up a flight of stairs. The only thing dampening this instant infatuation is the certainty she's twice his age. And that she currently smells like a wino.

"Yes?" she asks.

"Hi. Um . . ." He gestures to the house across the cul-de-sac. A small moving truck is parked out front, and attached to the back of the truck is a trailer holding a small SUV. A dark-haired man is pacing back and forth beside it, barking into his phone. Phoebe can't make out the words, but she wouldn't want to be on the other end of that call. "We're moving in across the street, but my dad can't find the house keys he swears he's had with him the whole time. You wouldn't, like, happen to have an extra key on hand, would you?"

Phoebe frowns at the house, which she does notice looks a little vacant. The lawn is somewhat overgrown, the front flower beds weedy, the trees just this side of untrimmed. It probably hasn't been too long since someone last tended things, a couple weeks maybe, but around here that's bordering on decrepit. "I didn't even realize that place was for sale."

He shrugs with a grin. "Well, it's empty and we're moving in, so I guess it must have been."

Phoebe does recall the former residents appearing to be roughly her father's age, and the stooped, delicate way the wife walked to and from the mailbox. Sadly, that's all she really knew about them. Not even their names. Pathetic. Maybe one of them died and there was a quiet auction. "Welcome to the neighborhood."

"Thanks."

"I'm sorry to say I don't have a key. I only ever saw them in passing. Folks kind of keep to themselves here." She wants to add: *In fact, kid, this conversation represents the most words I've ever spoken to one of my neighbors in a single go.*

His face falls a bit and he glances over his shoulder at his ranting father. "He's not exactly making me want to go back there to deliver bad news."

Phoebe realizes she's perfectly fine if he doesn't want to go just yet. This is the best distraction she's had in months.

"We might as well introduce ourselves, then. I'm Phoebe Miller."

He stares at her for a second. Maybe he isn't sure how much he wants to interact with someone who smells like a wine barrel. Can she blame him? Then he grins, extending his hand. "I'm Jake Napier."

"That's a strong grip you have, Jake." Oh wow. Now she sounds like a bad actress in the opening scene of a cheap porno. It's hard to believe that once upon a time, she knew how to talk to men. "Your dad seems a little pissed."

He flushes with embarrassment. "Yeah, it's been kind of a rough trip. He's Ron. My mom is Vicki. She's driving our other car, but she's stuck in traffic about an hour behind us. I'm just glad they didn't ride in together. There would have probably been a roadside murder scene somewhere in the middle of Utah otherwise."

"Oh man. Moving is the worst," she says. As if she would know. She's moved once in her life, coming here from her father's house fifteen whole miles away. Hired help handled everything, even the unpacking. She had only to point to where she wanted things, like a demanding princess. The Napiers seem to be more the DIY type, even though it's clear they have money. They'd have to if they're settling down here.

"Yeah, it's been a real roller coaster for everyone," Jake says.

"Where are you from?"

"Los Angeles," he says. "But my parents are actually from out here."

"Ah, so a homecoming for them. What's the occasion?"

"My dad took a job at a hospital here. He's a doctor. I'll only be here a couple months, though. I'm starting Stanford this fall." It's hard to miss the note of relief in his voice, which is understandable. The last thing a kid his age wants is to pick up and move halfway across the country with his parents, but at least he has an upcoming escape.

"Oh wow, congratulations. Starting college is a major milestone."

"I also turned eighteen on the way out here. Lots of milestones."

The math running through her head is both reflexive and nauseating. He isn't half her age, but just shy of a decade and a half is a wide enough gap for decency to get lost in. *At least he's not a minor*, she thinks. *You have that going for you, right?*

"Even if you're heading back west soon, you'll still be visiting during the holidays, won't you? Pack a parka. We have real winters here."

"That's what I've heard."

"So, Stanford, huh? Let me guess. Philosophy, political science, or premed?"

He laughs, adorably. "That's three strikes. I'm actually going to be pre-law. I want to be a criminal defense attorney."

"Law school would have been my fourth guess. I weep for another young heart soon to be crushed by the drudgery of the American justice system."

"You sound like you have experience with that," he says.

"No, but I watch a lot of *Law & Order.*"

They grin at each other, and she's tempted to ask him in so she can look a little harder for the spare house key she knows she doesn't have, but his father yells from across the street. "Jake, I could use your help down here!"

He turns and gives a wave. "I guess I should go." He lingers a bit, like he doesn't want to leave. Whether it's more because he enjoys her company or because he doesn't want to return to his father, she isn't sure.

"You might be able to get a key from the house at the corner." She points to her left. "Don't know their names, either, but I'm pretty sure they socialized more with the former owners."

"You don't know any of these people, do you?"

"Well, I know you now, don't I?"

He flashes a brilliant California surfer-boy smile that makes her heart flutter. "Good point. I'll go ask them."

"Good luck. See you around, Jake."

"Okay. Great. Bye, Ms. Miller."

Oh, look at his adorable manners making her feel like her mother-in-law. "Please call me Phoebe," she says.

"You got it. Later, Phoebe."

She watches him go, admiring his long, confident strides and the solid roundness of his shoulders. He isn't exactly built, but he also isn't skinny like a lot of guys his age. There is substance to him, she suspects inside as well as out. She closes the door before anyone can catch her staring, but her belly is burning in that special way it used to when a hookup felt imminent. And he's going to be living only a couple hundred feet from her front door, at least for a little bit. This could be interesting if she wanted it to be. Maybe even a little dangerous.

"He's barely eighteen, you cougar," she blurts out to the empty house. The commonsense part of her, having spoken without warning, quashes her fantasies before they can take root. She trudges upstairs to clean herself up. By the time she's showered and in a pair of soft, clean leggings, she feels a bit more like herself again, and she hates it.

■ ■ ■

W ATCHING YOU ISN'T the only hobby I have. I guess you
could say I collect things, which doesn't sound strange at
all until I add in the minor detail that I sneak into people's houses
to get those things. It's mostly just scraps and trinkets I'm after—
little figurines, labels from pricey bottles of wine or liquor, the tassle
off a curtain—stuff no one would miss, though sometimes I'll steal
a dirty secret or two if they're readily visible. Those secrets are a little
more interesting in ritzy neighborhoods like this one, probably because they feel more hypocritical or unexpected. BDSM rooms are a
recurring theme in the homes of the ultra-wealthy, but that's fifty
shades of unsurprising, as are the amazing drug stashes. Child por-
nography is depressingly common as well. In those cases, I don't
mind leaving any exposed caches out in the open to drive them crazy
night after night, wondering who knows their filthy truths.

I've been breaking into houses so long that it feels normal to me.
A bored kid growing up in the Indiana sticks will do anything for a
little entertainment, and I didn't have video games, a computer, or
even cable TV, so I took to watching people instead. Eventually I

found work doing chores for them, and I would use their bathrooms and check the medicine cabinets. Typical enough. But after that, if the coast was clear, I'd move on to their dresser drawers or their pantries. I had to know if they were living anything like me, this dirty little farm girl whose mother still sewed patches onto jeans and darned socks like someone from the frontier days. After a while, I stopped looking for reasons to be invited in and waited until they weren't home. It seemed easier that way. And here I am, sitting in one of the wealthiest suburbs in the country. I'm proud to say I've explored a great many of its houses so far. Not yours, though. Not yet.

We've met a few times, but you wouldn't remember. I was able to land a part-time job at the local fancy grocery store a mile from your house in the hopes you might shop there, and again, you didn't let me down. In fact, you've come through my checkout lane a couple of times, which is how I learned about your love of wine and Ben & Jerry's. You didn't look twice at me, which is fine. I would be concerned you'd see something familiar in my face, and then you'd ask that question people do when they can't quite put their finger on something. "Do I know you from somewhere?" I've rehearsed all sorts of possible answers to that question, but none of them feel right yet.

If you were hearing all this, you'd likely think I was sitting out here waiting for the right opportunity to break into your house and add a piece of your life to my collection. Things aren't quite that simple when it comes to you; it's not a piece of your life I want. Soon enough, you will know why I'm here. In the meantime, I'll keep watching for that telltale twitch of the blinds letting me know you're there and that you see me. I never have to wait long.

CHAPTER 4

PHOEBE'S SO BUSY glowering into her coffee cup, trying to find her thoughts in a swirl of cream, that she doesn't hear Wyatt the first time. "Hmm?"

"I don't have to go into the office today," he repeats.

"Oh." She can't help but sound disappointed. It's getting harder to hide. "How come?"

"The keynote for the anxiety seminar I'd planned to attend in the city canceled. I have no other reason to go, and I'd cleared my schedule for the day. So I'm a free man."

"Congratulations. What are you going to do with your day?"

He doesn't answer right away, like he's thinking about it. Phoebe picks up her phone and starts scrolling through the morning headlines, hoping he will decide to play golf or run any business errands he's been putting off. Instead, he says the last thing she wants to hear today: "Let's go do something fun."

She looks up from her phone, hoping her irritation with him isn't as visible on her face as it feels. Why does he have to make his day off about her? "Like what?" she asks.

"We could hop a train into the city, grab lunch, maybe do some shopping. We haven't done that in ages."

Part of her softens. He's trying, at least, which is more than she can say for herself since the fight a couple days ago that she now thinks of as the Big Ugly. He hasn't said a word about any of it, but she's been waiting for it to pick back up where it left off. Instead, he seems determined to move on.

It isn't working, though. Despite his attempts to be chummy, she can feel a well of contempt churning away just beneath his placid surface, and an afternoon of eating fancy food and spending money on more things they don't need isn't going to make it go away. Wyatt advises clients all week on how to deal with dysfunctional thinking. Why can't he recognize his own? Avoidance is such a weak glue.

"I'm not feeling up to going out today," she says.

"Come on, honey. Don't stay in this rut. Sometimes you have to make yourself do things even when you don't feel like it."

"Why do I, though? It isn't a rut if I'm completely fine with staying in. I have things I need to do here, anyway."

"Like what? Obsess over a car outside that has nothing to do with you? Work on your book?" His expression reveals no sarcasm, but it's roiling in subtext. A couple years ago, she told him she wanted to try her hand at writing. She managed to scribble down two chapters before losing interest, but she kept up appearances for a good bit longer. Her looking busy with a project seemed to make him respect her time more. It also gave her something to talk to people about on their rare social outings. Instead of being the pampered, apathetic princess, she was an interesting author. The act started to wear thin once she realized she would have to produce an actual book before too long. Wyatt seemed to sense this, because he'd stopped asking her about it, at least until now. His congenial mask is slipping. Fine. Let it. She'd rather deal with him at his ugliest than watch him struggle to act like everything is okay.

"What I do with my time around here is none of your business. I never nag you about that, do I? When you say you don't want to do something, I don't force you."

"In case you forgot, we're *married*, Phoebe! Married people spend time together. If all you wanted was a roommate who left you to yourself, why didn't you just say so ten years ago?"

"You were a lot less annoying ten years ago."

"Oh, that's nice." He stands up. "Let's just ask the obvious question here, since it's clearly been on your mind lately, but you're too much of a damn coward to actually say it. Do you want a divorce?"

This is the part where she should tell him yes. The marriage has run its course. It's time to divvy up the consolation prizes and move on. The process shouldn't be too difficult. They were smart. He signed a prenup. She would have to pay him alimony, but she doesn't see him being vindictive about going for more, and she doubts she would have to pay him for long anyway. Wyatt should have no problem finding a Good Wife to spit out ten kids for him.

But it isn't logistics that keep her from saying yes. With Wyatt gone, Phoebe fears she would lose herself completely. She loves the taste of wine a bit too much these days. Most of her family is dead or so dispersed they don't matter. They arrive here in the form of yearly Christmas cards, which are really just placeholders in their portion of the family trust. When she kicks off one day, they'll descend like vultures to pick her carcass while reciting her best virtues, all of them lies or assumptions. She's used her father's money to build herself a hollow excuse for a life. Nothing would magnify that more than being completely alone, all day, every day. *Of course, this is also why people have children.* She stiffens at the sound of her mother's voice piping up in her head, uninvited.

"If you want to leave, I won't stop you. But . . . I don't want you to go."

He rubs his hands over his haggard face. "Okay. This is good, right? We have something to work with."

"This doesn't put kids back on the table. That ship has sailed. If you can tell me you accept that, we can move forward."

His jaw clenches. "Can you at least tell me why you're being so adamant about this? Is this really all you want out of your life? A big, empty house. No dimension. No depth. No job. Just . . . you. And your little imaginary friend in the car outside, I guess."

She sighs. "I don't know if I could explain it in a way that would satisfy you, any more than you can explain why you want kids so badly in a way that would satisfy me."

"Of course I can explain why I want kids! It's natural human instinct to want to love something or someone outside yourself, to contribute to the world in some meaningful way."

"I'm sure Hitler's mom felt the same. But look what she unleashed on the world."

His face is first an O of incredulity, but it soon softens with a hint of comprehension. "This is about your father, isn't it? You somehow think whatever kids you raise are going to turn out like him or worse."

"This wasn't an invitation for you to analyze me, Wyatt."

"I'm not. But tell me I'm at least close."

"Daniel never liked kids. To him they were annoying, dirty, noisy nuisances better left to the care of someone else."

Wyatt shakes his head. "He obviously cared for you enough to leave you most of his money."

She shrugs. "He liked me more as an adult, I guess. A dislike of children is one of the only things I had in common with the man." She can't help but wince at how cold those words sound outside her head. Are they even completely true? Though she isn't interested in motherhood, she can safely bet if Xavier or any of those lost embryos had lived, she would have treated them better than Daniel ever treated her. But that still isn't saying much, and Wyatt doesn't need to hear anything that might bolster his hopes.

Wyatt stares at her. "That's it? You just . . . don't like kids?"

"You make it sound like that's not reason enough."

"Most people don't like other people's kids, Phoebe. But they do like their own."

She shakes her head. "That was not true in my house. You try growing up with someone who hates kids. It's not a fun way to live. I'm not going to do that to someone else."

"But see, that empathy you just showed for a kid who doesn't even exist tells me we can work on whatever this is."

The last grains of her patience finally run out. "Or you could respect my feelings and my decision and stop trying to think they're something that needs fixing. Do you have any idea how insulting that is?"

Little pinpricks of something approximating hate dot his eyes. "It's that final, huh? End of discussion. Phoebe's way or no fucking way?"

"You should be grateful I'm being honest about this. People who don't want kids are the last people who should have them."

"Well, if we're on the subject of conditions, maybe I have one too. If you don't want to take care of a child, you can at least stop acting like one and start taking care of yourself. Try a shower and a change of clothes once in a while. It makes me sick looking at you."

She gapes at him. He's never been so baldly critical of her. No, not just critical. Mean. Is this the mask slipping or is it a new mask he's trying on for size? She doesn't like it on him. But most of all, she doesn't like how his words have hooked under her skin like barbs. It's one thing to see your reflection in the mirror, another thing when someone else holds it up for you. Her eyes burn and her guts somersault, but she won't betray even the faintest tremble. She's well practiced at this part. Being Daniel Noble's daughter was all about maintaining a smokescreen, and he hasn't been dead long enough for her to forget how.

She gives Wyatt a cool grin and lifts her coffee cup for a sip. "I'll take that under advisement, Doc," she says, her voice cool, smooth. "Oh wait, you can't be a doctor without a doctorate."

It's an extremely low blow, considering he flunked out of his master's program after they lost Xavier, and though he went back eventually, he never mustered the gumption to go for his PhD. But they're aiming for each other's soft spots right now, and she can't deny that it felt good, at least for a second, to hit him back. His face flushes a deep scarlet and his hands curl into tight fists, white knuckles and all. For a tense moment, Phoebe braces herself for an escalation and regrets that she has nothing more than a mug of lukewarm coffee to defend herself with if he decides to leap on her.

Even her fingernails are too chewed to be of any use. But in all the years she's known Wyatt, she's never seen him react violently. It's simply not in his nature.

But it's in everyone's nature, she reminds herself. Everything that moves eventually breaks. That was one of her father's sayings.

Somewhere in the storm that must be swirling in his brain, Wyatt finds his calm again. He shrinks back a little, relaxing his fists, and then stalks off in the direction of his study. The door slams shut a few seconds later. Hard punctuation at the end of an ugly paragraph. Letting out a long, shaky breath, Phoebe gets up and goes to the front window and peeks through the blinds, expecting to see her companion the blue car sitting there like it was when she checked an hour ago, but it's gone now, and in that moment, she's never felt lonelier.

A second later, the garage door at the Napier house opens, and Jake steps outside wearing black spandex running gear and a pair of white earbuds. He faces her house for a long moment, and it feels like he's looking right at her. A low hum of dismay amps to an internal shriek. *Look away now! Don't let him think you're spying!* But a quick realization cuts that voice off, leaving a warm, titillated hum in its wake: isn't he spying on her too? A moment later, he turns away to give his legs a few stretches, then glides off up the street in long strides.

"I'm going into the office."

Phoebe startles and turns around to see Wyatt dressed for work. His eyes are red and watery. He only cries when he's especially angry, as if the tears help to wash away his rage. It's almost a relief to see them now after what nearly happened a minute ago.

"Okay. Have a nice day." Her pleasant tone clashes badly against the mood between them, enough to make them both wince a little, but her mind is somewhere else now. An idea is beginning to take shape. A really bad idea.

Once he's gone, the silence left in his wake, normally so comforting, is suddenly abrasive and smothering. Seeing Jake take off on his run unlocked something in her. His easy strides represented freedom at its most essential. She wants it. Not to actually go running, but to move nonetheless. She remembers when she could move through the world that way, unburdened.

Something she's never done before is cheat on her husband. There have been opportunities, especially in their earlier years when they were both getting out more, but she's never done more than flirt a little. But this feeling she has right now isn't about sex or even flirting. She just wants to be near someone fresh and new, even if it's only to say hello and possibly see if the chemistry from the other day still holds. If she can seem interesting to someone like Jake, she might feel inspired to see what else is out there.

But if she goes outside only to speak to Jake, his parents will probably have something to say about it. Phoebe knows a way around that problem. It requires a bit more work and a lot of nerve, but Wyatt's words this morning have galvanized her, knocked her mousy self comatose. She also knows how ephemeral this feeling might be, so if she is going to do anything, she needs to move now.

■ ■ ■

IN THE KITCHEN, she flips on the radio. As she measures and mixes her ingredients, she catches herself singing along to the music.

An hour later, the kitchen smells like caramelized sugar and berries, and a dozen of her famous jumbo-size blueberry muffins are cooling on a rack. Cooking was the one life lesson her mother taught her that actually stuck. Of course, Carol had taught it in the hopes that Phoebe could one day impress a man, and to that end, she supposes it was a success. Wyatt always loved her cooking. But it also helps that she enjoys doing it.

Finding she still has plenty of energy to carry out her plan, she dashes upstairs and takes a long bath, shaving and exfoliating every part of herself like she's preparing for a date that might move beyond first base, even though there will be no such thing. But she retrieves another bit of her mother's long-abandoned Good Wife wisdom: you only feel as good as you look. Maybe Carol was on to something there, because she's feeling pretty great right now. But she won't give Wyatt too much credit. She isn't doing this for him.

With her body and hair wrapped in thick towels, she crosses to her closet to begin the difficult process of picking the right outfit. If she puts on a dress, she might look like she's trying too hard, or give off a fussy 1950s housewife vibe. But she also wants to show off her best assets while hiding the ones she's neglected, and a dress is her best bet. She strikes a balance, choosing a soft pink jersey number that cinches above the waist and swings freely at her knees. After adding a pair of strappy sandals and some nude polish to her toenails, she'll be the epitome of cute and casual.

An hour later, she steps in front of the mirror one more time, fully dressed, her makeup light and sensible, her golden hair hanging loosely around her shoulders. After a moment's deliberation, she decides to put it up. She's aiming for "quickly thrown together but still managing to look rich and fabulous," and nothing says that better than a sloppy ponytail. It will also conceal the grown-out cut.

She still isn't completely satisfied as she presses in on her growing pooch of a belly, wondering if she looks inadvertently pregnant, but if she starts cycling through outfits again, she'll lose the last of her nerve and go right back to the leggings, and probably eat all those muffins by herself. She gives her head a shake. Not this time. Downstairs, she places the muffins into a reusable container that she intends to leave over there. Borrowed plastics are the perfect way to ensure future get-togethers. Maybe Jake will be a good boy and bring it back over here for his mom.

Before going outside, she peeks out the window to see if the blue car has reappeared. The street is still deserted. "Please just stay gone, whoever you are," she mutters. It's as close to a prayer as she ever gets.

CHAPTER 5

THE NAPIER HOUSE looks quiet and dark, almost like it's still vacant. Jake might be the only one awake, his parents no doubt exhausted after a long cross-country trip and all the unpacking. The short spread of blacktop separating their houses suddenly feels like a wide gulf, and for the first time since Wyatt left, she feels her nerve slipping. Then the front door opens, and a trim, petite woman in a black tank top and cut-off shorts steps outside and takes a seat on the bottom porch step. A red bandanna covers most of her dark brown hair, keeping it out of her face the way it might if she were busy dusting, scrubbing floors, and emptying boxes. This could be hired help, but it doesn't seem likely at this hour. Phoebe is sure this is Jake's mother, Vicki.

Taking a furtive glance over her shoulder, the woman pulls a pack of cigarettes and a lighter from her bra and lights up. Phoebe raises a brow. She didn't think people smoked actual cigarettes anymore, especially doctors' wives.

She sucks in a deep breath and sets off down her front porch steps, pulling together every resource she has in order to be the open, warm society girl she once was, or at least tried to be. Vicki looks up and sees her coming, and Phoebe's nerves begin rattling like train tracks right before the locomotive bears down on them. She also feels vaguely nauseated, but when she's most of the way there, she gives a final "fake it till you make it" push of sheer will and puts on her most brilliant smile. "Hi there! I live across the street and wanted to introduce myself. I hope I'm not coming at a bad time." Is she speaking too rapidly? Is she too shrill? She has lost her gauge for these things. It's like trying to fly a plane without knowing where the horizon is.

The woman quickly scrubs out her cigarette on the sidewalk and places the butt into her pack before standing up. Phoebe notices a bruise encircling her upper arm, deep purple fading to yellow around the edges. "Not a bad time at all. I've been meaning to come over and introduce myself, since I know you've already met my son, but I keep finding new fires to put out over here. You're Phoebe, right?"

So Jake has already spoken of her. Of course, his father already knew about the visit, but Phoebe lights up inside anyway. "Yep! And you must be Vicki."

"That's me. The woman of the house, though I look more like the housekeeper I wish I had." There are bags and purple rings under her eyes, sure signs of exhaustion. Why doesn't she have anyone helping her?

"I don't want to get in your way, but I figured since your kitchen might not be all set up yet, you'd want something homemade for breakfast." She holds out the container of muffins.

"Oh my gosh, thank you. All the fast food, pizza, and Chinese takeout has taken its toll. I'm ballooning from the sodium." Phoebe can't see an ounce of fat or bloat on the woman's body. If anything, she looks a bit underfed, but Phoebe knows how vanity works. "Why don't you come in?" Vicki says. "It's a mess, but I've already unpacked the most important thing."

"What's that?"

"The coffeepot, of course."

"Coffee sounds great. Thank you." Phoebe is amazed at how easy this has been so far. It's nice to play a well-adjusted human again, like stretching her legs after an overly long sit. Vicki makes it easy, though. She has the sort of rhythm anyone can fall in with. Inside the house, she's immediately impressed with how wide open the place feels, thanks mostly to the high ceilings and light colors. The natural wood and floor-to-ceiling windows in the living room bring the outside in. There isn't any substantial furniture or rugs in place yet, only boxes and a couple chairs, so their footsteps and voices echo off the hardwood floors. "It's beautiful in here. I've never been inside."

"Unfortunately, it needs more work than I was anticipating. Plumbing, gutters, maybe even a roof, but given the market, we're still quite lucky."

"The previous owners were pretty old, if I recall. I imagine they must have let a lot of things go."

Vicki gives a faint nod. "Boy, did they ever."

She escorts Phoebe into the kitchen, where a few boxes sit among not much else. It looks like they didn't bring a lot of stuff, maybe enough to fill a small apartment or dorm room. She seems to notice Phoebe noticing. "We came only with the essentials.

Moving across the country with everything you own is too much of a burden, so we had a big yard sale out there with the plan to fill this place with new things."

"Starting with a blank canvas sounds like a perk to me," Phoebe says.

"Most definitely." Vicki gestures to a set of stools parked beneath the breakfast bar, and then quickly clears away the pizza boxes and empty soda cans. "Like I said, it's a mess."

"It's really okay. You should see my house, and unlike you, I have no excuse." It's a giant lie. She maintains a spotless house even now, without the help of the housekeeper who used to come by twice a week until Phoebe grew paranoid about prying eyes after the Daniel media fallout. But there was never much for the help to do anyway. Cleaning is Phoebe's one major compulsion and remaining source of pride, but Vicki seems to need some reassurance. Taking a seat, Phoebe watches her prep an electric kettle. The coffeepot is actually a glass Chemex beaker. Points for being a coffee snob. "Where are the men?" Phoebe asks, knowing perfectly well where one of them is.

"Jake is out for a run, and my husband, Ron, is entering the sixteenth hour of an eight-hour shift at the hospital. He's going to be in a great mood when he gets home." Her sarcasm is about as subtle as a neck tattoo. A few minutes later, they're both sipping delicious cups of brew and starting in on the muffins after Vicki's profuse apologies that she still hasn't been to the store to buy any real groceries, including butter. Phoebe is taking small, delicate bites befitting what one does in new company, but Vicki doesn't appear to value such conventions. She bites off half the muffin top and rolls her eyes in ecstasy. "Oh my God, these are perfect," she says with her mouth still mostly full. "Adding butter would have been an insult."

Phoebe, both amused and relieved to cast the invisible corset of social decorum aside, follows suit and takes a real bite too.

"So, Phoebe. That's a cool name. Makes me think of the girl in *Fast Times at Ridgemont High*."

She grins. "If only I still looked like that in a bikini."

"That you ever did puts you several steps ahead of me. Tell me about yourself."

Her stomach flip-flops. Why does meeting new people always begin like a job interview? Then again, she's lucky Vicki doesn't appear to know who Phoebe really is. She sifts through her collection of canned responses and finds one that puts her as far away from her father and family name as possible. "I'm a Chicago girl, born and raised. I've lived in Lake Forest for ten years, since I got married. Wyatt and I met while we went to Northwestern. No kids." The last two words turn bitter on her palate, her latest argument with Wyatt still fresh in her mind. Vicki seems to be waiting for her to say more, and Phoebe realizes she has nothing even remotely interesting to say about herself that wouldn't invoke her father in some way. "Um, I also like sunsets and long walks by the lake. My favorite flower is the orchid."

Vicki laughs. "Sorry for putting you on the spot. It's a bad habit of mine. You went to Northwestern, huh? That's great. Ron is working at the hospital there. What was your major?"

"Communications. After I graduated, I worked for my father doing marketing and research for his company. That was fun." They were actually the worst years of her life, at least until recently. Most of her coworkers either hated or feared her, thinking she would be promoted ahead of them or snitch on them for the old man. None of them knew that he'd been gunning for Phoebe to fail. She didn't understand it then, but she now knows that Daniel didn't have much use for women in the workplace if he couldn't coerce them into banging him.

"It sounds like you don't work for him anymore."

"No, I didn't last long at that, actually."

"So what did you do next?"

She draws a blank. The answer is precisely nothing, but she can't say that. "I've dabbled in writing." There she goes with the god-damn book lie again. It's hard not to wince, especially given her fight this morning with Wyatt.

Vicki's eyebrows predictably raise with interest. "Writing books?"

"I wouldn't go so far as to use a plural. I got maybe thirty pages down before I realized no trees deserved to die for my lack of talent."

"Ouch. You're being a little hard on yourself, don't you think?"

Phoebe shrugs. "Maybe. But it wasn't my calling. I guess I haven't really had one yet. My father was an engineer, but I wanted nothing to do with that, and he never pushed me one way or another."

Vicki's jaw drops open. "How cool! My mother was also an engineer. A great one too. But I agree, it can be boring if it isn't your thing. It wasn't really mine, either. I always wanted to go into law, take on the big bad corporations Erin Brockovich style."

Phoebe is suddenly glad she hasn't revealed who her father was. "Is that what you do? Practice law?"

Vicki shakes her head and looks down. "I was only ever a

humble domestic provider, I'm afraid. The way life shook out for me, I didn't have much opportunity to follow in my mother's educated footsteps. So I was married and a mother myself by the time I was twenty, and I focused on that while Ron completed med school and all his residencies."

"Sounds to me like you did the right thing. After my mom died, I was basically raised by staff. Heck, even before she died, really."

"Well, I don't think I would have done it differently, but my only child is nearly all grown up and about to fly the coop, which feels like the equivalent of being laid off without severance." Her tone is light enough, but Phoebe can sense an ocean of discontent just under this woman's cheerful façade. Their circumstances couldn't be more different, but Phoebe can relate to the feeling that somewhere along the way, life sort of left her behind, and now she has to figure out the directions on her own.

"I've been thinking maybe it's time to get a dog," Phoebe says.

"I was more in the mind of starting an affair with a much younger man."

Phoebe is glad she wasn't sipping her coffee just then, or she might have choked. Instead, she offers a crooked grin. "That's always an option too, I guess."

They sit for a minute, drinking their coffee, thinking their thoughts. The silence doesn't feel as awkward as it should for two people who've known each other for less than an hour. In fact, it's almost companionable. Phoebe wishes she didn't like her so much. Is this really the best time in her life to make friends with someone? Then again, when has she ever thought it a good time? That's probably half her problem right there. It helps that Vicki isn't like the other women around here. She doesn't seem uptight enough to crack walnuts with her pelvic muscles. Just the fact that she stepped outside without being in full makeup puts her in a different league. Hell, she even smokes something that isn't battery powered. Maybe it's because she's a few years older than Phoebe, but Vicki is . . . authentic. She could be the kind of friend Phoebe has been needing most of her adult life. Why does she have to have such a hot son?

"You know, I'm really glad you came by," Vicki says. "The last couple days, I've been kind of going out of my mind wondering if I did the right thing."

"You mean moving here?"

"We took a bit of a crazy chance, and it's been hard on all of us. I never imagined I'd come back to the Midwest. California will probably always feel like home to me."

"That's right. Your son said you were from here originally."

"Oak Park, actually. But I was just a little girl then." She pauses again, staring into her coffee. "When my mother fell ill, we relocated west to be closer to her family, but they've all gone now. But I grew up there, met Ron. Turned out he was an early transplant from here too. It's what drew us together, I think, because we sure didn't have much else in common." She laughs. "Anyway, here we are again, coming full circle."

Why the sudden move back here when clearly Vicki didn't want to do it? Phoebe wonders. But she knows that posture well: averted gaze, crossed arms, shoulders slightly hunched. It's how Phoebe looks when the conversation strays too far in the direction of her father. Clearly, Vicki has some sore spots. Now isn't the time to prod. Maybe it never will be, and that's okay.

"It's not so bad here," Phoebe says brightly, hoping to insert some levity back into the conversation. "The winters suck, but we have a lake that pretends to be an ocean, and our hot dogs are covered in salad so you don't have to feel as guilty about eating them."

Vicki grins. "I don't know whether to laugh or cry."

The door leading to the garage opens and Jake walks in, drenched in sweat, music leaking from his earbuds. When his eyes land on Phoebe, a jolt of warmth floods her belly like she's just taken a shot of whiskey, and immediately she feels like a horrible person. The unexpectedly decent conversation with Vicki has stirred up a strange stew of competing emotions.

"Hey, Phoebe." He yanks out the earbuds and grabs a dish towel to dry himself off.

Vicki raises her eyebrow at him. "Wow, manners much?"

"She told me the other day I can call her Phoebe."

"That's true. I did. And hello, Jake. How was your run?"

"Sweaty. It's really humid out there."

"I was using that towel, you know." Vicki glares at him, but there's enough of a grin to indicate she doesn't really mind.

"Calm down, woman. I'll get you a clean one." He tosses the wad of white terry cloth at her.

Vicki catches it just before it hits her face. "Oh, gross!" She looks at Phoebe with faux exasperation. "You see what I have to deal with around here?" She slides the container of muffins toward him. "Eat something, you brat. Phoebe made these, and they are awesome. There's a little coffee left too, if you want it."

"I'll have some, after I grab a shower."

"Wait. Before you clean up, could you mow the grass? I swear I can practically hear it growing out there. The last thing I need is someone from the city knocking on the door, wielding a ruler."

"I would, but we didn't bring a lawn mower, remember?"

Vicki sighs and rubs her forehead. "Isn't that just great? Another goddamn thing we'll have to buy. Your father is going to be so thrilled."

"I thought you already knew."

"As if I haven't had enough on my mind lately! Is it asking too much to get a little help around here with this stuff? Jesus."

Phoebe glances at Jake and sees him staring at his feet, like a scared, shamed little boy. Something has shifted between mother and son, taking the jovial vibe of moments ago with it. "Sorry, Mom," he says, not looking up. "You're right. I should have said something sooner."

Vicki rolls her eyes. "Forget it. I'll just add it to the list of other crap I have to do still." She looks at Phoebe as if remembering she's still there, embarrassment spreading across her face. "Jeez. I'm sorry. You've only known me for five minutes and you're already smelling my dirty laundry."

"Hey, don't worry about it," she says. "You have so much on your plate, I can only imagine how hard it is."

Her shoulders relax a little. "Thank you. Would your landscaper be able to come on short notice, by chance? I swore to Ron the lawn would get done today along with the rest of this stuff."

Phoebe wonders what Ron would actually do if his wife failed to follow through on that promise, and then she eyes the bruise on Vicki's arm again and remembers the man she saw pacing the sidewalk the other day, screaming into his cell phone. Maybe this isn't a conclusion she should be drawing so early about a man she's never formally met, but at best, Ron seems like someone with an anger problem. She does, however, have a solution to the Napiers' lawn dilemma. "I don't know the landscaper's availability, but I have a mower in my garage that you're more than welcome to."

Vicki's whole body sags with relief. "Oh my God, are you sure it isn't too much trouble?"

"It's none at all. Sometimes Wyatt will mow between visits from our guy if we've had a lot of rain, but that's rare. I think he's used it once in the last two summers."

"You are a real lifesaver, Phoebe. You have no idea." She doesn't sound like she's exaggerating, and that's a little worrisome. "I'll send Jake over to get it whenever you're ready. Maybe he can get the number for your landscaper too."

"Actually, Jake can follow me over now. It's time I get out of your hair anyway." Phoebe stands, hoping she doesn't look too eager, especially with Jake's eyes now boring into her.

"I owe you big. Come back over tomorrow, if you want. Ron's working another shift and I should have this kitchen whipped into shape enough to cook us breakfast. No pressure."

She wants to decline. At this point in her life, this one social visit feels like it should do until at least Christmas, but it's hard to say no to someone who could clearly use some friendly company. "All right then. I'll see you tomorrow."

"Maybe bring your book over so I can read it." Vicki winks.

"Very funny," Phoebe says with a grin.

Jake follows her out the front door. It's grown a lot hotter since she was out here earlier, but she isn't sure she can blame it all on the weather. What exactly is she trying to do, anyway?

"So, you wrote a book?" he asks.

"Not really."

"Well if you were to write one, what would it be?"

"Something for the soccer mom S & M crowd. A sure blockbuster."

"Ah. I'm more of a sci-fi guy, myself. Make it soccer mom S & M in space, and I'll definitely check it out."

She laughs. "I'll keep that in mind." Once they're in front of the garage, she keys in the code to raise one of the doors, preparing herself for the reaction he's about to have when he sees what's inside.

"Holy shit! Is that a 458?"

Daniel's precious Ferrari is a guaranteed show-stopper. She thinks of the scene from *Ferris Bueller's Day Off*, when Ferris lusts after the forbidden one in Cameron's garage, but she doesn't reference this, despite knowing the dialogue almost verbatim and all the places where it was filmed locally. The movie is a decade and a half older than Jake is, much like her.

"It's actually a lot rarer than that," she says. "Don't really know much about it, though." *Don't care, either,* she thinks.

"It's yours and you don't know about it?"

"It was my father's. He was a big car collector. For some reason, he thought I should end up with this one when he died." She knew the exact reason she ended up with it. He'd been quite aware of how much she hated his compulsion to hoard anything remotely ostentatious, like, for instance, the rarest cars in the world. This Ferrari was his most prized of the whole lot, not just of his cars, but of everything he owned. It arrived here on a flatbed truck about three weeks before he died, with a note that said his two most precious treasures belonged together, a sweet enough sentiment to anyone who didn't know what a manipulator he was. Daniel had counted on her feeling too conflicted to sell it, and he'd been correct. So here it sits, hidden away in her garage like a secret lesion. But she often fantasizes about taking a baseball bat to it. Maybe even a can of lighter fluid and a match.

"Your dad sounds like he was an interesting guy."

Phoebe pastes on a grin. "He definitely wasn't boring."

"Have you driven it?"

"Oh God no. The husband did take it for a spin around the block once, though, but it was terrifying." *Like Daniel was*, she adds mentally, while also noting her odd linguistic choice about Wyatt. Not "my" husband, but "the" husband. Already, she's unmooring herself from her commitment in the hopes of seeming more available. But given the way things are going with her marriage, is a little detachment that far off base? "The guy I happen to live with" is probably the most accurate descriptor of all, but it would only make her sound weird. Honesty is not always the best policy.

Meanwhile, it doesn't appear Jake even noticed. He's studying every swoop and curve on the Ferrari's body.

"It's pretty ridiculous, isn't it," she says.

"I would say 'amazing' is a better word."

She rolls her eyes out of his view. Outsiders never get it, even ones like Jake who haven't exactly grown up poor. Maybe when he's older, he'll see what a distraction this kind of stuff is. Her father amassed so many things in life, hoping their sheen and exorbitant price tags would cover for the fact that he was a terrible person. It worked well enough when he was alive, but not so much now. He's only lucky people didn't come forward about him until after his death. Then again, he probably knew the truth bomb was coming and expected her to shoulder that burden too, like this goddamn car.

"You're a gearhead too, I take it?" she asks.

Jake shrugs. "A little. But even if I wasn't into cars, I'd still be drooling over this one." His hands are clasped behind him, like he's in a museum viewing a priceless artifact. It makes his already impressive shoulder muscles stand out in bold relief. She realizes now that they're out of view of the street, and every part of her begins crackling with an energy she hasn't felt in years. She remembers having this same sensation as a much younger woman easing into her sexuality, testing the effect she had on boys her age and older men alike. That's when she discovered something that felt almost like a superpower. It wasn't only that she was pretty and well developed, though that didn't hurt. It was something more invisible, a deep, magnetic well of charisma that made anyone she used it on stupid for her. At some point, around the time she met Wyatt, she walled it off and gradually forgot it was there. It no longer felt like something she needed, not when she found someone who seemed content to be with her at her worst. But the mortar between those bricks is crumbling now, and she can feel a bit of that power again, even if it's unwieldy in her older, out-of-practice hands.

"You can touch it if you like," she says, stepping a little closer to him. "Maybe I could even let you get inside."

She's done it, and now she's screaming internally. The words hang between them like a potent musk that could either bring him closer or drive him away. Or maybe he'll be utterly clueless and take her at face value. In fact, maybe it would be okay if he was so absorbed in the allure of the Ferrari that he didn't hear her at all. Yes, let that be the outcome, because this is stupid. So goddamn stupid. She isn't seventeen anymore. *Grow up, Phoebe. You want excitement, maybe go for a run instead. There are better ways to get an endorphin rush.*

He turns away from the car and looks down at her with the steady, confident gaze of a much older man. "I might embarrass myself if I did that."

There's no doubt at all now that he heard her, in both text and subtext, and this is a pivotal moment for them both. The door between them is standing wide open. Either one of them is free to pass right through it if they choose. But he's waiting for it to be her. Of course he is. How many girls has he been with at this point in his life anyway? One? Two at most? He might even still be a virgin. That's the icicle that pierces the bubble for her.

She clears her throat and takes a step back. Her craving has subsided, leaving room for sanity to reassert itself. The only thing she wants now is to be in her bed. Alone.

"All right, let me show you where the mower is," she says. Shame has won, for the time being, at least.

···

THERE'S A NEW family in the neighborhood, but when did you get close to them, Mrs. Miller? In all the weeks we've been locked in this standoff I've never seen you actually set foot outside your front door. It's been so long I stopped hoping you would, so I could hardly believe my eyes when I spied you walking back home from the newbies' house with a young piece of eye candy in tow. You were so engrossed in him you didn't even notice me pulling up in my usual spot. Since then he's been 'round several times, as has a woman who looks like she might be his mother. But never together. What are you up to, I wonder—playing house or playing with fire? Don't get too distracted. I wouldn't want you to forget who really matters.

I've been a bit preoccupied recently too. I knew from the moment I met Jesse Bachmann that he was a Class-A jerk. It started with the way his dead-fish eyes wandered over my body like it was a nice coat he wanted to try on. It continued with the off-color jokes, usually about women, I'd overhear him make in the break room or by the loading docks with the soda vendors and other male

employees, most of whom would grin out of politeness before re-
treating. I took notice of the way the other girls reacted around him
too, tensing up and clasping their elbows, like a malevolent spirit
had just entered the room.

And did I mention this creep is the shift supervisor for customer
service? He technically isn't my boss, or anyone's boss for that matter, but he likes to stretch the title as much as he can get away with.
You might have even seen him. He's the slouchy ginger whose idea
of a smile is a slight lip curl, like someone trying to pass a particularly hard bowel movement. I would have been happy to continue
ignoring him, but over the last week or so, I started noticing him
skulking more in my peripheral vision, watching me when he didn't
think I could see. Oh, the irony.

I think he'd been waiting for me to ripen on the vine a bit, to get
more comfortable at the job before he made his move. I imagine
this is what he's done with nearly every woman at this place. So I
started mentally preparing myself for the moment that finally came
yesterday when I was clocking out and turned around to find him
standing directly in my personal bubble, spewing cocky entitle-
ment with every musty exhale.

"The answer is no, Jesse," I said.

He jumped, clearly startled. This hadn't been part of his rehearsal. Rejection, he probably did expect, if not hope for. Guys like
Bachmann depend on rejection to fuel their worldview that all
women are bitches and hate them. But preemptive rejection? They
never see that coming, and it denies them the pleasure of seeing
their targets squirm. "You don't even know what I was going to say,"
he sputtered.

"The answer is still no." I pushed past him.

"So that's it, then? I don't even get a chance?"

"No." I never stopped walking.

He muttered something under his breath that sounded suspiciously like "Fucking whore." Right on cue. There always has to be a parting shot, and he went with the gold standard. My only mistake was thinking it would end there.

But between late last night and this morning alone, I've received three anonymous emails from different addresses. I've also received a series of hang-up calls from various numbers that I suspect are all spoofs, and this morning, I stepped out of my car to find the lovely c-word painted on the driver's-side door in pink nail polish, which means he was right outside my car in the dead of night while I slept.

So I guess I've gone and made myself an enemy. Normally I'm the one sneaking around in the dead of night. For now, Bachmann has my attention. He's bought you some time.

CHAPTER 6

PHOEBE OPENS THE door to find Vicki holding what looks like a quiche and a bottle of white wine. She's a half hour early. Then again, running a few minutes ahead seems to be Vicki's default setting, as if she can't wait any longer to be somewhere else. Phoebe can't relate to this at all, but since she has nothing else going on in her life, she can accommodate Vicki's quirk easily enough.

"Good morning," she says, stepping aside to let her in, glancing furtively over Vicki's shoulder out of habit. The blue car isn't here yet. Someone is running late. She pauses for a moment. It never showed up yesterday, either. When was the last time it was here? Her little notebook ought to tell her, but Vicki is already making a beeline into the house. It'll have to wait.

"I'm ready to dive headfirst into this," Vicki says, hoisting up the bottle.

"You really didn't have to go to so much trouble." Phoebe takes the quiche and pops it into the oven to warm up. "I only bought precut fruit. You're making me look bad."

"Trust me, it isn't any trouble. You know I like to bake."

It's their fifth meal together in the three weeks that have passed since that morning in Vicki's kitchen. Two of those meals have been at local eateries, upon Vicki's insistence that Phoebe show her what's on trend around town, though the subtle suggestion seemed to be that Phoebe needed to shed her hermit skin and get out more. She groused internally about it, but ultimately she would always be glad to chow down on a burger from the Lantern or sip on a mule at the Maevery Public House, spots she and Wyatt used to haunt regularly when they first moved up here. The rest of their times together have been spent in Phoebe's kitchen or on her back patio, though she's sure next time, Vicki will drag her out in public again. She's already mentioned a few other spots that have caught her eye.

Next time. She supposes this must make Vicki a real friend now. Not only are they sharing food, but they've swapped phone numbers, text messages, recipes, and celebrity gossip. They haven't delved much deeper than that. They also haven't made friends on social media, but that's only because Phoebe deactivated all her accounts after her father died. And that's a good thing, because she still hasn't opened up to Vicki about any of that. Maybe she's already made the connection and isn't saying anything out of common courtesy. If so, that only makes Phoebe like her more.

Wyatt would probably be proud of her for making an effort at friendship, if she ever decided to tell him. That she hasn't yet is more a function of their living in separate ends of the house now, but she supposes she also likes keeping this part of her life to herself. If Wyatt knew, he might want to join in and try to make it a double date situation, and that is out of the question. Thankfully

Vicki hasn't mentioned doing any such thing. Like Phoebe, she seems content to maintain this little girlfriend oasis of theirs.

Of course, it isn't exactly an oasis. There's another person on their island, though mostly unbeknownst to Vicki or anyone else: Jake. He comes over regularly enough now to mow the grass that Phoebe went ahead and canceled her landscaping service. His attempts to find a summer job here in town this late in the season were unsuccessful anyway, so she's doing him as much a service as he's doing her. Wyatt hasn't mentioned anything about the change, but he rarely has a hand in maintenance matters.

She's also employed Jake for other random jobs around the house that she long ago stopped nagging Wyatt to take care of: replacing lightbulbs she can't reach, unclogging a downspout, hanging art she bought years ago but never put up, touching up a little chipped paint on the porch railings and outside door frames, organizing her shed and attic, and, of course, dusting off the Ferrari. It's been nice accomplishing certain tasks, but she isn't blind to her real motives. Having him around perks her up like a triple espresso. She likes watching the easy physicality that a lifetime of tennis has given him, but he can hold a great conversation too. That high-dollar private school education shows in his knowledge of books, politics, and language.

The stares between them linger a touch longer than they should, and it's amazing how many unspoken words can crowd into a single second, but Phoebe figures as long as she doesn't touch, she can continue to enjoy those quiet gazes. Which sounds just like a pyromaniac who tells herself that as long as she sticks with safety matches, she won't ever burn a house down.

But at least he'll be going away to school soon. By Labor Day, this ridiculous little infatuation will be extinguished for good.

Vicki grabs a wineglass from the cabinet and the corkscrew from its ready spot near the wine rack and takes her usual seat at the table, the same place Wyatt used to sit in the morning when they ate breakfast together. Her new friend has definitely grown familiar with the surroundings. Then again, they've gathered in Phoebe's kitchen the last three times, and it looks like that will continue for a while. Vicki says her house is still too spartan for guests, because she and Ron can't seem to agree on even the simplest things, like paint colors and furniture. Phoebe thinks there's a bit more to the story, like perhaps Ron doesn't like his wife having guests, but she's happy to host either way, because even though she's let new people into her life, she will always feel more comfortable within her own walls.

Phoebe watches Vicki struggle to uncork the bottle for a minute before deciding to intervene. "Want me to do it?"

Vicki gives her a sheepish look. "Would you? Knowing my luck, I'll drop the damn thing."

Well practiced at this particular skill, she makes quick work of it and hands the bottle back. Her friend doesn't look so good, pale and a little weak, like maybe she's using this wine to nurse a hangover, something at which Phoebe is also well practiced. While Vicki fills her glass well beyond the halfway mark, Phoebe notices how gaunt the woman looks. She must have lost a few pounds from her already petite frame, but it's kind of hard to tell based on what she's wearing: a billowy pink gingham blouse that's both long sleeved and buttoned a bit too high. Unusual for midsummer. She remembers the bruise she saw on Vicki's arm the first day they met and feels a little uneasy. Is there something new to cover up?

Though they've both spent some quality time ragging on their husbands, they've avoided anything serious. But the questions have lingered in Phoebe's mind. Vicki always seems a bit too high-strung, nibbled around the edges, like her fingernails. Phoebe did finally meet Ron up close the morning after she loaned them the lawn mower. He'd come home from his shift at the hospital early, complaining of a headache, so his mood wasn't better than it had been on moving day. He was polite enough and thanked her for the mower, but he sounded bitter about it too, like the gesture had embarrassed him more than anything. People can be weird about accepting help, though, and Ron seems like someone who takes his manly pride seriously. Which also makes him the type of guy who would put his hands on his wife.

Phoebe decides it might be time to take things to the next friendship level. "Hey, is everything all right?"

Vicki takes a deep sip from the glass and lets out a sigh. "I look that bad, huh?"

"I wouldn't go that far, but I can say from personal experience that when I'm ready to guzzle down a bottle of wine with breakfast, I'm not having a great day."

"Your insight is not inaccurate. But let's just drink and have some food first."

Phoebe nods and reaches for the bottle. "I can get behind that."

After the quiche comes out, Phoebe plates big slices of it next to the pineapple and strawberries she bought, and they move out to the back porch, because Vicki normally likes to smoke while they chat. Phoebe bought an ashtray for her last week, which she promptly cleans and hides away after Vicki leaves. Wyatt would be glad knowing Phoebe is having a friend over, but he would have a conniption over any evidence of cigarettes.

"All right, we have our food," Phoebe says after a few bites. "Spill."

Vicki puts down her fork and wipes her mouth. "Ron and I had a pretty bad fight yesterday. No big surprise there, but it was worse than usual. I'm worried he might leave me. Especially after Jake goes away to school." Her voice cracks on those last words, but she clears her throat and manages to hold it together.

"What was it about?" she asks, refraining from wondering aloud why Ron's leaving would be any great loss. At best, he's a surly jerk. *Take his alimony, honey; let the rest go.*

"I don't even know where to begin." She's quiet for a minute, as if gathering her thoughts. "Everything's just coming at me from a million different directions. Ron's job, our marriage, my mom."

"You mentioned your mother was ill. That must be stressful by itself."

"She's actually been in a nursing home most of my life, which is hard to believe now that I think about it. I still remember how she was before . . . before she got sick, but I can't believe it's been more than twenty-five years." She sighs and lowers her head. "It's really hard for me to talk about her. The hardest thing, actually."

"It's okay if you don't want to. I understand."

Vicki suddenly lets out a short, shrill laugh, the sort that makes it difficult to tell if someone is amused or angry. "Do you?"

"I know what it feels like to lose parents. My mom died when I was thirteen." A defensive note enters her voice. Is Vicki trying to challenge her on who's suffered more? *Let it go, Phoebe. The woman is clearly stressed out.* She takes a long swallow of her wine.

"I had a plan when we came out here, you know? We've been through absolute hell these last few months, but I was sure we were going to make a fresh start, put everything back together again like it was before. But it hasn't exactly worked out. I feel like a fucking idiot." Vicki is speaking louder and faster, gesturing with her much emptier glass. The alcohol must already be going to work.

"You're still adjusting," Phoebe says. "It's only been a few weeks."

Vicki continues as if Phoebe hasn't spoken. "Ron hates his new job, says he feels like he's been *demoted*." She rolls her eyes. "Yeah, okay, dude. I know you don't have your fancy practice in Beverly Hills anymore, but you're still a goddamn neurosurgeon in one of the country's top hospitals. Demoted. He's lucky he's still a doctor at all and not a janitor at that hospital."

She falls silent for a minute, the words hanging between them like a vapor. Phoebe is tempted to ask what exactly happened with Ron's job, but it doesn't feel like the right time yet. Vicki is still winding herself up to let more out. "And then there's my son. I get the sense he's spinning his wheels too. He hardly mentions Stanford anymore. You know how many years I put into making sure that kid had the grades and the athletics to get his scholarship? He has a full ride, and now it's like he's ready to blow it. I suppose that's my fault too."

Phoebe raises her eyebrow. Jake has a scholarship? Interesting, given Daddy's prestigious line of work. Neurosurgeons from Beverly Hills can usually afford to send their kids to college without that kind of help. She's almost curious enough to ask more about this, but Vicki keeps talking.

"Ron and I do nothing but scream at each other these days. I'm surprised you can't hear our fighting. Or have you heard it? Don't worry, you won't embarrass me if you say yes. I'm already mortified enough for all of us."

"I haven't heard anything. This place is like a fortress."

Vicki pulls out her menthols and lights one. "Lucky you. Our house is like Swiss cheese. Drafty windows, roof leaks, bad central air. You name it, it needs fixing. The place is a total lemon."

Phoebe frowns. "Didn't you need to have all that inspected before you bought it?"

"I guess I should come clean on that. We're actually just renting it." She bows her head, as if in deep shame. Phoebe can understand a little of her distress, at least from a status standpoint, but it seems far from the end of the world. If anything, Vicki should be relieved not to be saddled with a mortgage on the place.

"Well, then the owners should be responsible for repairs and things, right?"

Vicki sighs. "You would think that. But the way we did the lease . . . it was kind of rushed and slapped together. Basically I thought we could handle whatever little problems popped up. I assumed a house around here couldn't need that much work. I was stupid."

"That really sucks." It's her stock answer when she can think of nothing supportive to say, because yeah, Vicki was pretty stupid. Lake Forest is lush with generational family estates worth millions of dollars, but they're still just houses, and many of them are pretty old. They'll fall apart like any other pile of wood and brick when they're not maintained.

"Ron was on board with everything too." She pauses. "Well, mostly, anyway. He didn't want us to get the place, but he eventually came around. And he was fine until things started going south with it. Now it's all *my* fault, and he reminds me every chance he gets. But we were also rushed into a move in part because of *him*." Vicki takes another long drag from her cigarette and wipes her eyes.

"Why did he rush you to move?"

"He lost his job."

"Oh. I'm sorry to hear that."

"Don't be. He's really a quack. The only reason he has this Northwestern gig is because he still has a few friends in high places. Isn't that how it always works? They say the cream always rises. People forget that turds also float. Eventually, he'll screw this up and get flushed, and we'll all go down the drain with him."

Phoebe winces. Vicki, clearly buzzed and well on the way to drunk, drains her glass and empties the remainder of the bottle into it, bringing the chardonnay nearly to the rim. "Do you mind?" she asks, as if Phoebe would object now.

"Have at it." For the first time in a while, she feels like her current sorrows aren't as much in need of drowning. At least she has a good roof over her head. At least her chunk of the Noble fortune is insulated from the current fallout over her father's stupidity, almost as if he saw to that. Phoebe feels guilty now, though she isn't sure why.

"It's strange how everything can fall apart in a way that makes you wonder if a higher power not only is in charge, but has a vendetta against you in particular, you know?"

"I do, yeah," Phoebe says. Though not in the way Vicki means it. She thinks of her father's many ill-fated wives, to start, and all the other damaged lives he left in his wake, more coming out of the woodwork every day. She can understand how it can feel like a higher power is ruining your life, because for many people, Daniel Noble was that higher power.

"It's been a nightmare, Phoebe. No, not a nightmare. Nightmares. Plural, all running together. All I do anymore is wait for shoes to drop. Maybe Ron will get another malpractice suit and blow this job too. I almost count on it."

She shakes her head. "Wow."

Vicki looks at her with a crooked grin. "Speechless, huh?"

"I'm sorry. I never know the right thing to say."

"It's okay. I get it. My life is a clusterfuck. Every day I get up and look in the mirror and I'm also, like, wow."

Phoebe is beginning to regret opening this can of worms. As much venting as Vicki has done this morning, it seems like she's holding back a tidal wave more of pain and rage, which begs the questions: how much worse is it going to get, and will there be some special request at the end? A sourness fills Phoebe's mouth as she remembers why she always avoided getting too close to people. Those expectations, they always come around eventually, don't they? And in many cases, they're holding out a hat.

Shame washes over her as she realizes how much she just reminded herself of her father. Vicki is only looking for someone to listen. It isn't fair to assign any intent beyond that. And what if she did happen to ask for some kind of assistance? Five minutes ago, Phoebe was happy to call her a friend. Helping each other is what friends do.

But wouldn't it also be a little unfair of Vicki to put her in a position where she has to say yes or risk making things permanently awkward with her neighbor? She doesn't seem like that kind of person, but they've only known each other a few weeks. If she's learned anything about people recently, it's that you can know them your whole life and still discover they're strangers.

Despite her doubts, though, Phoebe says the only other thing she can think of, the only thing that seems appropriate when a friend opens up about her troubles: "Is there anything I can do to help?"

Vicki's expression is part relief, part surprise, part . . . resentment? Phoebe wonders if she stepped wrong, but Vicki drains the last of her wine, sets down the glass, and takes a deep breath. "It's really about my mother. She—"

The doorbell rings twice in quick succession, and they both jump. Vicki upsets the plate of mostly untouched food on her lap and lets out an irritated squawk as the quiche and her fork slide off onto the patio stones. "Oh damn it!"

"It's okay." Phoebe stands up. "I'll be right back."

She glides to the door, relieved at the break in the tension. It doesn't matter who it is at this point. Could be a traveling Bible salesman or even a reporter asking about her father for all she cares. When she sees Jake, however, her heart takes its customary leap and she smiles big. She wasn't expecting to see him at all today. "Hey, what's up?"

He isn't smiling back. If anything, he looks a little pale. And his T-shirt is wet all down the front. "Is my mom still here?" he asks.

"Yeah, come on in."

She leads him toward the patio, but Vicki is already in the kitchen depositing her plate into the sink. When she sees her son, she frowns. "What's wrong?"

He clears his throat and immediately begins to fidget. "So, uh, the kitchen is flooded."

Vicki gapes. "*Flooded?* What did you *do?*"

"I only ran the dishwasher like you asked me to. Water started coming out from under the sink. It looks like one of the hoses gave out. I went to turn off the water at the cutoff valve, but I think we need to, you know, call someone."

"Please. If it's just a bad hose and a little water, I can take care of that myself."

He heaves another sigh. "It isn't just the hose. When I was turning off the water, the valve kind of broke off. I have duct tape holding back the spray, but just barely."

Her face goes nearly the color of a beet. "Why didn't you turn off the water at the main valve?"

"I don't know where that is. I looked around by the water heater, but I'm not a plumber."

Vicki balls her hands into fists and shakes them at the sides of her head. "This is great! Just . . . just *perfect!*" She turns to Phoebe, her face branded with rage that seems almost accusatory. "See what I'm dealing with here? I can't catch a break for even one goddamn hour!"

Phoebe opens her mouth, but she isn't sure what to say that

won't sound grossly inadequate. "Wow" certainly won't do it. But it doesn't matter, because Vicki is storming toward the front door, with Jake trailing along behind her. He throws several apologetic glances back at her over his shoulder. Seconds later, the door slams closed, leaving Phoebe shuddering in a vacuum of silence. She's considering helping herself to another slice of Vicki's quiche when her phone rings. It's Wyatt. She's tempted to let it go to voicemail, but she needs to fill the void with another voice, even if it hasn't been very friendly of late. Also, she can't remember the last time he called her from work. It could be an emergency of some sort. Though would she still be his main point of contact if he was having one of those?

"Hello?"

"Oh. Hey." Papers shuffling in the background.

Phoebe waits a few seconds and frowns. "So . . . what's up?"

"Sorry, I wasn't expecting you to pick up. Was just going to leave you a message."

"You could have texted or emailed if you didn't want to actually speak with me."

"That's not what I meant." He sighs. "Listen, sorry. I was just calling to let you know I canceled that thing we had planned with Gene and his wife a while back. It was coming up this weekend."

It takes her a second to make all the necessary connections in her head. Gene. Gene Fielder, Wyatt's office mate. He runs a small practice specializing in behavioral therapy for kids. He and his wife, Sarah, are the closest things Phoebe and Wyatt have had to mutual friends in the last couple years, but she can't even remember the last time she saw them. Christmas? "What thing was that again?"

"The jazz festival in Englewood."

"Ah."

Silence. Then he says, "I know you don't like jazz anyway."

"Yeah, I hate it. Funny how you said we wanted to go in the first place." She knows this is only going to escalate things between them, but she can't help herself. Every day he seems to bring her a new reason to be annoyed. It isn't the first time that Wyatt agreed to an activity one or both of them wouldn't enjoy, just because he doesn't know how to say no. The jazz festival doesn't sound like it would be as awful as, say, the time Gene invited them to a sales pitch for a shady timeshare in Florida, but her night would still end with a headache.

"It was just an attempt to be social. You know, spend time with some friends."

She could tell him she actually does have friends and that she's been plenty social lately, thank you very much, but there has already been one emotional meltdown in this kitchen today, and she's not going to add to the count. "Then why don't you go? You don't need me to be social."

Silence for half a minute, then, "I don't know. Maybe."

"All right, well if that's all you wanted, I'll talk to you later."

He starts to say something, but she's already hanging up.

■ ■ ■

AN HOUR LATER, the doorbell rings again. Phoebe nearly decides to ignore it and continue watching the mindless reality show she put on to drown out the echoes in her head. But it's probably Vicki, and she'll undoubtedly want to smooth things over after this morning. If there even is anything to smooth over. It isn't like they had a fight. Nevertheless, Phoebe feels like they did, or like some of Vicki's anger was directed at her, though she can't understand why.

Wyatt, in his esteemed-mental-health-expert wisdom, would say it's projection. Phoebe hasn't been too pleased with herself lately. Hiding away from the world like a coward to avoid inheriting her father's disgrace. Lusting after a teenage boy. Allowing her marriage to tumble into disarray. Gaining weight. Drinking like a fish. She's guaranteed to see her loathing reflected back at her from almost anyone. That's her problem, not anyone else's. Vicki isn't mad at her. She's just mad all around. And she needs to know someone gives a damn. They both do. Maybe Phoebe will have a turn and tell her all about her so-called charmed life as a ruthless tycoon's kid.

She gets up from the couch and peeks through the window to see not Vicki standing on the porch, but Jake. He looks even more solemn than he did earlier, but at least he's dry in a plain white tee and a pair of jeans. She opens the door.

"Can I come in?" he asks.

She stands aside to let him pass and checks the street again. Still no blue car today. This time she takes a second to consult her notebook. The last day she recorded anything was Tuesday morning. It's now Friday. Maybe a cop paid a visit when Phoebe wasn't looking. She can't help but feel a pang of disappointment at the possibility.

Jake is in the kitchen leaning against the island, his arms folded pensively across him. The silence is so unpleasantly thick she feels close to bursting out with, *Gee, isn't everyone in a fine mood today!* Instead she leans against the island next to him. "Want something to drink? Some of your mom's quiche, maybe?"

He shakes his head. "I wanted to apologize for what happened earlier."

"There's no need for that. Is everything all right?"

"For now. We got the water shut off before things got any worse. A plumber is coming this evening. My mom's over there right now trying to meditate herself out of having a stroke. All of this is so stupid."

He runs a hand through his hair, and a few strands flop down near his eye. Almost reflexively, she reaches up and brushes them away, and then realizes immediately how intimate the gesture is. Familiar. She hasn't actually touched him before. His unwavering stare tells her he's having a similar thought, but he doesn't seem put off. Instead, he reaches out to tuck a small wisp of her own hair behind her ear, moving slowly, deliberately, fingertips lingering and then gently gliding down the line of her jaw before falling away. "You had one out of place too," he says.

Phoebe busies herself by going to the sink for a glass of water. Even with her back to him, she can still feel his gaze. "It's only been a few weeks since you got here, you know," she says. "Things will ease up for your mom soon, I'm sure." She could just as easily be talking about herself, though inside her, things seem to be doing the opposite of easing up. She forces herself to drink the water. It goes down in hard, audible gulps.

"I doubt things will get any easier for her."

"I'm sure that isn't true," she says.

"Oh, it is. Things aren't normal for Vicki Napier if she isn't struggling. A big part of her loves what's happening right now, because she gets to play victim. It's just so embarrassing when she goes off like she did earlier. She doesn't care how it makes other people around her feel. It's all about her, you know?"

"Pain and stress can make people selfish without realizing it."

"Of course now she feels terrible about how she acted. I told her that wasn't good enough."

"Don't be harder on someone than they are on themselves, Jake."

He sighs. "I know you're right. But the longer you know her, the more you'll see what I mean. I know she seems pretty cool at first, but trust me..." He trails off. She nearly presses him to finish the thought, but does she really want to know more? At this point, Phoebe feels like she's peered deeper into the dysfunctional diorama of the Napier household than she cares to. Maybe it's time to insist on a little more opaqueness, for the sake of remaining good neighbors.

"Well, I'm prepared to cut her a break and move on. She's mortified enough. I would be too."

"Yes, but I doubt you'd ever act like that."

She turns back to him. "You know that for a fact, do you?"

"I think I have a pretty good idea what you're like by now." He grins. A warm ember in her gut pops alight. "You're cool. Like ... Blake Lively or Keira Knightley."

Phoebe bursts out laughing. "Wow, Jake. Have you been drinking?" She wishes she was. It will take a gallon of wine to mute the girl in her head who's shrieking over being compared to two beautiful actresses.

He joins her at the sink, standing close enough to make their shoulders touch. The proximity is maddening, as is the scent of his cologne. "Do you have anything I can do around here today?"

She tilts her head up to look at him. His eyes are so blue she's sure she'll fall in them and drown if she keeps staring. "Jake," she begins, wondering where exactly she plans to go with this.

"I just need some kind of distraction. Don't make me go back over there."

"You could always go for another run," she suggests.

"I thought about it. But I kind of prefer your company." He gently nudges her shoulder with his, another tiny motion bearing a truckload of intimacy.

Okay, that's it. Time to be the adult in the room yet again, Phoebe. Acknowledge this thing between you and then send him on his way before you do something really stupid. But her balance is so weak after the morning she's had. It's hard to make the right words come out, but she brings them to the edge of her lips and, with effort, pushes them through: "I don't think you should keep coming over here."

He shakes his head. "Please don't say that."

"I have to do the right thing here." *Yes, that's it. It's never easy, but it's always worth it.* Is it really, though? The right thing means she'll go back to sitting alone and eventually drunk in front of the TV. The right thing means likely still being in that same sunken divot in the couch when the guy who knew she hated jazz but still made plans for them to go to a jazz festival comes home to remind her with his sad, mopey face what a coldhearted bitch she is.

The prospect of doing the right thing isn't what's turning her heart into a trip-hammer at full power, or making her feel like she's standing on a high, narrow ledge with a dubious pair of wings and a strong urge to jump. Maybe that makes the right thing the wrong thing. At least for right now. *Oh, the lies we tell ourselves.* She shoves that needling voice away.

Jake turns to her, effectively removing any room for air between them. "I'll go if you want me to. But why does it feel like we both want something else?"

Where does he get such confidence at his young age? She opens her mouth to speak, but she can't make the necessary lie come out. *Just see how the next few minutes go. You won't be able to move past this little infatuation until you've let it have its way with you a bit. Think of it as an attempt to cure yourself.*

She kisses him before she can offer up a sane rebuttal to this ridiculous idea. He returns it eagerly, his mouth experienced, but not overly so, more than willing to follow her lead. "We can't have sex," she whispers. "I don't have any condoms."

"It's okay."

The longer they kiss, their hands wandering first over each other's clothes, then beneath them, the more tortured she feels, knowing she can't have him the way her body craves him most. So she chooses the next best path to satisfaction, taking his hand and guiding it between her legs. He's more deft than she expects. She pulls him tightly against her as he works, and her orgasm takes her so completely she doesn't notice until he cries out that she's dug her fingernails deep into his shoulder. "Sorry," she breathes, letting him go and leaning back against the counter, her legs too wobbly to hold her upright for the moment. Jake doesn't look like he's doing much better as he lets out a long, shaky sigh and resumes his position next to her.

"Did that really just happen?" he asks.

"Yeah, I think so." Acknowledging that part is easy enough. The hard part is admitting that it wasn't enough. The thing she hoped to exorcise is now fully awake and hungry.

As if he heard the run of her thoughts, he asks, "Will this be the only time?"

"You know it can't become anything more than this, right? I'm married. You're heading off to school." *I'm also friends with your mother* doesn't feel like it needs to be said. It's the invisible elephant in the room, one that will likely suffocate her if she lets it.

"I can handle that." He lightly strokes her arm, sending a wave of goose bumps down her body.

She lays her head on his shoulder, and his arm slides around her hips, pulling her closer. Already she feels herself warming to another round, but not before they get some ground rules out of the way. "We have to be so careful. God, if anyone found out about this . . ."

"Don't worry. I know how to be careful."

She thinks of her friend in the blue car, a potential witness. "You know about the bike path that cuts through the woods behind our cul-de-sac, right?"

"Sure. I run on it all the time."

"Take that when you come and go from now on. Less risk of anyone seeing you."

"Okay." He grins. "I feel a little bit like your coconspirator now."

"Yeah, I guess that's one way of putting it." She'll take it over "boy toy," anyway.

He faces her. At first, he looks serious, but then a glint of fun pops into his eyes. "So I have to ask again. Do you have anything I can do around here today?"

She can think of a few things.

■ ■ ■

I KNOW YOU'VE been busy lately making friends with your new neighbors, but you must have noticed I haven't been around as much, either. I'm pushing it by being here even now, but I had to stop over before my morning shift. I can't have you thinking I've forgotten you, though at first, I thought maybe you had, with nary a twitch from those front blinds once your husband left for the day. But eventually you came through. A little late, but better than never. It feels good to know you're still looking out for me.

You can blame Jesse Bachmann for my absence; the oily little shadow man's behavior is escalating. He started making things at the store a lot more difficult for me right away, threatening to report me for the tiniest infractions, like clocking in a minute or two late, or not collecting carts from the parking lot at the designated times even though we're shorthanded at registers. From there, I started noticing more disturbing things, like that the food and drink I'd been leaving in the break room fridge had been tampered with—the sandwich flattened, the seal broken on my bottled water. I threw it all away untouched, and started just buying food from the deli next door.

And now it's spilling over into this part of my life. A couple days ago, I received an email containing pictures of my car sitting in this very spot, letting me know he's been following me outside of work. In spite of this great inconvenience, I can't help but be impressed by his stalking skills. Where he'll take it from here is anyone's guess, but I suspect it won't be good for me.

If you were a girlfriend hearing all this, you'd probably think I should be scared right now. You'd probably also ask why I haven't taken this to the management, or even the police, yet. Unfortunately, everything he's done so far has been hard to pin directly on him without making me look overly paranoid. So, bearing that in mind, I lined up a little insurance policy against the creep by doing what I do best.

Yesterday just happened to be inventory day, which tends to go late into the night. I was able to arrange to have the evening off. Bachmann, being on the lowest rung of the supervisor ladder, was not so lucky. He made sure anyone within earshot knew how displeased he was about that. I already knew where he lived. He isn't the only one who can dig into employee files. Management is lax on keeping that stuff secure.

True to the cliché of angry social rejects, Bachmann does live with his mother, just not in her basement. He stays in a room above her garage, which is situated behind a tidy little house about eight miles northwest of Lake Forest. There were no cameras or alarms on the premises, at least that my brief sweep could pick up, but the biometric lock he installed on the door was adorable. I only had to pull out a paper clip to pop it open from its manual key backup. But just knowing that he thought it was so much more secure than a high-quality traditional dead bolt told me he had stuff to hide. It felt like Christmas when I made my way inside.

For all the stock Bachmann put into that fancy smart lock, he didn't make much effort to conceal things behind that door. Sure, his computer was password protected, like anyone's these days, but I didn't need access given what I found left so brazenly in the open. Namely the dozens of printed photos tacked to the wall next to his bed featuring still frames from the store security cameras, all of them female customers and employees, including me. He'd labeled each of them with charming nicknames. Our general manager: Thunder Tits Theresa. One of our night cashiers: Barely Legal Bailey. I was simply labeled "Nasty Whore," not even worth a clever alliteration. It was the same way he'd addressed me in the emails. Not that I'd needed any more proof that he was the one behind the car photos, but it was a nice bit of corroboration, nonetheless.

I also discovered his affinity for good old-fashioned yellow legal pads. The towering stack of them next to his bed would have provided days of entertainment if I'd had the time or stomach to read the petulant manifesto of a chronically rejected narcissist, but the one on the very top was good enough for my purposes. I took several pictures of the pages, as well as his photo collage on the wall, before making off with my little jackpot.

Now I just have to decide what I'm going to do with this information. Do I tell Bachmann what I have on him and force us into a reluctant stalemate? Or do I use the nuclear option and deliver it to

Thunder Tits Theresa? Both are tempting for their own reasons. I'll give it some time to stew.

I'm here past my normal time, but something else has grabbed my attention since I arrived today, and I want to see it through. Did you happen to notice your new neighbors are running a bit of a drama factory over here? They like leaving their windows open in the middle of summer, which is odd. Maybe the air-conditioning is broken, but whatever the reason, the sound of their fights carries all the way out here, and this morning is no exception. Most of the time, I hear only the husband, but sometimes I hear her too, a softer undercurrent, like the lone flute in a symphony of brass and percussion. It's hard to make out actual words, but the tone and pitch are telling enough. People who yell like him are broken inside. It reminds me a bit too much of home.

And speak of the devil. The gentleman of the house appears to have tapped out early. He's now on the front porch, pacing back and forth, raking his hands through his hair. Cool down, bro, before you have a heart attack. He delivers a swift kick to the porch rail, which must hurt. Those loafers don't look like they have steel toes. And now he's glancing my way, which feels like my final cue to go. I know you're still keeping your eye on me, but I do hope you're looking out for these people too.

CHAPTER 7

THEY'VE BEEN BURIED under the sheets for the last hour, pressed together like a pair of spoons, drowsing in and out of sleep. If she keeps her eyes closed, she can almost pretend this isn't the boy next door she's been sleeping with every afternoon for nearly the past two weeks. But if she lies in still silence for too long, a curtain pulls back in her mind, revealing a dark gulf filled with all the worst thoughts. Like that Wyatt could have a canceled appointment and come home early. They may be only a step away from divorce, but the shame if he discovered this would overwhelm her. Even worse would be if Vicki found out, and there are myriad ways she could. Young people in particular can be careless. He might leave his phone in the wrong place, exposing some lurid text or picture they've shared. Or one of his shirts carrying Phoebe's scent might get too close to Vicki's nose; she's already complimented Phoebe twice on her choice of Black Opium.

But plaguing her worse than any nightmare scenario of discovery is the voice of her own conscience, whispering to her that she's no better than her father. Cheating on her spouse with someone so young is textbook Daniel. As is wallowing in the thrill that such a power dynamic brings. She hates that, of all the behaviors she couldn't relate to—his drive to hoard money, his crude humor that often strayed into cruelty, his tacky taste in décor and cars—this is the one to which she can. And because of her father, she's more vulnerable to scrutiny right now. She isn't directly part of Daniel's world—doesn't work for the company, doesn't speak for him in any capacity—but the Noble name is on a lot of lips lately. If this affair became part of the media's conversation, the fallout would crush her. And has she forgotten so soon that someone is still watching her? Someone who might be looking for anything at all to blackmail her with? The blue car hasn't been coming around quite as often lately, but the visits haven't stopped yet, and she isn't sure what will need to happen before they finally do.

She's behaving more and more like a drug addict, where the fix is everything. It comes in many forms: the first kiss of the day, the feel of his warm skin pressing against hers when they quickly jettison any clothing between them, that moment when she isn't sure she has one more orgasm in her and then proves herself wrong. The pleasure eclipses any threat of consequences, no matter how dire. Unchecked, it will be her undoing.

At least there is an expiration date for all of this. In a handful of weeks, he'll go off to Stanford with a nice packet of memories to keep him warm until he finds someone his own age. Meanwhile, they've worked overtime to cram as much as they can into the few stolen hours they have together every day, and in doing so, they've rapidly evolved into something more than a fling, which is as lovely as it is troubling. They cook for each other. They watch each other's favorite shows. They have similar wits, falling more into the irony and humor of a mature couple than the saccharine romantic platitudes of the young and naive. She's also opened up to him about her father, and all the pain he's caused her in both life and the aftermath. Jake's youthful way of seeing the world in starker terms of justice and injustice, fair and unfair, means he can comfort and validate her in a way Wyatt and his middle-aged pragmatism never could. In their best moments, she feels like she's back in the earliest days of that relationship, which in turn makes her feel nineteen again.

But age and experience are never too far away to remind her these feelings are an illusion. When Jake leaves out the back door every afternoon, Phoebe returns to reality with a man who can no longer disguise his contempt for her. He slams every door he closes, chops every other word he must exchange with her down to a single frost-rimmed syllable. He's emptying far more bottles of his beloved bourbon, but mostly behind the shuttered door of the spare bedroom, where, not so coincidentally, he's been playing a lot of John Coltrane and Miles Davis at just a high enough volume to dig at her. But isn't this the last stage of ugly limbo for most relationships before the inevitable fade to black?

She doesn't see this fling with Jake as being any exception, and wouldn't, even if it didn't already come preloaded with so many moral failings. She's carrying this knowledge of the future around with her like a secret tumor. And there's no use telling Jake that he'll have one just like it someday. He'll have to grow one himself, and only then will he understand. It may not bear her name when it finally happens, but she's definitely planted the seed.

As much as it might pain her to think about it, he really can't leave for California soon enough. Let her have this *Bridges of Madison County* moment and return to some semblance of sanity. Her marriage is beyond saving at this point, but there is life on the other side of a divorce, if she can find the courage to get there.

She rolls over to face him and is taken all over again by how handsome he is. It's far too easy to imagine sleeping all night with him, and then waking up and planning their whole day together.

"What if we stop doing this now?" she asks. "Would you be upset?"

"Yes." He isn't one to waste words, which is one of her favorite things about him. He knows what he wants, which is so rare in a man even twice his age. "Are you saying you want this to end?" He's sporting a crooked grin, but it isn't entirely playful.

"No, but it will soon no matter what we want. Stanford calls."

He sighs and rolls onto his back. "I'm trying not to think about that. But my mother won't shut up about it, almost like she can't wait to be rid of me."

He hasn't directly mentioned his mother since they started this, which has been a good thing, considering Phoebe and Vicki have more or less resumed their old rhythm from before the awkward brunch, and she's struggled to keep these two very distinct worlds separate in her mind. But now she sits up and takes interest, because it isn't quite the same between Vicki and her, is it? Vicki seems more distant, not as keen to open up. She hasn't spoken again about problems with the house or Ron, and Phoebe has been reluctant to trigger another emotional torrent by asking her. It just seems easier to be a cheerful harbor from whatever storms Vicki is dealing with, and if such a time comes that she needs something more, Phoebe will do whatever she can.

But she can't help but be curious about whatever's happening over there. How could she not be after the little peek she's had behind the curtain?

"I very much doubt she's looking to get rid of you. She just wants you to enjoy this opportunity you have and realize how lucky you are."

He laughs silently. "The funny thing is, when she made the decision to move here, I wanted to stay in California. I had this plan in mind to live with some friends until I started Stanford in the fall, but she wasn't having it, said she didn't want to separate the family any sooner than she had to. My dad sided with her, because he didn't want one more thing for them to fight about. I finally gave in, and I hated her for it all the way out here. I wanted this whole thing to blow up in her face. Part of me still does, actually, because all she's done is upset our lives over some crazy belief . . ." He stops and stares at his lap for a minute, and then shakes his head. "It doesn't really matter anymore, because I'm glad it happened. Coming here is actually the best thing that ever happened to me."

Now it's Phoebe's turn to shake her head, because she sees what's coming next. It's bearing down on her like the high beams of a truck on a lonely country road, and panic has rooted her to her spot. "Jake . . ."

"Maybe Stanford is overrated. Chicago has some great schools. You and your father both went to Northwestern, right? The way I see it, if it was good enough for the Nobles, it's good enough for me."

She pulls away from him. "Why are you doing this?"

"Doing what?"

"Reneging on your plans. You can't just make snap decisions like this. Stanford is a big deal, and it's too late to enroll anywhere else for the fall anyway. You're not jeopardizing your education because of me."

"So I take a gap year and think things over. I'd hardly be the first person to do that. Why would it be so terrible if I decided to stick around?"

She wants to scream all the obvious facts into his pretty face. Because the longer this goes on, the more likely it is that they'll get caught. And the promise of its being short-lived was the only reason she allowed this to happen in the first place. *The Bridges of Madison County* doesn't become *The Bridges of Madison County* until Francesca refuses to leave with Robert. Remembering her obligations is Phoebe's only path to redemption; otherwise she's no different from Daniel, ruining the lives that stand between her and whatever she wants.

"I said from the beginning this couldn't go anywhere, and you agreed. You said you were just fine with this being casual."

He grins. "But you don't want me to go. Not really. Admit it."

"It doesn't matter what I want. You know the position I'm in. Carrying on like this much longer is dangerous."

He raises his eyebrows. "Dangerous? That's a little dramatic, don't you think? So what if people find out? I think it would actually be a relief to stop treating this like it's this filthy secret."

"But it is a filthy secret! My god, you're just a kid, Jake."

He winces, and his face reddens. She's never said such a thing to him before, never wanted to condescend to him in such a way, because it would only make her feel like a hypocrite. "I'm not a *kid*. I'm eighteen. And I wasn't too young for you a half hour ago," he points out, correctly of course.

She feels like she's going to be sick. "You're right. I'm sorry. But your mother and I are friends, Jake. That puts us in a very tenuous situation, wouldn't you agree?"

He gives a grudging shrug, which is not the acknowledgment she's looking for.

"And you know the situation with my father. If this got out with all the other things people are saying about him, that his daughter is a . . . a pervert . . ."

He sighs. "Phoebe, I think you're blowing that whole thing out of proportion."

Her mouth falls open. For a moment, she thinks she's been hallucinating Jake's face over Wyatt's, because the two of them sound identical. "How can you be so dismissive all of a sudden?"

"I'm not! I'm just saying the bad press will blow over eventually. You're not your father."

"You don't know my father, Jake, and you really don't know me all that well, either."

He stares at her with hurt confusion. "Maybe you're right, but I know you're being selfish, and you can't even see it because you've shut yourself away from the world and you can only see things your way."

She stands up like the covers have suddenly started burning her skin. Her robe is draped over a nearby chair and she grabs it to cover herself. "Don't you dare try to analyze me. I'm already married to a goddamn shrink."

He gets out of bed too but doesn't seem the least bit concerned with covering up. Why would he be? He's arguing from the position that he has nothing to hide. "Listen, I'm not saying it will be easy, especially at first. Yes, my parents will be mad. Yes, it's even possible a gossip reporter will have something to say about the daughter of Daniel Noble in some blog post or tweet no one will even see. But you have to admit you're happy when we're together. Why don't you want more of that? Why are you so afraid of whatever this is?"

She feels like she did when Wyatt brought out his adorable adoption pamphlets, and yet again, she's wielding the needle to burst someone's bubble. But she hates this even more, because they were never supposed to fight. This wasn't that kind of arrangement. "Happiness is bullshit. It's only meant to define small moments, not a whole life. Nothing we've done means shit outside this room, where you actually have to live."

"You really think you can make me believe that? This is more than just sex."

"Do you think you're the first person I ever fucked for amusement?"

His face darkens. "Don't. You're just trying to hurt me now." There it is, the nerve she was searching for.

"I know what happens when people get stuck on happy, okay? They think, hey, sex is fun, and we like some of the same things. That must mean we're happy! Let's stay together forever and we'll be happy forever! But it's a lie, and I'm done telling it to myself. If you're smart, you'll listen to me and stop buying into the bullshit too. And you'll stop believing that a few doses of happiness are worth ruining people's lives over. That's what my father spent his entire life doing, and I can't do that. I've clearly already done enough damage."

"You don't mean this. You don't mean any of it."

"If you tell me one more time what you think I believe, I'll end this whole thing now, for good."

He's pacing now, holding a bullish posture startlingly similar to his father's the first day Phoebe saw him. She wonders how deep his resemblance to Ron really goes. Will he leave bruises too? She almost wants to test him just to see, to give him one more nudge. But he turns away and quickly dresses himself. The knot in Phoebe's gut releases itself, but only a little. Behind it is a fresh nausea as the fun little distraction she's built for herself goes up in flames. When he's done, he goes to the bedroom door and looks back, waiting to see if she'll change her mind. Part of her, and not a small one, wants to do just that, to return to the soft sheets and warm silence and beg him to forget everything she just said, but she maintains her stone face. If she doesn't stick to her convictions now, she'll lose what little self-respect she has left.

She goes out to the landing as he stomps down the stairs. He places his hand on the doorknob, and she cries out, "No, don't go that way!" The car was out there when last she checked, and it's too early for it to be gone. And what if Vicki is on the porch having her midmorning cigarette? If she saw her son storm out of Phoebe's front door like a jaded lover, she would certainly have questions.

Jake turns to her, his jaw jutting with defiance, eyes blazing. Oh how she hates that furious gaze on her. "You've had your way on everything so far. Now it's my turn."

She rushes down the stairs and blocks the door. "Don't be stupid! People will see you!"

"After all this, do you really think I care?" He pushes her aside and opens the door. Time slows to a crawl as Phoebe's eyes land on the blue car parked in its usual spot. The absence of Vicki on the Napier porch is a tiny mercy as the hot summer air hits her exposed skin. In the midst of their argument, she didn't tie the robe, and she's naked underneath. She quickly slams the door shut, but it's too late.

Gripped by panic and rage, she wants to scream. She wants to break things. Instead, she takes a deep breath and goes to the kitchen in search of her trusty cabernet. But then she has another thought, and veers instead for the liquor cabinet, where she finds Wyatt's bourbon. It isn't her favorite, but she needs something that'll make the walls of this house and the voices in her head stop mocking her. Once she's settled on the couch, she takes three deep swigs straight from the bottle and then flips on the TV. It doesn't take long before she finds a game show with a live audience, and she turns it up loud. If she tries really hard, and keeps sipping from the bottle, she'll eventually feel they're in the room with her.

CHAPTER 8

SHE SNAPS AWAKE to the sound of the phone ringing, the sun glaring in her eyes. *Jake. Please let it be him.* All she can think of is how yesterday was a mistake, and she needs to fix this.

But it isn't him. It's Vicki, and her mouth goes dry. What if she saw him running out the front door yesterday, and in his upset state he told her everything?

"Then she wouldn't be calling," Phoebe says to the empty bedroom. Either Vicki or Ron would be over here beating down Phoebe's door. She answers.

"Hello?"

"Good morning, sunshine. Or afternoon, technically. You stood me up. I've been calling all morning."

Phoebe glances at the clock. It's just a few minutes past twelve, about two hours beyond their typical brunching time. A quick glance at the phone shows a series of missed calls from Vicki's number. This just happened to be the one that caught her on the edge of consciousness. Luckily, Vicki doesn't sound grumpy about it. "Shit. Sorry. I never even heard the doorbell ring. Was so out of it."

"I understand. Rough night?"

In the fog of her hangover, she recalls a brief discussion with Wyatt.

"I can give you the number of someone you can talk to, Phoebe," he began.

"Talk to about what?"

His eyes fell onto the mostly empty bourbon bottle in her lap. "Do I really need to say it?"

"Yes. For once, just tell me exactly what you're thinking instead of being so goddamn mealy-mouthed. I've always hated that about you. So did my father."

His face darkened like a thunderhead, and she braced herself for the lightning. But it never came. Instead, he strode off, though she isn't sure if he left the house or hunkered down in his jazz cave, because she lost consciousness soon after. At some point, she managed to drag herself upstairs, though she doesn't remember that, either.

Vicki laughs softly. "I can tell by your silence it was indeed a rough night."

"You could say that. Can we rain-check for tomorrow?"

"No way. I've decided that as your newest and, let's be honest, only girlfriend, I am sworn to uphold all our standing plans lest we both drown in the murky waters of suburban white-girl ennui."

Phoebe laughs despite her pounding headache. No more bourbon for her, ever. "Did you double up on your happy pills today or something?"

"How did you know it was Double Dose Wednesday? Now get up and make yourself look decent for real. I am taking us out today."

Cold strings tighten around her gut. "Out?"

"Yes, Rip Van Winkle. *Out*. Let's go flaunt our Amex cards in the village. I've been wanting to hit all those cute little shops since I got here."

Phoebe quietly groans. Her favorite thing about Vicki has been her complete lack of interest in things like going out or having girly shopping excursions. But at least she only wants to go down the road and not to the Magnificent Mile. In the middle of a weekday, it will be quiet. "All right. I'll be ready in an hour."

"Bazinga!" she cries. "People are still saying that, right? Come over when you're ready. It's nice enough that we could even walk if you want."

She nearly groans again. Exercise? "Sounds great!" she says, trying on chipper for size and finding it a poor fit.

After the phone call, she lies back down for a few more minutes, hoping to pump herself up. Maybe Vicki could give her a little bit of whatever she's having. She wonders if something happened to change their fortunes. An influx of cash, perhaps? Hard to go on a shopping spree when you're broke.

Letting out a deep sigh, she gets out of bed and drags herself into the shower. When it's over, she feels almost human again, and more open-minded about the day's prospects. How long has it been since she left the house to do anything but buy a few groceries, anyway? A little retail therapy would do her some good. It's actually a nice day too. Not too hot or humid, perfect for a leisurely stroll. And there is that great little European bakery where they could eat every calorie the walking would burn. That officially sells her.

After combing her wet hair and stepping back into the darkened bedroom to get dressed, she sees someone sitting on the corner of her bed and screams. Then recognition kicks in. "Jake?" She fantasized about a moment just like this last night, where he'd use the key she gave him to let himself in and slip back into bed with her like nothing happened. And then she chastised herself for being so quixotic.

He comes to her, his eyes shining in the dimness. "I was such an asshole. We don't have to do anything you don't want to do. I'm so sorry."

"Shut up." She grabs his shirt and yanks him toward her. "We only have a few minutes. Show me how much you've missed me."

Thirty minutes later, Phoebe is walking with Vicki along the quaint cluster of shops in Lake Forest known as Market Square, and feeling far less burdened by her conscience than she expected to. Before parting ways for the day, she and Jake mutually agreed to just enjoy each moment together as it comes, and she's applying that same principle to this one too. It does mean building thicker walls between the compartments in her mind, going out of her way to keep conversations from straying to personal things that remind her exactly who Vicki is. This puts her dangerously close to the waters of self-delusion, but she only needs to do it for a couple hours at a time. *It's simple, Phoebe. Just maintain your hard boundaries, and you might be able to end each day not curled into the fetal position.*

Phoebe hasn't walked this much in a long time, but she's always loved strolling through the historic cluster of buildings that comprise Market Square. With its brick and stucco façades, gabled roofs, open courtyards, and elegant foliage and landscaping, which is particularly lush this time of year, the outdoor shopping district brings her back to the trips she took to Europe with her parents growing up. That she lives within walking distance of such a place and rarely musters the effort to even leave the house most days fills her with shame, and she makes a promise to herself to get down here more, at least once a week. Yet she knows the promises people make to themselves are the most brittle of all.

However, the number of bags they've amassed so far makes her wish she'd insisted on driving. When they reach the checkout at Williams-Sonoma, she's about to suggest they text Jake to come pick them up (so much for those strong boundaries), but they hit another snag entirely when the perky young woman ringing up Vicki's sprawling pile of housewares becomes a little less perky. "I'm sorry, ma'am, but it says your card has been declined."

Vicki frowns. "Excuse me? That can't be correct. Can we run it again?"

"Of course," the girl says, more out of an obligation to maintain rapport than any belief that running a dud card again will make it a nondud. A second later, she shakes her head, this time with a bit of fear creeping into her eyes as she braces herself for what could be a DEFCON 1 situation. "I'm really sorry. It declined again."

"Well that just makes no sense!" Vicki cries, making the girl shrink back a bit. "I assure you, there should be no problem with these cards. I've been using them all afternoon, and I know my balances." She begins digging in her wallet for another card, muttering under her breath, ruddy blooms of color rising in her cheeks. Phoebe's anxiety mounts as she remembers Vicki's outburst the day the dishwasher sprang a leak, and wonders if being in public will be any deterrent to her having a similar meltdown. Phoebe makes brief eye contact with the clerk, hoping to assure the poor girl that she won't let this get out of hand. Vicki sticks a different card into the card reader's chip slot. "This one should give you no troubles."

The girl grins nervously as she waits. After a torturous fifteen seconds, during which Phoebe wonders whether Vicki really is trying to shop on nearly maxed credit cards, the telltale beep of rejection sounds again. Color drains from the clerk's face, but she's only just opened her mouth when Phoebe steps up with her card. "Here, try mine."

"Phoebe, no!" Vicki sounds as if Phoebe is stepping in front of a bus to spare her life.

"Vicki, yes. I told you I wasn't going to let you leave here without that wine aerator, and I meant it."

"There has to be something wrong with their system. I can put the stuff back and come for it later." Her voice doesn't carry much conviction, and the tears in her eyes only underscore that she knows very well it isn't the system malfunctioning. Phoebe also notes with considerable discomfort how much those eyes resemble Jake's.

"Whatever the case may be, I'm happy to get this. So settle back, all right?"

She pats her friend gently on the shoulder, hoping to calm her down, her guts stirring with embarrassment on Vicki's behalf. Anything else she might try to say to make her feel better ("I have more money than I know what to do with" or "A few hundred bucks is as inconsequential as a sneeze") would only make things worse. When the register produces its mile-long receipt, the clerk hands it to Phoebe with a grateful look. "Thank you so much, ladies! Have a wonderful day!" Her overly chipper voice makes Vicki wince.

"Our pleasure," Phoebe says, taking their bags and leading Vicki out of the suddenly oppressive store. On the sidewalk, she hands Vicki her bag.

"You really didn't have to do that," she says.

Oh, I believe I did, Phoebe thinks. *At least to save that poor employee in there a bout of unearned wrath.* "Hey, there's this amazing European bakery just up the block. Let's go stuff our faces with sugar."

Vicki shakes her head. "I don't know. I think I just want to go home."

"Listen, this part was going to be my treat, regardless. I absolutely insist on cake."

She smiles weakly. "Cake does sound pretty good, now that you mention it."

"That's the spirit." They link arms and walk. The tiny bakery is blessedly empty, so they can take their time admiring the confections showcased behind the domed glass like edible art pieces. Vicki asks Phoebe to pick something for her. Phoebe goes with a slice of Black Forest gateau, a raspberry-almond tart, a small selection of French macarons, and two coffees. At a back corner table, Phoebe arranges their spread between them.

"We'll never be able to eat all this," Vicki says.

"Not with that attitude." Phoebe picks up a fork and goes right for the gateau. It tastes as glorious as she remembers, and she makes a note to come down here more regularly for a slice. To go. "Find me a better combo than cherries and chocolate. I dare you."

Vicki takes a bite and her eyes roll back in her head. "You're right. My God."

They eat in silence for a couple minutes, sampling everything. Vicki puts down her fork with a sigh and sips her coffee. "Thank you, Phoebe. Really. I . . . I don't even know what to say."

"How bad are things right now? You can tell me."

After a long pause, she says, "Bad. And apparently much worse than I thought since I can't even go shopping without embarrassing myself." The tears overflow and start streaming down her cheeks. "I've been feeling for a while like the walls are just closing in on me. On all of us. Sometimes I think the only reason I'm still breathing is for Jake, knowing he has a chance to get out and make something of himself. At least I did that one thing right, you know?"

She breaks down sobbing. Phoebe, now feeling hollowed out by shame, lets her cry it out, in part because it's often the best thing you can do for someone in pain, but also because she needs a moment to think. What will it do to Vicki when she learns her one remaining hope is an illusion? Maybe if everything else wasn't so dire, it would be easier. When the storm begins to wind down into sniffles, Phoebe makes a decision. It goes against every single thing her father ever taught her about friends and money, but she's also happy for any opportunity to defy him now.

She opens her purse and pulls out a small brown Italian leather case Daniel gave her for her eighteenth birthday. The irony of what she's about to do with it almost makes her smile. She flips it open and grabs the fourteen-karat fountain pen tucked inside, also a gift from Daniel. "What will be enough to float you guys for a while?" she asks.

Vicki looks up at her with a tear-streaked frown. "What?"

Phoebe starts filling out the check with Vicki's name. "Will ten grand do it? That should get you caught up on some bills and house repairs, right? Make it a little easier for you to breathe." *What about when you find out I've been having an affair with your teenage son? Because if he decides to break your heart by ditching Stanford, it's only a matter of time before you find out why. Is there a price for ameliorating some of that pain?* Maybe she should tack on another ten just to be sure. Guilt money. That's what this really is, isn't it? So much for thinking she was defying her father. This is right up Daniel's alley. Her stomach burns all over again, but it's too late to stop what she's already started.

"Oh God," Vicki says, covering her face again. "This isn't how I imagined any of this would go."

"Any of what?"

"Just . . . everything. Look at me. I'm sitting here crying over a demolished piece of cake after you've already paid for my goddamn kitchen supplies, and now you taking pity on me by doing this. I made a fool out of myself again."

"Well, I can tell you from my own experience that things rarely go how you think they will. I can also tell you that I want to help you, and so I will." Phoebe signs the check, tears it out of the book, and hands it across the table. "Now shut up and take my money."

Vicki eyes it for a few seconds, and then dissolves into gales of laughter.

"What is it?" Phoebe asks, confused.

"It's nothing. It's just . . ." She starts laughing again, making Phoebe wonder if the woman has begun to have a genuine breakdown. "I'm so sorry. I know it's inappropriate as hell to laugh at a time like this. But your checks . . . are those kittens wearing tiaras?"

Phoebe snorts laughter of her own. "You got me. I'm a total girl. Now, are you going to take this thing or do I have to beg?"

Vicki takes the check and stares at it. "I'm speechless, Phoebe. Truly. My son says no one under the age of sixty writes checks anymore. Maybe if I told him someone as cool as Phoebe Miller had checks, he would get some. Probably *Star Wars* ones, though."

Phoebe, who knows this particular interest of Jake's quite well—they've already watched the original trilogy together, and plan to start on the newer movies soon—nods. "I guess I'm a little old-school. My dad taught me to always have paper at the ready just in case." *And it isn't as sexy to dash off a quick emotional bribe by asking someone for their PayPal address,* she thinks. *You do it with a five-hundred-dollar leather checkbook and a gold fountain pen.*

The smile fades from Vicki's mouth as she studies the check a bit longer. "I bet Daniel is still teaching you a lot of things."

Phoebe's breath catches. She never told Vicki about her father, though she supposes it's easy enough for anyone to do a quick Google search and get all the sordid details. She nearly brought it up a few times in their conversations, but something always stopped her. Lack of a good segue, maybe, or the desire to avoid unpacking things all over again for someone new, only to have that knowledge sitting between them like a rotting carcass. It was hard enough just to tell Jake.

Vicki seems to realize she put Phoebe in an awkward spot, and her expression turns regretful. "Oh jeez, I'm sorry," she says. "I guess I'm guilty of some online snooping. Given all the women who've been coming forward with horror stories about him, I can't blame you for wanting to keep it quiet."

"No, it's okay. I know I can't hide forever. It's kind of terrible of me to think I can, given what he put so many people through."

She places her hand on Phoebe's arm, her eyes taking on a hard glint. "His mistakes aren't yours, Phoebe. And being his daughter, you're as much a victim as anyone else in all this." Vicki looks like she's holding back another mouthful of words.

"What is it?" Phoebe asks.

Vicki leans closer and lowers her voice. "I completely understand if you don't want to tell me, but . . . he didn't, you know, hurt you that way too, did he?"

It takes Phoebe a moment to comprehend what she means, but when it clicks, she gives her head a rapid shake. "Oh God no. He never laid a hand on me. If anything, it was a struggle getting him to acknowledge my existence half the time."

"Well, it sounds like the motherfucker did you a favor. Also, pardon my language."

Phoebe's about to tell her there's no offense taken when Vicki's phone rings. "Hold that thought." Vicki looks at the display and rolls her eyes before answering.

"Hello, dear." Her smile fades a little. "Just having coffee with Phoebe down at that little bakery in Market Square." She pauses, frowning deeply. "Yes, we did a little shopping. Why?"

Her jaw drops. "Are you monitoring—" Another pause. This time Phoebe can hear an angry voice spilling from the speaker, and her nerves begin to crackle again.

"This is ridiculous, Ron. Don't bother, all right?" A few seconds later, she pulls the phone away and looks at it for a second. "Did that bastard just hang up on me?"

"What's going on?" Phoebe asks.

"My husband is pissed off again. Nothing new. Jake told him I was out shopping, and he put a stop on my credit cards. Says he's on his way to pick me up. Like he's my goddamn father!"

They look toward the door. As if on cue, Ron steps in front of the glass and peers inside for a moment. Phoebe feels a stab of inexplicable guilt, as if she's been caught red-handed doing something naughty. Like it was her idea to venture out on this little shopping trip. If only they'd stuck to brunch, this wouldn't be happening.

"Do you want me to say something to him?" she asks, and then feels like an idiot. As if now that she's wielded the magical checkbook and fountain pen, this gives her the authority to be Vicki's bodyguard in all domestic disputes.

"I'll handle this," Vicki says, and gets up to go meet her husband outside.

Phoebe watches the scene unfold on the sidewalk as if it's a silent movie. The two bakery employees also gaze in fascination as Ron begins pacing almost immediately, tossing out the occasional wild gesticulation to punctuate his rant. Vicki's hands are perched on her hips as she tries to strike a confident pose, but it isn't long before her shoulders droop and her arms cross in front of her. She then appears to make a tearful plea, and Ron stops pacing and closes his eyes. As Vicki continues to speak, he moves in closer, placing his hands on her shoulders. Phoebe tenses up, wondering if this is the moment he starts either slapping or shaking his wife. She notes there are people across the street who have also stopped to watch the Napier drama unfold. But instead of escalating things, Ron places his forehead against hers, utters a few words, and kisses her temple. He says a few more words in her ear, and Vicki nods. Then he walks off, casting a withering glare toward the bakery. Phoebe is far enough inside to know he can't actually see her, but she still feels certain that glare was intended for her.

Vicki quickly wipes her face and walks back inside, head high, posture sturdy. She doesn't sit back down. "He's waiting for me in the car," she says. "I hate to leave you like this. Especially after everything..."

Phoebe shakes her head. "You don't need to worry about me. But I am worried about you. He looks like he's at the end of his rope, Vicki."

"I know how it looks. Ron can definitely be an asshole, but I'm every bit his match. Trust me. And things are going to be better soon. Thanks to you." She bends down to pick up her bags and kisses Phoebe's cheek. "I'll call you later."

After she's gone, Phoebe stares in a daze at the remains of their sugar binge, telling herself it would be best to start walking home now to avoid the temptation of finishing it. But she doesn't go very far down that particular path of common sense. She picks up the fork and lays waste to it all. And then, in a final farewell to the interests of good health, she summons an Uber to take her home.

'VE MESSED UP, Phoebe. Bad. It won't be more than a day, maybe two, before they connect all the dots between the dead guy in the stockroom and the female employee who got him fired yesterday, and who's now mysteriously absent. I guess I don't have to tell you what I ultimately decided to do with those pictures I took in Bachmann's apartment. I did sit on them for a bit, waiting to see if conditions would improve, but the messages haven't stopped. I even warned him to back off. He thought I was being cute.

In light of what's happened, part of me wonders if I should have found another way to deal with him, but I can't help feeling something else would have triggered him, leading to the same outcome. Guys like Bachmann operate on rails, usually toward disaster.

My phone has been ringing all morning. Theresa, my manager and unwitting sister-in-arms, probably hadn't figured out right away who'd left the blank envelope on her desk yesterday morning containing copies of the pictures, along with a brief note explaining whose they were. Going the anonymous route was the best way to handle things. I couldn't very well tell her I'd broken into his place. She likely would have fired us both.

I never heard a word from her as I worked my shift. A few employees noticed Bachmann's absence from his regular post, with some hoping aloud that he'd either quit or been canned. I happened to notice Theresa looking a bit pale and quiet, despite her professional façade, and I knew the answer.

On the voicemails, she sounds almost like a worried friend. She probably knows now who put that envelope on her desk, and I would bet everything she's turned it over to the police by now. It's equally easy to imagine a detective standing over her shoulder, feeding her lines encouraging me to come to the store so we can talk. Why wouldn't she cooperate fully? She was only doing her job. And now she has the Lake Forest police department, yards of yellow tape, and a looming slew of bad press blocking townsfolk from buying their overpriced produce and supplements.

Bachmann might have taken it better if Theresa were a Tom. Being fired by a woman was just one hit too many to Bachmann's straw-house ego. We're lucky he didn't come into the store and start shooting it up. Instead, he decided to just go after me.

Given that things were quiet until about six this morning, I have a feeling it was Andy Dailey, the dock manager, who found him behind the towering pallets of soda where I'd left him, since he's usually the first person back there in the early-morning hours. Sorry, Andy. You're a nice guy who doesn't deserve the lifetime of nightmares you're likely to have from all this. That's my fault.

At first, I thought I could show up to work at the normal time and play off my shock like any other innocent employee, but the second I got a look at all those red and blue lights and uniformed men crowding the store entrance, I knew I had no chance of walking away from this clean. So I kept driving, and I haven't really stopped moving all day. I know I should get as far away from this town as I can. That would be the smart move. But every time I start thinking of a new destination and how I will have to start my life all over, I remember why I came here in the first place. My business isn't done. You can help me.

I just wish I could scrub the memory of it away.

I don't think he left the store after Theresa canned him. He must have gathered his things and then holed up in the stockroom. It's not hard to do. It's a dim and dingy cave stacked to the ceiling with product, and it's far less monitored than one might think. And since we had no scheduled deliveries that day, the room stayed more or less unattended. We do have outside vendors coming and going back there throughout the day, but they wouldn't have thought twice about seeing Bachmann.

That none of this occurred to me as I headed back there to dispose of my trash near closing time is precisely why Bachmann is dead right now. My mind was more focused on a potential ambush on the way to my car, but in hindsight, that shouldn't have concerned me nearly as much. The parking lot is well lit and has cameras. This is not the case in the stockroom, where there are no cameras at all. It's the first time in my life I regret not being caught on surveillance.

If there was tape, the police would know without question it was self-defense. Without it, there is just my word. There were some red marks on my throat, where he grabbed me. Sadly, they've since faded. My scalp still hurts where he yanked my hair, but pain isn't visible. Also invisible are the memories of the fishy stench of his breath as he pressed himself against me, whispering, "You owe me, bitch. Now hold still or I'll snap your fucking neck."

He had been trespassing back there, though, and the cops have likely sifted through everything in his garage apartment by now. But even with those elements in my favor, the cops would wonder how I managed to hit his femoral artery so squarely with my knife while he was attacking me. They don't care for answers like "luck" or "coincidence" even when they're true. They would also ask why I didn't run out into the store when I saw him slither out from around the wall of soda pallets closest to me. My answer would be equally dissatisfying and cliché: I froze. By the time I realized it was Bachmann, he'd grabbed me. He was stronger than I expected him to be, like either he'd done this sort of thing before, or he'd been fantasizing about it so long it amounted to years of practice.

The police may very well accept all of these answers, but then the matter of the text messages we exchanged a few hours before the attack would come up. They would see that he made a very specific threat ("I'm coming for you whore"). And my flippant response ("I'd like to see you try") might read as egging him on.

They'd also have questions about the butterfly knife I used, like where I got it and why the engraved monogram on it doesn't match my initials. Someone might even recognize it as stolen from the dresser drawer of a local accountant, if said accountant filed a police report. Then the real probing would be under way. They'd corral me into a dank, dingy room and use every weapon in their arsenal to break me down over several hours. Even if I got rid of my whole collection of stolen trinkets, the courier disguise, and the robbery tools, somehow they'd find a way to get me to confess to every sin I'd ever committed, along with several I didn't. I've seen enough true crime shows to know how that works.

So for now, I'm cowering like a scared animal during a bad storm. And yes, I'm using that word. "Scared." It feels more appropriate now. Every time I think I've found a quiet enough place to take a breath and close my eyes for a minute, I feel him grabbing me all over again, crushing me against the wall as he clumsily worked on the button of my jeans with one hand while he kept his other wrapped around my throat; the cold steel of the knife handle as I ease it out of my pocket; the warm gush of his blood on my hand when in the blind fury I began stabbing his thigh wildly and quickly; I see his lips going white, his eyes glazing over, locking the hatred in place forever. And finally, I see the naive plans that brought me to Lake Forest ripped apart.

But as dire as all this sounds, the game isn't over yet. Interestingly enough, I think you might have given me a new card to play the other morning without even realizing it. I wouldn't have realized it either until circumstances forced me to start considering all my options. And the thing is, I might actually be doing you a favor, since you're in a bit of a pickle too.

Don't worry, I'm not judging you for sleeping with your teenage neighbor, even if his mother is your BFF. That's none of my business, and since I just killed a guy, I have no room to talk about bad decisions. But you might have thought to put some clothes on before he opened the door to storm out. I'm guessing there wasn't any time. Judging by how upset he looked, it must have been one hell of a lovers' quarrel. Did you happen to notice me sitting out here?

Given how quickly you slammed that door, I'd bet on yes. Don't worry. I didn't see a lot. But I did see enough.

It would be a real shame if anyone else were to find out. His daddy already has anger issues, and Mommy Dearest seems to care a whole lot about her new friend next door. And then there's your husband, of course, dutifully leaving for work every morning, probably clueless about what, or who, his wife is doing. Again, not judging, but it really is a delicate web you're weaving. It's in such a vulnerable spot too, easily snagged by any old passerby.

I guess you can see where I'm headed with this. It doesn't make me proud, but I'm running out of options. It's time to give you a little nudge.

CHAPTER 9

As a way to further smooth over the bumps of their recent spat, Phoebe surprises Jake with a belated birthday celebration in bed. After sharing gourmet chocolates and a bottle of champagne, she gives him a small present. It took some effort to think of something right. It couldn't be too extravagant, or it might raise suspicions if either of his parents happened upon it. Most important, it needed to have personal meaning, something he could always look at and be reminded of her, no matter where he ended up in life.

She settled on a framed original print of Daniel's Ferrari's concept art, which had arrived along with the car itself, and had been sitting in a guest room closet ever since. On the back, she wrote a little note (*Your other favorite ride . . .*). No signature necessary. Even though he still hasn't been able to drive it, she has let him sit in it and start the engine a few times. They've also christened it in other ways, which felt like a satisfying middle finger to Daniel for dumping the car on her in the first place. It's nice to see the print go to someone who will actually appreciate it, but even better to have one more piece of her father out of her life. Since unwrapping the gift, Jake has demonstrated his immense gratitude a few times. Phoebe plans to stick this day into a mental time capsule and visit it regularly.

Since their fight, she hasn't asked him if he's had any further thoughts on his college plans. Her mind keeps turning back to Vicki in the bakery yesterday, speaking with tears in her eyes about how Jake's future is her one remaining hope. The conversation can't remain on pause forever, but Phoebe has decided not to fight him if he chooses to stay. She doesn't want to repeat what happened two days ago. They'll figure things out together.

She hasn't seen Vicki since their strange shopping trip, though Vicki did send a text last night letting her know everything was okay, and thanking her again for the money. Phoebe has been debating the wisdom of that gift ever since, wondering if this might be the start of Vicki's tapping her like she's an ATM. And does Phoebe have any right to refuse more requests for help, given what she's been doing with Jake? What if they already know and are just waiting for a chance to blackmail her if she tries? The thought turns her guts to jelly, but she quickly shoots it down as ridiculous. Phoebe freely offered the money to her; Vicki didn't ask for it, and probably would have died at the thought. And she especially doesn't seem like the sort of mother who would pimp her son out as a bargaining chip.

But everything is for sale at the right price, and everyone has a circumstance under which seemingly inalienable bonds and morals dissolve like superglue in acetone, especially when one's very survival is thrown into question. How much money would Phoebe part with out of a desire to protect her vanity? She knows it's higher than ten grand, but there has to be a limit, one where she'll have to be ready to go all in on Jake and say he's worth whatever humiliation might come from exposure. He certainly seems prepared to face that for her, but he has so much less to lose. If anything, he would come out of this something of a folk hero, the boy next door who nabbed the aging heiress. She could see him fielding offers for interviews or spots on third-rate reality shows. America would lap it up.

And she hasn't even thought about what Wyatt might do if he found out. She imagines he would be upset in his typical half-repressed way. But what if she's taking that for granted? Recent events have eroded what little mutual respect is left between them to nearly nothing. He could decide to hire a pit bull for a divorce lawyer and drag things out in court, or possibly even find some other way to cash in on both his victim status and the debacle with her father. How about an exclusive interview with a media luminary, or a shocking tell-all book about life with the daughter of the infamous Daniel Noble? They could call it *Like Father, Like Daughter*.

She squeezes her eyes shut and shoves all those thoughts away, pressing herself against Jake's chest, absorbing the comforting and steady thump of his heartbeat, timing her breaths with his. Whenever reality or karma finally does come calling and she needs an escape, this is the song she will always cue up. She's just on the edge of sleep when the doorbell rings. They both sit up reflexively, like two people caught dead to rights in the middle of a terrible sin.

"Don't answer it," Jake says. "It's probably just a salesman." He doesn't sound convinced of his own theory.

As if in response, the bell rings twice more in rapid succession, triggering an avalanche of all her worst-case-scenario thoughts. It's Vicki. She's figured out everything. Her vengeance will be swift as she fights with all the brutality of a lioness protecting her cub. Phoebe's adrenaline surges, making her both hot and shivery, but she feels a trickle of calm when Jake places a hand on her shoulder. "It isn't my mom. She's at a dentist appointment. I saw her check in on Facebook fifteen minutes ago."

She breathes a little easier. Thank goodness for the modern need to share every mundane detail with the public. The bell rings again as she gets out of bed and wraps herself in a robe. "Stay put. Whoever it is, they'll have no reason to come up here."

Closing the door, she makes her way down the stairs and gazes through the peephole. Her stomach gives a little lurch when she sees Ron standing there. It isn't her worst nightmare come true, but she has no reason to think he's here bearing good tidings, or that he'll give up and leave if she doesn't answer. He's already rung three times, and he doesn't look like he's moving yet. She takes a deep breath and opens the door, glancing over his shoulder to check for the blue car. It was here for a bit this morning, but it's gone now.

Ron doesn't appear to have slept or eaten in the last week, judging by the dark luggage under his eyes and the way his clothes hang from his body as if on a rack. The sour-sweet stench of beer wafts off him, troubling for someone who is supposed to be a brain surgeon.

Phoebe has always sensed that Ron doesn't care much for her, but today his contempt is as plain as the alcohol on his breath. Then she glances down at his feet and sees a white Williams-Sonoma shopping bag, and the picture is starting to come a bit more into focus. He's here about yesterday. She should have known.

"Phoebe. I must have caught you at a bad time." He glances at her robe, silently judging, as if he has any room.

"Not really. What's up?" She gives herself an invisible pat on the back for sounding so light and friendly.

"I need to speak with you. Can I come in?"

The thought of his being in her house with Jake hiding so close by fills her with churning dread, but she can't think of a reason to say no that wouldn't come off as hostile, and it seems unwise to provoke hostility in Ron right now, or ever, really. She stands aside to let him through and then leads him to the living room, her back stiff, as if bracing for him to lay a hand on her. In the living room, she tells him to have a seat anywhere and offers him a drink.

"Scotch and soda if you have it."

She pours without comment. "Need ice?"

"No, it's fine."

She pours generously and hands the glass to him. He doesn't guzzle it down in a single gulp, but the faint tremor in his hands says he wants very much to do so. It suddenly occurs to her that he might be drinking like this because he's more anxious than he is angry. This settles her stomach, but only a little. "Is everything okay?" she asks.

"You're aware of our predicament." It isn't a question. Just a statement of fact.

"What predicament?"

He gives her a deadpan stare and pulls a slip of folded paper out of his breast pocket. Phoebe immediately recognizes it as the check she wrote Vicki yesterday. The princess kittens stare back at her, mocking her with their sweet innocence.

"Why are you trying to be coy?" Ron asks.

She sighs. "Okay, fine. I helped your crying wife, all right? She told me you've been struggling and I offered some short-term assistance. Is this some kind of wounded-masculinity thing?"

A frown crosses his face. He seems confused. "She didn't ask you for this? Tell me the truth."

"Of course not! Why would you think that?"

He bows his head for a long moment, as if in deep prayer. When he looks back up at her, it's like he's added another ten years to an already ancient and crumbling façade. "You know, it really doesn't matter. I'm giving it back, regardless. It's time for me to put an end to this madness once and for all. We don't need your help. I'm doing just fine taking care of my family. Maybe you forget, but I am a doctor."

"No, I didn't forget. Vicki told me you were having a . . . professional crisis." She specifically remembers Vicki using the word "quack." Phoebe might not know the specifics of what went down, but if any doctor walked into the room looking like Ron does right now, she would run for the hills.

His eyes glitter and narrow. There's the anger. It only took a little prodding to draw it out. "You really need to be careful here. You don't know a goddamn thing about me."

"You're right. I don't know you, and I don't want to. But I've seen enough to know you're a bully. You put a stop on your wife's credit cards when she went to do a little shopping. And I've also seen the bruises on her arms."

She's prepared for him to explode, and she has her phone at the ready just in case. But he only stares at her for a second, and then drops his head again, shaking it. "My God, it's amazing how she's got your mind all twisted around. I really have to hand it to her. You think she's the only one with marks?" He unbuttons the top three buttons of his shirt and exposes his shoulder and a series of scratch marks scabbed over.

A floodgate opens in her head, spilling out all kinds of questions. Did Vicki really leave those scratches? What else might he be implying about her? But it's pointless to ask him, because he's probably lying too. The truth lies somewhere between the two of them, and Phoebe doesn't have the energy to go digging for it. She'd rather they both left her alone. It's like that saying about circuses and monkeys. They aren't hers.

"You know what? I'm done here. All I did was try to help. She was grateful for that help. You're the only one who seems to have a problem with it. I'm not the bad guy here!"

"Drop the act, sweetheart. The apple rarely falls far from the tree, and yours is pretty fucking rotten. I smelled it on you from the beginning. I told my wife the last thing we needed was to try and make friends with a Noble, but she never listens."

She flinches at being called out. Of course he knows who she is, because Vicki knew. They probably talked about it over breakfast one morning, swapping idle gossip the way she and Wyatt would sometimes do when they were still speaking. She suddenly feels cold and transparent under Ron's gaze. They're doctor's eyes, peering at an MRI of her soul and seeing a malignant mass even she didn't know existed.

"I want you to leave now," she says. If he doesn't get up, she'll call the police. If he comes at her, she's only one good lunge away from the kitchen island, where she keeps her knife block.

For a moment, it looks like he might adhere to her expectations and refuse. His expression says no one tells him to leave; he tells you when he's ready. But somewhere in the turbulent froth of his mind, he snatches a piece of good sense, and the fight gradually fades from him, wilting his posture. He empties his glass and sets it on the end table before standing up. "You're right. It's best I leave before this gets even more out of hand." He trudges toward the door. When he gets there, he stops and turns around. "I think this goes without saying, but you need to stay away from my wife. And my son. *Especially* him. Do you understand me?"

She opens her mouth, but only silence comes out. It seems to satisfy him. After he leaves, she closes the door and turns the dead bolt. The adrenaline that has been holding her upright for the last several minutes drains away, and she sags to the floor, bringing her knees to her chest to calm herself. She stops just short of putting her thumb in her mouth for additional comfort, like she did when she was a little girl. Wine is her thumb now, or a spoonful of ice cream. Or solitude and trashy books by the pool. The simple things had always been enough. Before Daniel's death. Before the blue car. Before her marriage fell apart. Before the Napiers showed up.

She hears footsteps on the stairs and jumps. It's Jake coming down; she forgot he was up there. "What just happened?" he asks. "That was my dad, wasn't it?"

"Yes, but it was nothing that concerns you."

"Okay." He clearly doesn't think it's okay. He's confused, like someone who's watched a play with the scenes out of order. "But it sounded bad."

"Sure. Because that's just my life these days. Bad seems to be seeking me out. I guess the universe decided it was my turn."

He stares at her with visibly mounting concern. "What did he say to you? Does he . . . know about us?"

"No." Or at least she doesn't think he knows, though his warning to stay away from Jake especially had jumped out at her. She nearly tells him some of what happened, but it isn't her place to fill him in on his parents' problems. It was never her place, as Ron just reminded her. She should have kept her nose out of it, even if she hasn't kept her hands off their son. "It doesn't matter."

He leans down to place his hands on her arms, but she goes rigid. "This really isn't a good time to touch me."

He pulls away, wounded, like his favorite puppy just nipped at him. "All right. Whatever you need. What can I do to fix this?"

She looks up at him, mentally rolling back the notion from their earlier postcoital cocoon that Jake could stay here and everything would still be okay. "You need to go to Stanford, Jake. Get away from this place. You don't need to be here. Everything is too messy, and it will only get worse."

He shakes his head. "My mind hasn't changed on that. I'm staying here."

"Jesus, Jake. Why are you doing this?"

"Because I love you." He doesn't hesitate even a little. His certainty is as strong and unwavering as gravity.

She puts her head back down on her knees. "Why did you have to say that?"

Jake kneels in front of her. "I know you feel the same way. You're so afraid. Why can't you just trust this? Whatever else is going on right now, we can face it together."

She raises her head to look at him again. "How well do you think you know me?"

"I'd say I know you better than most."

"Oh really? You know what shows I like and how I take my coffee. You know the preferred temperature of my shower water and my favorite sex positions."

He sits up straight. "I also know how hard it was for you growing up with a father who hated women, and you weren't surprised when so many of them started coming forward with stories. I know you felt trapped into starting a family, and this is why your marriage is ending. I know that you love cooking and writing. Your favorite artists are Dale Chihuly and Henri Matisse. You've thought a lot about starting a food blog."

She's impressed he's paid so much attention, but he still doesn't understand her point. "So you've memorized a few surface details. Good for you. But it's impossible to know anyone completely."

"You're trying to push me away again. It's not going to work."

"My husband used to look at me the way you do. And it was mutual. Now we're like a couple of cats circling each other in a dark alley. Have a chat with your parents. They probably felt like they were in a fairy tale once too, and if they're even a little bit honest, they'll tell you the same thing I'm telling you now. It's all bullshit. People fall in love with what they want to see, and eventually that illusion fades."

His face is working as he gears up for another impassioned, romantic rebuttal, but if she hears one more time how the right person can change everything, she's going to fly into a rage. All she wants now is the soothing, empty womb of her old life. "I need to be alone right now. Please give me that."

"We promised we weren't going to fight. That we weren't going to let this sort of thing break us up again."

She reaches out to him and takes his hand. "I'm not breaking up with you." Though the desire to wash her hands of all this has never felt stronger. "My brain just needs a rest. I'll call you later. I promise."

He's clearly not satisfied, but he nods. She admires this about him, his ability to pull back when asked, even when it's difficult for him. "Okay. I'll talk to you tonight, then?"

"Yes."

"Promise me again."

"I promise." The words feel sour in her mouth, but enough wine should wash them away.

■ ■ ■

AFTER QUICKLY POLISHING off one bottle of cabernet, she decides it's going to be a two-bottle day, possibly more. Why the hell stop there? It isn't like she has anything better to do. The warm flush from the alcohol is a poor substitute for the contented glow she'd felt in bed with Jake earlier, but it will have to do.

The doorbell rings just as she pulls the cork, and she jumps hard enough to knock the bottle over onto its side, spilling a glug of its precious contents onto the counter. "The fuck is it now?" she mutters aloud to the room, noting the slur with some amusement. Maybe it's Vicki, here to add another block to this toppling Jenga tower. She goes to the door and looks through the peephole. No one's there. Not even a delivery truck, or her old friend from Executive Courier Services. A small jolt of fear penetrates the drunken cloud. Who would ring the bell and run in this neighborhood? Or did she hallucinate the whole thing?

"Drunker than I thought," she mutters to herself, but opens the door anyway just to be sure. Nope. No one there. But something catches her eye, a small white envelope lying on the welcome mat. Her name is scrawled across the front in red ink, and the wine in her gut suddenly feels like it needs to go somewhere. She would much rather have the auditory hallucination than this. Nothing good ever comes in mysteriously delivered envelopes with names scrawled across the front in red.

She glances around, certain the person who left this here is watching. They couldn't have gone too far. Everything feels too still. Not even the birds are singing; it's as if they're taking a pause in their day to bear witness. She quickly bends down to scoop up the strange delivery and slams the door shut again.

She should throw it away. Better yet, take it to the barbecue out back and burn the sucker. But she can't dismiss this any more than she could ignore a tangle of snakes in her bed. She rips open the envelope before her doubt can intervene and pulls out a thin slip of paper. Covered in red letters. The color of warning and blood. The note is just four sentences long, but they have the impact of buckshot at close range, and for the second time today, all the strength has run out of her legs, sinking her to the floor.

I know your secret about the boy next door. I can't promise I'll keep it. What's it worth? I'll be in touch.

...

'VE PUSHED OVER a very big domino, though I'm afraid to predict how exactly things will fall from here. A lot of it depends on you, I suppose. No matter how things go, I want you to believe me when I say this isn't how I envisioned things would end up for us. I never thought I'd wind up killing a man, either. So much for thinking we know our limits.

It's too late to take back now. I just have to see it through and pray you don't do anything foolish. There's no need to make this more difficult than it already is.

CHAPTER 10

S HE TRIES TO drink her panic away for the next hour or so, but it doesn't budge. If anything, the booze is making her more aware of it, and sicker to her stomach. This is no time to obliterate her mind. She needs to think. Better switch to coffee.

Who left the note? It was clearly a blackmail attempt with its coy, *What's it worth?* This takes Ron, with his check-returning wounded pride, off the list—along with anyone else under the Napier roof, for that matter. They had money in hand. It wouldn't make sense to threaten her for it now. The most obvious answer is her friend in the car, the one who has been there, with few exceptions, watching all this time. But how much could she—Phoebe has come to think of the driver in feminine terms—really know? Sure, there was the day of her fight with Jake, when he stormed out the front door, leaving an undressed Phoebe in plain view for a couple seconds, but is this all the proof she has? If so, that isn't much on which to base a whole blackmail scheme.

Unless she snapped pictures. Those could pop up next, probably somewhere on the internet, if she blows this off. Phoebe groans and nearly goes for her wine again before stopping herself. It's time to make an approach. She's scared to death, but it's the only way to know for sure. Phoebe gets up, goes to the front window, and peers through the blinds as she has every day for weeks, this time actually hoping to see her little sentry waiting.

Instead, she finds a completely empty street. It's been empty a lot lately, come to think of it. What if after all this, the car never comes back? What if the goal was to mess with her head by keeping her waiting for a bomb to drop? What a cruel joke that would be, worse than the threat in the note itself.

The phone rings, and she nearly cries out. Grumbling, she goes to where she left it on the couch. It's Vicki. She wants to let it go to voicemail. This charade has become exhausting. And it is a charade, if Ron can be believed. *My God, it's amazing how she's got your mind all twisted around.*

Phoebe grits her teeth. If she doesn't answer now, the calls will keep coming. And then her doorbell will start ringing. *You could always trash the phone, barricade the door, and never set foot outside again. Sure, Wyatt would probably put in a call to one of his psych colleagues at the hospital and stick you in a suite with Nerf walls, but at least you would be free of this place, right?*

"Hello?" she answers. It's hard to scrub the edge completely out of her voice.

"Hey, doll. How's your day going?"

Pretty great! It began with a lovely morning with your son in bed, followed by a scary confrontation with your husband, and then for the ultimate chaser, a blackmail note from my mystery stalker threatening to expose me for the lying tramp I am. You know, typical weekday crap. "Oh . . . it's going. What's up?"

"I need you to tell me not to eat this giant slab of Black Forest cake I picked up from our favorite little bakery just now. I haven't stopped thinking about it since yesterday. This is my last chance for redemption, Phoebe. You're the angel on my shoulder."

She tries to smile, but her whole face feels like a brittle mask that might shatter at any moment. "That costume never did fit me well. Eat the cake."

"This is probably why I liked you from the start." The words are a little muffled, like she's speaking around a mouthful of the decadent slice. After a few seconds of silence, Vicki asks, "Are you okay?"

"I guess so. Why?"

"You sound a little down."

She debates shrugging her off with a lie, but the topic of the money is going to come back up sooner or later now that Phoebe has her offering back. "Your husband came over today. He returned the check I wrote, and your Williams-Sonoma purchases. Did you know about that?"

Vicki is silent for a long time. Or at least, it feels like a long time under the present circumstances. "That lying, arrogant *prick*." Her voice is low, the words sharpened daggers. Phoebe can picture Vicki sitting over there and stabbing her cake repeatedly with her fork, rendering it chocolate-cherry mud.

"Whatever is going on between you two, I think I need to just stay out of it from now on. I thought I could help, but clearly that only caused more problems, and I have enough of those to deal with, you know?"

"Listen, I've gone about this all wrong from the very beginning, but I think you and I being friends now . . . It's time for me to explain some things. Can I come over?"

"This isn't a good time for me." And it will never be a good time. Trapped between the dueling words of a married couple who are as stable together as vinegar and baking soda, Phoebe can feel herself closing off, and she knows once that happens, she won't open back up again.

"Okay then, tomorrow," Vicki says more empathically. "I know I've been a real drag, but this is important, Phoebe. Please."

She can't help but feel curious about what Vicki has to say, but Ron's words echo again: *She's got your mind all twisted around.* And on the heels of that, the note on the doorstep: *I know your secret about the boy next door.*

She suddenly feels cold enough to start shivering. Are all these things swirling around her like debris in a tornado—the car, the note, the Napiers' issues, the sordid revelations about her father, and now Vicki's urgent request to meet—related somehow? How else to explain this growing certainty that a trap is about to spring around her ankle?

Come on, you're being paranoid. Just because you have dots in front of you doesn't mean you have to start connecting them.

Maybe so, but this is still one big mess of dots, and they aren't going away. They actually seem to be multiplying at a pretty alarming rate. Soon they'll all start to merge into one ugly blob. Whatever Vicki has to tell her, it won't stop that. Things you have to make an appointment to say in person because you can't say them over the phone or in a text are rarely good. By the end of tomorrow's brunch, Phoebe is certain she'll be in a deeper rut, or at least a different one.

"Tomorrow will work," she says, mostly to move the conversation to the end. Her heart is thudding hard enough now to make her chest hurt.

"So should we do our usual brunch time, then?" There's a note of relief in Vicki's voice.

"That sounds great." No, it doesn't sound great. In fact, she's pretty sure she won't answer the door when Vicki comes over tomorrow. Better yet, she might just make a quick escape before her neighbor shows up. That way she won't have to wait for the doorbell to stop echoing off the walls like a taunt.

Her breath catches. Escape. Now there's a thought.

"All right. I'll see you tomorrow, then," Vicki says, her tone seeking some sort of reassurance that Phoebe can't provide.

"Okay." She hangs up. Alone again in her too-quiet kitchen, one word begins twirling like a dervish in her mind: *Escape.*

Oh sure, just run away from all your problems. How grown-up of you, Phoebe.

With a resigned sigh, she begins to swipe the idea away. But then . . . isn't that something her father would have said? She can hear it perfectly in his deep register, curved into the sarcastic scythe he'd always cut people off at the knees with if they stood too tall. Especially the women in his life. Her rebellion against all things Daniel flares anew, and she swipes him away instead. Daniel doesn't deserve a say, not now or ever, given his role in bringing her to this point.

And besides, is it really such a terrible idea? *Escape.* The word is like ice cream on a burning tongue. *Escape* from all this muck that's heaped in her life and is now piling up on her doorstep, turning her home into a prison. *Escape* from the prying eyes and whispered gossip of the people in this town who know who she is only because of her disgraced father. *Escape* from the Napiers and their drama. *Escape* from her own scandalous, hypocritical acts. *Escape* from Wyatt's perpetually wounded gaze and her resentment of him that's waxing more into loathing by the day.

Phoebe takes a long gulp of her lukewarm coffee and starts turning her idea around in her mind, like an archaeologist who might have stumbled on a rare artifact that initially looked like petrified garbage.

On a strictly technical level, she *can* do this. She has the economic freedom, and no employer to answer to. She has no family who would miss her. Wyatt would likely be relieved to avoid another unpleasantly revealing conversation like the one they'd had about adopting a child.

There are a few downsides she can't ignore, though. Leaving won't solve the problem of her blackmailer, who might decide to drop a bomb out of spite if she runs away without responding to any demands. That said, the bomb would be falling onto an old, discarded life. If pictures or gossip about the now infamous Daniel Noble's daughter hit the internet while she was kicked up on a beach somewhere out west, would she even notice? What about if she were on another continent entirely? Her passport is gathering dust, but it still has some years left.

God, will you listen to yourself? You're really considering this? Have you even thought about what it would do to Jake?

Yes, she can't ignore that this would hurt him. But with her gone, he would have no excuse to ditch Stanford. And if the blackmailer let the secret loose and Vicki or Ron learned of the illicit affair between their son and the woman next door, Phoebe's self-imposed exile could at least make it easier for them to weather the shock. Wyatt too, for that matter. Everyone would be better off in the long run.

She tries to drum up more rebuttals urging her to stay put. *Your problems will only follow you. You've lived on the North Shore your whole life. It's all you know. You're overreacting. Only cowards cut and run.* But none of them can match the volume of the voice shouting at her to go. Running away only seems irrational to people without the full context, and those people don't matter. She doesn't have to answer to them. She doesn't have to answer to anybody. She's had the freedom to do this all along, and now she has the motivation.

But Jake won't leave her mind, his declaration of love still so fresh. It's callous to think that because he's young, he'll get over the heartbreak quicker. He's an older soul than most, and sensitive; it's what attracted her to him in the first place. She would kill that part of him. After the initial grieving passed, he would be left bitter and distrustful.

It doesn't have to be this way. She has an opportunity to end things on a good note, to give him a proper good-bye. And if she's really being honest with herself, she needs it too. She's prepared to burn every bridge she has connecting her to this place, but she won't burn him.

She checks the time and is shocked to find it's only two thirty. A lot has happened in only a few hours. Almost too much. But she

can't remember the last time she felt this level of clarity and optimism about something.

Now she only needs to decide where to go. California, maybe?
Or maybe not. It's too close to home, at least emotionally. Too easy
to get lost in daydreams of crossing paths with Jake someday. New
York is a good place to get lost, but the flavor is similar enough to
Chicago that it wouldn't feel like much of a change. She's always
loved London, though. And if she's looking to clean the slate, why
not drag it through an entire ocean? At the very least, it would be a
place to start. She'd stay for a couple weeks, a month tops, and then
move on from there. It's an enormous world. What's stopping her
from seeing it all?

Taking a deep breath, she picks up her phone and texts Jake:
Can you come back over? We need to talk. There she goes, making an
appointment for a difficult in-person conversation. Hopefully it will
end well.

Not even ten seconds later, he replies: *Be right there.*

Pacing while she waits, butterflies swirling in her stomach, she
rehearses various takes on good-bye, all of them too melodramatic
for her liking. It would have been easier to write him a letter instead, same as she plans to do with Wyatt. Avoid the sticky stuff. It
isn't too late to consider that.

"Coward," she mutters to herself, just as the patio door opens.
Jake comes in, smiling.

"I didn't think I'd see you again so soon," he says, leaning down
to kiss her.

Before their lips touch, she blurts out, "I'm leaving town." If she hesitated even for a moment and let him kiss her, she would have given herself over to the ether they create together.

He pauses and stands up straight, the smile replaced with a bemused frown. "Are you for real?"

"Yes."

"How long?"

This is where it gets hard. "For good."

"Okay. Wow." He runs his hands through his hair and begins to pace for a few seconds before he stops, probably realizing how much he resembles his father when he does that.

Phoebe fumbles for something to say that doesn't sound lame. *It's for the best.* Groan. *I'll never forget you.* Gag. She finally settles on, "I'm sorry. I know this hurts." Not much better.

"Why are you doing this all of a sudden? It's something to do with my dad, isn't it? He comes over here, and now you're just . . . leaving?" His voice rises as he speaks, his brow deepening with furrows.

She could elaborate on her reasons, but Jake needs to be able to return home without any doubt and paranoia in his head, otherwise he'll never move on with his life. "I had an epiphany after you left. All this talk about you going away to school and living your life forced me to look at my own and see all the ways it's gone wrong. I should have considered this a long time ago, really. Even before my father died, things had stopped moving, and I've realized it's not going to get any better unless I do something about it."

He's standing with his arms folded, eyes fixed on the ground, silent. But Phoebe can see the wheels turning. He's listening. At least she hopes so.

She places her hand on his shoulder. "If anything, I would say my decision has everything to do with you, Jake. During our time together, you've made me feel like I can do more. And you need to remember that too, because I can tell you, in another fifteen years, you're probably going to find yourself feeling stuck too, and I want you to know you really aren't."

"I don't think I would ever feel stuck if I was with you."

She closes her eyes and lets out a sigh. Why do the young always have to be so idealistic? "Jake, please stop. This isn't making things any easier."

"I'm serious, Phoebe. Let me come with you."

She stares at him, her mouth hanging open. He says he's serious, but is he really? And is her inability to utter an immediate, firm rejection of this terrible idea indicative of something? *Oh God, Phoebe, no. You built yourself a solid enough case for leaving. Absconding with Jake would completely defeat the purpose of starting over.* Yes. It would fan the flames of her burning bridges into a nuclear mushroom cloud.

She finally musters the will to shake her head, hoping it will be enough to let the light of good sense through. "I'd never forgive myself, and something tells me it would eat at you too."

"It wouldn't eat at me, trust me. Being anywhere with you is the only thing that would make me happy. And you'd be happy too."

"What did I tell you the other day about happiness?"

"Okay, I get what you were saying about that. I know it's not a permanent state. And I'm willing to accept the possibility that at some point down the line, you and I will see we're too different and we'll go our separate ways. But that doesn't mean I should give up on what I'm feeling right now because we don't know the future. I want you to believe in the now. We'll cross whatever bridges we have to when we get to them."

"Your mother . . ." The memory of Vicki sobbing in the bakery floats up. Phoebe closes her eyes against it, as if that will help.

"My mother will have to stop depending so much on other people to make her life better. That's been her problem all along. And I'll tell you something: you probably care a whole lot more about her feelings than she cares about yours. Or mine."

"She cares a lot about your future. You worked really hard to get into Stanford."

He shakes his head. "She worked me hard to get into Stanford. There's a difference."

Phoebe cocks an eyebrow. "I seem to remember you telling me the first day we met you were going to be a criminal prosecutor."

He manages a small grin. "Actually, it was criminal defense. But there are more ways to get there than Stanford, if I decide that's something I still want to do after I've lived my life a little and seen the world. With you."

She needs to stop this, but she's putting all of her strength into keeping the whole idea alive. Besides, shouldn't Jake have the opportunity to make his decisions and learn from his mistakes? Right now, their secret little tryst feels sexy specifically because it's a secret. The allure of stealing away to a far-off location with a forbidden lover is difficult for anyone to resist. But when it's no longer their sexy secret, when the truth has been dragged into the light upon their departure, they will see it for the selfish, distasteful betrayal it was all along, and the glue holding them together right now will likely dissolve. He'll come home, and Vicki will take her boy back with open arms. Life will go on.

Something else occurs to her. Taking Jake with her would essentially neutralize her blackmailer, who's banking on Phoebe being willing to pay any price to keep her affair locked up tight. Well, it wouldn't be a secret anymore once they're gone. Some might call that a pyrrhic victory, but she's in no position to be picky. "Do you have a passport?" she asks, feeling simultaneously filthy and exhilarated.

"I do." His face breaks open into the sunniest smile she's ever seen and he pulls her into a long kiss. When they finally part, he says, "You've made me so happy. You have no idea."

She wishes she felt as excited as she did before; a new discordant thread is twisting through her gut now, but she supposes it's just nerves. They'll fade once they're up in the air, and by the time they're wheels-down at Heathrow, she'll be glad he's there. "I have a lot of packing and planning to do, so you should head back and get your things ready too. I'll text you when the coast is clear in the morning, so you can come over here. I want to be gone as early as possible."

A frown creases his brow. "You want to leave tomorrow? That's fast."

She's never felt more like a fugitive. "I know. But I'm pretty sure if I don't leap now, I probably never will. I don't expect it to make sense."

He kisses her forehead. "I get it. And I'm ready to jump with you."

She breathes a small sigh of relief. "Okay. Good. I hope."

"No, it is good. So where are we going?"

"Hope you like fish and chips."

His face lights up. "London?"

She nods. Her smile feels natural enough. "Righto, old chap. Now get going. I'll text you when the reservations are booked."

They hug again before he leaves. "I love you, Phoebe."

Her skin prickles at the words, but it's mostly nerves she feels. "I love you too," she says. Maybe she even means it.

She heads upstairs to her underwear drawer, where she keeps her passport as well as an envelope filled with a few thousand dollars that she used to jokingly call Apocalypse Cash. It doesn't feel so much like a joke now, at least on a personal level. She contemplates getting even more cash out of the bank, or better yet, traveler's checks. It's even more old-school than her leather checkbook with its princess kittens, but it's easier to disappear when you don't have a digital trail. That's a criminal's way of thinking, and she hates having to view it that way, but she can't discount the possibility that Vicki or Ron might go to the trouble of tracking them down to try to bring their son home.

From her closet, she pulls out a small bag. It seems sensible to pack only what she can fit in a carry-on. She can buy whatever she needs once they get settled. Looking at the vast amount of clothes she's collected over the years, most of them expensive enough to pay someone's rent for several months, she realizes she won't miss any of it.

CHAPTER 11

SHE POURS A bowl of cereal and taps her foot to the steady, predictable beat of a day that is set to be anything but steady and predictable. No room for any new riffs this morning. Wyatt needs to walk in here at ten minutes to eight, pour coffee into his favorite travel mug, and leave without discussion. She has a few things left to do, but at least her bag is packed and waiting in her bedroom closet. Once he's on his way to work, she'll text Jake and they'll drive to the airport. She considered ordering a ride service, but she doesn't want to chance Vicki's spying them both climbing into the backseat of a strange car. The last thing she wants is a scene. Now, if only Wyatt would get going already.

Yesterday, she reserved two first-class seats on a nonstop flight to London departing at one. By the time Wyatt gets home this evening, she and Jake will be over the north Atlantic with chaos at their backs and the unknown stretching out before them. Overnight, the dread in her gut eased into a more friendly sort of anticipation. She hasn't been to London since she was a teenager. Jake hasn't been at all. It will be fun to watch him gaze in wonder at the stunning architecture and the double-decker buses, to walk the streets holding hands, even if they do look a bit mismatched age-wise.

Late last night, she began an email to Wyatt that she hopes to finish in a few minutes. She plans to keep it brief. He would only find an apology hollow or patronizing, and she doesn't particularly want his forgiveness. She just wants the separation to be quick and clean.

She's considering composing something to Vicki as well, but her mind keeps shooting blanks as far as what to say. No words from Phoebe could ease the woman's pain. Only time can do that, and even then, it's only fair to expect Vicki to hate her for life. She can't envision any friendly reunions or Christmas gatherings. It's best not to think of the elder Napiers at all from this point forward, not if she wants to maintain the steely nerve she needs to get through this. She checks the time again.

It's now ten past eight. But Wyatt is still sitting out by the pool, a non-travel coffee mug in hand, taking in the morning like he has the day off, which she knows isn't true. He has appointments. She checked his calendar. What gives?

She suspects she knows the answer. He's ruminating on last night. This is what she gets for cooking him dinner, for making a nice parting gesture, even if he didn't know that was what it was. But an evening of chicken marsala and civil conversation wasn't enough for him. He had to get drunk and try for a little dessert too. She indulged him for a brief, clumsy kiss, and then told him it was late and she wanted to get some sleep. *I have a long day tomorrow,* she nearly said, and stopped just short of it. But the bourbon had made him cavalier enough to try again. He nuzzled her neck, nibbled on her ear. There was a time when the gestures used to give her the most delicious tingles, but now they only reinforced how removed she felt from Wyatt's orbit. After she pushed him away again, firmly, he pleaded, "Come on, Phoeb. I miss you. Don't you miss this?" His hand wandered down to the curve of one of her breasts and began to squeeze. She slapped it away, unable to hide her distaste.

"Go to bed, Wyatt. You're drunk."

He glared at her. "So are you half the time. Why did you even bother with any of this?"

"I'm asking myself the same question," she said. He trudged off to his room and spent the rest of the night nursing his rancor with the remainder of his bourbon and his precious jazz. She didn't see him again until this morning. Likely he's hungover. Any other morning, she would let it pass, but there isn't any time for drama today.

She's considering ways she can nudge him out the door when he comes back in. His face is a little pale, and he didn't bother shaving today. The alcohol has been rough on him, all right. In many ways, he looks a lot like Ron did yesterday. At least he's dressed for work, and only has to read minds rather than cut into brains and spinal cords. "I expected you would have left fifteen minutes ago," she says.

He turns to stare at her. "Our marriage is finished. Just say it."

She slumps. Of course he wants to have this conversation now, of all mornings. It's almost like he knows he has to stall her for some reason. "I'm really not in the mood for this right now."

"Too bad. You can't keep dictating the terms."

She can't help but flinch a little. Hadn't Jake said something similar to her the day of their big fight? "Fine. Our marriage is finished. I said it. Happy?"

He blinks and then shakes his head. "So that's it, then? Ten years of marriage and you're going to end it by mocking me. That's all I'm worth to you?"

"God, Wyatt! What more do you want me to say?"

"I want to know why you started hating me overnight. What did I do to you? I loved you. I was faithful."

Her impatience grows. There isn't any time for this, and even if there was, she doesn't see the point of opening up a wound just to make it bleed more. But he doesn't look like he's going anywhere, and if she wants him gone in the next few minutes, she sees no choice but to give him the fight he wants.

"I was nothing but a baby factory to you."

"*Excuse me?*" There's the fire in his eyes now. It never takes long when the subject turns to pregnancy.

"Did you ever care about what it was putting me through? How many miscarriages would it have taken before you finally got it, Wyatt?"

"Of course I cared!"

"Yes, you cared so much that you watched me go through four failed in vitro cycles without even once suggesting we give it a rest. You'd probably still be jerking off into a cup if I hadn't said anything."

"What did you expect me to do, read your mind?"

"No! I expected you to *see* me! How was it not obvious to you, a shrink of all people, that I was falling apart and I needed help?"

He shakes his head. "It's so typical of you to put your share of responsibility on someone else. You insist on complete autonomy, but only when it suits you."

"And it's so typical of you to wait for me to be the bitch, so you never have to do any of the heavy lifting."

"Oh, so now I never did anything for you? Incredible!"

She stands up. "Am I really so far off base? What did you bring to this marriage, exactly?"

"There she is. There's Daniel's daughter. I knew sooner or later, you'd make this about money."

"This was never about money! It's about emotional support and your inability to provide it."

He rolls his eyes. "Yeah right. Keep telling yourself that, princess."

He's turning away from her, signaling he's finished. She should be relieved, but she's too fired up now. He doesn't get to claim victory on some false belief that their demise had anything to do with his lack of wealth. It's just another way to make himself into a victim, and she refuses to let him get away with it again. "Thank you for proving my point. You prod me to tell you how I'm really feeling, and then when I do, you're done."

He whips around. "That's right, Phoebe. I'm done, with all of this. Are you really surprised? It's clearly what you wanted."

"You were never interested in the truth. Just a pat on the head. You act like you're one of the good guys, but you're just a spineless fraud."

His eyes narrow as his cheeks deepen to the shade of beets. The hand wrapped around his coffee mug is trembling, white-knuckled. "What did you just call me?"

She draws herself up to his height, strong and defiant. The dragon inside him has stirred awake, but she isn't afraid. She's fireproof, and there are wings on her back. Soon she'll take flight, and he can burn himself and this prison to the ground for all she cares. Phoebe Miller doesn't live here anymore.

PART 2

THE OTHER MRS MILLER

CHAPTER 12

SOMEWHERE A PHONE is ringing, but Nadia barely notices. Internally, she hasn't stopped screaming since she got here. The raw, almost meaty stench of blood in the room reminds her of the slaughterhouse back home. She's clinging to that memory now, staring down at Phoebe's lifeless body, hoping it's enough to keep her from falling apart. And as she fights against wave after wave of shock, she realizes she almost expected to find something like this after what happened earlier this morning.

Phoebe's husband backed out of the garage at speed, clipping the mailbox post with his Audi's bumper and then swerving to avoid hitting Nadia's car, which was parked a bit closer to the driveway this morning as she waited for her moment. Then he stopped and got out, arms waving as he approached her thankfully locked door. "You! Get off my street! You've harassed us long enough! I'm calling the police!" After unsuccessfully trying to open the door, he pounded on her window for emphasis, instead.

And there was blood on his hand. He left behind smudges, but the skies had opened up in a torrent of rain only minutes before, and they quickly washed away in the downpour. The fog inside her windows gratefully obscured their faces, but she could still make out the whites of his eyes in the murk, blazing bright with fury.

She sped away in a panic, no particular destination in mind, her mind whirring with questions all the while. What happened back there? Was this because of her note, or something else? What should she do now?

She'd wound up heading south, and then west on I-90. The storm cleared just as she spotted the blazing white turrets of Medieval Times all the way out in Schaumburg. The sun brought back a measure of courage and sanity, enough to convince her to stick to her original plan and go back. It was all she could do, short of going on the run with nothing but what she had on her now, enough money for a few tanks of gas and a little food, assuming nothing else went wrong. Besides that, she was worried something might have happened back there. How right she'd been.

The phone stops ringing, and silence rushes in to fill the void, trapping her in a vault of nightmares new and old. This is nothing like the Jesse Bachmann scene, where the lighting was dim enough in the stockroom to make the blood look more like crude oil. By contrast, in the gleaming bright of the Miller kitchen, the blood has nowhere to hide. It's screaming for attention. There are obvious signs of struggle. Broken dishes, overturned chairs, spilled coffee on the floor near the large island, a crock of kitchen utensils overturned across its surface.

Near the puddle of coffee is Phoebe sprawled in a wide pool of blood that appears to have spilled from two separate wounds: one on the temple, one in her chest.

A veil falls over Nadia's mind as she tries to piece together what happened here. A fight of some sort, obviously. Then the weapons came out. A blunt object for the head, and a knife for the chest.

Nadia scans the area for a knife block, finds one on the island. The top center slot stands empty, the one reserved for the biggest in the collection. That definitely would have done the job. She next spots a swatch of dark red on the nearest corner of the island's white quartz slab countertop. Perhaps in the middle of the scuffle, Phoebe slipped and hit her head there. She goes down, and then the attacker finishes the job. The wound is on the appropriate side of her head given the position of the body. Nadia would bet, if she checked the soles of Phoebe's bare feet, she'd find coffee on them.

She looks down at herself. Red on her hands from when she slipped in the blood puddle and caught herself; smears across the front of her shirt where she wiped it off; more of it on her legs, especially the knees, from when she knelt next to Phoebe's body to see if there was any chance of saving her, as if all the blood weren't clue enough about what a waste of time it would have been to try. Instead, she closed Phoebe's open eyes. It was unsettling how much effort it had taken, but having them remain open and staring would have been worse. It also felt like the only decent thing she could do in the moment.

The blood on the floor is already beginning to coagulate, revealing yellowish plasma at the edge of the pool. Her stomach begins undulating, verging on revolt. She stumbles away from the body, slipping in the blood and nearly falling. Where's the bathroom? She's studied the floor plan of this house, as she has so many of the houses in the public records of this town. It's part of the hobby. But she might as well be in a maze now. Going left around the first corner, she finds herself in a formal sitting room that probably never gets used. Exiting through the other side and making another left lands her in a dark and cavernous dining room with an enormous table running the whole length of it. Straight ahead is the front foyer, which puts her back in the main hallway. Now she has a choice of several doors, one of which has to be a bathroom. First one on the left. No, that's a closet. *Fuck.* The first door on the right, however, is jackpot.

The phone starts ringing again as she flips on the light. The series of chimes would be cheerful in any other setting, but it feels hideously out of place now, like giggles at a funeral. She needs to find that phone and see who's calling, but she's too preoccupied with not missing the toilet. Her throat burns as she raises the lid. Invisible hands wring her guts like a wet towel for what feels like several minutes and then subside just as the phone falls silent again. Red smears mar the toilet bowl where she gripped it, and she distantly notes how pristine this bathroom is, even the floor behind the toilet. In all her time watching, Nadia never saw evidence of a maid. If Phoebe was this much of a clean freak, she must have hated her very messy death.

She flushes the toilet and rests on her knees for a bit, reeling from the severe turn of events, the sense of loss. So much time spent waiting and watching, building up her nerve just to introduce herself to Phoebe, only for all of it to go as wrong as anything can. Nadia can't help but feel she played a role by leaving that note, but she'll never know for sure. And she'll never know Phoebe, either. Not the way she'd wanted to when she came all the way to Lake

Forest, her mind burning bright with something completely foreign to her: hope. If only she introduced herself sooner, before Jesse Bachmann forced her into a shoddy, desperate attempt at blackmail. They could be sitting in the kitchen right now having coffee instead, swapping stories. Now she has to plan all over again for her basic survival.

Uh, in case you didn't notice, Phoebe has been murdered. If you're smart, you'll hightail it out of here before the husband comes back to clean up his mess. A man who killed his wife is probably going to be a lot less discriminating when it comes to the stranger who just discovered his ugly deed.

She closes herself away from the harried animal in her brain and stands back up. "One mess at a time," she says. It's a mantra she's used a lot in difficult circumstances when the walls started closing in: the other night after Bachmann; three months ago, as she watched her mother take her final breaths in the wee hours while her stepfather, Jim, slept in a chair nearby, oblivious. One mess at a time. Get through the next minute. Then think about the next one.

"I can't go anywhere looking like this," she says aloud. Yes, excellent point. She's already a person of interest in one murder. Probably a good idea to avoid witnesses while covered in blood. *First wash your hands, then change your clothes. If he shows up, do what you've always done when there's a sudden fork in the road: improvise.*

Under water so hot she can barely stand it, she scrubs her hands. It's hard work. She learned from her years on the farm that blood doesn't wash off without a fight. It bonds to clothes and sticks to the skin like an incrimination, staining the cuticles and nails. She needs a brush to do it right, but she makes do with a hand towel she wets under the faucet, turning it and the water instantly pink. Eventually, she's satisfied and dries off with the other towel on the rack, then wipes up the bloody smudges she left on the toilet and floor, making a mental note to take these towels with her when she goes. She risks a glance at herself in the mirror. Pale skin, haunted glassy eyes. It's a face she's seen far too often lately, what she's coming to think of as her Murder Face.

"I'm not a murderer," she says, but her voice quavers with a lack of conviction. There are now two people dead because of her in the span of a week. She can argue that she didn't plunge the knife into Phoebe's chest the way she plunged it into Bachmann's leg, but there's no denying she was alive before Nadia delivered her that little note, and even she has a hard time believing in that level of coincidence. *You got the ball rolling, didn't you, foolish girl?* That's Jim's voice. He only ever pops up when she's really hating herself.

She closes her eyes and breathes. Clothes. But before she takes another step, she dips into her pocket for her trusty butterfly knife just in case a certain someone decides to come home. She feels a bit safer with it now that she knows she can use it when she has to, but hopefully it won't come to that. No more blood. Please.

She is just grasping the rail of the staircase when the front door flies open, startling her so hard she drops the knife. Helplessly she watches it skitter across the tile toward the dining room just as a man storms in.

In her dawning panic, Nadia isn't sure if this is the husband, one of the men from next door, or some other player in this drama she hasn't accounted for yet, but it doesn't matter, because her guts have frozen into a solid brick, weighting her to this very spot and removing any hint of the forward momentum she mustered only seconds ago. Recognition finally filters in, thanks to not only this morning's encounter but the dozens of mornings she's watched this face pass her by from the driver's seat of his shiny black Audi. He's still wet from the rain, but he's since bandaged his hand. Little rosettes of blood have seeped through the gauze. Must be a nasty cut.

Stages of comprehension slowly dawn on his face, from dazed bewilderment to horror. *This isn't my wife. This is a stranger. This stranger is covered in blood.*

"Who the hell are you?" he asks.

CHAPTER 13

O F ALL THE clever things she might have thought to say before this moment, she can only manage to say, "Nobody." Bravo, Nadia. Bravo.

His Adam's apple bobs as he swallows hard, tracking his eyes down her body and back up again. "Is that blood?"

"You know very well it is."

The color drains from his face. "What have you done?"

Before she can answer, he rushes off down the hall, calling out Phoebe's name. She grabs her knife from the floor and follows him at a distance, certain this is all theater. When he sees Phoebe's body, she expects him to go full maudlin, screaming and sobbing, maybe even trying to resuscitate the body with grotesque and inaccurate CPR. Anything to convince his audience that he didn't kill his wife this morning. But when she finally enters the kitchen and finds him standing over Phoebe's body, many silent seconds pass. A faint tremor in his shoulders betrays some distress, as does his sickly pallor, but otherwise he's a statue.

"Ph-Phoebe?" His voice is small, almost frail. "Oh *God* . . ." He covers his mouth.

For the first time, she doubts his guilt. This stance of shock is too familiar. Didn't she and Jim both stand over her mother's body this same way for several minutes when it was clear she was really gone? It was like waiting at a station for the grief train to arrive and whisk her away to some tear-filled landscape, but it seemed like it was running a little behind. And while she waited, she struggled to find a piece to complete the circle of this newly extinguished life, something that would give it a little meaning. Nadia tried for so long to remember her mother's last truly conscious moment, what her last word was before she slipped off into a coma. It didn't come to her then, and it still hasn't, but she's sure it must have been something mundane, dredged up from a brain short-circuiting from all the end-of-life demands the body makes.

Right now, Phoebe's husband is probably thinking of the last moment he had with his wife before he stormed away, trying to match it up with what he's seeing now and coming up empty. If Nadia still wasn't half-convinced he did kill her, she would tell him that it will never make sense. One minute, Phoebe's heart was pumping blood through her veins, her brain crackling with electrical impulses, carrying myriad thoughts. The next, she's lifeless, all those thoughts, all that electricity, obliterated. How can something so simple be so impossible to understand?

He leans down, peers a little closer, careful of all the blood, and then rears back when the truth of it really hits him. "*No no no.* Oh, fuck. Oh God, what is this?" He looks around at Nadia, confusion and despair etched into every feature. But fear is quickly supplanting them as his eyes go wide and glassy, especially when he sees the knife in her hand. He falls back a few steps. "What do you want? Is it money? It has to be money. I can get that for you. Just please put down the knife, okay? There's no need for anyone else to be hurt here." Does he think she's robbing him, or does he know about the note Nadia left? It's impossible to tell. She needs to be careful.

"I didn't do this. I found her like this."

"You're lying."

"I promise I'm not. I tried to save her!"

"That's not right. None of this is actually happening." He staggers away toward the farthest corner of the room. By the time he reaches the wall, he's wracked with shakes and his skin is practically translucent. Nadia flashes back to just the other night, when she sat shuddering behind the wheel of her car, her brain pulsing with the words, *YOU KILLED HIM YOU KILLED HIM YOU KILLED HIM.* Is that what's happening here? Is a similar truth settling into him like a fever?

When he doesn't say anything, she grips the handle of her knife just to remind herself it's there and then goes to him. Mercifully, they're out of view of the body. "Look, you can drop the act, all right? Just tell me why you did it."

He looks up at her. "Who the hell do you think you are, accusing me of anything?"

"It's not hard. Remember your rage fit this morning? The bloody prints you left on my window when you pounded on the glass? That cut doesn't seem like a coincidence to me. But I guess she just tripped and fell, right?"

Recognition fills his face as he glimpses the logo on her shirt, a three-dollar thrift store find that gave rise to the idea that if she was going to be creeping around wealthy neighborhoods, she should try to look like she's on some official business. A courier seemed like the perfect ruse. No one wants to be responsible for interrupting someone else's deliveries. "Oh, that's right, you're the little spy in the blue car, aren't you? The one who had Phoebe in a fit for weeks. Jesus . . . to think I told her she was being paranoid. Turns out she was right all along to be worried."

"It isn't like that, trust me."

"So I guess it's just a coincidence that the day I finally tell you to scram, she ends up dead. Christ, I should have listened to her. I should have confronted you on day one."

She wonders wildly how things might have turned out had he done that. Would that have forced her to run away, or make her introduction sooner? Either way, Phoebe might still be alive. Jesse Bachmann too. "I swear to you, I didn't do this."

He takes a step toward her. "Then what did you want with my wife?" He gestures to Phoebe with a glance and a wave of his arm and shudders.

Nadia nearly blurts out the truth, but she isn't sure this is the right time to milk him for sympathy. And there's no hope of pressing him for the getaway cash she'd intended to demand from Phoebe, not without looking even guiltier. The tightrope she has to walk right now is in a high wind. Any wrong move, and it's all over. "That's a long story that we don't have time for right now."

"Tell me!" He advances even closer.

She holds the knife out to ward him away. Her hand is trembling a little, but she's still confident she can use it if she has to. "Don't you take another step."

He throws another cautious glance at her weapon. "And she has a knife. What a coincidence. So is this where I end up joining my wife in the hereafter?"

"I never would have done anything to hurt her. I don't want to hurt anyone!" She wishes she didn't sound so defensive. It's the fear at work, but also more than a little guilt and distrust. He's pushing her onto the ropes, trying to break her down, but is he doing so because he's genuinely innocent and afraid himself, or because he's trying to deflect? Until she has a better idea, she has to keep him mostly in the dark. "Look, Phoebe and I had . . . mutual interests, okay? I'd been working up to introducing myself. Was actually planning to do it today, but someone killed her, and that's all I know."

He's frowning at her. "Mutual interests? What sort of mutual interests? You actually know who she is?"

She nods. "Looks like we both have a lot of questions."

"You're also the stranger in my house standing over my dead wife!"

"Whom I found after watching you leave here in Hulk mode."

He shakes his head. "I'm telling you, that's impossible."

"And yet, here we are."

Neither of them speaks for a minute, pondering their impasse. Then he says, "So who let you into the house if she was . . . like this when you got here?"

"After you raved at me like a psycho, I went driving around for close to two hours before I decided to come back. I needed to see her. Speak to her. I knocked and rang the doorbell, but when she didn't answer, I got a bad feeling in my gut, because she . . . you know, doesn't go out much. I walked around back, to the patio. When I peeked through the doors, I saw her feet splayed out . . . so I came in. Found her like this."

He closes his eyes, takes a deep breath. "The door was just unlocked?"

"Yes."

"And you saw no one else around?"

She shakes her head. "The only person I saw near your house this morning was you."

"So why didn't you just call the cops? That's what anyone else would have done." Her mouth goes a little dry. The truth definitely wouldn't help her, so she says nothing. He nods, like he's heard the basic run of her thoughts telepathically. "Right. Something tells me you're the type to avoid cops when possible."

"You didn't exactly dive for your phone, either," she says.

"I'm fixing that right now." He reaches into his pocket and pulls out his phone.

"They'd arrest you first, you know." She hopes she doesn't sound too eager to dissuade him. "They always go after the husband. Always."

"The evidence will speak for itself." He doesn't sound entirely convinced of that. He's also no longer tapping on his phone screen, which is a relief.

"It's screaming to me now that you did it, and I guarantee you they'd agree. You have the best motive. She's rich. Also, your marriage was falling apart."

He flinches. "How would you know that?"

She won't mention the affair, unsure what emotion it might

trigger, but she doesn't really need to. "I was actually just bluffing, but your reaction pretty much said it all."

He looks away, adequately chagrined. She continues. "You also had the most opportunity to do it, since you live here. And there's the cut on your hand, the blood on your shirt."

"I broke a coffee mug and cut myself! It's my blood!"

"Doesn't matter. They'll say you cut yourself while stabbing her. And then there's the witness. Me. I'll tell them what I saw, a clearly distraught man speeding away from his house right around the time of his wife's death, but not before stopping to threaten me." It's another bluff. She wouldn't be within fifty miles of this place when the cops showed, but again, he doesn't need to know that.

He's visibly shrinking as she speaks, and it satisfies her greatly. But then something occurs to him, because he frowns and straightens his posture a little. "What about when I tell them you've been spying on our house for weeks? I'm sure they'll find witnesses around the neighborhood to back that up. Phoebe even keeps . . . *kept* a logbook. I thought she was being ridiculous . . ." He bows his head and gives it a grim shake. "That's on me now, for not believing her. But given that you don't want to involve the cops, you must have something to hide, no matter what your so-called mutual interests were with Phoebe." He looks at her a little more closely. "Why do you look so familiar, anyway?"

Nadia stiffens. It's very possible he's seen her picture in recent news, but she'd rather he didn't make that connection at the moment, or see how desperate she is to avoid facing any police at all. *This is why you should have just left the second you saw those splayed-out feet, foolish girl. Now here you are, trying to bargain with a likely killer.* "Listen, we can go back and forth all day about who did this, but it's not going to change the fact that we both are in a bind here. Would you agree?"

His jaw clenches like he's reluctant to admit it, but nevertheless he says, "I guess so."

"At best, they'll have reason to arrest us both. Maybe they'll eventually be able to exclude us as suspects, but is that something you want to take a chance on? This will be everywhere in the news too. Even if by some miracle they catch someone else for this, people will talk and they'll dig, and it will live on through the internet forever."

After a long moment, he cries, "God, this whole thing is so fucked!"

She doesn't raise any objections about that. He paces a few times, keeping his head turned in an effort to avoid looking at Phoebe. Nadia says, "Look, maybe we should take this into the other room. I think we'd both find it a little, you know, easier to talk."

He doesn't respond verbally, but the relief that crosses his face is plain enough. She follows him into the sitting room adjacent to the kitchen, which is mercifully out of view of the body. The lighting is better in here, which allows her to see how bloodshot his eyes are. "So?" he asks. "What are we going to do?"

"So you now see this as a 'we' problem?" Nadia asks.

"Would you disagree?"

"No. Just making sure we're on the same page."

"Same page? I don't even know what book this is. Will you at least tell me your name now that we're considering being coconspirators?"

"Okay, fair enough. I'm Nadia."

He studies her face for a moment, as though trying to determine whether that's her real name, and then gives a resigned nod. "All right, Nadia. I'm Wyatt. But I guess you already knew that."

She doesn't tell him that she might have known it once but eventually forgot it. He's never really been on her radar. Phoebe was always her priority. Nadia was just fine thinking of him only as "the husband." She's about to ask him if he wants to open with any suggestions on next steps when she notices his face working, like he's trying to hold back tears. She realizes she's still holding out her knife. Not as prominently as she was before, but enough to keep him at a safe distance. She lowers it fully to her side but doesn't fold the blade back in yet or move any closer. Baby steps, at least until she's sure he isn't putting one over on her. "Do you need a moment?" she asks.

He closes his eyes, takes a few deep breaths. "No. Just fighting off a little panic attack. I feel like my brain has been short-circuiting since I woke up this morning. Emotions all over the place."

"I gathered that by the way you left."

"We'd had a bad fight. Probably our worst one ever, and we've been having a lot of them lately." He looks at her sharply. "But she was very much alive when I left. That was my biggest mistake, leaving. Of course at that moment, I thought it was the smart thing to do, because I was so angry. You always think you're going to have a chance to go back and fix things."

Doubts about his guilt begin creeping back in. At the very least, his regrets seem genuine, and she wants to ask what they fought about. After all, Phoebe was leading something of a double life. Of course, that also means there are more suspects to consider. Three of them, right across the street. With a little digging, she might be able to find out for sure. But to what end? Revealing who killed Phoebe won't do a thing to alleviate Nadia's Bachmann problem.

What she should be doing is getting out of town before all that catches up to her. Meanwhile, even if she helps hide the body, Phoebe will have to be reported missing. Wyatt can buy some time by saying she left town for a little while, but that won't work forever. Eventually, someone somewhere is going to expect Phoebe Miller to show up for something, and when she doesn't, the police will get involved. They'll grill Wyatt, and then, to cover his own ass, he'll put them on Nadia's trail.

Of course, Phoebe was kind of a hermit. She didn't have an outside job or even a Facebook page anymore. Aside from the neighbors across the street, how many people would even notice her missing? He could just fake her signatures for the occasional check or tax documents. Stick to email for everything else. A female voice might be needed for a phone conversation now and then, but . . .

Nadia nearly gasps as an idea blooms to life, but she's not going to get her hopes up just yet. It's way too good to be possible. It's actually downright absurd, but therein lies its genius. "Does Phoebe have any close family who would miss her?"

He wipes at his eyes and shakes his head. "No. Her parents are both dead. All the other relatives are either distant or not really in contact."

"What about her business or financial interests? Any lawyers, family trustees or busybodies, that sort of thing?"

Now he's staring at her with guarded interest. "You've been spying on her for weeks, so I assume you know who she was."

"Yes. I know she's Daniel Noble's daughter." Nadia's stomach sours a little as she thinks of how she'd been intending to use this knowledge to her advantage.

"She was an only child, so she received the bulk of the personal inheritance. The rest went into a trust for the few remaining aunts and cousins, who feed off of it like vultures. They've always kept their distance. And since you know who Daniel Noble is, then you've probably been paying attention to the news recently."

Had she ever. "Yes. He was a rapist." The words come out harsher than she intended.

He raises his eyebrows. "Not one to mince words, I see."

"Should I have said 'alleged' rapist?"

"You'll never catch me defending the man. Anyway, as you can imagine, I think anybody with ties to Daniel's money is looking to keep a low profile right now. Phoebe was no exception."

She nods. This is good. Very good. "What about her accountants and lawyers? Does she work closely with them? What about any side work for the company?"

"Around tax time, she might go into the accountant's office to sign some documents, but that's about it. She hasn't worked in any real capacity for the company in years. What little correspondence she gets is all through email."

"And since you're her husband, you can act in her stead, correct?"

"That's not how ultra-rich families operate. Outsiders are pretty well isolated from things, and my father-in-law was particularly keen on keeping me at arm's length."

"Why's that?"

Wyatt shakes his head as if to say *some other time*. "I would have received a substantial chunk upon Phoebe's death, but even then, I'm sure there are some ridiculous conditions in the will I don't know about."

This is another mark in Nadia's favor, but she stops short of pumping her fist in triumph for now. There's another important matter. "What about her friends?" She already knows about the two people Phoebe spent most of her time with lately, but he would likely have more insights on any others. She senses there won't be much, though. Given that Phoebe had no social media accounts that Nadia could find, and rarely left the house for any other reason than to grocery shop, it stands to reason that all her other friendships have withered on the vine.

"Phoebe didn't do friends. Getting her out of the house, especially in recent months, was like pulling teeth. I suspected some agoraphobia in addition to depression, but she refused to let me diagnose her or refer her to someone who could. I'm a therapist." He sounds almost apologetic about it.

"She was friendly with the people who moved in across the street recently." Nadia decides to leave out any mention of lover boy for now. One mess at a time. "The wife came over to visit a couple times a week during the day. Sometimes they went out together."

He seems almost taken aback by that news, but then he shrugs and shakes his head. "I never noticed. We were barely speaking anymore these last weeks, and my head has been in a fog. She could have been running a drug and prostitution ring out of the garage for all I knew."

He's ticked all the boxes for her, and she's nearly trembling with excitement. Phoebe was a hermit with no real social life, apart from the neighbors. They will be an issue, especially if one or all of them did have something to do with Phoebe's death, but she can deal with them soon. The real beauty of her idea is it utilizes the one thing that brought Nadia all the way to Lake Forest in the first place.

"So I think I have a plan. You may not like it, but it's the best chance we'll have to buy ourselves all the time we need to get to the bottom of what really happened here."

He inhales and squares his shoulders. "Okay. I'm listening."

"By the end of the night, it will be like this never happened. We're going to undo the murder and make Phoebe live again."

CHAPTER 14

WYATT STARES AT her like she might have sprouted a second head, which isn't all that far from what she has in mind. Then he shakes his head and looks down at his feet. "I got nothing."

"It would be better if I showed you," she says. "Do you mind if I go upstairs for a few minutes? You can come with me if you're worried I might do something."

"What do you need up there?"

She clears her throat. "To be honest, I'd like to clean myself up a little. Would it be okay if I changed into something of hers?"

He sighs and stands up. "Fine. I'll come too. I don't want to be alone down here."

As they climb the staircase, Nadia takes a moment to admire the bold abstract paintings on the walls along the way. Phoebe clearly loved modern art, a sharp contrast to the classic Tudor exterior of the house. This seems to encapsulate the Phoebe she came to know, at least in her head, over the last several weeks. Traditional and elegant on the outside but full of surprises.

"Are you ever going to tell me who you really are?" Wyatt asks when they're nearly at the top.

"You'll figure it out on your own soon enough."

"That's a little cryptic for my liking."

She turns to him when they reach the landing. The big set of teak double doors at the end of the hallway can only be the master bedroom. How grand. "I just think if I simply told you, you wouldn't believe me anyway." She pauses before opening the doors. "Are you coming in with me?"

"You think I wouldn't?"

She shakes her head. "I need the insurance as much as you do right now."

The bedroom is nearly pitch-black thanks to the heavy curtains covering the windows. She fumbles blindly for the light switch for a few seconds, but Wyatt beats her to it. Bathed in clean LED, the room isn't much cheerier. Walls the color of concrete. Metal and glass furnishings. Even the lap-pool-sized bed doesn't feel at all cozy or inviting, thanks to the stark white bedding and the brushed steel bed frame. Plants or colorful fabrics would help soften the space, but it would still feel like a mausoleum. It's interesting that Phoebe would have chosen such a spartan look for the most intimate room in her home.

She glances at Wyatt, who's even more solemn than before. "Is it okay if I look in the closet for some clothes?"

He nods and points to another set of double doors. "You'll find everything in there."

When she opens the doors, she stops breathing for a few seconds and then lets the air out in a whoosh. "Wow. She sure loved to shop, didn't she?"

"Not as much recently. But yes." He sits down on the tufted leather ottoman at the end of the bed.

The place holding Phoebe's wardrobe is about the same size as the living room in the house she grew up in. Hundreds of garments line the walls in three stacked rows clear to the vaulted ceiling, all of it organized by color. The entire back wall is devoted to shoes, count-less pairs perfectly lined up in long rows, also to the ceiling. There's an enormous island with drawers in the center. It's bare on top, save for an iron and an empty laundry basket. A quick check of the draw-ers reveals stacks of bras and panties, all laid in flat, color-coded rows with retail precision. The one thing throwing off the balance is the big empty hole on the other side of the space, which is presumably where Wyatt once kept his clothes. All that's left are a couple suits hanging in their dry-cleaning bags, and an old-looking winter coat. So he's living in another room of the house, after all. Good thing they agreed to keep the cops away. This closet would've provided all the answers they needed about the strength of the Miller marriage.

Nadia's eyes fall on an item on the floor that seems out of place: a small wheeled travel bag, the sort of thing people use for a carry-on when flying. She can't imagine the overly fastidious Phoebe would just leave this lying out. "Looks like you had some travel plans," she murmurs, giving the bag a quick lift to check its weight. Heavy. Definitely packed for a trip. Nadia will riffle through this thing soon, but for now the only task she must concern herself with is performing a resurrection.

"What's taking so long in there?" Wyatt asks.

"Are you kidding? It's like a Macy's in here." Or like one of the posh boutiques she's driven past in downtown Lake Forest, though she's never gone inside any of them.

She sifts through the dresses, most of them her size, though she finds a few that are a size bigger, likely to accommodate Phoebe's recent weight gain. Most of the larger ones are more on the plain, casual side, like she bought them just to have anything at all to put on rather than to make herself look pretty. If this closet were a geological sample, Nadia would conclude by these frumpy frocks that this is about the point in Phoebe's life where she started giving up.

Unfortunately, regardless of the sizes, nearly everything in here is some shade of pink or purple. Nadia wears a lot of black, which is both her preferred aesthetic as well as a necessity of car living and limited laundry access. She can live with purple, but as someone who grew up on a pig farm, she really hates pink. But she'll have to get used to it, at least for now.

She finally selects an eggplant-colored maxi dress with a white sash around the waist. It looks like a normal knit fabric, but the silky feel of it is unlike anything she would find at the discount stores where she normally shops.

Next, she scans the enormous library of shoes and notices with relief that she and Phoebe are both a size seven. The range of brands and styles is completely foreign to her. She recognizes a couple of them from popular culture or the occasional fashion mag she's flipped through in the break room at work. Most of them look like they've never touched actual pavement. Most of them also look like they'd make her feet weep in agony five minutes after putting them on.

As she settles on a pair of simple white sandals, she feels a rare elation. This Indiana farm girl has ascended to the summit. All she needs to do is clean away a little more blood and dirt.

She steps out of the closet to find Wyatt sitting with his face in his hands. "I found something to wear. Can I use the bathroom now?"

He looks around at her, his dark eyes exhausted and brimming with emotion. "Sure. Just try to be fast. I don't much like being in here."

She considers mentioning his empty spot in the closet, but he likely already knows she noticed. "It's okay. I've always been quick."

The master bath is a fortress of white tile, glass, and gleaming water fixtures. Only after hastily washing and dressing does she let herself look at Phoebe's expensive dressing table. As expected, it contains an array of cosmetics and perfumes that would rival the aesthetician counter at any high-end department store. Though Nadia does have some experience with beauty products, she never became passionate about them. With limited money, one must choose between looking beautiful and eating. On the days when she couldn't make it into a YMCA to shower, she cleaned her face with moist towelettes and dabbed on a little concealer and mascara with the help of her rearview mirror. Quick and simple. Phoebe's collection of potions, however, suggests someone who thought about her appearance almost obsessively, or at least used to once upon a time.

She isn't going to spend too much time doing herself up, as she's only trying to prove a point, but first she removes the tiny rhinestone stud from her nose. A nose ring doesn't fit the look she's going

for. Next, she washes her face with a black soap that contains acti-
vated charcoal "to purify the pores." It looks like a horror show but
feels like money. Once she's properly scrubbed and moisturized,
she applies foundation from a bottle covered in French words. The
shade is a tad darker to match a more golden complexion, but it's
good enough for the time being.

She brushes on some shimmery shadow the color of champagne
and adds a touch of dark purple eye pencil around the lids, mascara,
highlighter on the cheeks and forehead, and a swipe of translucent
pink lip gloss. When she's finished, she brushes her hair and smooths
it with a serum to give it that rich-girl glow.

As a final touch, she gives herself a few spritzes of perfume and
then stands back to view the whole package in the mirror.

Phoebe Noble Miller stares back at her.

Nadia lets out a breath as she takes in her reflection. If this
doesn't convince Wyatt to go along with her plan, she'll just have to
tie him up and keep him in the basement until he changes his mind,
because as far as she's concerned, she is Phoebe, at least enough to
fool people on the first pass. What more do you need in a world
where people are spending more time looking at their phones than
each other?

She emerges from the bathroom. When Wyatt glances up at her,
he jumps to his feet. "Jesus!"

That guy took three days to come back to life. Nadia is pretty
sure she has him beat. "What do you think?"

He seems frozen in place, eyes wide with wonder. When he
speaks, he sounds like a man coming out of a trance. "It's remark-

able. I don't know how I didn't notice the resemblance before, but . . . God."

"Well, before I was in a hat." And covered in his wife's blood, but no need to remind him of that. "But good to know I clean up okay."

"It's hard to believe it's even possible. If I didn't know Phoebe was an only child, I'd believe you were sisters."

Nadia drops her gaze to her sandals. "I'm glad I'm convincing."

He continues to study her face, like he's slowly warming to the potential of this idea, and she feels a little ashamed at her building excitement over a future that includes private showers and a real bed, a diet beyond food in grease-spotted bags handed out through drive-thru windows, money for every possible desire and necessity. She will be able to make Nadia disappear completely, shedding her troublesome old skin for one far more luxurious and easy to wear. Sure, it won't be without problems, especially in the immediate future, but down the road, once all the kinks have been worked out, she can't imagine a better outcome.

Wyatt seems to notice he's staring, and he clears his throat. "So this is your plan. We . . ." He pauses, appearing to struggle with his next words. "We . . . bury Phoebe and then you impersonate her?"

"What better way to avoid a murder investigation or even a missing person report than to have no murder or missing person?"

He shakes his head. "I still think it won't work."

"Why not?"

"Because it's preposterous. Your hair shades don't match."

He's not exactly wrong there. Nadia's natural color is dark brown, but in an attempt to have a new look to go with her new life, she'd tried lightening it to an ashy blond using a drug store kit not long after she got to town. It turned out a little brassier than she wanted, and the roots were showing, but the point is moot. "That's an easy fix, and you know it."

"That may be, but you can't just fill a person's shoes and expect people not to notice the differences. Even if you look a lot like Phoebe, you're not a carbon copy."

Nadia predicted most of this conversation while she was getting dressed. She knew Wyatt would initially balk at the idea, as would most sane people. But she intends to wear him down. It won't take much work. He's already latched on to the idea at least a little bit, judging by his gaze.

"I think people will buy it just fine," Nadia says.

"How?"

"Can you really see yourself challenging someone's identity to their face, even if you sensed something was a little different about them?"

He frowns. "No, I guess not."

"We see celebrities every day getting face-lifts, Botox, and implants that change their looks, but we don't actually stop thinking they are those people."

He sighs. "True, but I still think this is completely nuts."

"It *is* nuts, which is why it will work. Because no one would ever expect an actual impostor. That isn't to say people who know Phoebe won't sense something different about her. But rich women get work done practically every week, right? They'll just chalk it up to that. Also, her having been a shut-in works to our advantage. No business outside the home, no real family or friends. If we keep up appearances, no one will be the wiser."

"Except the new neighbors, as you mentioned earlier. That will be a sticking point."

Nadia thinks they'll be problematic for a few different reasons, namely that one of them could be Phoebe's killer, and the sudden appearance of a decoy will cause one hell of a stir. She's counting on it, though. As much as this is about not rocking the boat by alerting the world to Phoebe's death, she wants to know who did this.

"I'm not worried about that right now," she says. "Let's just focus on getting everything in place first."

He rubs his face and then looks back at her with a frown. "When you said 'keep up appearances,' you mean we have to live here together? Like we're married?"

Her expression is pure deadpan. "I've been in Phoebe's closet. It's obvious you're living in separate areas of the house, Wyatt. Do you really think it's going to be that much more of a stretch for us to share a roof?"

He mumbles something that sounds like "I guess not."

"Besides, I think you're forgetting a much bigger opportunity in all this."

"What's that?"

"Once I learn how to be Phoebe, or when you and I get to a place where we do trust each other, we can divorce"—she makes air quotes around the word—"and go our separate ways."

"That's a good point," he says, still a touch dubious.

He frowns and begins pacing back and forth on the landing,

arms folded across him, eyes focused on the brilliant white carpet. He's thought of something else. She's trying to remain patient with him, as it's important to work out any possible complications ahead of time, but it's so hard, because she suddenly feels desperate to make this work. "What is it now?" she asks.

"Why are you so willing to throw your own life away over this?"

This is one question she was hoping to avoid. "Has it occurred to you that I'm trading up? I can't think of many people who wouldn't give up their drab, dead-end life to become a billionaire."

One of his eyebrows goes up. "Any baggage you have right now is going to be a liability for us both."

"You have nothing to worry about." She says it with such confidence, she believes it herself. They really should have nothing to worry about, if they do everything right.

He doesn't look like he's any closer to believing her, but he shakes his head and continues pacing. Then he says, "Her killer is going to know you're an impostor. Assuming the killer isn't you."

"Or you," she snaps back.

"Correct. If it isn't one of us, then there is still a murderer out there. They could even be watching the house right now, waiting for this place to become a crime scene."

"You're worried they'll become a problem for us?"

"Yeah, I'd say that's more than likely. If their plan doesn't come to fruition, and if they see a new Phoebe walking around, they won't know what the hell is going on. It will make us both loose ends in their book. They may not be able to rest until they take care of us too."

"Or they might be relieved we covered it up for them and move on," Nadia suggests.

"We can't afford that kind of optimism. This person could be unhinged. Seeing someone else impersonating the woman they expect to be dead could make them crack even further."

"Then what better way to smoke them out and deal with them?"

He rubs his face like someone trying to scrub away a bad dream. "And how do you propose we deal with them?"

She hesitates to answer. The phrase "deal with" in this context has an ominous quality she doesn't much care for, especially in light of her recently "dealing with" a nuisance of a former work colleague. "I think it's safe to say that if we go down this road, we need to be prepared to get our hands dirty. It's either that, or we get used to the feeling of handcuffs."

He nods slowly, like it takes most of his energy to do it. "I still can't believe this is actually happening."

Nadia shares the sentiment. Everything still has an unreal quality about it, and that feeling is only going to intensify for a while. And that's assuming Nadia's own problems don't follow her here. "We have a lot to figure out still, but right now, I think this is the best option we have. Are you in?"

She holds out her hand for the most important shake they'll ever make. *Please be on board, Wyatt. Both our lives depend on it.* After a few seconds that feel like an eternity, he finally takes her hand. "I am. God help us both. Now what?"

CHAPTER 15

BEFORE THEY GET started, Nadia takes out her phone and asks Wyatt to do the same. "What's this about?" he asks.

She opens her camera app. "I want you to stand next to Phoebe."

The color drains from his face. "Are you serious?"

"Yes. And then you'll take a picture of me on your phone."

"Let me get this straight. You want us to *pose* with my *murdered wife's* body? Jesus, what kind of sick game is this?"

Nadia sighs. Patience, girl. "If you can think of a better way to ensure that one of us won't run off on the other at the first given opportunity, I'm all ears."

"But we'd be implicating ourselves in a murder, which innocent people don't do."

"Like I said, I'm open to suggestions. Until we trust each other, we need something."

He stares at her with his mouth open, but no words come out. Finally, he shakes and lowers his head, a sure sign of resignation. "I don't like this at all. Not only is it just . . . *grotesque*, but nothing is safe in the digital age."

"We'll figure out how to encrypt the files or whatever. Unless you have a better idea, Wyatt, we need to get this done. Time is really getting away from us here."

He finally surrenders, and holds up his phone. "I'm not putting all of her in the picture. We only need to see her . . . her face, right?"

She thinks about it and nods. It's a fair enough compromise and enough to serve the purpose, given Phoebe's head injury. "That will be fine."

They both snap pictures. Wyatt puts his phone back in his pocket with a shudder. "I feel sick even having this on my phone."

"Perhaps one day we'll mutually decide it's time to delete them."

"Let's hope," he mutters.

Nadia volunteers to wrap the body, but Wyatt insists on helping. "She's my wife. We'll do it together."

She appreciates his egalitarian outlook, but his skin has grown remarkably sallow, probably because the smell of death in here is even stronger now than it was earlier. Hopefully he won't puke or faint. Nadia is barely holding it together, and she can't spare the energy to babysit him or clean up even more mess. She decides to give him a distraction.

"Do you have a tarp or some plastic sheeting we can use?" she asks.

"I'm sure I have something downstairs. Be right back." While he rustles around beneath the house, Nadia begins planning the next stage of the game. Their best option is also the riskiest. They'll need to drive a few hours south of here. It's a long distance to go with a dead body in the trunk, with the potential for disaster increasing exponentially with every mile. A wreck. A phantom flat tire or breakdown. A bored sheriff or state trooper looking for any stupid reason to pull someone over.

Nadia briefly considers other options. The lake. She's disposed of a lot of things in that ubiquitous body of water over the years, but it's too public, and there is too much of a chance Phoebe will either wash ashore or be discovered by some boater. They could dig a big hole in the backyard right now and never have to take another risk after tonight, but that would only sour the space for them both, even if they only stayed here for a short time. There would also remain the possibility that long after they departed this place, someone could accidentally dig her up while doing a little remodeling. At least where Nadia is thinking of taking her, total elimination is as close to guaranteed as she dares hope.

Wyatt returns with a large roll of brown canvas covered in various colors of dried paint. An old drop cloth, by the looks of it. He also has a tangle of nylon bungee cords. "Will this stuff do?"

"That should work."

A phone starts ringing and they both jerk. It's the same one she heard earlier. "Is that Phoebe's phone?"

He nods. "Just ignore it. We have enough to do."

Despite her curiosity, she agrees the phone will have to wait for now, but she has another thought. "Do you know the passcode for her phone?"

"She uses her birth date for everything."

"Good. Because we'll need to get into it later if we want to learn anything."

"Fine. Let's just do this."

She takes the canvas and spreads it open on the cleanest segment of floor she can find away from the main blood puddle. They'll have to lift Phoebe onto it, but it shouldn't be too hard with both of them working.

Silently, Wyatt moves into position at Phoebe's head, while Nadia takes the foot end. Now they'll have to touch her, and she'll be pretty chilly by now, possibly even entering rigor mortis. Nadia hopes not. It would only make them both more squeamish. "Ready?" she asks.

Wyatt stares at Phoebe, not moving.

"You steady?" she prods. He looks dumbstruck, vacant. Pity stirs within Nadia. Poor bastard. If he really didn't kill Phoebe— and she's starting to think he might not have—then she can only imagine how much of a head fuck this is for him.

"I'm okay," he says eventually. "I'm not feeling much of anything right now." He looks up at Nadia, bewildered. "That sounds really bad, doesn't it?"

"Not really. I get it. Your mind wants to separate itself from this." She felt the same way after she realized Jesse Bachmann was dead. Still feels it.

"Yes. Dissociation. I've studied this sort of thing academically, but I guess it's different when you're living it."

"Are you sure you didn't kill her? At this point, you might as well tell me."

He lets out a deep sigh and Nadia's heart skips a beat.

"No. And I would never have done it this way if I had. I hate blood. It's why I didn't go to med school. Let's just get this over with." He bends to grasp Phoebe's wrists. Nadia is just grabbing the ankles when the doorbell rings, stopping her cold. She glances at

Wyatt and sees his mouth drawing down into a silent scream worthy of Edvard Munch.

"Just ignore it," she whispers.

The bell rings again, followed by a knock. Nadia can't remember if the door is locked. Someone who sounds this determined might go ahead and barge in, and if so, her plan will be over before it even gets off the ground.

"What do we do?" Nadia asks, her voice little more than a squeak, the terror a tight band around her midsection. Could someone have called the cops? What if the ones investigating the Bachmann murder tracked her here after all? What if Phoebe's killer is executing the perfect setup by sending in the cavalry while the body is at their feet?

Wyatt straightens, letting Phoebe's arms fall back to the floor. He turns away from Nadia, bowing his head and pressing the heels of his hands to his eyes. After a few hard breaths, he stills for a moment. When he turns back, it's as if he'd flipped a switch. His expression is as serene as she's seen it all morning. It's a form of self-control Nadia can't help but envy. Must be one of his therapist tricks.

"Don't worry. Stay here. I'll take care of this." He checks himself over to make sure he doesn't have any blood on him and then leaves. Thankfully the kitchen is invisible from the front door, but she still wishes she was close to a bathroom, because now, in addition to needing to puke, she needs to pee. And maybe die.

She hears a door open, followed by, "Oh, hello there! You must be Wyatt."

A woman's voice. Cheery and bright. Not very policelike. Nadia calms down a little.

"Yes. Hi. Uh, you're our new neighbor, right? Phoebe has mentioned you."

Oh fun, Phoebe's current bestie. Nadia would bet she's the one who's been calling all morning.

"That's right. I'm Vicki Napier. My husband is Ron, son is Jake. Phoebe has told me so much about you." The voice sounds warm, but Nadia can detect the slightest bit of contempt oozing from around the edges. Vicki and Phoebe probably did that catty thing a lot of girlfriends do, dissecting their mates right down to the marrow, zeroing in on all the nastiest parts. This woman probably knows things about Wyatt's sexual habits and other private rituals that would mortify him.

Speaking of sexual habits, does Vicki know that Phoebe was spending a bit too much personal time with young Jake? Maybe the husband clued her in. That could explain the carnage here. But Nadia shakes her head. From what she's seen of this woman, she's pretty slight. It would take a lot of mama-bear adrenaline to pull off a feat like this. Not impossible, mind, just unlikely. Papa bear, on the other hand . . . he gets angry a lot.

"She told you all about me, huh? That can't be good." Wyatt tries on a joking tone, but it comes off a little shaky. Vicki's responding laughter matches it, a shrill peal that belies any humor. Nadia feels a little seasick just listening to them.

"Is Phoebe around, by chance? We were supposed to meet up for brunch this morning, but I haven't been able to reach her. I'm starting to get a little worried." *Oh, I don't know if Phoebe is up for visitors right now or at any point in the future*, Nadia thinks, glancing down at the body.

"She picked up a nasty stomach bug," Wyatt says. "That's actually why I'm here. She needed someone to hold her hair back." Nice one, Nadia thinks.

"Uh-oh! I hope it isn't too serious."

Oh, it's dead serious, Nadia thinks. *A real killer virus. Lots of stabbing pains.* Mad laughter bubbles up inside her, but real humor is a star in another galaxy right now. This is more like creeping hysteria.

"These things tend to pass pretty quickly," Wyatt says. "But I'll tell her to answer her texts at least."

"I appreciate that. And if there is anything I can do to help her, don't hesitate to call."

"Thanks, Vicki. I'll do that."

Nadia lets out a quiet sigh. Thank God that's done.

"Oh, hey. What happened to your hand, there? It looks like it's bleeding."

Well, fuck. "I broke a mug this morning and cut myself. Clumsy mistake, but it's nothing serious."

"If it's still bleeding after this morning, you might need some stitches."

"Yeah, maybe. I'll look into that when I have a minute."

"My husband is a doctor. I could ask him to have a look if you'd like."

"That's very nice of you," Wyatt says. "I should be fine, though."

"All right, then. Let me know if you change your mind."

"Okay, great. Thanks again."

A second later, the door shuts, and Nadia falls against the wall behind her. Wyatt's a little hunched over when he comes back, like he's aging a year or more for every minute that passes. "That was really fucking scary."

"You did fine. How did she seem? Like maybe she knew something?"

He shrugs. "She seemed normal enough, a bit high-strung, I guess. Wasn't giving me any vibes one way or another."

Nadia was hoping for a more astute analysis from a shrink, but she'll forgive him under the present circumstances. He'll have more time to evaluate her later. Dr. Ron too, and maybe the prodigal son if they're really lucky. "I think we should go over there this evening and let him stitch your hand."

"Are you insane? I'm not going over there. And did you just say 'we'? I just told her Phoebe was sick."

"Well like you said, stomach bugs pass quickly. I'll act weak, but we have to go. We need the intel, and it's a good idea to present as normal a front as possible."

"What sort of intel?"

She raises her eyebrows and gestures toward Phoebe's body. "Uh, hello? We need to look for a murderer here, unless you're happy with us continuing to suspect one another."

He lifts his hands in surrender. "All right, I get it. I just want to know what you think we might find that would tell us anything helpful."

"Namely reactions. The one who acts like they've just seen a ghost when they lay eyes on me is probably our guy. Or gal."

"Okay, then what? We just start duking it out?"

She shakes her head. "I have a feeling this will be a longer game than that. But I guess anything could happen."

Wyatt exhales. "Do we really need to start the Nancy Drew thing now? We haven't even done the most important part yet."

"We can't move until after dark, anyway. So let's wrap her up and stow her in the trunk of whatever car we're taking, clean up, you know, the rest. After that, we can head on over and see what we can see."

"I still don't like it. Feels like walking into a lion's den with fresh meat around our necks." He makes a move of disgust, as if realizing too late how close to home the bloody metaphor is.

"If any of them are guilty, they're going to be too shocked and afraid to break cover. We'll be over there just long enough to take the temperature of the place, and you'll get free stitches on your hand as a bonus. And you're going to need them. You don't want to risk infection at a time like this." And the place they're going is far from clean.

He sighs and shakes his head. "Fine. Let's just get this part over with before I lose my nerve."

They bend down again to move Phoebe onto the drop cloth. Though neither of them says how they feel about handling dead flesh, it's hard to hide their respective difficulties: Nadia's overall distaste, Wyatt's silent, grief-stricken tears, not to mention the physical strain for them both. Once the body is on the canvas, they roll her up into it, blessedly removing her from sight. The burden on Nadia's chest lifts just a little bit more, even though it's the easiest part of the whole ordeal. They secure the fabric with the cords and duct tape, making Phoebe into a sausage.

"And now we move her to the trunk?" Wyatt asks, his complexion pale enough to appear translucent, skimmed in sweat.

"Yes. We're driving separately on the way down to Indiana. I'll need to abandon my car as well."

"Why abandon it? You could always just sell it."

It's too soon to explain why that's not a viable option, and she'd rather not go into the Jesse Bachmann situation at all. She's been nervous enough driving the car around town, though she's already swapped the plates once and is sure the Executive Courier magnets have done enough to divert attention. But her luck with that is destined to run out before long. This is her best chance to ditch the thing for good. It also seems appropriate enough for the trail of Nadia to end not far from where it started.

"It's easier to deal with it this way."

He looks dubious. "If you say so. What's in Indiana?"

"That can all wait until we're on the road."

They spend a few minutes lugging the heavy human parcel out to the garage, where Nadia sees something she didn't notice before in all her weeks of spying, mostly because this side of the garage was never open to the street. "Holy shit, what is that thing?"

Wyatt doesn't say anything until after they have the body covered in blankets and sealed inside the Audi's trunk. "That right there is one of the rarest Ferraris you'll ever see, and it's crammed into a dusty garage. Almost funny when you think about it."

"Yours?"

"God, no. It wasn't really Phoebe's, either. Her father had it delivered here not long before he died."

Nadia stares at the red beast, then turns back to Wyatt. "Why don't you drive it? I mean, if it's here, you might as well enjoy it."

He shakes his head. "This isn't the sort of car someone just drives. One of these things was auctioned off for over four million dollars not too long ago. It's better to think of it as an exotic sculpture on wheels."

She whistles and runs her hand along the rear fender. It's now the most expensive thing she's ever touched. "Seems like such a waste hiding it in here like this."

"Oh, it is. Phoebe hates . . . hated flashy shows of wealth. Don't get me wrong, she liked having money and she didn't let it go to waste, but her father was always a tacky bastard, and spiteful too. Phoebe always thought he left her this car as a taunt, to see if her loyalty to him would outweigh her disgust. It's just the sort of passive-aggressive move he was known for."

"What an asshole."

"I told her it would be the perfect act of revenge to get rid of the thing in the worst way. Hand it over to any schmuck on the street, maybe fill it with toddlers and hand them ice-cream cones and markers. I know she agreed deep down, but she couldn't quite bring herself to do it."

The more Nadia looks at the car, the more she dislikes it. "Hell, I would have set the thing on fire."

Wyatt gives her an appraising glance. "This seems almost personal for you too."

"Maybe it is a little."

"That mutual interest you mentioned you had with Phoebe. Would that happen to be Daniel?"

"It might be."

"Ah. Were you one of the women he, you know . . . hurt?"

She shakes her head, knowing these questions won't stop coming until she answers him satisfactorily. In such cases, only the truth will do. "Only indirectly. The person he really hurt was my mother. He knocked her up and left her stranded."

"I see. But why the fixation on Phoebe? Did you think you could get to him through her somehow?"

Nadia stares at him. "Let me clarify. He knocked up my mother and left her stranded, oh, *twenty-six years ago.*"

He doesn't speak right away, but Nadia can see the pieces coming together in his head, like the tumblers in a lock. "Hold on a minute. Is Daniel . . . your father?"

"I would hardly call him a father. But would he pass a paternity test? Sure."

His jaw drops open. "It's all starting to make sense now. But wait. Holy shit, that means Phoebe . . ."

"Congrats. You figured it out."

"Is that why you've been sitting outside our house? Were you planning to intimidate her? Get her to give you money or something?"

She shifts her feet, finding it harder to make eye contact. "No, my plan was to introduce myself and get to know her. But we never made it that far." Her self-loathing burns in her guts. Not only was she too much of a coward to introduce herself properly when she had the chance, but she ended up blackmailing her half sister and possibly set in motion the chain of events that got her killed.

"I think Phoebe would have really loved to know she had a sister," Wyatt says quietly.

"Well, thanks for making me feel like shit. Can we get back to work now?" She turns and walks back inside.

"I'm sorry. I didn't mean to be insensitive. If you want to talk about it, though . . ."

"I'm good, all right? Now can we drop it?"

"For now, sure."

She glares while her back is still to him. In the kitchen, Nadia takes inventory of Phoebe's household cleaners, which easily rival her health and beauty collection. "You two didn't have a housekeeper, right? I never saw one, but just making sure."

"Not for a while now. Phoebe liked doing it herself. Was a little obsessed with cleaning supplies."

"I can definitely see that." She opts for an old favorite: oxygenated bleach. It's what she used to wash all the farmworkers' clothes, as well as sanitize the room in which her mother died. It seems like morbid marketing for the makers of this stuff to say there's nothing better to wash death out of things, but that's what it does best.

They spend the next two hours washing, rinsing, and repeating on the kitchen's every surface. Without a dead body in the room, she can almost pretend she's scrubbing the slaughterhouse floors, a common enough chore from her childhood, especially before a health department visit. Except, at least there they had hoses and floor drains. Here, they empty more than a dozen buckets of red water into the sink. By the time they declare things clean enough, it's nearly five o'clock, and they're both exhausted, filthy, and stinking of a nauseating cocktail of blood, bleach, and sweat. Wyatt pours himself a drink to take the edge off, but Nadia refuses when he offers. She doesn't have a tolerance for the stuff, and she needs to be especially clearheaded for the next stage of this wild ride.

"What now?" he asks.

She watches him fidget with the bandage on his hand. "I think you know the answer to that."

"I was hoping you'd changed your mind."

"I still think it's a good opportunity to get a read on them."

"Do you really think one of them killed her? It's hard to imagine Vicki would have come over here, or invited us over there, if so."

"That's precisely what guilty people would want us to think."

He stares at her. "What do you know about them that makes you so suspicious? You saw something when you were sitting out there, didn't you?"

"I promise you, when all this work is done tonight, we'll sit down and talk everything out. Right now, we're up against the clock."

"I don't like that you're holding all these cards I can't see. How are we supposed to work together when I don't know everything you know?"

He's going to dig in his heels until he gets something. Nadia decides to relent, at least a little. "Okay, fine. The Napiers have a pretty troubled marriage. I heard screaming matches over there all the time, though I could never really tell what they were fighting about."

"How does their bad marriage lead to Phoebe's being . . . killed?" He's still struggling to acknowledge it. That will likely take time.

"I'm only pointing it out because Ron seems like a really angry guy. My suspicion is if Phoebe managed to get on his bad side, he would have been trouble." And Phoebe was definitely doing something that would have gotten on his bad side, but if Nadia went into what she knew about the younger Napier, Wyatt would likely cease to be useful tonight. She hopes this will be enough to keep him moving for now.

He pours another short drink, knocks it back, and closes his eyes for a moment. "Phoebe seemed to be a magnet for bad marriages. Her dad had a long string of them. We had our share of problems too. And now this. Jesus." He shakes his head and knocks the liquor back. "All right. Let's get cleaned up."

CHAPTER 16

THIRTY MINUTES LATER, they're crossing the street together, with every potential outcome spooling through Nadia's head: cold, cordial, awkward, violent. It might actually end up
being fun, with Vicki breaking out the Parcheesi board. On second
thought, that would make things doubly awkward.

Gazing at the oversize stone cottage façade of the Napier home,
she catches a twitch of the blinds on the expansive front bow window. Nadia can't help but feel both a little alarmed at being watched
and nostalgic for the simpler days when it was her in her car and
Phoebe peeking out at her. Who might the Napier lookout be?
Someone who has something to hide?

Well, whatever happens over there, at least she looks good. Wyatt helped her get ready this time, selecting a pair of black leggings
and an oversized light pink T-shirt for her to wear. ("This is definitely something Phoebe would wear when sick," he said, and then
paused. "Honestly, it's what she wore most of the time these days.")

It took a little while to get the makeup right this time. Subtlety
was key, to make her look like she wasn't wearing anything at all,

while defining the features they had most in common, like the eyes, chin, and cheekbones, and downplaying the ones that more resembled Nadia's mother: nose, lips, the hair, the latter of which Nadia covered with a pink ball cap to hide the visible roots. If she manages to make this work, she might consider going back to her natural brunette at some point. Why wouldn't Phoebe have decided to experiment a little? The upkeep would definitely be easier. Phoebe's skin was also more golden than Nadia's ivory complexion. For now, she can at least use it to her advantage playing sick.

After her third attempt at eyeliner, she fell into a pocket of doubt. She couldn't see Phoebe's face in hers anymore. For several minutes, she sat frozen before the mirror, trembling with a dysphoric certainty that everybody was going to see right through this ruse. Wyatt must have noticed how long she was taking, because he came in to ask how it was going. Nadia stammered, "I ... don't know if I have this. Maybe you were right."

"Hold that thought," he said, and left the room for a second. He returned with a framed photograph of Phoebe in front of the house, holding a sign in her hand reading *SOLD!* Her smile was radiant. She looked fit and trim in a pair of white shorts and a purple sleeveless top, with a golden tan and blond hair past her shoulders. Although Nadia had never really gotten to know her, she could say the woman she saw in the grocery store never smiled like that. Maybe she did when she was with Jake. Nevertheless, the resemblance was remarkable enough to take her breath away.

"I know I said I thought this whole idea was nuts, and I still do, but I think you have it," Wyatt told her, gazing solemnly at Phoebe's picture. "Trust me. Trust yourself." Everything came back into focus after that.

Standing side by side on the Napier porch, they look at each other. He seems okay right now, considering what they're about to do. "What's my name?" she asks.

"Phoebe. Honey. Babe. Sometimes Phoebs. You hate that, though." He grins a little, but his eyes are unreadable.

"That'll do, sweetie." She reaches out and rings the doorbell.

The door opens, but only wide enough for a woman's head, capped with a shaggy brown pixie cut, to peer out. This is the first time Nadia has seen her up close. Her face, with its delicate feminine features, might appear kind under other circumstances, but right now, drained of color, she looks cold and wary. Maybe even afraid. Her pale blue eyes seem to be studying Nadia's features rather intently, which she expected, but did those eyes just dart up to her temple? The same spot where Phoebe had received a nasty blow? Nadia can't be sure. Maybe she's just eyeing the hat Nadia is wearing. Her frayed nerves could also be playing tricks on her.

"Phoebe?" she asks, sounding alarmed. "Are . . . are you all right?"

It's difficult for Nadia to discern Vicki's intent. Is she asking because of Phoebe's alleged illness or because she knows Phoebe is a corpse right now? She tries on a stoic grin. "I am now. You know how stomach bugs are. They come out of nowhere and leave just as fast."

Some of the wariness leaves Vicki's eyes and after a few seconds, she opens the door a little more. "Oh. Oh good. I'm a little bit of a germophobe. Part of being a doctor's wife, I guess." She crosses her arms over her body. Still defensive.

"Which is why we're here, by the way. Wyatt decided to take you up on your offer for Ron to look at the cut on his hand. After I nagged him half the day."

Vicki grins. Reluctantly, but at least it's there. "I'm glad good sense prevailed. Come on in." Once they're inside, she glances up at Nadia's ball cap. "Never figured you as one for hats."

"It's from my 'head in a toilet all day but feeling just well enough to be upright' collection."

This time, she laughs a little. Good. Maybe Vicki really was just worried about catching the stomach flu. She still seems a little stiff as she leads them through the foyer and into the main living area, but since Nadia doesn't know her, she doesn't have a baseline to compare to. Nadia briefly wonders if Vicki is picking up anything different about her "friend's" voice. That detail didn't even occur to her until now. She thinks she can chalk it up to being sick tonight if she has to, but she's going to have to work on that later. Maybe Wyatt has some videos or voicemails to help her.

Throughout her years of breaking and entering, Nadia has encountered a spectrum of style and taste, and the Napier home is definitely more on the spartan end of things. Though the more she sees of it, the less she thinks it's an intentional décor choice. There's minimalism, and then there's just having nothing. Their footfalls echo hollowly off the walls and vaulted ceilings. Some rugs would help with that, as well as furniture, but both are lacking. In the living room, the only seating options are a cheap-looking brown love seat and two folding chairs, like what one would find at a banquet hall. A couple of cheap end tables have been pushed together to make a coffee table in the center of the room, and one more table beside the love seat is holding a plain lamp that looks more like it belongs on a desk. A college student's desk. In fact, the whole ensemble looks like something assembled by a young couple who had just enough money to pay the security deposit and first month's rent but not enough to furnish the place with, so they went scavenging at thrift stores.

A vast expanse of built-in bookshelves flanking the fireplace would offer a great opportunity for more warmth, but they're currently empty, save for a few paperbacks on a bottom shelf. The homiest feature is the huge array of framed photos on the mantel. There are a lot of pictures of Jake throughout the years in that display that show him progressing from cute kid to awkward teen to current heartthrob. Apparently, he enjoys tennis and surfing in addition to older married women.

The family first arrived here when? A month ago, give or take? Nadia had been coming here a few weeks already when they showed up. Seems like a long time to still have that whole "just moved in" look, especially if you're wealthy enough to move to Lake Forest. Maybe they aren't so wealthy after all, which is odd. Of all the Chicago suburbs they could have picked, they went for one of the most exclusive. Either they were ignorant of that, or they picked this area for another reason.

"You're noticing my appalling lack of furnishings," Vicki says, a playful element creeping into her voice. She's loosening up a little more. "You ought to be proud that I at least have a couch in here now."

"It's a nice couch," Nadia lies.

Vicki looks at Wyatt. "Your wife probably hasn't told you, but it's been slow going replacing what we sold before the move. We're making some progress, though."

"Selling everything and buying new on the other side makes the most sense," he comments mildly.

Vicki nods. "Yes, or so I thought at the time. I was trying to be frugal, and I also thought it would be healthy to wipe the slate clean and start from scratch, but it's been harder than I expected. We've had a lot of unforseen expenses. But even under ideal circumstances, how do you replace a whole life overnight, you know?"

"I can only imagine," he says, his voice a bit fainter now.

An awkward pause ensues. The house's silence drapes over them like an unwelcome blanket. Nadia grasps at anything to fill it. She detects the aroma of cooking food. "Something smells good. I hope we're not interrupting dinner."

Vicki shakes her head. "Oh, no, it's just a sauce simmering." She pauses. "Would you like to stay and eat after Ron fixes up Wyatt's paw? I made a bunch."

Nadia and Wyatt pass a quick glance. "I probably shouldn't eat yet," she says. "My stomach is still little unsteady."

Vicki rubs Nadia's shoulder and offers a sympathetic look. "No problem. We'll just add it to our growing stack of rain checks." She lifts her head and yells toward the hallway, "Ron! Your patient is here!"

After a moment, they hear a muffled, "Hang on!"

"He's been locked away in his study all day. Lord knows what he's up to. I'm so over it." She gives Nadia a knowing eye roll, and Nadia returns it in a way she hopes reads, *Men, am I right?*

Vicki takes a step back and looks Nadia up and down, a grin

playing on her face. "How much did you barf, anyway? I swear you've lost ten pounds in the last twenty-four hours."

Nadia cringes inside. She had a feeling the weight difference would be noticed, even with the baggier clothes. There's only one way to play this off, though: catty humor. "Are you trying to call me fat?"

"Well not anymore, skinny bitch," Vicki replies, laughing. Nadia joins in, unsure whether to be relieved at how much easier the banter has become, or more on guard because of it.

Vicki brings them into the living room. "You take the love seat, Wyatt. Ron will be with you shortly. Like most doctors, he likes to run at least thirty minutes behind. Makes him feel more important."

A door down the hall closes a moment later, and Ron walks in holding a big orange American Red Cross bag. Upon seeing Nadia, he gives a start so faint that she might have missed it if she weren't looking right at him. It's hard to get a good read on either of them now. They're either really good at pretending they're not seeing a walking dead woman, or there's nothing for them to hide.

"Nice of you to join us, sweetie," Vicki chirps. "You and Wyatt haven't officially met, have you?"

"No. Seems like you ladies are having all the fun." Nadia has only ever heard Ron's voice from a distance, and at yelling registers, so she's surprised by how deep and serene it sounds, almost like Harrison Ford's. He extends his hand toward Wyatt and then pulls back when he sees the bandage. "Well, I guess we should fix that first."

Nadia watches Ron closely as he takes a seat next to Wyatt. The two men are of similar age and build, and both look like they've been having a rough go of things lately with their bleary eyes and scruffy facial hair, but Ron's weariness looks more ground in somehow. The daily fights with his wife probably aren't helping. Neither is the barren state of this house. The question is whether he's worse now than he was this morning.

"Thanks for doing this," Wyatt says. "I was going to head to the ER, but Vicki suggested I come here." He sounds natural and affable enough, which is a relief. If they both can stay this cool under pressure, they might just survive this weird little playdate.

Nadia clears her throat. "I also insisted."

"It's no trouble," Ron says, sifting through the paper-wrapped parcels from his med bag. He sounds distant, distracted. Nadia senses he's avoiding her gaze. What would the reason for that be?

"Would you actually mind if I used your restroom before we got started?" Wyatt asks. "Phoebe was in such a rush to get me over here."

Vicki grins. "Sure. It's down the hall. Second door on the right."

His eyes flit briefly in Nadia's direction before he heads off. They didn't discuss going on any scouting missions before they left, but she admires his initiative. Hopefully he'll find something interesting to report.

"Phoebe, you want something to drink? I have some ginger ale if your stomach is still bothering you."

"That sounds nice, thank you," she says, more interested in something to help lubricate her dry mouth.

Vicki glides off toward the kitchen. "Would Wyatt like the same, do you think?" she calls over her shoulder along the way.

"Sure. Can I help?"

"No, you just sit tight."

Wyatt is taking longer back there than she likes. She starts to fidget a little, but then notices that Ron is watching her with a chilly, speculative expression that says either he can see through the sham of her disguise, or he has particularly nasty business with Phoebe that precludes any attempt at small talk.

Vicki arrives moments later, a dubious savior bearing glasses of ginger ale on ice, just as Wyatt returns from the bathroom. It's only after she's drained half her drink at a single go that she wonders if it was a good idea to accept anything to eat or drink from these people, given what they may have done. She supposes if the room starts spinning in the next couple minutes, she'll have her answer.

"I have to say, Wyatt, it's great to finally meet you," Vicki says. "You are my bestie's husband, after all." She smiles at Nadia, showing a few too many teeth. A cold, invisible finger tickles the back of Nadia's neck, but she returns the smile and prays Ron is a quick hand with the needle and thread.

"This is a pretty nasty little gash," Ron observes once he gets Wyatt's hand unwrapped. "I was hoping I could glue it shut, but I think it's going to require a few sutures."

Vicki takes a closer peek. "Wow. All that from a piece of broken mug?"

He jerks as Ron pours disinfectant over the wound. "It shattered in my hand when I put it down. My lucky day, I guess."

The doubt she's still nursing about Wyatt's innocence flares alive again like an ember in a fresh breeze, burning her gut. He's lying, and the brief look he gives her confirms this.

"You broke it just putting it down?" Vicki asks, her eyebrow raised in a playful way. "Come on, admit it. You slammed that sucker. Were you two having a little tiff?"

"Damn, Vic. Stop interrogating him," Ron says, swabbing the cut and surrounding skin with Betadine before grabbing a syringe filled with clear fluid that Nadia assumes is lidocaine. "Shit just happens sometimes."

"True," Vicki replies, though she doesn't sound convinced. "Some people just don't know their own strength."

"This is going to burn a little," Ron says, positioning the needle. "But it'll numb up quickly." Wyatt looks away with a grimace.

Nadia says, "It probably had a hairline crack that finally gave way." *You know, like some people,* she wants to add. *Someone here, perhaps.*

Vicki searches her face for a few seconds. "Something is really different about you. Did you, like, do a chemical peel? Your complexion is like porcelain now."

Nadia plays off her nerves with another exaggerated scoff. "First you say I'm fat, and now I'm old? Christ, some friend you are."

She laughs. "I'm just wondering who I should be crediting, that's all. You look like a whole new woman."

Nadia doesn't breathe or so much as twitch a facial muscle. If this were an old Hitchcock movie, there would be alternating close-ups of their faces, with a strings-heavy score building to a taut crescendo. Then Vicki would pull out a gun—or a knife, since it's the weapon du jour—and demand answers. *Who are you? I know you aren't Phoebe, because I last saw her at the end of this blade.*

The front door opens, and a few seconds later, the third and youngest Napier walks in wearing sweaty running gear and earbuds, and sorting through a bundle of mail. "Hey, Jake," Vicki says. "I was just beginning to wonder if you'd show in time for dinner."

When he looks up and sees Nadia in particular, the small stack of envelopes and circulars falls from his fingers, and his eyes go glassy with terror. Lover boy is not quite ready for prime time, it would seem. But something more than his reaction catches Nadia's attention. Red scratches mar his pretty face, as well as his arms and neck, like he ran through a blackberry bramble, or perhaps struggled with a woman fighting for her life. Come tomorrow, he might even be showing a few bruises. All the boxes in Nadia's mind fill with checkmarks. Alarms begin sounding, raining down balloons and confetti. Ladies and gentlemen, I believe we have our killer!

Vicki quickly gets up to collect the dropped mail. "Jesus, Jake, don't be rude. It's just the neighbors. What's your deal?"

Jake pulls out his earbuds and clears his throat. "Hey, everyone. Sorry. I didn't think anyone was here. Just startled me is all." He shuffles from foot to foot for a few seconds, like a kid who has to use the restroom. "I'm going to hit the shower."

"By all means, boy. Go clean up." Vicki watches him dash off up the hall and shakes her head at Nadia. "I really don't know about that kid anymore."

"He's fine," Ron mutters, bent over his suturing work.

She looks at Phoebe. "He's hiding something. I can feel it. I asked him if he's started packing up for orientation. First semester is right around the corner. He just grunts and shrugs. This kid, who literally couldn't talk about anything but Stanford this spring, is like . . ." She makes a "poof" gesture. "Gone."

"Vic," Ron grumbles. His tone is likely a preamble to most of their fights, and Nadia feels the hairs on her arms stir.

"Excuse me, but I am allowed to express my concern for my son with *my* friend." Vicki's emphasis on "my" increases with each utterance. "Between you and Jake, it's like I can't have anything to myself. Peace of mind, a bag of kitchen supplies, hope for a goddamn normal life."

She's glaring at her husband now and gritting her teeth. It feels almost like a silent dare. Nadia is reminded so much of how her mother would goad Jim that she can almost feel herself shrinking back into a much younger form, watching helplessly as two adults who should have known better spun each other up into a mutual rage, and then by the end of it demanded that she pick a side.

Ron's face goes the color of a beet, but he miraculously keeps a lid on it for now. In the silence, Nadia thinks of those old nuclear bomb test reels, and how eerily placid everything looked right before the light flashed and the mushroom cloud appeared. Vicki takes a deep breath, holds it in, and turns back to her. "Sorry. It's been a day." She laughs wildly. "Or maybe more like a month. Or a year. Who am I kidding? My whole fucking life."

"It's going to be okay," Nadia reassures her, wondering if that's what Phoebe would have done. Vicki doesn't look like she believes her much either way.

"I'm done," Ron says, and for a moment Nadia thinks he's referring to his ability to hold on to his temper. But she understands he means his little surgery when he snips the suturing material and begins wrapping Wyatt's hand. He's clearly rattled and keeps dropping the gauze roll, but once he's cut it and secured it with tape, he wipes his brow and declares, "Good as new."

Wyatt lets out a sigh that Nadia reads as clear relief, because now they can leave. "I really appreciate it," he says.

"Just keep it dry. Change the dressings every couple days. In two weeks, I'll remove them for you. Need anything for pain? I can give you a few Vicodin."

Wyatt shakes his head. "That's not necessary. Thank you, though."

"If you change your mind, just ask."

For a moment no one says anything, like they're waiting for another shoe to drop. Then Nadia stands. "Well, we shouldn't keep you from dinner."

"Ah yes, a woman's work must continue," Vicki says glumly.

"Nice meeting you, Wyatt," Ron says, and then turns away to start cleaning up. He doesn't even acknowledge Nadia.

Vicki walks them to the door. She looks at Wyatt. "Hey, big guy, can I borrow your wife for a sec? Important girl stuff to discuss."

Wyatt and Nadia exchange a quick glance and he nods. "Of course. I'll be on the porch, babe."

Once he's gone, Vicki turns to her. "Aren't you two nice and cozy now."

Nadia's chest feels tight. This is what it's like to flail in the deep end without a life preserver. "We're working through things."

"That's great. Really great. Good for you both."

Nadia touches the doorknob, and Vicki places her hand on her shoulder.

"I was really upset with you this morning for ditching me." She sounds a little shrill and wobbly, like she had to force herself to admit this. That makes at least a couple people who were upset with Phoebe this morning, and Nadia knows she has to tread carefully.

"My stomach was pretty upset too, believe me." She smiles, but Vicki isn't smiling back. This time the snarky-bitch angle isn't going to cut it.

"Ron says I always expect too much out of other people. I'm starting to think maybe there's something to that." Her eyes well up with tears, and she swipes them away almost violently.

Even under the best of circumstances, Nadia has always sucked at finding the right things to say to people in distress. Right now, she feels like her tongue is stapled to the roof of her mouth, and it takes physical effort to pry it loose. "I really am sorry."

"Don't apologize," she snaps. "I really hate the sound of those words right now. They make me feel like shit."

Nadia recoils at the force of her words. It's impossible to read Vicki's face in the deepening shadows, but she senses a nakedness in her eyes that wasn't there a moment ago. It's something bordering on hate. Or is Nadia reading into things?

"Go home to your husband, Phoebe."

Nadia exits the house and flinches as the screen door slams shut behind her.

■ ■ ■

I'LL NEVER FORGET the moment you died. Or when you came back.

As you were struggling to take your last breaths, I told you it would be okay. I think you must have heard me, because a second later, you stopped fighting and let go. It went so fast. Only a few seconds from the moment the knife went in. I think you knew at the very end that you were free, like all of us want to be, and your face became so peaceful. I think I helped you.

No one else would understand that. They'd say I murdered you and that I deserve to pay for it. But I think I must be paying already, because here you are, alive again, and I don't know how to handle it. I know she isn't *really* you, but my feelings can't tell the difference, and my eyes barely do, either. She even sounds like you. Hearing her talk made me want to crawl out of my skin.

How does anyone move on from something like this? Death is hard enough, but it's even harder when the dead don't stay dead.

CHAPTER 17

TEN MINUTES LATER, they're both sitting in the living room and still panting from the adrenaline rush of it all. For the first time, she wants some of what Wyatt is sipping from his glass, but she guzzles down water, instead.

"I can't believe that worked," Wyatt says.

"Are we sure it actually did? It felt to me like we were all putting on a performance." She tells him about the short conversation she had with Vicki at the door.

He thinks about it. "Do you think it means anything?"

"Hell if I know. My nerves are shot right now."

"Same. There were moments over there where I felt completely unmoored from reality."

"I see more of that in our future. So what did you find on your little recon mission?"

He frowns. "What recon mission?"

"Duh, when you conveniently said you had to use the bathroom. Did anything jump out to you?"

"Oh. I really did have to go to the bathroom."

She can't hide her disappointment, but they can't all be snoops like her, she supposes.

"The bathroom is as bare as the rest of the house, if that helps." He throws back another gulp of whiskey. "Who do you think looks the guiltiest?"

"Let's both name someone after the count of three."

Wyatt nods.

"Okay," she says. "One . . . two . . . three . . . Jake."

"Ron."

Nadia raises her eyebrows. "Ron? Really? Why him?"

"I've seen a lot of guys like him in my practice over the years. High-pressure jobs, unhappy marriages. They're bombs waiting to go off. Ron seems like he's on the . . . severe side."

She nods in agreement. "Yes."

"He sees his wife getting a little too chummy with the woman next door, and we already saw how he doesn't like Vicki airing their dirty laundry. Who knows what she and Phoebe have talked about. Ron decides he's had enough of Phoebe's interference. Comes over, maybe flies into a blind rage." His face reddens with anger of his own, but he lets it go in a long breath. "We know the rest."

She can't deny the theory is solid. After all, Ron was her number one guy too, and his likely knowledge of something going on between Phoebe and Jake provides another motive that she isn't sure Wyatt needs to know about right now. Ron also went out of his way to avoid interacting with her the whole time, like her mere presence was a strong irritant. That could have been due to basic dislike, though, rather than his aversion to seeing a dead woman resurrected. "I think you could be on to something, but after seeing Jake . . ."

Wyatt sighs. "Yeah. That reaction, the marks on his face. I admit, it doesn't look good for him, either."

"I sense a 'but' coming."

"But I can't quite see the motive. I suppose he could be a Ted Bundy in practice, but he didn't ping my psychopath radar."

She's been dreading this part, but it's too important to keep to herself. Same with the blackmail note, but she hopes to hold off on telling him about that one a bit longer, if not forever. Her initial worry that he might already know about the note has dissipated. Given their mutual level of distrust, Wyatt certainly would have brought it up by now as a reason to doubt her character, and if he found out about it now, and the event that drove her to write it in the first place, he might never trust her at all. Phoebe likely kept it to herself, like the rest of her secrets, it appears. "So . . . here's the thing that makes Jake a bit more suspect. I was waiting to see if you already knew, but I guess you don't."

Wyatt's frowning. "Knew what?"

"I'm nearly a hundred percent certain that Jake and Phoebe . . . were up to something. Together."

His face goes slack and he blinks. "I'm sorry, what?"

"Well, he was over here a lot. Mowing the grass, doing odd jobs around the place."

He gives an irritated shrug. "Just because she hired him to do chores doesn't mean anything else was going on."

"No, but he was around . . . a lot." She speaks gently, hoping not to upset him more since he's already on the defensive. But now he looks like he just took a bite out of a lemon.

"Look, our marriage was far from ideal, but even if Phoebe was having an affair, I doubt it would have been with a goddamn kid, okay?"

Okay, so we're firmly at denial, Nadia thinks. She supposes she can't blame him, but he can't remain there anymore, not if he really wants to get to the bottom of what happened here. "I also watched him storm out of your house a few days ago while Phoebe stood in the doorway. It looked like they'd had a bit of a, you know, lovers' quarrel." Wyatt opens his mouth to reply, but she holds up her hand to stop him. "She was basically naked."

He closes his eyes and props his forehead against his balled fists. Seconds pass, and he doesn't say anything, but the slump in his shoulders seems to hint at acceptance. "Did you see anything else?"

Isn't that enough? she nearly asks, but it would only sound cruel. "No. And look, I don't think we should count out Ron, either. For all we know, he might have seen the same thing I did that day, and that would give him plenty of motive. We just can't overlook Jake, because of the possible jilted, um, lover angle. He's also the only one who reacted strongly to seeing me tonight."

"Not true. Vicki didn't exactly roll out the welcome mat when she answered the door, either," Wyatt reminds her. "She looked like she'd had the fright of her life. I saw the way she studied you. And you said anyone who looked like they'd seen Phoebe's ghost was probably the killer."

Nadia can't argue with that. "I can't blame her for noticing the differences, though. She was Phoebe's closest friend. And she did seem to warm up a little." At least until the very end, when she was nearly out the door.

"Yes, she loosened up some once she realized you weren't going to give her the plague. If you buy the mysophobia excuse, anyway."

She stares at him. "What's that?"

"Sorry. I got clinical for a second. Fear of germs."

"Ah, yeah, that. I don't know if that was real or not, but it's easier to believe she was afraid to let a sick person in the house than it is to believe Jake got those scratches from anything other than finger-nails. Phoebe fought her attacker."

Wyatt sighs. His hands make a rasping sound against his stub-bly cheeks as he rubs them. "I don't think that trip over there got us closer to the truth, did it? We have three people who might have done it but nothing more concrete than that they're acting a little weird, and nothing pointing to why. Unless you can think of any-thing else."

Nadia hesitates for a moment and then tells him about the packed bag she'd discovered in Phoebe's closet. "It's possible she was about to leave town. Could factor in somehow." *Oh, it most cer-tainly does factor in. Do you think the shut-in housewife you'd been spy-ing on for weeks suddenly made travel plans before she received your note? Not impossible, but it seems unlikely. She was probably going to run away because you threatened to spill her secret. The mystery is who else found out, and what did they do about it?*

After a contemplative silence, he says, "This is unbelievable."

"I've told you the truth about everything I know."

"It's not that. It's just that if you'd asked me a day ago what I thought the odds were of Phoebe leaving this house for more than groceries, I would have said a million to one. Now I feel like I barely knew this woman at all."

"We all have blind spots."

He shakes his head. "Feels a lot bigger than a spot. I've just been blind, period. She told me as much this morning. Of course I argued with her about it. But she was right." He sighs. "I want to have a look at that bag."

Nadia looks out the window to find the sun going down on this very long, weird day. Too bad it's only about to get weirder. "There will be time for that later. Right now, we have something more important to take care of."

Wyatt runs his hand back through his hair. "I guess you're right."

"I'll give you the address for your GPS, but just do your best to stay behind me. And it's probably also a good idea for you to drive my car."

"Why?" He looks immediately suspicious.

Because they aren't looking for a middle-aged white guy in a blue Ford Focus, she thinks. "It just seems easier this way. For you."

He closes his eyes and sighs. "It's not going to be easy, regardless."

"Listen, the hardest part will be the trip down. Once we're there, the rest is just coasting downhill." She knows she's oversimplifying it. The actual disposal part won't be any picnic, either, but that's no way to give a pep talk.

"All right. Fine. I just want this day to end."

"That makes two of us. Now, let's get going. We can talk on the phone on the way down. Maybe it'll make everything feel a little less . . ."

"Terrifying?" he asks.

"I'll go with that."

———

ONCE THEY'RE ABOUT twenty miles out of the city, traffic opens up and her dual worries about having a body in the trunk and the cops' taking notice of her car fade to background noise. All they need to do is keep the cruise control set to the speed limit and drive between the lines, and they'll get there without incident. When the last vestiges of pink fade from the western sky, her phone rings through the car's Bluetooth system, which displays Wyatt's name.

She answers. "How are you doing?"

"Wishing I was anywhere but here," he says.

"Same."

"I'm not sure I can do this whole drive with only my thoughts for company. Do you mind if we just sit on the phone?"

"Sure." She's glad of the distraction, something to keep her guilt about her half sister at bay. There's a long silence, so long Nadia almost thinks they've been cut off.

"No offense, but your car is crap."

She grins. "Careful. That's my house you're talking about."

"Wait. You *lived* in here?"

"Cheaper than a studio apartment. Fewer roaches. No roommates."

"Good point. I've lived among roaches a few times. I wouldn't recommend it."

They don't speak for a few minutes and she wonders if he's going to hang up. "So this place we're going, you're from there originally?"

"Yes. Monticello, Indiana, born and raised. Though I was conceived in Chicago, so part of me feels like I'm really from there."

"So . . . how did your mother end up in the path of Daniel Noble, anyway?"

"She emigrated from Serbia back in the nineties, during the war over there. Got a job with some catering company that happened to do work for a lot of his functions. They met at one of those."

"Ah. Daniel always did have a soft spot for the help. Phoebe had a lot of nannies in addition to stepmothers after her mom passed."

"Yeah, well you can imagine how much interest he had in my mother after he got her pregnant. He wanted her to get an abortion, but she was way too religious for that. When one of his people took her to the clinic, she snuck out the back and hooked up with some other immigrant friends of hers, who put her in touch with a widowed farmer in Indiana who was looking for a little help around the house. That's where I was born. Eventually she married that farmer, probably out of some sort of sense of obligation. Jim's his name. I never got the feeling that she loved him all that much, but she took pretty good care of him until she died of liver failure a few months ago. One of the last things she told me was who my real father was."

"That had to have been a shock."

She snorts. "Honestly, I thought she was delirious. Then, not even a month later, Daniel died. And all of a sudden, his name was everywhere. It felt almost like my mother sending messages from beyond the grave, if I believed in that kind of thing. So I started paying attention. I'd heard the name Daniel Noble, knew he was some famous rich guy, but had no reason to care before. Didn't even know what he looked like until I started clicking on the various headlines."

"Bet you noticed a resemblance," Wyatt says.

"Definitely. The Noble genes are strong, it seems. It didn't exactly make me feel good at the time, mind you. Still doesn't. Maybe it's not as bad as finding out you're Charlie Manson's kid, but you know, same ballpark."

He laughs a little. "I think Phoebe would have agreed with that."

"It was actually when I looked her up that I decided it might be worth it to pursue this whole thing. I noticed right off the bat how much we looked alike. And given everything going on in the news about Daniel, I thought, *Hey, maybe she could use a friend*. It sure sounded good to me. I never had many of those."

Listen to how altruistic she sounds. She supposes it's easier than admitting to the not insignificant spark of jealousy that also fueled her journey to Lake Forest. Two sisters, one with everything, including the family name, the other one a bastard, kept in the dark her whole life, destitute. Nadia felt long overdue for a taste of her birthright. It's what made writing that blackmail note so easy at the time. It felt good to rattle a privileged rich girl's gilded cage.

"You'll have to forgive yourself eventually, you know," he said quietly. "For being afraid to reach out to her when you got here. It wasn't your fault. It was Daniel's."

"So, am I going to get billed for this therapy session?"

"Nah. This one's on the house."

More miles pass in silence. Then he asks the question she's been waiting for all night. "What exactly is the plan when we get where we're going?"

She already knows he isn't going to like it. No decent person would. But it's still their best choice. "There's a pit for dead livestock on the outer edge of the property. It's deep and the animals are covered with lime and dirt as they're piled in. Once the pit gets full, it's capped off with more dirt and sown with grass seed."

"You want to bury her in a mass grave with farm animals?" He sounds almost numb now, like someone who's resigned to the never-ending series of punches that just keep coming.

"It isn't about what I want to do. It's about no one ever finding her. If she ever turned up, we would be done for. That means no water, where she might eventually wash up on shore. And no shallow grave out in the woods, where she'd be dug up by animals."

"Couldn't someone dig up the pit at some point?"

It is possible the county could force Jim to move a burial pit if they didn't like where he placed it, especially if it was too close to a water source. But despite Jim's always complaining about government regulations, he seemed to do a good enough job staying in line. His livelihood was too important to him. The only possibility of discovery might lie several decades, or maybe even a century, from now, if Jim's land is ever sold off and subdivided. Developers digging deep into the earth may find some human bones mixed in with all the livestock, but by then, anyone who could be directly affected by such a discovery would be long gone. "It's highly unlikely," she says.

"Are we ready to bet our lives on it?"

"I am, yes." She speaks with conviction, but he sighs like he isn't quite sold. "I can run through some other options at the farm, if you like."

"Jesus, how is this happening? Sure, might as well lay them all out."

"Not all the dead livestock gets buried. They compost some of the pigs in big piles, but it's a slow process and the workers turn them every few weeks, which means someone will find her there."

"I see." He sounds like he's going to be sick, but he also doesn't tell her to stop.

"There is also a manure lake, but with the drought this summer, there probably isn't enough rainwater to submerge her, and we would have to keep her weighted, which gives us the same risk of failure as any other water burial. The final option would be to, um . . . feed her to the—"

"Don't even say it!"

"I ruled that one out for obvious reasons."

"Yep. Burial it is."

About an hour later, they pass a sign informing them they have ten miles to go until they reach Monticello, but Jim lives on the farthest outskirts, so familiar sights are already starting to pop up. The park with her favorite swing set. The crooked old house everyone swore was haunted. The Stop & Go, where she used to ride her bike to buy junk food and other wastes of her meager allowance. Sometimes she would get her mom the latest issue of the *National Enquirer* or the *Weekly World News*. Mom had loved tabloids, the more ridiculous the better. Jim used to roll his eyes and sip his Wild Irish Rose as she shared articles about the latest in strange creature or alien sightings, pointing to the badly edited photos as irrefutable proof.

They pass the sign welcoming them to Monticello, and Nadia breaks into a cold sweat, like a force field will soon drop down around her, preventing her from leaving again. *You got out once. Did you really think you could do it again? Foolish girl.*

"So this is Monticello," Wyatt says.

"Home to about five thousand lost souls."

"Doesn't look so bad."

"It isn't, I guess." There are far worse places for a kid to grow up. Fishing and camping at two nearby lakes. Roller-coaster rides at Indiana Beach. Plenty of open spaces and secret places to get lost or make trouble. But she wasn't able to enjoy it as much as other kids her age did. Responsibilities on the farm took up most of her time, and when she was finally old enough to have relinquished some of those, she was off into other things. Breaking and entering, for instance.

She sees the sign for Callahan Farms ahead. *Fresh Meats All Year!*

"It's coming up in a bit. Let's go ahead and pull off." Per their plan, Wyatt drives Nadia's car as far off the road as possible. The feeling is bittersweet. It had been her one major possession, purchased from a private seller with nearly all the savings she'd amassed over the years from money Jim had paid her for her farm work—a pittance compared to what the regular employees there made, but better than nothing. Now it's just an empty shell. Before leaving, she'd removed all the important items from it: her collection of stolen trinkets, her laptop, the few clothing items she didn't want to give up, like her leather jacket (pleather, actually, but nice pleather) and her Converse sneakers, both lucky thrift-store finds. All of it is in a duffel bag on the seat behind her.

"Is this on private property?" he asks.

"Probably. Aim for that stand of trees to your right. Cover it with any loose brush you might find."

"Okay. Hanging up now so I can do this. See you in a few."

Nadia can't see the car anymore from her vantage point. Hopefully that means the car won't be noticed for a long time. She also doubly hopes a cop won't pass by now. Assuming everything goes smoothly, it could be months before anyone finds the vehicle, and Nadia will be in full ghost mode by then. And in the unlikely event the Chicago police ever get hold of it, they won't find much in terms of new information. Even the address on the registration is from a UPS Store mailbox that she abandoned months ago. It's a two-ton dead end.

A few minutes later, he emerges from the trees and climbs into the passenger seat. "I found plenty of fallen branches to cover it with. Wiped it down really well inside."

"Thank you."

"You are going to tell me why this was so important, correct?"

"I am. But for right now, you need to brace yourself a bit. Things are going to get pretty bumpy."

"Metaphorically or physically?"

"Probably both."

She drives a mile or so past the farm entrance until she finds the narrow service road that she sometimes used for make-out sessions with local boys during her briefly tumultuous teenage years. It was always nicely secluded, but also close enough to the house that she could send them on their way and then walk back home with no one suspecting a thing.

Once she turns onto the packed-dirt lane, she switches off the headlights, confident enough in the terrain without their aid. In the distance to her right, she sees the farmhouse lights and shudders. Jim could still be awake now. Nadia wonders if he's alone or if he's already found himself a replacement, one who will give him a bit less grief over his drinking and other bad habits. For whatever reason, no matter how old they get, men like Jim always seem to have women willing to hitch their wagons to them. She once asked her mother why she never left Jim when he treated her the way he did. "Sure, I could leave him," her mother said. "Start over in a new place, find another man. But it will always be the same." Nadia asked her how that could be possible. The woman rolled her eyes and shook her head, like she always did when she thought her daughter was being intentionally dense. "Because I will always be the same."

She wonders what Vera would think of all this. *I'm not going to be the same after tonight, Ma.*

The shovels rattle in the back as she drives along the dips in the road, rocks pinging the undercarriage, branches from the trees to her right slapping against the windshield. She glances over and sees Wyatt gripping the handle above the window, his face a drawn mask in the green dash lights.

"How can you even see?" he asks.

"I've used this road a lot. Besides, it's better to drive in the dark than for him to look out his bedroom window and spot headlights where they shouldn't be."

"What would happen if he did?"

"You know many rural fellas who take kindly to trespassers?"

"But he was your stepdad, right? I doubt he'd shoot you."

"I'd rather not bet my life on that. He only tolerated me because he loved my mother. I doubt I've crossed his mind at all since I left."

Wyatt says nothing more. The burial pits are at the top of a short rise, and she brings the car to a stop just shy of the crest. "Let's be quick about this," she says, and gets out. Immediately, she stifles a gag. Though Jim uses plenty of lime to speed the decaying process, the smell is still world-endingly bad out here, especially from this vantage point. Nadia remembers how it would sometimes catch on the wind just the right way and blow into the house like a putrid ghost. But there is no breeze tonight, and it makes the stench feel thick enough to coat her skin. She brings her hand up in a futile gesture to shield her nose and mouth. Wyatt gags too, and it has a bit more oomph than hers. Respirator masks would have been a good idea, but it's too late for that now. "If you need to throw up, do it in the tall grass over there." She points to a patch about ten feet away.

He nods and stumbles off in that direction. A few seconds later, she hears him quietly retching and decides to start scouting around while he's busy.

She grabs the flashlight from the passenger floorboard, hooding it with the bottom part of her T-shirt to cut the glare, and scans the surroundings. The trench can't be too far; the smell is too thick. But she hasn't been out to this patch of land in a couple years, well before she left here, and a little bit of low-lying fog has crept into the landscape, swallowing her feet and limiting her visibility even more. After about twenty paces, she starts to feel disoriented. It's too dark, and the gravity of their errand weighs heavier than ever.

She calls out to Wyatt in a grated whisper. Seems like it's been a minute since she last heard him. The only response is the distant chatter of frogs and crickets.

She turns around, peering as best she can into the distance. "Wyatt, you okay?"

Still nothing. Goddamn it, where is he? A voice in her head, cool and wispy like the fog swirling around her ankles, speaks up: *He's got you now. Killed the wife and then played you just long enough so you'd bring him to a place where he can easily dispose of you both. Well done, Nadia. But hey, you'll get to spend plenty of time with your long-lost sister now.*

No. She refuses to believe that, even if it makes a sick sort of sense. It's just her fear talking, making her think the worst. "Wyatt!" Louder this time. Too loud, but she doesn't care now with panic beating down her door, demanding entrance.

On her next step, her foot comes down on empty air. She lets out a terrified yelp before plunging down a short hill, skidding to a stop on her belly within kissing distance of a hump of rotting carcass. The soil is wet with what can only be liquefying remains.

Horror finally overwhelms her, making her lose the ragged remainder of her calm as well as her stomach, but she vomits in lieu of screaming. Afterward, racked with shudders and exhausted nearly to the point of passing out, she isn't sure what to do next, or if she can even stand. This is it. This is where they'll find her. *Where Wyatt will find you,* that wicked voice corrects. *And finish you off. He'll bury you where you sit, in this stinking sludge.*

"Oh, shit, are you okay? What happened?" She looks up to see

Wyatt's pale face highlighted by his own flashlight. His genuine expression of concern silences the voice in her head.

"So . . . I think I found the trench," she says. For a moment, they say nothing, and then they begin laughing. It's equal parts humor and terror, a painful partial exorcism of this singularly mad day. It also gives her the ability to find her feet, though she's still more than a little wobbly. He reaches down to help her up, and she hesitates for a moment, checking her wracked gut before dismissing her earlier thoughts as the emissions of an overworked mind. She takes his hands and lets him hoist her back up to level ground again.

Once she's sure her knees will hold, her momentary gratitude morphs into anger and she yanks her hands out of his. "Where the hell did you go?" she demands. "I was calling out for you. Didn't you hear me?"

"I grayed out a little after I puked back there." He drops his eyes. "I'm really sorry."

She sighs. The morbid weight of all this is still nearly unbearable, but her irritation dissipates. "It's fine. Are you ready to get this over with?"

"God, yes."

"I'll need help moving her down into the hole. I can do the shoveling part if you want, though. I'm used to the smell now that I'm covered in it."

Wyatt shakes his head. "We both need to do this, I think."

Together, they open the trunk and lift out Phoebe's wrapped body, which feels even heavier than before. Now that Nadia's eyes have adjusted to the darkness, she has a better sense of the slope and where to place the body.

The soil is wet and sandy, which makes for easy digging. After thirty minutes of quiet but frenzied work, they scoop out a hole that's about six feet long, three feet wide, and three feet deep. They look at each other, faces streaked with dirt and sweat, the whites of their eyes bright with the horror of their deed. "This is good enough," she says.

A few minutes later, it's finished. Nadia can see no evidence of either a canvas or newly disturbed ground. She looks at Wyatt. "Is there anything you want to, you know, say?"

He's silent for a moment, and then shakes his head. "She knows."

On their way back out of the pit, Nadia uses her shovel to erase their footprints.

CHAPTER 18

SHE STIRS AWAKE with a sore body and a groggy, unrested mind. The combination of yesterday's events and the spatial disorientation of being in a real bed made it impossible to keep her eyes closed for more than a few seconds at a stretch. By the time sleep finally found her and stole her away for a little while, daylight was beginning to kiss the horizon. The sun now pouring through the blinds has the quality of early afternoon, which she confirms after glancing at her phone. One thirty. She smells food. Is Wyatt cooking down there? Before investigating further, she gets up and heads for the bathroom.

Although she showered immediately after returning here last night, she can't resist doing it again. With all the jets in the walls, and the enormous showerhead hanging above, she feels like she's standing in a misty Amazonian hideaway. She covers herself in more of Phoebe's exotic soaps and shampoos, making up for dozens of speedy washups in homeless shelters and YMCAs, where time, comfort, and hot water are always limited. Now she has as much as she can stand. And not just for one or two days. This is *hers*.

Every time she has that realization, her mind lights up like a winning Vegas slot machine, but the feeling doesn't last more than a few seconds. Despite all the work she and Wyatt put in last night, it's all still under threat with Phoebe's killer out there. However, there's one question neither of them has quite grappled with yet. If they do figure out who did it, what will they do next? Is she prepared to face another deadly fight for her life? Will Wyatt be able to do the same? And that leads to her remaining doubts about him as the killer, and an echo of her brief but terrifying thought that when he disappeared on her at the farm last night, he'd been planning to jump her. That he didn't do so could signal either innocence or incompetence, even though her instinct still leans more toward the former.

Even so, until she learns anything more definitive, she'll stay the current course while making sure to keep both eyes open. He could be having the very same conversation with himself.

She shuts off the water and quickly dries off before throwing on a black tank and a pair of yoga pants. Today, she'll need to make arrangements to touch up the roots of her hair. They're increasingly peeking through, and it's more important than ever that, at least for now, she passes as a natural blonde. In the kitchen, she finds Wyatt standing at the stove, his back to her. A large stack of pancakes looms on a plate next to a skillet where he's cooking what smells like bacon. Jazz spills at a low volume from a small Bluetooth speaker perched on the nearest countertop, and he's whistling along a little.

"Uh . . . hey," she says, unsure of what to make of the sight before her.

He looks over his shoulder. "I hope you aren't gluten-free. I made roughly a thousand pancakes." He sounds almost chipper.

"I see," she says cautiously. This behavior is incongruous to say the least, given what happened in this room yesterday. She thought it would be weeks before eating seemed normal to either of them, let alone cooking and eating in here.

"I've already set out plates on the breakfast bar. Coffee?"

That she can at least do. "Sure." She takes a seat and watches him maneuver gracefully in his sweatpants and White Sox T-shirt to fill her mug from the French press.

"Cream and sugar?"

"I drink it black," she says.

He looks impressed. "Same. That'll simplify the shopping list. Phoebe always liked a little coffee with her cream and turbinado."

She stares at him while waiting for her coffee to cool. "Hey, are you all right?"

He brings the plates holding pancakes and bacon over to the bar and then goes to the microwave to retrieve a small carafe of maple syrup. "I'm fine," he says, though he doesn't make eye contact. "Now dig in. I know you have to be starving."

Quite the opposite, in fact, though the smells are beginning to tug at her a bit, and she'll probably force herself to nibble something before too long. She watches him drown his pancakes in butter and syrup. "Why are you acting this way?"

"What way?"

"Like nothing happened."

He sighs and puts his fork back down. "I know very well I'm standing in the middle of a murder scene. If it wasn't for my friend Klonopin last night and my other friend Xanax this morning, along with a tiny dose of Irish in my coffee, I would still be holed up in the fetal position in my room right now. Cooking breakfast makes me feel normal for a minute."

She sees the glassy, bloodshot state of his eyes and bows her head, properly chagrined. "I'm sorry. I hadn't considered that you might actually be, like, stoned."

"Therapist, medicate thyself. I think that's how it goes." He takes a bite and chases it with a sip of his doctored coffee. "But I wouldn't recommend trying this particular combination at home. I am a trained professional."

"You don't have to push yourself so hard. It's only been a day."

"On the contrary, I do have to push myself. I can feel the terror in me just waiting to grab hold and paralyze me forever. So this is me trying to stuff it into a box, so I can keep moving. The hope is eventually, with the help of a few chemical training wheels, that part of me will suffocate and die."

"Compartmentalization. I get it. Must be something you use a lot in your work."

"Necessary part of the job, I'm afraid." He picks up his fork again, and she follows his lead. Nadia didn't think she would have a taste for pork after last night, but the body wants what it wants. When they're finished, he clears their plates while she refills their mugs. They take their coffee into the living room.

"You're not a bad cook," she says.

"You have officially eaten one of three meals I can make without embarrassing myself."

"Oh yeah? What are the other two?"

"Nachos and boxed mac and cheese."

"You have the blue box in this house?"

"I might have one stashed somewhere. Phoebe was no stranger to junk, but she liked expensive junk. The ten-dollar pints of ice cream, the organic chips and frozen pizzas. But she also never had a ten-dollar weekly grocery budget, so our palates differed."

"You were poor once?"

He shrugs. "My folks had high times and low times, like most people in the middle."

"Good to see you've stuck to your roots." She laughs a little as she slowly falls into the easy rhythm of their banter. It's been a long time since she's talked to anyone about nothing, and after recent events, she didn't think moments like this would ever exist again.

"I'm only mediocre at golf no matter how hard I try, and I've never been sailing. Probably why I don't have many friends around here."

"That White Sox shirt probably doesn't help."

"You got me there."

They sit together in an easy silence, sipping coffee. Then he leans forward and rubs his face. "Look . . . now that we're up to our necks in this, it's time for you to be up-front with me about something."

She has a good guess what this might be about, and braces herself. "What's that?"

The humor winks out of his eyes, and he's all business now, save for a little bit of the medicated glaze. "I know the police are looking for you over the recent stabbing at the grocery store."

There it is. "I don't know what you're talking about."

He frowns. "Are you really being coy right now? This is serious, Nadia. Your picture has been in the news. I already had a feeling I'd seen you somewhere before. Something jiggled loose last night, I think when I saw an Earthbound Foods shopping bag in your car, but I couldn't be sure until I did some Googling this morning. And there you were. A person of interest in a murder investigation. Really fucking nice of you to tell me this in the beginning when I asked if you were in any kind of trouble."

"Do I get to explain any of this?"

"Explain why you lied to me? Go ahead. Though it makes a lot more sense why you came up with this idea of yours yesterday. Only a fugitive would be so willing to swap her own identity with someone else's. I feel stupid for not figuring it out right away, or I would have told you to take a hike."

"Listen, you're getting way too worked up over this. There is no Nadia now. There is only Phoebe. They're tracking a ghost."

"You're making a lot of dangerous assumptions right now, like that they won't ever trace you back to this street, or that this disguise of yours will even hold, or that they won't find your car. When that happens, we'll both get taken down. I was better off taking my chances calling the police yesterday when I got home . . . when I found her."

She shakes her head. "Everything would be a lot worse for us both right now if you'd done that. We've covered ourselves well. We just have to keep each other's backs and trust that this is going to work."

Another thought seems to hit him, and he sits up board straight. "What if they'd spotted your car last night and pulled me over? Were you prepared to just let me go down?"

His voice is rising. Soon his anger will override the power of the calming drugs in his system. "Listen, I'm sorry. It was bad of me not to tell you what you were getting yourself into, but it would have been far riskier for me to be spotted driving that car."

"You're goddamn right it was bad of you. Trust is hard enough to come by right now, wouldn't you say?"

"Yes. But I was worried that if I told you what I was dealing with too soon, you would refuse outright to participate."

He shakes his head. "And now neither of us has a choice but to deal with your baggage when it comes back to haunt us."

"*If* it does. And it won't."

"Forgive me if I'm not so quick to believe that, or anything else you've told me so far."

The silence that falls between them now isn't so easy this time. The guarded wall is going back up. "I know what you're thinking. If I stabbed one guy, then it wouldn't have been too hard for me to stab Phoebe."

He looks at her for a moment and then looks away again. "Something like that."

"He was attacking me. I did what I had to do to get free."

"And yet you ran."

"Do I really need to explain to you why that seemed like the best option at the time?"

"I guess not," he says grudgingly.

"Then I have to ask. Do you really believe in your gut that I killed Phoebe? Especially after what we saw across the street and discussed yesterday?"

More ponderous silence as he appears to consider her question seriously. "No," he murmurs. "In spite of all this, I . . . I don't think you did it."

"Good. And if it makes you feel better, I'm feeling pretty sure you didn't do it, either."

"God," he croaks before covering his agonized face.

Nadia frowns at the gesture, feeling a sudden hard weight in her gut. "Or . . . did you?" She can only get the words out in a shaky whisper. What would she do if he did confess right now? What might he do to her?

"No. But I still feel like I had a hand in it. That fight we had . . . I think I understood how people could be pushed into dark places, and she had me there, and I was on the ropes." He looks at his bandaged hand. "I squeezed a goddamn coffee mug until it shattered, and I'm not even a particularly strong guy."

"That's when you cut yourself," Nadia says.

Wyatt shakes his head. "Actually, not quite. When it broke, there was one perfectly pointed piece of ceramic left in my hand, and I . . . closed my hand around it, like . . . like I wanted to use it."

He's crying freely now, and Nadia watches him in paralyzed shock, her mouth increasingly like dried-out leather.

"I remember seeing the realization creep into Phoebe's eyes, first amusement, then fear. And it only spurred me on, because in all our years together, Phoebe never looked at me that way. She always looked down on me, always made me feel just a little inferior. I never believed it was intentional, but in that moment I figured something out too: that's why she kept me around for so long, so she could feel bigger than someone else, because her father had always made her feel so small. I was just boiling inside. I barely recognized who I was.

"She took a step back, and I grabbed her by the arm and jerked her toward me. That's when the shard finally cut into my skin, and the pain brought me back from wherever I'd been locked away for those few seconds. The whole thing, from the moment the mug broke to that cut, was only a few seconds, but in the moment, everything felt so slowed down. I dropped the piece and she immediately slapped me across the face. Then I left. The next time I saw her . . ." He trails off. Nadia can fill in that blank on her own. The next time he saw Phoebe, she was dead.

Phoebe's phone rings and they both jerk as if slapped by an invisible hand. Nadia gets up and heads toward the kitchen. Wyatt follows. "What are you doing?" he asks.

"I'm going to answer my phone." After some searching, she finds the device—a rose-gold iPhone, naturally—on the kitchen floor in the toe-kick space of the countertop farthest from where her body was, which is why they missed it when cleaning up yesterday. Phoebe might have had it knocked from her hand, or the killer kicked it there to keep it out of her reach. Nadia picks it up. The name on the screen doesn't surprise her, but she can't help but feel a jolt of wicked validation: Jake.

Wyatt peeks over her shoulder. "Ah, Jesus. Well, if he's calling her, he must not know she's dead, right?"

"You saw how he looked at me last night. He knows something." The ringing stops, and she can't help but feel like she just missed an opportunity. Maybe he'll leave a voicemail.

"Now what?" Wyatt asks.

The phone vibrates and chimes in her hand, indicating a message. "What's her passcode?" Nadia asks.

"Her birth date is May twenty-second, eighty-seven."

Nadia types in 052287. The phone rejects it. "Got any other ideas?"

"Try it again."

She knows she typed it correctly but indulges him. Same result. "She must have changed it."

Wyatt shakes his head. "That's not like her at all. She always forgot her passwords, which is why she used her birthday for everything. I always nagged her about how unsafe it was."

"People who have something to hide learn new passwords. Maybe she wrote it down somewhere."

He shrugs. "And now we've arrived at the needle-in-a-haystack part of the game."

"Not necessarily. She probably kept it close at hand." Nadia examines the phone. A smudge of blue ink catches her eye on the bottom edge of the clear silicone case. On closer inspection, she can make out actual writing. "Can you read that?" she asks. Wyatt comes in a bit closer.

"Looks like it's inside the case. Maybe pry it off?"

She removes the case and looks again. Another six-digit number. "I think we found it."

He shakes his head. "How could she be so stupid?"

She isn't sure if he's talking about Phoebe's affair or the method of storing her passcode, but it's a fitting enough remark for both. "We should be grateful for her stupidity. I was about to start regretting I didn't keep one of her fingers to use on the fingerprint sensor." She sees his wince out of the corner of her eyes. "Sorry. I wasn't thinking."

He clears his throat. "It's okay."

She types in 070901. "Could be another birthday. Maybe Jake's."

"Jesus Christ—if so, he's only just eighteen," he mutters.

The phone unlocks and she navigates to the voicemail list to select the most recent one. "This isn't the only message she has from him," she says, showing him the screen. "Far from it."

"Just play the damn thing," he says.

She taps the screen. Jake's voice is so low that even with the volume all the way up, they still have to lean in close to hear.

"I don't know what to say. Nothing feels real. When I saw you in my living room yesterday like nothing even happened, I thought I was going out of my mind, and I think I still am." There's a long pause, where they can only hear his shaky breath. *"You and I should be in London right now."* His voice breaks. *"And you know, I blame you for why we're not! I'm sorry, but I do. We could have done this my way, but you had to be so fucking . . . stubborn."* He takes another sniffling pause. *"I still love you. Always will. Maybe it's a curse I deserve."*

The message ends there, and Nadia immediately hits "play" again. A second listen doesn't provide her any new insight. "They were leaving town together," she says, and immediately switches over to the email app. The most recent message that doesn't appear to be spam of some sort is an airline ticket confirmation. "She bought two tickets to London the night before last, departing yesterday afternoon. One way. But what stopped them?" The answer is clear enough to her, but Wyatt doesn't respond. He turns on his heel and walks off toward the stairs.

Nadia follows him up to the master bedroom. He throws open the closet doors, looks for a second, and grabs the thing Nadia knew he was coming up here to get: the bag she told him was standing at the ready.

He tosses it onto the bed and unzips it. Inside is a stack of neatly folded garments and leather pouches she assumes are for toiletries and cosmetics. Basic travel fare. She packed light for such a big trip, but that was probably Phoebe's intention, to shed her old skin and buy a new one. She was also probably wanting to move quickly. *Because of me, and my note. Has to be. This is my hand in this.* Nadia feels like she's been gut punched and sits on the ottoman at the end of the bed.

Wyatt starts riffling through the clothing, turning it into a snarl of cotton and lace, so much pink it could almost belong to a young girl. Next, he unzips a toiletry bag and dumps out an assortment of cosmetics and small bottles of shampoo, toothpaste, and hair products onto the bed. The second one reveals more of the same. He then flips the lid of the suitcase back down and unzips the front pocket. Inside, he finds an envelope holding a passport and other vital documents one would take with them if one were looking to establish residency elsewhere. In the back of her mind, Nadia is grateful he located those. She'll need them herself someday.

"Wyatt, what are you looking for?"

"I don't know. Confirmation, I guess. Now I have it. She was flying away with the kid. I think Ron or Vicki must have gotten wind of this and put a stop to it."

"Jake sounded pretty upset with her in that message."

Wyatt shakes his head. "But did he sound like he was talking to a dead woman?"

Nadia thinks on it. "I guess you could read it either way. Let me see if there's anything else in here that can shed some light."

She unlocks the phone again and checks for other telling messages either sent, received, or saved. She finds one in the Sent folder for Wyatt with the subject simply reading, "Good-bye."

"Did you get the email she sent you the morning of?"

Wyatt frowns. "What email? Let me see that." He takes the phone before she can hand it over. A few seconds later, his jaw clenches tight as he reads. He taps the screen a few times and hands it back with a blank look. The message is no longer there. It doesn't seem like the right time to ask what the email said, but Nadia feels it's safe to assume it wasn't a love note.

She checks the call logs instead. There are several incoming from Wyatt on the previous morning, no doubt the source of the incessant ringing in the background while Nadia stared down at Phoebe's corpse. He was probably trying to apologize for the fight. There are a few calls from Vicki sprinkled here and there too, checking in on her friend, who'd ducked out on their scheduled brunch, the one Vicki had said was so important. There are no calls from Jake between the night before Phoebe died and the call he just made. That's interesting.

Satisfied she's extracted all the useful information out of Phoebe's phone, she sets it down on the bed. Wyatt is sitting on the edge with his back turned to her, his shoulders slumped. "Are you okay?" The dumbest question in human existence, and yet it's always the closest at hand.

He stands and turns to her, his expression blank. "I need to go out for a while. Being here is a little suffocating right now."

"Do you want company?"

He shakes his head.

"I understand." She supposes it wouldn't feel so much like a break to have his dead wife's lookalike tag along.

Once he's gone, she goes over to the closet and grabs the bag of essentials she kept from her old life. Inside is her trusty laptop, covered with stickers and scratches from years of heavy use. It has been her reconnaissance workhorse, and it's about to be put back into service once more. She could have chosen to use the newer and faster iPad now at her disposal, but it doesn't feel right. The world may see her as Phoebe Miller now, but this is a Nadia job, and it requires a Nadia tool.

CHAPTER 19

S HE BASKS IN the cool breezes coming off of Lake Michigan, while the sun warms her bare shoulders. No need for a hat to cover her hair, either. After another go with a home-bleaching kit this morning, as well as a few rounds of toning shampoo, her locks are as close to Phoebe-blond as they're going to get, and free of their dark roots. The summer dress she chose for today's outing is knee-length, with thin spaghetti straps and a bold geometric print in jewel tones that both flatter her figure and pop brilliantly against the turquoise-water backdrop.

After doing some quick studying on fashion, including designer brands and common faux pas, she's made sure her strappy silver Louboutin heels are not an exact match for her small white Fendi purse. Inside that purse are all manner of credit cards and a driver's license identifying her as Phoebe Eleanor Miller, age thirty-two, a resident of 4115 Gooding Lane. Nadia wasn't exactly thrilled to have gained six years in age, but she was amused to discover her zodiac sign has switched from Scorpio to Gemini, a sign represented by twins.

Now that the dust has settled a bit, she's had time to process this new life. It's the ultimate fruition of Nadia's dream, to make her way up here and assume her rightful place in the family she never knew she had. She has the house, the money, the clothes, the makeup and hair, and all the supporting documents to show for it. But in spite of the simple pleasure this brings, and the relief to be out of her car and the immediate danger of the cops finding her, she's never felt more cheated and sad, not to mention guilty over the role she very likely played with her meddling. It hits her a little at a time, like drips from a leaky faucet.

Because of everything that's happened, she can't be a Noble out in the open, as herself. She gets to have the lifestyle, but only in exchange for waking up every day a fraud, an avatar for a dead sister who never knew she existed. She has to assume Phoebe's fashion and way of life, both of which are different from what Nadia would have chosen for herself if given the opportunity. None of it feels like hers. She wonders if it will in time, if the pink clothes and painful shoes will feel less like a costume. If a full erasure of her former self will occur, simply because it must if she wants to stay out of prison, or worse.

It may begin to happen someday, and she will have to decide if that's really what she wants. But first, the questions around Phoebe's death must be answered. And given what she's learned about the people next door after her hours of digging, she only has more questions. Though also a few ideas. She doesn't like living so close to the Napiers right now. Every window in that house feels like a prying eye.

Today started a bit more low-key. She didn't come downstairs to find a stoned Wyatt cooking up a stack of pancakes, thank goodness. Instead, she was up before him, and after she finished with the last of her research, she went out to retrieve coffee and bagels, keeping a close eye on the Napier house while coming and going. When she got back, she caught herself peering from the same set of blinds Phoebe used to watch Nadia through every morning, and a wave of unexpected grief hit her. She's still trying to muddle her way through.

It was nearly noon when Wyatt finally exited his room. She didn't ask where he'd gone yesterday. That would have been a wife's question, and Nadia is no one's wife, no matter whose name she goes by now. But she does know he came in well after midnight, and his inability to eat more than a few bites of his bagel this morning, while being thirsty enough to drain three glasses of water and a large coffee, signaled he'd likely been out drinking. At least he was in an agreeable mood, even if he was quiet. When she asked him to pick a place where they could go and discuss things today, somewhere neutral, somewhere that didn't have a fog of murder and pain hanging over it, he chose the year-round carnival and tourist-choked destination of Navy Pier. At least it's cheery, and the views are great. They could use a bit of that right now.

But he's even more pensive than before they arrived. After failing to talk him onto any of the rides, she says, "Hey, are you going to make me drag it out of you or what?"

He looks at her. "What?"

"The stick up your butt, for starters. Talk to me."

His expression remains pensive, and Nadia's beginning to think he's going to keep quiet, but finally he speaks. "We used to come here together a lot when we were dating."

She sighs. "This does not sound like neutral territory."

"There aren't many truly neutral places in this city when it comes to Phoebe and me, but I figured this would be better than some of the others, because I loved it more than she did. She didn't care much for crowds, even back in our younger days. But I couldn't afford to take her to five-star restaurants or the theater like she was used to, either. It was hard dating a princess."

"It couldn't have been all bad if you married her."

He grins. "You're right. It was hard dating a princess, but it was also exciting. She was smart, intense. Fun as hell. She was well traveled when we met. Taught me a lot. Everything felt like an exotic experience. It's hard not to be drawn to someone so bright, even if deep down you feel so dull by comparison." He runs his hands through his hair. "Yeah, maybe coming here was a bad idea."

Nadia wants to be annoyed with him for dragging them all the way here when he had to know it was going to bring up painful memories, but she understands his need to grieve, to reconcile the good with the bad over the last fifteen years of his life with this woman. She felt much the same way when her mother died. There were a lot of reasons to resent Vera. Her judgmental nature, her constant negativity, the way she sometimes seemed so helpless that it made Nadia feel more like the mother than the child in the relationship. But mostly it was the cowardice Nadia resented—staying with that old drunken farmer when she could have tapped the Noble cash cow at any point to buy them a better life. She probably would have ridiculed the women who are now coming forward after Daniel's death to talk about the abuse they experienced, never mind that she was one of them.

But that doesn't stop the pain of her loss from creeping up on Nadia at the most unexpected times, or nullify the good things, like her wicked sense of humor, the generosity of her heart, the loyalty she showed to everyone she cared about, even if it was to a fault. Nadia doubts she'll ever stop hearing Vera's voice in her head during her most self-critical moments. She spots a bench overlooking the water and leads him there to sit. "Look at me," she says.

She doesn't much care for what she sees. It's a handsome face. She noticed that about him from the beginning, but even in the few days they've known each other, the stress has cut deep lines around his eyes and mouth, aging him well beyond his years. He also seems grayer at the temples and in his growing stubble. A shave would help, as would a yearlong nap.

"I'm Phoebe."

He shakes his head. "No you're not."

She grabs his hands. "Shut up. Right now, I'm Phoebe. I look like her. I have her ID in my purse. I'm wearing one of her stupid dresses, and we have the same shitty paternal DNA. I am more her than anyone else can be, and I want you to tell me exactly what you would tell her right now if you could. You said after we buried her that she'd know what you were thinking, but I think it's time for you to open up."

He hangs his head. "I know what you're doing."

"Good. So play along and be the patient for once. I'm giving you an opportunity no one ever gets. Sure, you can scream at a pillow or a wall, but it doesn't beat venting your spleen onto an actual person. So let's have it."

"Okay." He takes a deep breath and looks her in the eye, though Nadia can see it's hard for him to hold that gaze. "You were right. I stopped seeing you. But I'm not sure I ever saw the real you, until that last day. And then it was too late . . ." He pauses and looks down at his feet long enough that Nadia is beginning to wonder if he's finished, but then he continues. "A lot of my friends told me, when they could see I had it bad for you, that I was wasting my time. Look out for her, they'd say. She's cold. She's a mess. You won't get far with that one.

"I didn't see any of that, though. I saw strength and independence. I saw this gorgeous package filled with a million tinier packages that I couldn't wait to spend my whole life opening up, and I felt so goddamn special that out of all the guys in the world you could have had, you picked this nobody to do that. But at some point, I stopped opening those gifts and you stopped presenting them to me. I don't know which came first, but it doesn't matter now. Neither of us was perfect. But I'm still going. I'm going to find out what really happened. I'm seeing you, and I'm probably going to spend the rest of my life trying to make this right. Your kid sister is helping. I think you'd like her."

He lets go of her hands and turns back to face the water.

Nadia spends the next few minutes processing this intimate glimpse of Phoebe, now fully understanding the sadness she felt earlier when she peeked through the blinds. The thought of all those tiny gifts remaining unopened forever, when she could have had the chance at a few of them herself if she'd only mustered up enough courage to knock on the door sooner, is overwhelming. "Did that help?" she asks, her voice hoarse.

"I think so. But I don't want to do it again."

"That's fair."

She takes a breath and moves on to the bigger thing she's been holding on to. From her purse, she pulls out a folded sheaf of papers she printed off, containing the results of her digging on the Napiers last night.

Wyatt pages through them. "Ron and Vicki are from here originally, huh? Interesting."

"Yes. But they met out there, apparently. I'm guessing he tapped some old contacts here when everything out west fell apart."

"Fell apart how?"

She gestures toward the papers. "Keep reading. It's in there."

He flips through a few more sheets. "Wow. Ron lost his medical license in California?"

"Looks like he had a few malpractice suits. One girl ended up paralyzed during a spinal surgery that should have been simple enough, at least for him. Another person died after a botched procedure. But it looks like all of them were eventually dropped. I assume they were paid off, but that didn't stop the state board from dropping the axe on him. For all I know, there might be more than what I found on my initial dig. This was enough to give me the general idea, though."

"Yikes. I should be surprised he was hired out here, but I've seen more than a few Teflon-coated quacks, even in my less prestigious end of the health profession. The higher up the food chain they get, the more they protect each other. Even when people are getting hurt."

"This probably explains some of the tension in the Napier marriage too," Nadia says.

"I agree."

"You're lucky he didn't amputate a finger while he was stitching you up the other night." She grins a little to signal it was a joke. Wyatt smiles, but he also subconsciously covers his still-bandaged hand, as if he doesn't want to think about it.

"He also strikes me as a drunk," Wyatt says. "He smelled like a distillery the other night. I'm sure that doesn't help family matters much."

"Yeah. Did the alcoholism cause the malpractice or vice versa?"

He shrugs. "That's anyone's guess. Did you find anything on her?"

"Weirdly, no. She's a bit of a blank on the search results, apart from your standard social media accounts, none of which were remarkable, at least from what I could view publicly. I couldn't find any real employment history or credit."

"It's not as strange as you might think if she's been a stay-at-home mom all these years. Vicki is what, late thirties? She has an eighteen-year-old son, so that means she was a mom and married around age twenty. There's your blank spot."

"That's kind of sad. I didn't get an alpha-homemaker vibe from her."

"It's not sad if that's what she and her husband agreed on when they started their family." He sounds a touch defensive. Was this a point of contention between Phoebe and him? This doesn't seem like the right time to poke that particular bear.

"You're right. But I'm sure it's not helping her stress levels now. She put all her eggs into her husband's basket, and it turned out to have a giant hole in it. I watched my mom do the same thing."

"We're only getting part of the picture, so all we can do is speculate."

"It's funny you mention speculation. That brings me to the most interesting part of this. I looked up the property records for the house they're living in. And it turns out, they don't actually own it."

He shrugs. "So they're renting. Ron lost his job, they needed to move fast. Not enough time to buy."

She elbows him. "I'm insulted you think that's all I have. After a little more digging, I was able to track down the owners in a nice little retirement community in Buffalo Grove. Talked to the wife this morning. Very sweet lady named Imelda Johnson."

He nods. "Yeah, I know her. We didn't speak a ton, but we would exchange pleasantries if we were both out getting our mail at the same time. I never even knew they'd been planning to move out until they were already gone. I'd been preoccupied, I guess. How did you get her to talk to you?"

"Pretended I was a location scout for a movie. It wasn't hard. In my experience, old people are happy to talk to just about anyone. They're lonely. The woman practically told me her whole life story."

"I'm impressed."

"Well, according to my new best friend, Imelda, they'd never had the house listed for sale or rent. Vicki contacted them directly, said she'd fallen in love with the area and wondered if they'd be interested in parting with the house for a generous sum. Imelda saw it as some kind of divine intervention, as she'd been trying to talk her husband into assisted living for months."

"What did Vicki offer her?"

"Twenty thousand on a rent-to-own agreement. The Napiers are supposed to be paying them five grand a month."

Wyatt opens his mouth as if to respond, and then frowns. "And they didn't actually know each other before this?"

"Nope. Now, why do you think they would pick this one house out of all the houses in Lake Forest or the surrounding areas they could have found to live in?"

"You think they were trying to get close to Phoebe."

"Bingo. And get this. Sweet little Imelda wanted me to get a message to Miss Vicki as soon as I could. Apparently they're late on this month's installment, and Imelda hasn't been able to reach anyone. The poor woman was about to drive over there herself, but I told her I'd take care of things."

Wyatt is shaking his head. "This just keeps getting weirder and weirder."

"You saw the inside of that place. Frat houses are better furnished. They're broke."

"But why Phoebe? What's the connection there?"

Nadia shrugs. "That's where I came up empty. None of my digging pointed to any clues. If I had to guess, I'd say maybe something to do with Daniel. His death has brought all kinds of people out of the woodwork."

"You included," Wyatt remarks, though not unkindly.

"True. But I think I could find out more if I can just get a little closer to them."

"I don't like it."

"I don't, either, but I also have no reason to think that whatever scheme they're working on is going to stop just because Phoebe is dead. If anything, it might escalate the situation. One or all three of them could be sitting over there in a constant state of panic. We can't ignore this and hope it will go away."

He sighs and stands up. "Okay. I think that's plenty for us to chew on for now. Let's go somewhere else. A place with drinks."

"Another not-quite-neutral place?" she asks.

"The area around the pier has changed a lot in the last few years. I figure we can walk until we see something we both agree on. Something nice and gentrified, like an Applebee's or a Guy Fieri joint."

She laughs. "That'll work."

They've traveled about a hundred feet when Wyatt takes her hand. Before she can react, he mutters, "Two o'clock. Ferris wheel ticket counter."

She looks over and her breath catches in her throat. All three of the Napiers are standing in line. Jake, who was facing their way, abruptly looks back down at his phone.

"What are the odds?" she murmurs.

"You think they tailed us here?"

"Come on. Of course they did. What are the chances two sets of jaded neighbors from the suburbs trekked all the way to a giant downtown tourist trap at the same time?"

"You're probably right. I'm just surprised we didn't notice them on the way."

Nadia rolls her eyes. "Yeah, no way we could have missed a dark gray SUV that looks like every third car on the road. We wouldn't have spotted a tail in that traffic anyway."

"Just keep walking."

Nadia has no intention of following those orders. Instead, she raises her hand and waves. "Vicki! Hey, girl!"

"What are you doing?" Wyatt growls.

"Can't win the game if you don't play. Come on."

Vicki spins around on her sneaker-clad heel, her face blooming quickly into a grin identical to the one she wore the other night when she answered the door. "Oh my God! Hey, neighbors!"

Nadia leads Wyatt over, and despite his earlier protest, he doesn't break his stride. When they reach the Napiers, Nadia goes into hug mode first this time, fully embracing her role as this woman's bestie. Would Phoebe have done that? Maybe not, but there's no room left for doubt. If Phoebe wasn't a hugger before, she is now. It's called having a new lease on life. "How crazy is this, running into you here of all places? So great."

"I guess great minds think alike. We're just out for a bit of family fun. I can't believe how amazing this wheel looks in person. I used to ride the old one all the time when I was a little girl."

Wyatt tips a wave to Ron and Jake. Lover boy looks a little less haunted than he did the other night, but sunglasses obscure his eyes. The scratches have mostly faded, though there are still a couple on his neck. Nadia likes to think of them as Phoebe's contribution to the discussion. *Watch him.*

"Well, it's worth the wait in line," Nadia says. "The weather is perfect for it too."

Vicki's eyes widen like she just had a brilliant idea. "Oh, you should come up with us! My treat. These gondolas seat like eight people." She's the only one who looks remotely interested in this idea.

Wyatt squeezes Nadia's hand. Hard. But she isn't going to pass this up. In fact, she was hoping for just such an invite. Time to be proactive. "We'd love that." She looks up at Wyatt with her sunniest grin. "Come on, babe. You're not that afraid of heights."

"Sounds like I don't have a choice." The daggers in his eyes could cut glass.

"We're in!" Nadia says.

Vicki makes an amusing raise-the-roof gesture. "Woot! Let's do this."

Ron mumbles something that sounds like "The more the merrier," and Jake is still looking at his phone. Vicki seems to be the only one in the family with a pulse. But she also seems a little *too* cheerful, like she's trying to compensate for her husband and son. Is she always so "on" like this? It must be exhausting.

Once they have their tickets, along with a pass to skip the long line, they head over to the much smaller queue of people who paid for the privilege of a shorter wait. The sign says the ride is only ten to fifteen minutes long. Nadia wonders how long it's going to actually feel under the circumstances. As she gazes up at the towering structure, a bit of regret begins to seep into her guts. That's a long way up to be trapped with three people who might have an agenda.

Their gondola arrives and the five of them get on. The Napiers and the Millers sit on opposing sides, as the universe would seem to have it. Wyatt takes her hand again. It isn't a romantic gesture but more like he's maintaining a conduit of quiet communication between them.

Vicki looks all around the inside of the car and rubs the back of her seat. "Gosh, this is really nice, isn't it?"

"Yeah," Nadia says. "Cozy." A bit like an isolation chamber. Will anyone hear their screams if one of them decides to attack? *You didn't really think this through, did you? But you've always been too impulsive for your own good. Foolish girl.*

Ron grunts. "For eighteen bucks a person, it should have come with a free beer or something."

Vicki rolls her eyes. "Don't listen to the cheapskate. This view is worth every penny."

Ron looks out the window next to him as they ascend. "One of the most violent cities in the country, but everything looks so small and peaceful from up here, doesn't it?"

"Too bad we can't just stay in here," Vicki says. "Above it all."

Nadia can't think of a worse hell, but she affects a sigh of agreement and focuses on the sailboats cruising the gleaming water below. "That would be nice."

Nobody says anything for a few seconds until Jake blurts out, almost absently, "Too bad you can never really run away from anything." He doesn't look up from his phone.

"Uh, rude?" Vicki points to the device.

"I just want to get a few pictures. Is that okay with you?"

A moment ago, the gondola was spacious enough. Now it feels like a coffin with five people crammed inside. "Come on, Vic," Ron says. "Let the kid take a few pictures. What's the point of being up here if you can't bring some of the view home with you?"

Vicki looks like she's biting the inside of her cheek to keep from saying what she's really thinking. Finally, she sits back. "Have at it.

Just try to actually, you know, enjoy the view with your own eyes too, and not through a screen." She looks at Nadia. "People are obsessed with filters these days, aren't they? It's like reality isn't good enough."

"Reality isn't good enough for most people," Wyatt remarks. He's been so quiet, Nadia was starting to wonder if he'd join the conversation at all. "It's what keeps me in business."

"Hear hear," Ron interjects. "Capitalism thrives on existential misery."

"That explains your scotch budget," Vicki quips. It doesn't quite play like a joke.

"Don't worry, Ron," Nadia says. "You probably have nothing on my wine cellar." An obliging chuckle passes among them, easing some of the tension. He glances at her for half a second before turning back to his window. It's a bitter acknowledgment of her presence, but unlike the other night, an acknowledgment nonetheless.

Jake snaps a few shots from various vantage points while the gondola is at the very top of the wheel. Ironically, for all her berating about phones, it's Vicki who insists on his taking a selfie of them together, and then asks him to message it to her. It's like she can't decide from one moment to the next what kind of mom she wants to be. Nadia's hip vibrates with a text message. Jake is no longer looking at his phone; despite the darkness of his sunglasses, she senses he's looking directly at her.

As much as she wants to grab her phone now, it seems safer to wait until they're off the ride, which will be over in a few minutes, anyway. Jake finally turns to look out his window, and Ron asks Wyatt about what the mental health business is like. Vicki grins at Nadia, who feels like she has to say something to make this whole exercise in discomfort worth it. "So I'm thinking you three should come over for dinner tomorrow night." The invitation is as spontaneous as her decision to greet the Napiers in the first place, but already she's forming a plan for what she can do once she gets the Napiers out of their house for a bit. "That is, if you're available."

"Hey, guys," Vicki says. "Dinner with the Millers tomorrow?" As the three of them confer only with their eyes, Wyatt's fingernails dig briefly into the palm of Nadia's hand. He's not happy, but he'll deal with it, just like he's dealing with the ride. When no one voices any objections, though Ron and Jake don't exactly come off as enthusiastic, Vicki says, "Sounds like it's on. What can we bring?"

When they finally step off the gondola, Nadia takes a deep breath of fresh air. There is very little relief in it, though, as the reality of her plan settles in. After they part ways, Wyatt continues holding her hand until they're nearly at the car, and then he flings it away. Nadia can't help but feel a little hurt, but he looks furious. "Dinner at our place, huh? Are you crazy?"

Once they're in the car, Nadia faces him. "Your fear is again duly noted, but I have a reason for inviting them over." She tells him what it is.

He leans his head back and closes his eyes. "You're going to get yourself or both of us killed. You do know that, right?"

"Then at least we'll die knowing who killed Phoebe."

"I sincerely hope that was a joke."

She shrugs. "It's funny because it's true, right?"

He pinches the bridge of his nose. "Look, will you just stop being so impetuous? Maybe I'm being a bit of a wuss here, but you could at least pretend like caution matters to you. And I'd like the chance to have a little input before you go inviting three potential murderers into my house."

She folds her arms and tries not to sulk. He might have a tiny point. She could have consulted him first on the dinner idea after the ride was over, sold him on it, and then made the invite later. "I did jump the gun. When I get nervous, I tend to act without thinking first. I'll try harder not to do that."

"Thank you." They sit quietly for a minute, and then he says: "Another five minutes in that gondola and Jake probably would have puked. Guilty or not, the kid is not taking this well."

"Put yourself in his shoes. Even if he didn't kill her, he's stuck watching his girlfriend hold hands with her husband while she pretends not to know him. It has to be a mind fuck." This reminds her of something. Nadia pulls her phone, or rather Phoebe's phone, out of her pocket. As expected, there's a text message from Jake. She opens it and finds a picture of herself in the gondola, with the pier and the vast blue of Lake Michigan stretching off behind her. Her eyes are focused on something off-camera, likely Vicki. The caption is only three words, and they're icicles in her spine. *You're not Phoebe.*

"Well, that's one question answered," she says, showing Wyatt the picture.

"He was fucking my wife. He would notice if a strand of her hair was out of place." He grips the wheel tight enough to make the leather creak, and Nadia thinks of the mug that broke in his grip. He seems to realize this himself and lets go. "Maybe Phoebe had the right idea. Run away. We could hit the road right now, never look back."

She touches his shoulder. "If that was the right idea, I don't think she'd be dead right now."

He doesn't seem to have an argument for that.

■ ■ ■

I KNOW NONE of this is funny, but sometimes I want to laugh when I think of how ridiculous things have become since you died. But when I've tried to let it out, hoping it would make me feel better, like a big sneeze does when there's a tickle in my nose, it sounds more like a bunch of short screams strung together. Then I stop, because I'm scared that if I keep going, it will just become one long, endless shriek. Even in the quiet, I can still feel that scream trapped inside my body with nowhere to go. It makes me feel constantly like I'm going to throw up, but that doesn't help. Believe me, I've tried.

But I bet you're getting a kick out of this. I can imagine you right now, sitting on a cloud with a bucket of popcorn, laugh-screaming too. Are you rooting for me? I don't think I'm even rooting for myself at this point. I'll just be glad when this whole game is done.

CHAPTER 20

NOTHING EVER COMES *easy to people like us.*

Her mother used to say that a lot, and it always drove Nadia crazy. *What a bunch of fatalistic bullshit,* she would think. *Make your own luck. Never crown a champion before you play a game, and if you're in a roomful of losers, then find another room.*

But as Nadia hunkers down at the Napiers' back door, staring at her third broken tension wrench of the evening, and time falls through her fingers like talcum powder, she realizes Vera might have had a point. When has anything ever come easily to her? It's always been a fight to keep moving forward. No greased rails on which to glide but a slog through muddy wheel ruts. She's finally willing to admit exhaustion.

But she still has one wrench left. It isn't over yet.

Using a nifty, and highly illegal, remote gadget she purchased a lifetime ago when it looked like the breaking-and-entering thing might become more than a passing interest, she already disabled the rudimentary commercial security system. Only this one tiny task stands in her way. She can *do* this! The lock isn't even very good. The old ducks who lived here before probably hadn't upgraded anything since the eighties. She's just gotten a little rusty, that's all. And she's never had so much riding on getting it right.

Nadia gives the wrench a mean glare. "This is all on you." If this one breaks, she'll surrender and smash the damn window. No time for any of her other, subtler tricks. Placing the wrench into the top of the lock, she inserts her pick, being very careful not to add too much torque as she lifts each of the pins, remembering to breathe.

An agonizing fraction of a second occurs when she's sure she dropped the last pin right as she turned the wrench, which would have resulted in an immediate snap, but the lock turns freely and she hears the satisfying click of entry. She checks the time and sends Wyatt a quick status update: *I'm in.*

His response comes a few seconds later: *Hurry.*

Because of the time she lost on the lock, she can't search the house as thoroughly as she planned, but that's okay. There isn't much stuff here to sift through, anyway, and she really only needs to find something that can prove a link between the Napiers and Phoebe. Luckily, she's broken into enough houses over the years to become adept at finding people's secrets, many of them surprisingly left right out in the open.

She scans the kitchen. Counters are bare, save for a coffeemaker and toaster. A few dishes in the sink. There's a stack of papers on the breakfast bar. Nadia starts there. Know the bills, know the person.

There are a lot of them too. Phone, electric, internet, all of them either past due or threatening cancellation. Three credit cards, maxed or nearly so. There are several envelopes from a place called Wood Glenn, a nursing home in California. Nadia doesn't have the time to read them in the detail she would like, but a quick scan of them gives her enough of a gist. Someone hasn't been paying the rent for a resident named Donna Parker, and they're threatening eviction. Nadia recognizes Parker as Vicki's maiden name, which she combed up in her background search. Donna could be her mother. "Well that sucks," she whispers, putting down the stack of papers and moving up the hallway.

The door at the end is the only one with glass panels she can look through. The small computer desk, the stacks of books and papers on the floor, and the orange medical bag she saw the other night while Wyatt got his stitches all point to this being Ron's office, but the door is locked, and she has no desire to test her luck with picking again. Reluctantly, she moves on.

The next two rooms she checks are completely empty. They're paying for so much unused space. The next one at least looks like someone lives in it. Hideous wallpaper of giant pink roses, little Imelda Johnson's taste, no doubt. King-size bed with a plain white duvet, small dresser against one wall with a few perfume bottles and bras slung on top. A pair of men's slippers rest on the floor next to the bed. This has to be the master bedroom. She moves through it quickly enough, checking all the usual spaces: closet (mostly empty, but for some hanging shirts and men's jackets), dresser drawers (also no surprises), under the bed (not even a dust bunny), and her favorite spot for hidden items: between the mattresses. Nothing.

Disappointed, she moves on, past a guest bathroom she has no time to search, to a bedroom immediately adjacent. This one is free of wallpaper, thank goodness. Only dark blue paint with white trim. She imagines it must have had a nautical theme in a previous life. The unmade twin bed and piles of clothes on the floor scream "young dude." Definitely Jake's room. She notes a picture hanging on the wall above the bed that looks an awful lot like an artist's rendering of the Ferrari in Phoebe's garage. A possible gift from his lady friend? "Aw, sis, that was sweet of you," Nadia murmurs.

She sifts through the clothes on the floor and then searches for a dresser. No such luck. All his folded garments are in a series of laundry baskets against the wall. His other belongings are in the boxes they likely arrived here in, most of them containing athletic trophies, books, video games, tangles of electronics cables, and other odds and ends.

She would look under the bed, but she realizes the mattress and box spring are on the floor and not a frame, so she checks underneath the top mattress. It takes her a moment to register what she sees. Her knees begin to feel a little wobbly.

It's a long butcher knife, with a handle very similar to the ones in the Miller knife block. She'll need to compare it to be sure, but she's already certain this is it, because neither she nor Wyatt was able to turn it up when they looked for it, and the blade has that unique pounded-steel look that the others in the set have. The look of a lot of money to burn.

She turns on the phone's flashlight and examines the knife for any visible blood. There appears to be a tiny brownish speck where the blade meets the handle but no way to tell for sure if it's blood, rust, or dirt. Otherwise, it looks clean, at least to the naked eye. Gingerly gripping the knife by the very end of its handle, she places it in her tool bag.

Phoebe's phone, which has become Nadia's main mobile device, buzzes, and she jumps, dropping the mattress. It lands with a heavy *foof* but looks no more disheveled than before. Wyatt: *They're getting antsy. Won't eat w/o you.*

Nadia grimaces. She still hasn't found anything linking the Napiers to Phoebe, or even Daniel, but the knife is a big score. The biggest score, if the goal is only to prove guilt. What she plans to do with that information is a whole other dirty can of worms she isn't prepared to open just yet. Right now, she just needs to get out of here. Turning off the flashlight, she crosses the living room at a quick clip.

She doesn't see the folding chair adjacent to the love seat until it trips her. In stumbling to catch herself, her phone slips from her hand and slides across the bare wooden floor like a glass hockey puck and into a darkened area of the room, beyond the reach of the dim lamplight. "Stupid!" she cries.

After placing the chair back where she thinks it was before, she goes looking for the phone. There aren't any pieces of furniture for it to hide under, but that doesn't mean she has even a second to look for something she shouldn't have dropped in the first place. Like a blessing in the dark, the phone lights up and begins to vibrate as a call comes in, about five feet away from where she's been looking.

She runs over, sees it's Wyatt, swoops down, and answers it.

"I'm okay," she says.

"What are you doing?" His voice is a whispered shriek.

"I got held up. Leaving now."

"Vicki went to the bathroom right after I last messaged you. She still isn't back. I think she might be snooping around upstairs. Jesus Christ, hurry up."

Nadia grits her teeth. So Vicki's definitely in on this, huh? She isn't surprised so much as disappointed to think that Phoebe's closest friend might have murdered her. "See you in a sec." She ends the call and exits the house, taking off her heels so she can run flat-out for the walking path she used to get here, the same one Jake likely took to visit Phoebe on his regular jaunts, as it's invisible from the street.

Once she's through the back gate and back in Miller territory, panting and covered in sweat, she freezes at the sight of a shadow in her bedroom window. A svelte, petite shadow with a pixie cut. Add a pair of wings, and she'd practically be Tinkerbell. "Hello, Mrs. Napier," she whispers, her heart pounding hard against her sternum.

She's about to text Wyatt to find a way to get Vicki back down to the dinner table when the shadow moves away and the room's light switches off. Nadia darts across the backyard to the patio, and then races up the stairs that lead up to the balcony off the master bedroom, entering through the French doors.

Shedding her tool bag, she dashes across the bedroom and through the door leading to the hallway landing, where she catches Vicki more than halfway back down to the first floor. "Oh, hey, did you need me for something?" Nadia asks, taking deep pleasure in the way Vicki stiffens and nearly stumbles. "I was out on the balcony and thought I heard someone."

Vicki turns around and looks up at Nadia with the barest grin.

"You were taking so long on the phone. I just wanted to make sure you were still alive up here."

Funny turn of phrase, Vicki. Were you hoping to remedy that problem? "Everything's fine. Almost finished."

"You're looking a little sweaty. Must have been an intense conversation."

"It's a little humid out there still."

Vicki nods slowly. "Ah. That must be why I didn't actually see you."

Oh, but you were looking for something else, weren't you? "Must be. Let me freshen up, and I'll be right down."

"Okie doke." She winks and proceeds back down the stairs.

Once Nadia is alone again, she gazes around for obvious signs of tampering. Nothing jumps out at her, but there remains the closet, where the bag holding all that's left of Nadia's old life is currently sitting out in the open. In her hurry to dig out her tool kit, she didn't conceal it again. *Like a goddamn nitwit.*

She quickly ducks into the closet and finds the bag in the same spot as before. At first glance, it looks undisturbed, but she knows the goal of a thief is to leave things looking just so. She unzips the bag, hoping to find what she's looking for resting on top where she left it, but knowing in her heart she won't. Her phone, *Nadia's* phone, the one she never expected to need again, is gone. Frantically, she overturns the bag and dumps its contents onto the floor, on the off chance it slid to the bottom. Dozens of stolen trinkets, her journals, toiletries, hair ties, crumpled receipts, her old work badge and pay stubs, and other random junk scatter in every direction. No phone among them. Because when you have a person's phone, you have them. Cold hands clamp around her guts and squeeze.

Nadia backs out of the closet, balls her hands into fists, and begins punching the bed over and over, somehow holding back the bloodcurdling, primal scream she wants so desperately to let loose. There are things on that phone. *Very incriminating things* that she didn't get around to locking down yet, because she had so many other details on her mind. And unlike Phoebe's phone, the kind of device Nadia could afford in her old life doesn't have all the fancy fingerprint and iris-scanning tech to keep it secure. It's just a cheap burner she picked up at a 7-Eleven not long after she got to Lake Forest. She could have locked it down with a passcode, but she didn't even do that, because she always found it annoying to enter a number every single time she wanted to check a message or surf the internet. Isn't that how every plan fails? That one detail so simple and commonsense that it's easy to overlook.

"How stupid are you? How utterly dumb?"

Angry, humiliated tears burn her eyes. But she manages to put on the brakes before all her hopes go completely over a cliff. *Breathe, Nadia. This isn't the end of the game. Not by a long shot. You have definitive proof one of these assholes killed Phoebe. Vicki might have scored a touchdown at the two-minute mark, but there's still enough time to turn things around. Now isn't the time to go into "woe is me" mode like your mother.*

She takes a quick look in the mirror to assess the damage. It isn't as bad as she feared, given all the sweat and tears. *Thank you, Phoebe, for your high-dollar makeup.* She applies a bit of powder to dull the shine and straightens her hair with a brush before heading back down to the dining room, where fifteen minutes ago, she claimed she had to take an important call from her accountant.

They're all seated at one end of a shiny glass table long enough to accommodate at least a dozen with plenty of elbow room. Like much of this house, the cavernous formal dining space resembles a modern-art museum, complete with an eclectic assortment of colorful abstract paintings on the walls, and a huge twisted blown-glass sculpture for a chandelier that appears to almost float over the table like a psychedelic squid, and probably cost as much as Wyatt's Audi. Such a room, fit for the grandest of dinner parties, seems almost comical in a house owned by a woman who eschewed every pretense of a social life, aside from her more recent girlfriend lunches with Vicki. Maybe the Millers enjoyed it for its intended use once upon a time. Nadia has yet to ask.

The spread of roast beef, potatoes, asparagus, bread, and wine Nadia laid out nearly a half hour ago is still untouched. Wyatt slumps back in his seat, his face awash with relief, when he sees her. The two Napier men seem more interested in their empty plates. "I'm sorry that took so long. You didn't have to wait for me. Everyone dig in, please."

"Like we would even think of eating without our hostess," Vicki says.

"I don't know about that," Ron says with a sloppy grin. He might not have eaten any food, but he's clearly enjoyed plenty of wine. "I'm starving."

Vicki elbows him. "Oh, he wouldn't have dared, Phoebe."

There's something different about Vicki right now. Squarer posture, a sparkle in her eye, a new note in her voice that telegraphs pure triumph. Nadia wants to stab the bitch with her fork and wrestle her phone back. Wyatt and Ron move in for the platters while the women continue to stare each other down from their places across the table. Their disguises feel all but useless now, but neither of them seems ready to unmask just yet. Vicki could just be looking out for her son. Nadia watches her dote over him, filling his plate with meat and vegetables like he's five. But unlike a five-year-old, Jake has a full wineglass. The better to dull his frayed nerves with, Nadia guesses. He might be a few years shy of legal drinking age, but as the old saying goes, if they're old enough to bang and possibly murder one of their mom's married friends, by God, they should be able to have a drink.

"So is all well in the land of numbers and ledgers?" Vicki asks.

"It's all fine," Nadia says. "I try to involve myself as little as possible in the family business, but sometimes issues come up."

Ron looks up from his nearly demolished plate of food. "Yeah, but we all know you don't mind waving Daddy's money around from time to time."

"Ron, for God's sake!" Vicki looks mortified.

Nadia has no idea what any of this is about. She exchanges a glance with Wyatt, who seems equally clueless.

"Don't get hysterical. I figured since we returned Phoebe's generous offering, we could all joke about it now." He drains his wine and then grins at Nadia.

Vicki closes her eyes for a moment, like she's reciting the serenity prayer to herself. "Don't mind my husband. He spends so much time drinking scotch that I forgot wine can turn him into a real asshole."

"Guys. Stop," Jake says. He's sitting low in his seat, like a sullen child who might at any moment decide to hide under the table.

"The food is delicious, honey," Wyatt says. Bless him for trying to keep this slow-motion train wreck going.

"Thank you," she says. The room falls maddeningly silent, save for the clink of silverware on dishes. Nadia isn't sure what's worse, this or the awkward and stilted conversation, but at least it gives her a chance to ponder what Ron just revealed. It sounds like Phoebe tried to give them some money, but whose idea was it to return it? She would bet on Ron, given the cutting nature of his remarks. With the stack of bills Nadia saw on the counter and the size of the Napiers' monthly rent, they sure could have used the assistance. But maybe Ron resented Phoebe's interference in his family affairs. Sounds like a possible motive for murder, but what does that mean for Nadia's theory that the Napiers moved here specifically to get close to Phoebe, and ostensibly, her money? Every time she thinks she's lining up all the pieces, a wind comes through and blows them all around again.

"Did you get the meat at Earthbound?" Vicki asks her.

Nadia shakes her head numbly, forcing her bite of food down. "I went to the Jewel Osco."

"Well that's a good thing. I haven't been back to Earthbound since they found that guy murdered behind the store. Don't think they ever found who did it, either."

This topic can't be a coincidence. Vicki saw the Earthbound pay stubs and badge bearing Nadia's name, and now she wants to play. The gleam in her eyes is almost predatory now. *I know who you are,* those eyes say. *I have you in a box and I'm going to make you squirm.*

Nadia returns the volley; she can't help herself. "I hope everyone is okay with how I sliced the meat. I haven't been able to find my best knife anywhere. So weird. Not the sort of thing that just gets up and walks away on its own."

Vicki looks startled and Wyatt shoots Nadia a look. "It's just fine, honey," he says, a tiny note of warning in his voice.

Jake stands up. His face is a little pale. "I'm sorry. Can I use your restroom?"

"Jake, just sit down and finish eating," Vicki says.

Ron grunts. "He looks a little like he's going to be sick."

"Well, I guess I should trust the drunk doctor who let his underage kid drink wine," she snaps.

"I'm sorry," Jake says again, heading out of the dining room. A moment later, the sound of retching comes from the bathroom, the same one Nadia lost her breakfast in the other morning.

Vicki is rubbing her temples, like she has a bad headache coming on. "Ron, will you go check on him, please?"

"There's no need to coddle him. He's a grown man."

"He's still our son, so would you *please*." The words come out through clenched teeth, the classic sign of one who has about had it.

Ron's face clouds over and he takes a deep breath, presumably to launch a nasty barb, or a hail of them. Nadia clears her throat, and this seems to remind him that he's not home, where he can yell at his wife with impunity. Ron gets up, muttering, "Excuse me."

When Vicki opens her eyes again, there's a raw desperation in them. "I'm not sure how much more of this I can take," she says to no one in particular.

Ron returns. "Jake is heading back home. I think we should go with him."

Vicki doesn't move. Nadia can feel everything this woman wants to say pressing against the backs of her lips, straining to get out. Her slender fingers are still wrapped around her fork. Nadia notes only a plain wedding band, no engagement ring. *Must have pawned it*, she thinks.

Ron grabs his wife's upper arm and tugs, like she's a child who won't listen. "Vicki, come on."

She yanks her arm out of Ron's grip, which was significant enough to require a little wrenching, and picks up her wineglass. "Weren't you the one saying we shouldn't coddle him? He's just going to go straight to his bedroom anyway." When no one says anything, she becomes flustered. "We've barely even started the meal Phoebe worked so hard on."

Nadia wonders how this is going to end. Ron's complexion is deepening to an infuriated plum shade. "It was no trouble," she says. "We can pick things up again when Jake is feeling better."

Vicki shakes her head, drains her wine, and finally stands. "Oh, we're definitely going to be picking things up again. Sooner rather than later, I hope." She isn't smiling, but a bit of the sparkle from earlier has returned to her eyes.

"Just let me know when, and we'll be ready," Nadia replies.

As they stand in the doorway, watching the Napiers cross the cul-de-sac to their house, Wyatt asks, "What exactly just happened here?"

Nadia lets out a long breath. "We're nearing the end of this weird little masquerade, I think. And thank God."

· · ·

I'VE NEVER BELIEVED in ghosts, but I felt you with us at that dinner table. We sat there pretending like things were normal, and failing miserably at it because we all know you're really gone, but nobody wants to say it out loud. It's so stupid, but would you honestly act any different if you were one of us?

I did think about ending it all right there, just telling them what I did so all this pretending could stop before someone else got hurt, because I know the longer this goes on, the more likely it is that that's what will happen. The words rose to the back of my throat so many times, but they kept getting stuck there. I had to swallow them back before I choked.

It's clear to me now that we all have secrets when it comes to you, but because no one wants to break first, we're going to have to break each other instead. I'm just afraid of what that might mean.

CHAPTER 21

NADIA RETRIEVES HER bag from upstairs, and then they set up in the living room to escape the awkward vibe still lingering at the dinner table. There's a lot to unpack, between the dinner conversation, what Nadia learned from her trip to the Napiers' house, and what Vicki gathered from her little scavenger hunt. She'll leave that nasty tidbit for last. From her bag, she pulls out the knife, holding it gingerly by its wood-grain handle. "This was under Jake's mattress. Look familiar?"

He goes white when he sees it and then shudders before looking away. "Yeah."

"Are you sure?"

"The set was custom made. If you look at the handle, there's a stamp with Phoebe's monogram."

Nadia looks, and sure enough, she finds the initials PEM. Again, she almost feels like it's Phoebe's way of speaking from the grave. *You're on the right path. Keep going.* "Are you comfortable with thinking Jake did it now?"

"I'm sure he was at least part of it, but unless you can do prints or DNA on that thing . . ." He shrugs as if to say, *Who knows?*

Nadia reluctantly agrees. The knife alone isn't enough to point directly to Jake, regardless of where she found it. She sets it down on the ottoman in front of them. "And after Vicki's snooping tonight, we know she's involved too. At the very least, she's trying to cover for her boy."

"Or her boy is trying to cover for her."

"Right."

They sit thinking for a minute, then Wyatt says, "What's the deal with Phoebe trying to give them money? I couldn't believe when Ron mentioned that earlier. It doesn't really sound like her."

"She wasn't very charitable?"

He gives a *so-so* gesture. "She was more like her dad that way than she'd care to admit. Friends don't give friends money, that sort of thing. With Daniel, though, it was greed. For Phoebe, it was more of a self-protective thing."

"Maybe she felt guilty. She probably knew they were having money problems, and she was sleeping with their kid."

Wyatt nods. "Now, that sounds more like Phoebe. Did you find anything else over there?"

"Unfortunately no. There just wasn't a lot of time."

A quiet moment ensues during which Nadia tries to decide how she's going to tell Wyatt what Vicki took from her bag, but when she opens her mouth, Phoebe's phone dings twice in a row with text alerts, as if coming to her rescue. The messages are from Jake.

When she opens them, she realizes there's nothing rescuing about them at all. Her body ripples with sickening waves of goose bumps, and the phone slides out of her hand and lands in her lap. "Oh God," she murmurs, but why is she so surprised? The moment she discovered her old phone was missing, she knew this was coming. The only unexpected part was seeing it come from Jake and not Vicki. They must be over there comparing notes like she and Wyatt are doing right now.

"What?" Wyatt leans forward. "What is it?"

She hands over the phone. The messages contain no text. Only pictures. Two very familiar, gruesome pictures. One with Wyatt in the foreground, another with Nadia, but both of them featuring Phoebe's lifeless, bloody face behind them. So much for the insurance policies Nadia had been so intent they create to protect themselves.

Wyatt glances at the screen for only a second and then puts it down between them. He doesn't explode as Nadia had been expecting. Instead, he only slumps back into the couch cushions with an exhausted sigh, as if nothing can surprise him anymore. "I had a feeling if she took anything from upstairs, it would be this," he says. "How did this happen?"

"Vicki was in Phoebe's room snooping around when I got back from the house. When I checked to see what she'd taken, I noticed my old phone missing."

His face flushes red, but he's doing a remarkable job keeping his voice level. Probably employing every mental calming trick he has up his therapist's sleeve. "And now Jake has it, apparently."

She swallows the growing lump in her throat. "Looks like it."

"How did he access the photos so easily?"

"My phone wasn't locked. I'm so sorry," she whispers. "You

thought Phoebe was bad about her passwords. She and I had that in common."

Before he can reply, the phone dings again. Nadia grabs it.

Jake: *This was always about the money, okay? $1M should be enough. Just pay and these pics and your other secrets won't become a problem.*

Nadia reads the message aloud and then says to Wyatt, "The little shit is blackmailing us! He's a lot braver on a keyboard, isn't he?" She feels a little hypocritical given her own blackmail, but this is particularly brazen. And for him to say this was always about the money . . . does that mean he was only sleeping with Phoebe for financial gain? Nadia can't help but be pissed on her sister's behalf.

Wyatt rubs his face with both hands and then leans back in his chair. "Just agree to pay it. Get it over with."

"Whoa, what?" Nadia isn't sure, but she thinks Wyatt maybe just morphed into a complete moron.

"You said there was probably a reason they moved here—to get close to Phoebe. We know they needed money, probably after Ron botched those surgeries and lost his license in California. They were looking to relocate to Chicago and saw the whole Daniel Noble saga playing out in the news. They're just like everyone else trying to pick at his carcass to see what coins fall out, and you know what? Let them. He spent his whole life exploiting people. It's about time everyone else had a turn."

She shakes her head. On one level, it does make sense, but something isn't quite adding up. "Phoebe already tried to give them money, remember? Ron gave it back."

"Maybe Ron isn't in on the scheme at all. This could be some weird mother-son thing, with Jake softening Phoebe up one way while Vicki worked the best friend angle. Obviously something went wrong, or Phoebe would still be alive, but they're hoping they can still cash in."

Another message from Jake: *An answer tonight would be nice. Let's just make this all go away, all right? I can make things very difficult for you. Think Jesse Bachmann.*

"Jesus," Nadia says, showing Wyatt the phone screen. "This just keeps getting worse."

"I'm telling you, just pay them the damn money. This doesn't have to be messy. If they hadn't gotten your phone, I'd say we still have a play, but their cards trump ours."

She clenches her jaw and taps the reply field to ask where they want the money sent. But no matter how hard she tries, she can't send the text. This wouldn't be the end of it. She knows this down to her toes, and Phoebe would agree with her. Maybe the Napiers wouldn't come calling again for a while, but this time next year or even a couple years from now, when that first million has run out, they'll send another text. And then another. They'll make sure she and Wyatt will never be able to rest. They'll be prisoners.

She backspaces over what she wrote and types three simple words for a reply: *Go fuck yourself.* Pressing "send" this time is a piece of cake.

Wyatt sees this, and the color drains from his face. "Way to be a team player," he says, and stalks from the room. A few seconds later, she hears ice slamming into a glass. He's pouring himself a drink. She goes after him.

"Doing it your way wouldn't have made me more of a team player."

He shakes his head. "No, but you're being reckless. Again. And now we're both going to be fucked. My way would have at least bought us time to disappear."

Another message: *I really wish you hadn't done that.*

She doesn't share that one with Wyatt. "Look, letting them lock us into a lifetime payment plan is not a solution."

"And you'd rather be in jail?"

"We aren't going to jail. I guarantee you, they're bluffing." She sounds more confident about that than she feels at the moment, but she isn't about to let them slump off in defeat, either.

He knocks back his drink. "I'm not going to wait around and find out." He walks off in the direction of his bedroom, and Nadia follows. When he tries to close the door behind him, she pushes it open. He doesn't put up a struggle.

"What are you doing?"

He pulls a suitcase out of his closet and zips it open on the bed. "I knew I'd be packing this thing eventually."

"So you're just going to run away now? At the pier, you told Phoebe we'd figure out what happened."

"I didn't tell Phoebe. I told you. And I know enough now." He pulls shirts out of the closet and tosses them into the open suitcase.

"You're a goddamn coward, you know that?"

He pulls himself up to full height, opens his mouth to say something, thinks better of it, and then shakes his head. "Forget it. It's not worth it," he mutters.

She folds her arms. "Yeah, like I said."

A fist pounding hard on the door makes them both jump and look around. Wyatt glares at her. "Well done, Miss Go Fuck Yourself."

"I'll take care of it," she says. Her voice is tough, but her guts are churning. That kind of strike on the door doesn't come from a friendly visitor.

In the front hall, she peers through the peephole. It didn't seem possible that they could slide even further off the rails than they already have, but now it seems they're dangling over an abyss. The two men standing on the porch aren't Napiers. They're cops. One of them is a uniformed officer, the other one plainclothes, with a badge hanging from a lanyard around his neck. She wouldn't exactly call his tactical vest, fatigues, and smoothly shaved head "plain," though. If the idea is to blend in with people on the street so no one thinks he's a cop, especially in Lake Forest, he's failing miserably.

"Get ready for your close-up, Mrs. Miller," Wyatt says from behind her.

CHAPTER 22

S HE OPENS THE door, putting on her concerned-but-friendly expression. "Hi. Is everything okay, officers?"

The plainclothes cop is frowning deeply, though maybe that's just his default expression. It's hard to tell with cops. "Ma'am, could you please state your name?"

"Phoebe Miller. What's this about?"

"Who is that behind you?" asks the uniformed officer. "Sir, please step out."

Wyatt appears beside her. So he ventured out instead of hiding in his bedroom. Maybe he isn't a complete coward after all. "I'm Wyatt Miller, Phoebe's husband. What can we help you with?"

"I'm Detective Bob Kelly," says the plainclothes. "And this is Officer Dustin Watson. We're with the Lake Forest police department. A call came through alerting us to a disturbance at your residence. Were you two having some sort of argument?"

She and Wyatt look at each other, matching their surprised expressions, and shake their heads. "Maybe the TV was too loud?" Nadia suggests.

"Everything's fine here," Wyatt says.

The two cops relax their postures, but only a little. Detective Kelly says, "There is another matter we'd like to discuss, if that's okay with you. May we come inside?"

Nadia raises her eyebrows. "What sort of other matter?"

"I'm afraid it's best discussed in private, ma'am, but if you don't feel comfortable speaking inside your residence, you're welcome to come down to the police station."

Movement across the street catches her eye, and she sees Jake coming out to sit on the porch. He's made a miraculous recovery from his dinnertime illness. Of course, he wants to watch his handiwork.

"No, you're more than welcome to come in." She stands aside to let them through, passing a brief glance to Wyatt, whose calm veneer is stretched so thin she can see the panic writhing underneath. If she can see it, Kelly and Watson probably do too. She leads them to the living room. "Can I get you guys anything? We just brewed up some coffee a little while ago."

"I'd like that, thank you," says the detective. "With whatever dairy you have on hand."

"Cream it is," she says, suspecting he's only accepting a refreshment to try to make this feel more like a civil gathering than an interrogation. "Would you like any coffee, Officer Watson?"

He shakes his head. "No thank you, ma'am."

Nadia and Wyatt sit on the couch together, and he puts his hand on her leg, establishing that all-important sense that they're a connected unit, when only a few minutes ago they were about to dissolve their little partnership. Kelly sits in the chair across from them and sips his coffee while Watson remains standing like a guard on watch. If his goal is to intimidate them by letting his essential "copness" permeate the space, it's working on Wyatt especially. She can feel his heartbeat through her shoulder. Taking his hand, she gives it a brief squeeze.

Kelly looks at the ottoman. "Strange place for a knife," he says.

Wyatt stiffens a bit. Nadia stifles a grin. This is a softball. All these questions can be softballs if she keeps her nerve. "I used it to open a package earlier. Wyatt hates it when I do that."

"Yeah, I keep telling her thousand-dollar knives aren't for cutting tape, but she never listens." He laughs a little. Kelly doesn't react one way or another.

"First, a little more about who I am. I'm actually a homicide detective. Watson here was assigned to the disturbance call, but I rode along."

Nadia gasps. "Homicide?"

"I've been investigating the murder of a man named Jesse Bachmann. Are you familiar with the case, by chance?"

"The name rings a bell," Nadia says. Wyatt murmurs agreement.

Kelly nods. "I figured it might. He was found stabbed at an Earthbound Foods recently. It's been in the news."

Nadia nods with recognition. "Oh jeez, yeah. I do remember hearing about that. Poor guy."

"Truthfully, he was no angel," Kelly says. "We even have reason to suspect he was involved in some unsolved sexual assault cases." He leans forward. "If you ask me, I think one of his victims got the better of him."

Nadia's jaw drops. The shock isn't an act this time. "Is that right?"

"Yes indeed. Unfortunately, we still have to do our jobs."

Nadia can feel Kelly's manipulation at work. He wants to make them feel like he's letting them in on a little secret so they'll be more comfortable opening up to him. It's a good trick, effective on people who don't know better. "But what does any of this have to do with us?" she asks. Clearly he was waiting for one of them to ask this.

Kelly sits back. "We've reason to suspect you might be connected with our main suspect, and possibly even harboring her."

Reason to suspect, huh? Did he receive an anonymous tip? From a certain recently emboldened neighbor, perhaps? She does the only thing she can do in this moment of paralysis: laugh. "That's the most ridiculous thing I've heard. Honey, I think someone must be playing a prank on us."

Wyatt chuckles too. It's a little on the shrill side, but it's natural enough for anyone to feel nervous when there are cops in their house. "Yeah, sounds like it."

"I'm not surprised, given everything that's been going on lately."

Kelly raises his eyebrows. "What do you mean?"

"Maybe you were familiar with my late father—Daniel Noble?" She's not sure how well it will work, but hopefully evoking the Noble name will inspire at least a little deference from these guys. And maybe a little sympathy too. "He's been in the news recently. Unfortunately, he seemed to share some character traits with this Jesse Bachmann. And, well, all the media coverage of his misdeeds has made my life a little eventful, as you can imagine."

Understanding fills Kelly's face. "Ah yes, that. Well, I'm sorry for your loss at any rate, ma'am."

"I'm only sorry that it's created situations like this. My father was a, well, difficult person and we were never very close, but a few people around here must still want a scapegoat."

"I understand, ma'am. Nevertheless, I must at least ask what you know about a woman named Nadia Pavlica."

Wyatt stiffens, but all the attention is on her. Kelly has been speaking only to her since he got here. And the reason feels obvious. The woman he's speaking to now and the woman he's looking for have very similar faces, and Kelly's eyes are crawling all over her features.

"I can't tell you anything, because I've never met her." The lie glides out so easily it shocks even her.

Kelly's expression doesn't change. "Are you sure? Any chance of a long-lost relation of some sort?"

She shakes her head. "Sorry, no. I can't say I'm close to my extended family, but I certainly know every member."

"I think you'll understand my insistence when you see what Miss Pavlica looks like." He holds up his phone to show them a picture. Nadia knows this picture well, because it graces her most recent driver's license. Pale skin, dark hair, gaunt like she's just on this side of malnourished, smudged eyeliner. It looks more like a mug shot of a drunk hooker.

"See a resemblance to someone you know?" Kelly asks.

Nadia peers a bit closer and then acts like she finally gets it. "Oh, I see. Well that's a little unsettling, isn't it, babe? Look at her."

Wyatt examines the picture with a pursed mouth and then grunts. "Yeah, I guess she does look a little like you, if you were younger and going through a Goth phase."

"She was last known to have blond hair. Would that change anything about your recollection?"

"I'm afraid not," she says.

"And you're sure you don't have a sister?" he asks her.

She laughs. "I'm sure if I did, I'd know it. Everyone hated Daniel, but they all want a piece of the Noble estate."

Kelly sighs and puts his phone away. "I study faces a lot in this job. I see some dead ringers now and then, but it's just uncanny, the resemblance between you two. The only thing different is the hair."

A frightening thought occurs to her. Can he ask for DNA or prints based on a hunch or a phoned-in tip? She doesn't think he can, but if he does, she knows the game will really be over. "It's pretty incredible," she agrees. "But it's also creepy. I don't like the idea of having a doppelgänger who runs around town stabbing people."

"Well, we don't know for sure if she's done that. We'd just like to talk to her." He pulls a card from one of his vest pockets and hands it to her. "If you do see her or think of anything else that would help us out, would you call that number? It goes right to my cell."

She takes the card with numb fingers. "Of course."

As she leads the men to the door, Kelly says, "You know, we've actually met before, but I doubt you remember."

"Oh really?" she asks, dreading the prolonging of this engagement.

"Your dad used to hold fund-raising events for the police department way back in my rookie days. He always brought this pretty blonde with him that I assumed was some young girlfriend or hired eye candy. But that was you, wasn't it?"

Her grin feels frozen in place. "It might have been."

He nods. "Yeah, it definitely was. I remember now. All the single guys were determined to get a dance with you. You even danced with me once, though I think I stepped on your toes a few times."

She has no idea if any of this is true, but she suspects Kelly isn't one to give up until he uses every tool in his kit, including making up an anecdote to trap her in a lie. "My dad dragged me out to a lot of events back then. They all kind of blur together in my memory. I think it's when I developed my hatred for dresses and high heels. But I'm sure dancing with you was the highlight of the evening for a young woman who probably secretly wanted to be anywhere else." She opens the door to let them out. Jake is still sitting on his porch, though Vicki has since joined him, because of course she has.

Once he's outside, Kelly turns around. "Like I said, ma'am, if you can think of anything at all, I'd appreciate a call."

"Okay. Be safe out there." She watches them walk back toward their cruiser and then waves at Jake and Vicki before closing the door and locking it behind her. "That was fun."

Wyatt looks at her like a stern, merciless general who's surveyed the battlefield and knows he's lost. "Go pack your bags. This is over."

"We aren't going anywhere."

"That cop saw right through you. He'll probably be back with a warrant for your DNA and to search this place in the morning, if not sooner."

"Oh come on. He has no evidence for a warrant! What, that I look kind of like the girl he's looking for? A judge will laugh him out of the building."

He rolls his eyes. "Your capacity for wishful thinking is astounding."

"Listen, the improbability of this whole situation is what's keeping us safe right now. No one would believe it if you told them."

"Are you paying attention? We're not safe at all! Those people across the street killed Phoebe. They have pictures of us with her body. They know who you are, and now they're looking to get paid. The building is on fire and the whole thing is about to come down on our heads. We were stupid to stick around this long."

Phoebe's phone rings. Nadia doesn't so much as twitch. She's been waiting for a call ever since she closed the door behind Detective Kelly and his trusty mule. "Hold that thought," she tells Wyatt, and then answers, putting the call on speaker. "Well hi, Vicki." She lays on the saccharine extra thick.

"Hey, is everything okay over there?"

She rolls her eyes. After all this, the woman still wants to put on an act? "No one's been arrested or shot if that's what you were hoping for."

Dead silence from the other end. *Come on, Vic. My mask is off. How about you take off yours now?* Finally, a long sigh, and then in a low voice, almost a whisper, "This isn't at all what I was hoping for."

"Oh come off it," Nadia snaps.

Wyatt puts his hand on her shoulder with a gaze that says, *Easy.* "How can we fix all this, Vicki? Let's just talk it through." He speaks clearly and calmly, like a hostage negotiator, which the situation almost seems to warrant. Except, of course, he's one of the hostages.

Another long silence, and then, "Come over here tomorrow. We can talk then."

Nadia snorts. "You think a third awkward hangout will be the charm? How do I know you aren't planning some kind of ambush?"

"I swear to you I'm not!" she cries. "I just need a little time to pull myself together, all right? Wouldn't you say we both need that? So no one else gets hurt?"

Nadia sighs. "Okay, then. Tomorrow evening?"

"Sure. Six o'clock."

"Six it is." Nadia hangs up. "There we go, our one chance to handle this extremely fucked-up situation like adults. I'm sure it'll be great, like a meeting between rival gang members."

Wyatt shakes his head. "I still think our best option is to bail right now."

She goes to him and puts her hands on his shoulders. "Either we try to settle this now, or we take a chance that they scorch the earth at our backs so we have no choice but to run for the rest of our lives. I don't know about you, but I want to be free, or at least if it all goes to hell over there, to be able to say we took a chance." He begins to speak, but she overrides him. "Listen. You were totally right earlier. The building is on fire and it's all about to come down. But you're forgetting that *we* can be the fire too."

She's amused to discover her hands haven't moved from his shoulders after several seconds, and that, for the moment anyway, she likes them there. The simple act of calming touch, the barest hint of human intimacy, brings her a stillness she hasn't felt in so long she'd forgotten she ever needed it. Wyatt too, from the way he's closing his eyes and letting out a soft sigh. His muscles, pleasantly solid but too tight with tension, are smoothing out just a little beneath her hands. *I'm doing that*, she thinks, warming to the idea that she can both bring him pleasure and take pleasure from it in return. Acknowledging both the existence of an attraction and the barrier she'd built around it, out of respect to Phoebe, to herself.

But is she misreading all of this? It's possible. They're exhausted, a pair of flags made threadbare from an endless storm of anxiety. Maybe if she caresses just a little more . . . only to be sure.

As her hands begin to gently knead, he opens his eyes and fixes them on hers. He also doesn't pull away. A low heat has crept into his dark gaze, quickening her heart to a gallop. After a moment, his hands move to her hips, drawing her in more.

They're now in the thick of a new physical awareness, which, in this brief moment of calm, before everything goes sailing over the edge of a cliff tomorrow, doesn't exactly feel wrong. Yet enough of her sanity still remains that she hesitates. "This would be a bad idea," she says. "For more reasons than I can count."

He looks down, nodding. "I know."

His voice is low, rough, yet she heard a silent "but" after those two words, one that says in a slew of bad decisions that have brought them both to this point, there are also worse things they could do. One expressing a yearning for escape, a craving for the luxury of vulnerability, even if it's just a tiny taste, before they get back to the grim business of survival. He closes his eyes again and seems to pause for a beat, as if to ask himself if he's really sure, and then he kisses her. She holds back at first, questions flowing through the turnstile in her mind. *Do I really want this? Can I trust him? Does this even feel good?*

The answers are all yes. For now. Nadia finally allows herself to open, anchoring herself to the present, melding her body against his. In a language neither of them expected to speak to each other, they declare a bond.

CHAPTER 23

"H OW DO YOU see this all going down?" he asks her.

He's lying on his back, staring at the ceiling, covered in a bare minimum of white top sheet and the shadows from the window blinds falling across his chest. Nadia, clad only in the black T-shirt she was wearing before their interlude began last night, is sitting up against the headboard sipping a cup of coffee, legs crossed. They blindly fumbled their way to his room once the kissing began, and they haven't left it since, except to fill their mugs and grab a bite to eat from the kitchen. They're low on groceries, but they remembered the leftovers from their roast beef dinner gone awry the evening before, and they ate them cold.

The sex seems to have fulfilled its therapeutic purpose. They're calmer and more comfortable around each other. Pent-up angst has given way to a smooth pragmatism about what difficult duties lie ahead. There's no telling how long this will last, though she hasn't objected to additional "treatments" throughout the night, and would continue to accept them if they live beyond tonight. She senses the feeling is mutual, even if she's curious to know who Wyatt thinks he slept with: Nadia or Phoebe. And on the heels of that comes another question, this one for herself. Who does she really want to be? Hopefully there will be time to figure that out later. For now, she stows those queries away to focus on his more pertinent one.

"They're going to ask for money. Either we pay them or we don't. You know my feeling on it."

"Now would be the time to let me know whether you plan to tell them to go fuck themselves. I'd like the opportunity to source a bulletproof vest."

"Caving to extortion will only empower them."

"We don't negotiate with terrorists, yeah, yeah, I get it."

"Look, you're the shrink among us. Why don't you use some of your mind juju to talk them down off of whatever ledge they're on?"

"You have a lot of confidence in my abilities."

She casts him a small grin. "I didn't say that. I'm just saying it's an option." After a moment's contemplation, she asks, "Do you have a gun?"

"Well, that escalated quickly."

"I hate the things, myself, but even I know we shouldn't go over there unarmed." Money, murder, and emotions make for a volatile mix. Add in that demands have already been made, and she would be surprised not to see a Napier pull a weapon over there.

"I have a stun gun at the office. Phoebe bought it for me, thinking I'd need protection from my clients, which I always thought was ridiculous. I never even took it out of the box. Anyway, her perception on these things was skewed. Like most people's."

"I'd probably shoot my foot off with a real gun anyway," she says. "Stun gun should be fine. I still have my knife too."

"And you do know how to use it." He glances at her. "Just saying."

"That was blind luck. I was just trying to get him off of me." She turns fully to him. "You do believe me about that, right? You never really said one way or the other . . ."

He stares at the sheets for a moment. "I wasn't sure at first, to be honest. But I believe you now."

"Because of what that detective said about him?"

"No. I didn't need his help. After the past few days I've just seen enough to think you wouldn't do something like that without having a damn good reason."

She sighs. "Thank you. I hope I never have to do anything like that again. Even if I had a reason, the experience was . . . awful."

He rubs her shoulder. "I know. But I think we can avoid violence if we're careful. The Napiers aren't hardened criminals. They're just terrified, stupid humans trying to survive."

"That's a good point. Maybe you can bring that up during tonight's therapy session, that we're all just stupid humans here." She slips back under the covers again. He's so close and still mostly naked. It's tempting to touch him again, but she hesitates, both unsure of what he wants and unwilling to risk rejection. But he scoots closer, opening the door for her, and she rolls over to study him. Their faces are only a couple of inches apart, their bodies nearly overlapping. She likes feeling his warmth down the entire length of her body. His eyes seem to darken as he places his hand on her bare hip, giving it a light squeeze. "We still have some time to pass before this nightmare begins," he says. They pass it.

———

JUST BEFORE SIX, Nadia and Wyatt step out their front door, not as husband and wife, or even boyfriend and girlfriend, but as partners of a different breed. The house across the cul-de-sac, with its stone façade surrounded by trim landscaping and lush, mature trees, is well lit and inviting to anyone who doesn't know any better.

Nadia is wearing a white tank top, skinny jeans, and the black pleather jacket she carried over from her old life, pieces that define her more than Phoebe's designer duds ever could. If the idea is to approach the Napiers without pretense, to be real, then she has to be Nadia. It didn't take long for the cheap, rough fabric to rub away at her new softness and find the callused girl still living underneath. But that's not necessarily a bad thing, either. She feels an evolution taking place within her, one that's merging parts of herself with her sister. Staying blond, for instance, and enjoying some of the finer things in life, but embracing the Indiana farm girl's rougher edges rather than covering them up. This is still Phoebe's story, but Nadia is the storyteller now, and she has to do them both justice.

Wyatt takes her hand. "You're trembling."

She looks at him. His eyes are a little bloodshot from the lack of sleep, but he's cleaned up nicely in a pair of black slacks and a dark gray button-down with the sleeves rolled up to his elbows, what he called his "therapist fatigues." Their styles couldn't be more different, but somehow it still works together. "I think we're both a little shaky."

He takes a deep breath. "I think you're right."

"As long as that stun gun of yours is charged, we should be fine."

"You're assuming I know how to use it."

"This probably wasn't the best time for you to bring that up."

"At least you still have your knife."

She grips his hand tight. "Let's go."

As they draw closer to the Napier house, a curious change begins to take hold. She stands up taller. Her shaking subsides. For the first time really in weeks, she's able to breathe fully. It's the realization she doesn't have to pretend anymore, not for these people, anyway. What she's feeling is liberation.

"Okay, act natural," Wyatt says. He rings the doorbell.

■ ■ ■

I T'S HAPPENING. The brake lines have been cut, the car has been pushed down the hill, and we're all careering toward the bottom. Will I walk away from this? Will anyone? That endless scream is still trapped inside my body, and I think soon it's going to find its way out. But just underneath that scream, I hear something that sounds like a lullaby. It's faint but growing louder and sweeter by the moment. It's telling me to stop struggling, to let go and accept whatever happens. Did you hear that lullaby too, at the very end? I think you're the one singing it.

CHAPTER 24

NADIA IS BEGINNING to believe she's a magnet for death as she stares down at a third dead body lying in a pool of blood in the space of a month.

The four of them who are still alive have to be ready to explain what happened here, but in the chaos of blood, death, agonized sobs, so many overlapping stories and lies, and the lingering whiff of gunpowder, she can't get everything to jell, and if she can't, how will the rest of them be able to? It's all too much this time.

Panic has been a big, bad wolf beating hard at her door for so long, demanding entry. The structure she's built around her has been stable enough, but it can't take much more. Once it breaks through and has her in its hungry jaws, this little plan of hers, tenuous from the start but still better than any of the alternatives were, will dissolve into failure, and her life will be over before it ever has a chance to start. She and Phoebe seem to have that in common.

But there's still a whisper of her pragmatic self left. *Forget five minutes from now. Forget even right now. Let's just walk through it from the beginning. One mess at a time, Nadia. Remember?*

She grabs on to that thought like the trusty life preserver it has always been and closes her eyes.

THE NAPIER HOUSE hasn't changed at all since Nadia was last in it nearly twenty-four hours ago, but somehow it feels emptier as she and Wyatt step over the threshold, like a tumbleweed might blow by any minute. Vicki leads them to a large dining room—not quite as large as the Millers', though with the potential to be equally impressive if someone actually decorated it. It's currently an empty box, save for a small, round table and five metal folding chairs. Ron and Jake are already seated.

There is no food or drink, or any other pretense of hospitality. That said, Vicki does seem to be choosing her steps carefully as she goes to her seat. She must have liquored herself up a little beforehand. Both Ron and Jake look a bit glazed over too. Come to think of it, Wyatt also took a few long swallows of whiskey before they left. Is Nadia the only person in this room with a full set of wits?

"Please sit down," Vicki says.

Nadia can't resist a little sarcasm. "Another gathering around a table? This is starting to feel like déjà vu."

Vicki offers a cold smirk. "Gosh, I guess we should have had a pool party instead."

"Come on, just sit," Wyatt urges her gently.

Nadia acquiesces, and an agonizing minute proceeds where no one speaks; they simply pass glances as if they're playing a game of hot potato. Enough already. "Are we just going to sit here and stare at one another all night?"

"Hardly," Vicki says. "I see you have a purse with you. Empty it on the table."

"Why are you running this show?" she asks.

She tilts her head. "I have you dead to rights, *Nadia*. Stop thinking you can wiggle your way out of this, and empty the goddamn purse."

"Okay, fine. No need to get worked up." Nadia unzips the bag and upends it on the table in front of her. Out tumble all the things she transferred over from the purse Phoebe had been using, and some additional odds and ends Nadia added on her own, like her favorite lip balm and chewing gum. "No weapons, if that's what you're so worried about." Her trusty knife is in her jacket pocket. Wyatt has the stun gun. No one had quite the forethought to pat them down.

"I'm not worried about that." Vicki reaches behind her and pulls out something her billowy blouse was concealing before. It's a shiny, black snub-nose revolver that fits perfectly into her graceful hands. In the stunned silence that follows, Jake's troubled murmur of "Oh God, Mom" might as well be a shout.

Ron is more direct. "Jesus Christ, Vicki! Where did you get a gun?"

Vicki ignores them both and points the barrel square at Nadia. "You see that brown leather checkbook? I want you to show me those princess kittens inside and write a nice seven-figure number. After that, I'll give you your phone back, and we can all go about our business. I don't even care who you really are at this point. I just want my life back the way it was."

Nadia doesn't move. "That's it? That's what all this has been about this whole time? Why does every murder always have to come down to money? It's so tacky."

Her eyes narrow. "That's rich, considering the pictures of both of you with her body."

She knew Vicki would be quick to bring that up, but she isn't going to let it knock her back. "Why did you have Jake do your dirty work, anyway? Having him send those texts when you could have done it yourself. That's also pretty tacky."

Vicki flinches. Nadia logs a point for herself.

"She didn't make me send them," Jake says. His face is gaunt, filled with shadows. "I already knew she wanted money. I was just trying to finish it so we wouldn't all end up here, like this."

"Yes, like this," Ron pipes up. "With you two accusing us of murder. Who the hell do you think you are?"

"Oh, forgive me," Nadia snaps. "You're only guilty of extortion and trying to profit from a murder, is that it? I guess it's possible she just accidentally wound up dead in a pool of blood on her kitchen floor, that a knife just magically—"

"Nadia, stop it," Wyatt cuts in. "None of this is helping." He looks at Vicki. "We came here to see if we could end this whole ugly affair amicably without anyone else getting hurt. Can we all agree that this is our goal?"

Everyone around the table nods, though Ron adds, "For the record, I think you're all fucking insane."

Vicki rolls her eyes. "Duly noted, doctor. Now can the adults please proceed?"

"Excuse me?" Ron says. "After the mess you've made of everything, I'd hardly call you the adult in the room."

"Yes, but *I'm* holding the gun, so I think I outrank you."

"All right, that's enough!" Wyatt looks irritated, but he takes a deep breath and proceeds. "Now, Vicki, could you please stop pointing the gun? If it accidentally goes off, we'll all be in even more trouble. Hospitals have to report gunshot wounds to the police, and we don't want that, do we?" He's speaking gently, like a therapist. And it seems to be working, because Vicki slowly lowers the gun and sets it on the table in front of her. Nadia would prefer it was out of the room entirely, but at least it isn't pointed at her.

"This is good, very good," Wyatt says. "Now, it's clear you need financial help. We just want some answers. I'm pretty sure we can work this out so we all walk away happy, or at least satisfied."

Miraculously, Wyatt seems to have taken control of the situation, but he's being crushingly naive if he believes this will end so neatly. Nevertheless, this was the plan they agreed on. He'll play the diplomat. She'll be here to ferry them to safety when things finally blow up.

"This isn't about cashing in," Vicki says. "I'm not going to let you cheapen it like that."

Nadia asks, "So then why the move to Lake Forest, to this particular house, no less? Why target Phoebe specifically? You saw her family in the news lately and thought she'd be easy to milk for money, is that right?"

Vicki sighs and rubs her temple. "Ron, please get the pictures from the mantel for me."

He looks at her like she just asked him to make a soufflé. "Are you serious? *All* the pictures? There are dozens of them."

"You know the ones I'm talking about! God, why can't you be supportive and do what I ask just once without fighting?"

His face reddens, and he looks like he's going to unleash a nasty retort, but his eyes flit down to the gun on the table and that's enough to bring him around. He leaves the room, and half a minute later returns bearing an unwieldy armload of picture frames.

"Arrange them down the middle facing the two of them," Vicki orders. When she sees that Ron isn't working to her satisfaction, she grumbles to herself and stands up. "Just let me do it. You never appreciated why this was important to me, anyway." She spends the next minute or so swapping the order of the pictures, apparently so they can demonstrate some kind of narrative.

When she finally stands back, she gestures toward the far left end. "They say a picture's worth a thousand words. For me, it's only a start. This is a condensed version of my life story. A visual aide, if you will. I want you to start with my childhood and then work your way up to the present. By the time you reach the last one, this should all make a lot more sense to you."

Nadia wants to chide her for being so dramatic, but her curiosity gets the better of her, and she begins with the first picture, which features a young dark-haired girl of about four, sitting on a woman's lap. Presumably, this is Vicki and her mother. It's hard to miss the matching hair, eyes, noses, and chins. Next, she sees snaggle-toothed Vicki a few years down the line sitting in front of a birthday cake with a candle shaped like the number seven on top. Mom is peeking in from the right side of the frame, both thumbs raised, all smiles. Then there's Vicki around the age of nine or ten dressed for a ballet recital, all dolled up in her pink tutu, her hair pulled back tight into a bun, cheeks rouged bright pink, clutching a small bouquet of white roses while her kneeling mother beams proudly beside her. Nadia is starting to sense a theme. Vicki really loves her mom. She keeps going.

The next frame features Vicki in her awkward acne-and-braces years, but she's still pretty in a pink taffeta monstrosity of a dress. Maybe freshman homecoming? Next to her is a woman in a wheelchair, unsmiling, staring off into space, withered to a husk with her talonlike hands bunched up at her chest. Recognition hits Nadia like a hammer to the head. This is Vicki's mother. Something happened to her between her daughter's middle school years and high school. And unlike in the other pictures, Vicki's smile looks almost sewn on.

It's the same for the rest of the pictures down the line, from Vicki's prom to her high school graduation, and finally her wedding. Mom is there in all of them, a wraith in a wheelchair positioned just behind and off to the side of her daughter, as if haunting her.

It all makes some kind of sense in how it demonstrates Vicki's emotional fragility, but it doesn't really achieve that perfect narrative magic until the final picture, which whisks the observer back in time, so that they can understand how the promising story of a young girl's life could evolve into this current nightmare. There's Vicki's mother in her prime, resplendent in a red off-the-shoulder cocktail dress, her raven hair—which reminds Nadia painfully of her own mother's—styled in the feathered puff that was popular for the time. She's raising a champagne flute, her nails and lips lacquered the same shade of red as the dress. Standing beside her—a handsome gentleman who needs no introduction, because he turned out to be no gentleman at all—is Daniel Noble.

"She was a brilliant engineer," Vicki says when Nadia picks up the picture for a closer look. "Graduated at the top of her class from

MIT and started with Noble Industries as an intern. She spent years working her way up the ladder, which for women of that time was no easy feat. And of course, he only sees the skirt and what's under it. I didn't learn about all that until years later, from the aunt I went to live with in California when my father couldn't take caring for an invalid wife anymore and shipped us both out there. I never saw him again. When I was fifteen, my aunt told me everything about Mom's affair with Daniel, and that she'd become pregnant and then had an abortion at his insistence, so she could maintain her status with the company, and—let's face it—him."

Nadia is reminded painfully of her own mother's similar experience with Daniel, and wonders how many other unwitting Noble half-siblings there might be, or could have been, in the world.

"Only the procedure didn't go as planned," Vicki continues. "They punctured her uterus and she nearly bled to death. Then she went into cardiac arrest and was starved of oxygen for several minutes. The doctors had the nerve to claim they'd saved her life. I guess living out the rest of your life with such severe brain damage you're basically a turnip was good enough for them." She laughs. "But one thing I can say for Daniel is he sure knew how to pay his debts. He quietly kept the money coming for her care for nearly thirty years. One of the best facilities in California. But we all know from the news that he didn't have a plan to keep his hush money flowing after he died. The bills started coming to me almost immediately. Maybe that was his plan. 'Hey, I'm outta here. You deal with it now, suckers!'"

Nadia and Wyatt sit silently as Vicki delivers this stunning summation. A million questions swirl around Nadia's mind, but none of them feel quite formed enough to bring into the world. Then Vicki says, "And you could argue that Daniel's responsibilities should end when his life does. Why should his family continue to pay for his sins? I agreed. When the bills first started coming to me, I paid them. I was mad, but I didn't want to be vindictive. I just wanted to live my life and take care of my family. Besides, my husband is a big-shot neurosurgeon, right? We can swing this. But then, of course, that neurosurgeon turned out to be a butcher of patients." She flings those last two words at her husband like fecal matter. He winces accordingly.

"I watched your drinking get worse year after year, Ron. I begged you to get help. I threatened to leave, but you knew I couldn't, because I had *everything* tied up in you." Her voice cracks, and she swipes the tears from her eyes. Ron keeps his mouth shut for once. Maybe he's feeling especially wary given the gun on the table.

Vicki turns her gaze to Jake. "So I focused everything I had on you. I made sure you had a good future waiting, that you got into a great school. I pushed you hard to earn a tennis scholarship, even though you always asked why we couldn't just pay for school ourselves like all your other rich friends. But I didn't want you to know how shaky things were getting, that your father was in serious trouble at work and was being investigated after his second botched operation. I didn't want you to know that I couldn't shake this feeling that things weren't going to end well for us . . . But you were all set, Jake. I pushed you to greatness, even though you threw it all away." Jake, red-eyed, opens his mouth to speak, but she holds up her hand. "Don't. Just don't."

"We know Ron lost his license to practice in California," Wyatt says, finding his voice. "And about the patients who were hurt."

Vicki nods. "I guess it would all be public record, wouldn't it? It took a couple years for it all to happen, but right around the time Daniel Noble was taking his last gasps, the medical board decided Ron was finished practicing in California. They also imposed a stiff financial penalty due to the costs of the investigation. With all our debts and legal expenses, we were wiped out basically overnight. But then Ron swooped in to save the day he'd helped ruin by getting a job with one of his old pals back here, with the promise he wouldn't turn any more of his patients into corpses or quadriplegics." She looks at him. "Good thing you got licensed to practice in other states back when your record was still clean, honey. I always wondered why you bothered, but it's like you always knew you would need an escape hatch."

"Vicki, goddamn it," Ron warns through gritted teeth, breaking his silence.

She places her hand on the pistol and looks at him. "Do you really want to challenge me on this right now?"

He slumps back in his seat. Vicki turns again to Nadia and Wyatt. "The job didn't pay nearly as much, and we had to leave my mother behind, but Ron insisted we'd get over the hump and we'd bring her out here when the time was right. I wasn't so sure, so I presented him with another idea. If we're coming back to this hellhole, why don't we get in touch with the Nobles, explain our situation with Mom. We can at least keep her in the place she's been all these years. It's only right since, you know, it's Daniel's fault she's there to begin with, and unlike the others looking for a piece of the pie, she has actual medical needs."

"That sounds fair," Wyatt says neutrally.

Vicki tosses up her hands. "Thank you! But tell that to my husband here. He thought it was a terrible idea."

"It was," Ron mutters. "I didn't want anything to do with their money, and you of all people shouldn't have, either."

"Oh, *you* didn't want anything to do with it. Because it's all up to you, right? It didn't matter that we were in a crisis of your making. You couldn't bend even a little. When Ron speaks, we're all supposed to just shut up and obey. Is there a diagnosis for something like this, Wyatt? Is it some form of narcissism?"

Wyatt treats the question as rhetorical and says nothing.

"Anyway, I was done letting him hold the reins after the ditch he'd run us into. I took initiative. Of course, there was no getting through to anyone at Noble Industries after the media shitstorm started over their fallen god, and I didn't want to get myself caught up in the tangle of accusers, either, especially given Ron's recent professional woes. So I came up with a different plan. Using most of what liquidated resources we had left, I got us this house. I drove a hard bargain and made it happen. Hell, I could practically be a Noble myself for how ruthless I was. I researched, planned, and rehearsed."

Nadia feels a little sick at how similar this sounds to her own mind-set as she geared up for her journey to Lake Forest. Phoebe had probably thought she was at a safe enough distance from the storm of events her father's death had triggered. Meanwhile, here sit two people who had her directly in their sights because of it, if for different reasons.

"When I met Phoebe, I knew it was going to be perfect, because I actually liked her right off the bat. It surprised me. I expected this cold, stuck-up fish. But she was just cool, you know?" She directs this at Wyatt, expecting him to echo her in agreement, but all he can do is continue to stare at his hands. "Of course, she didn't tell me she was Daniel's daughter at first, but who could blame her given what people have been saying?"

"So how did you go about asking her for the money?" Nadia asks.

Vicki shakes her head. "That didn't go at all how I planned. Every conversation we had, I kept looking for the right opening, but never quite found it. It always seemed too soon or like the mood wasn't right. Then other drama started getting in the way. This house ended up needing a ton of work. The remainder of our money was draining faster than my already dwindling patience. But I was also on borrowed time with Mom and the nursing home, so I couldn't put it off too much longer."

Despite her feelings of bitterness, Nadia can't help but relate. She nods quietly.

"But I finally achieved success," Vicki continues. "As we got closer, I told Phoebe about some of our recent struggles. I didn't mention Daniel's connection to my mother, but I didn't need to. The problems with the house, my marital stress, and Ron's professional setbacks seemed to be enough to inspire her to help out. She wrote me a check before I ever had to ask. It wasn't going to solve all our problems, but it could catch us up with the nursing home, at least, and maybe we could breathe a bit. But then I made a very big mistake." She turns a withering look on Ron. "I told my husband. I should have just quietly cashed that check and taken care of things, but I had to gloat a little. I thought I'd earned it. And what does he do? He gives the goddamn money *back*!"

"I wasn't going to let you just . . . whore out our family for a handout!" Ron shouts. "I was getting us back on our feet."

Vicki laughs and gestures at her barren surroundings. "Is this what you call 'being back on our feet'? Sitting in an empty house with the bills piling up, and you still swilling booze night after night?" She shakes her head. "Whoring out our family. Nice choice of words, considering what was going on behind my back. I'm sure that's why she really wrote that check."

She looks at Wyatt, her gaze hardening. "Did you know what Phoebe and my son were up to?" Jake winces as the subject of the affair is finally broached.

Wyatt only shakes his head. The therapist in him has gone into hiding as the situation has escalated well above his pay grade. Though the doctor in the room doesn't seem much better equipped to handle it.

"She had us all fooled, I guess," Vicki mutters.

"Mom, please stop this." Jake has never looked or sounded more like a scared little boy since Nadia met him.

Vicki doesn't seem to hear him. "Phoebe once said her father didn't care much for her, but I'm sure he would have been proud of her for going after a teenager."

"Shut up!" Jake cries.

That gets through at least. Vicki gives a small, pained flinch, but she fixes her gaze on Nadia. "She was going to run away with my son! She knew he was all I had left that mattered. I admit that I came into this whole thing with an agenda. But I also came to see her as a friend, and I was so sure she felt the same about me. Her level of betrayal . . . I still can't wrap my mind around it. How could she look me in the eye day after day, and then turn around and sleep with my *son*?"

"So you killed her because of it," Nadia says. "You discovered she and Jake were about to run away together and it set you off."

Vicki is momentarily speechless and can only shake her head.

Nadia rolls her eyes. "Will you just come off it already? You've spent all this time detailing every single excuse you had for killing her. Money, anger, revenge, et cetera. So why not just admit it?"

"You have no idea what you're talking about!" Vicki shouts, finally finding her words.

"It was an accident," Jake says, bringing all the eyes in the room to him. Vicki freezes in place alongside an equally shocked Ron. Nadia and Wyatt trade a glance, but neither seems inclined to interrupt. After a long, shaky breath, Jake forges ahead. "Phoebe was running late giving me the green light to come over that morning so we could go to the airport. My guess was something was going down between Wyatt and her." He glances at Wyatt, but only for a second. "I got tired of waiting and decided to head over anyway. When I walked in, Mom was there."

Vicki jumps in. "I went over to check on Phoebe after I saw Wyatt drive off like his hair was on fire." Wyatt's jaw clenches, but he doesn't try to defend himself. "Jake came in through the kitchen door and I saw the luggage he was carrying—it didn't take long for me to put it all together with their guilty looks, but it wasn't like either of them really denied it. I told Jake to go home. He tried to argue, but I convinced him I deserved to speak to Phoebe, my closest friend, about this alone."

Jake shakes his head. "That isn't really how it happened, Mom.

Stop trying to take me out of the equation." He turns away from Vicki and focuses on Nadia, probably because it's less awkward for him than talking to his dead lover's husband. "I admitted everything, that Phoebe and I were in love, that we were leaving town together. Mom blew up. I'd seen her and my dad throw down at home a lot over the years, screaming at each other, sometimes getting a little physical. But that was the first time she'd turned that anger on me." He looks at both of his parents, who are suddenly studying the pattern of wood grain on the table. Neither of them denies it.

"She started screaming at Phoebe first, though. But when Phoebe could say nothing other than how sorry she was, Mom only got angrier. She didn't want to listen. I think she wanted to fight. I got in between them to try and break it up." Perhaps unconsciously, he rubs at the remnants of the scratches on his neck. "That's when Mom turned on me, telling me to get out and go home so she could settle this with Phoebe herself, but I refused to back down. She pushed me a few times. Then I pushed her back." His chin trembles.

"Jake . . ." Vicki murmurs.

He looks at his mother, his face brimming with heartbreak. "I told you I was done letting you control me, that Phoebe and I were both adults who'd made a decision. But that only made you angrier. Your arms just started flying at me."

Hence the scratches, Nadia thinks. Vicki covers her face, overcome with shame. Ron looks at his wife with a mix of shock and distaste. A faint "My God, Vic," is all he can manage at first, as if he's only a bystander who didn't play any role in the eventual breakdown of his wife. Nadia itches to slap him herself. He takes a breath. "You told me he fell into some bushes on one of his runs."

"Then Phoebe stepped in and told me to get out," Jake continues, looking at no one again, his voice roughening. "She'd been taking Mom's side, but Mom only rounded on her again. Then it all just . . ." He trails off.

Vicki rubs her face with a trembling hand, streaking her eye makeup. "I was so out of my mind. It didn't matter anymore that I had been counting on her for help. That ship had sailed. All I could see was this woman who had made a fool out of me, taken my son, ruined me like her father had ruined my mother. She was Daniel Noble all over again. The rage was overwhelming." She takes a deep breath, as if to compose herself. "She tried to get away. I chased after her. And then sh-she slipped. I think there must have been something wet on the floor."

"Spilled coffee," Wyatt grates out, eyes closed.

"She fell hard," Vicki continues. "Her head hit the corner of that heavy granite countertop. The crack was so loud. It happened so fast. I didn't realize it at first, but when I really looked I saw she was hurt . . . bad."

"Okay, I think I've heard enough," Wyatt says. His skin looks like wet paper, like he's about to throw up.

But Nadia isn't done yet, because as close as Vicki has gotten, she still hasn't finished the story. "It happened so fast that you then grabbed a knife and plunged it into her chest to finish the job?"

"*What?*" Jake leaps up as if burned, his face blazing.

Vicki looks at her son, wide-eyed and tear-streaked. "It didn't—"

"That's why you ran me out of there? You said you didn't want me to see how bad it really was . . . and so I left. Like a coward. I'll never forgive myself, but I was so scared, and I didn't want to fight with you anymore. And you came home a few minutes later and told me she'd fallen, that there was nothing we could do for her."

"She did! There wasn't!" Vicki cries.

"And you swore me to secrecy. Told me if I said anything about this, it would ruin everything for me. You said I needed to move on, act like we'd never even met the Millers."

Vicki shakes her head. "I was protecting you, Jake."

Wyatt gives Nadia a brief glance. He hasn't looked this grim since he discovered Phoebe's dead body, but there's something else in his eyes. He turns to Vicki. "Stop denying what you did. You got this far into the story, so just finish it. I was ready to believe everything you said until you left out one crucial detail. You stabbed her."

She shakes her head. "No, I didn't."

"You did," he insists.

Vicki collapses to her chair and starts rocking back and forth, racked with shuddering sobs. "That's not how it happened. Jake, you have to believe me!"

"Stop *lying*!" Wyatt snaps.

"We found Phoebe's butcher knife in Jake's room, Vicki," Nadia chimes in. "Did you plant it there? Why would you do something like that?" Was it some vindictive twist to frame her own son if anyone happened to go searching? Or had she been hoping Jake would find it? Nadia can't imagine a mother performing such a power play on her son, but Vicki had one hell of a vendetta going all the way back to her childhood, and it had warped her mind.

"That's impossible," Vicki chokes out.

"Jesus Christ, Vicki!" Ron shouts, shaken from his previous stupor with this new revelation, his face slack with fresh horror. "What are they saying?"

Jake rocks back on his heels and grabs his chair for support. He's clearly on the ropes, like the breeze from a weak punch might knock him out. "Mom, tell me that isn't true . . ."

She shakes her head almost convulsively. "No, Jake . . . please just listen to me."

Wyatt continues, and it's as though all the pent-up grief, anger, and fear are spilling out of him all at once. He's an unstoppable force, a laser focused on Vicki. "Look, obviously you don't want your son to think even less of you than he already does. You want him to think it was an accident, and that's at least partially true. She slipped, fell, and hit her head. I buy that, even if it still doesn't paint you in the best light, since you're the reason she fell and you did nothing to help her.

"But I'm not going to let you worm your way around the rest. Phoebe and I had reached the end of our marriage, but I was still her husband and I loved her. I stared into her lifeless eyes that morning and I told her so. It was the hardest thing I've ever had to do in my life. But you know what really sucks about all this? You didn't only kill my wife and the woman your son loved. You also killed *her* sister." He thrusts a finger at Nadia. She nearly jerks in her chair with the force of it. Everyone but Vicki turns their eyes on her.

"Phoebe died before she ever got to learn she had a sibling. Nadia had been working up the nerve for weeks just to introduce herself when all this happened." He looks at Vicki again. "And for what, exactly? This selfish bullshit that you could have solved in a million better ways. Nothing you mention as justification will ever make up for what you did. Blame Daniel for what happened to your mother, sure. I even get that you feel entitled to monetary compensation, though it's pretty fucking unforgivable that you've stooped so low as to blackmail us now that you can't bleed Phoebe for money."

She shakes her head, her eyes wide and glassy. "No. You're trying to twist this and turn my family against me."

"You did that on your own, Vicki. If you can't admit the truth to me or to her sister, at least try for your son, whose only sin in this whole thing was falling for the wrong woman and then choosing unwise ways to clean up the mess *you* made." He's leaning in now, pointing a finger at Vicki.

Despite everything Vicki has done, Nadia can't help but feel a trickle of uneasiness watching Wyatt push this broken woman. She wants to cut in, pull him back, tell him they got the truth they were after, but Jake speaks first.

"I can't even look at you anymore. I'm still leaving after this. But not for Stanford. Not anywhere you can find me. I can never forgive you for this."

"Jake," she murmurs through her tears. "Please don't say that. I can't lose you too." She looks at Ron, pleading, "Don't let him do this."

Ron clears his throat, shifts his eyes between his wife and his son, and then lowers his head. "I won't stop you, son."

Jake's shoulders square more, his frown deepening as he regards his mother. "I know I was about to run away, and that she hurt you. But it wasn't all her fault. She tried to break things off, a couple times, but I convinced her not to. She was ready to leave town alone, but I begged her to take me with her, because I couldn't stand being here anymore. You were so miserable, but you tried to act like everything was normal, and that was worse than the truth. I could have told you I was leaving, but I knew you would have fought the hardest to make me stay. And I was right. You fought so hard you killed her." His voice breaks. "I know it wouldn't have been easy, but at least she'd still be alive if you'd just let us go."

Vicki's swaying in her chair like she can barely hold herself upright anymore. With the truth finally out, and her son turned against her, the fight seems to have gone out of her. "You're right. I should have let you go then. I've lost you anyway." Her voice sounds oddly flat now. She raises her head to look at her son. Nadia can't recall ever seeing such a shattered face. "Jake...honey, I'm so sorry." She grabs the gun. Both Jake and Ron scream in tandem. The report is deafening and a second later, Vicki is on the floor.

It happened so fast.

AFTER NADIA STOPS her own mind from flailing, she manages to regroup them long enough to get their stories straight before they call the police. The simpler the story, the easier it will be for them to remember it: the Millers came over to have a few drinks with their new friends the Napiers when Vicki, with no prior warning, pulled out a gun and killed herself. Before they make the call, Nadia tells Jake to retrieve her stolen cell phone. It takes a bit to motivate him through his shellshock, with his mother bleeding out on the floor, but when Nadia tells him they could all go to jail, he moves. After verifying that the incriminating pictures are no longer on Jake's phone, she asks him if the pictures were backed up anywhere. He shakes his head. Having no choice but to believe him at this point, she makes the call.

Moments after the police and paramedics arrive, they discover Vicki is still breathing.

CHAPTER 25

THEY SIT IN the hospital lounge with Jake most of the night, waiting to hear whether Vicki pulled through surgery. Even though they aren't at Northwestern Memorial, Ron can't put aside his need to be a doctor. He's spent the hours pacing the halls on his phone and consulting with the staff, likely bordering on harassing them. Anything to avoid sitting still.

Thanks to small doses of Xanax administered by his father throughout the night, Jake is in a bit of a haze but lucid enough for conversation. "Phoebe was really your sister?" he asks her long after Nadia thought he'd dozed off.

She nods. "Half sister, anyway."

He's silent for a few more minutes, then he says, "You're still going to pretend to be her, right?"

His question touches at the heart of the conflict that's been raging in Nadia since she took over Phoebe's identity. "I don't see that I have much choice. At least on paper. Not unless we want the world at large to know she's dead. And that would create a lot more problems."

"Would make more problems for you too, about that Bachmann guy."

She nods. The Xanax hasn't spaced him out completely. "Being Phoebe serves many purposes."

"I like that the world thinks she's still alive. Makes me feel kind of like she is too." A peaceful grin spreads across his face, but after a moment it falters. "Where did you guys, um, put her?"

"I think the fewer the people who know that answer, the safer she'll be," Nadia says.

He seems satisfied with that.

After a long lull, Nadia asks if he knew anything about the connection between Vicki's mother and Daniel. He shakes his head. "I never even saw that picture of Grandma and him until recently, and I still didn't make the connection. The only story I got about Grandma growing up was that she had a heart attack and suffered brain damage. I see her once or twice a year at most. It's always been really upsetting for Mom to go out there. Now I might get to know firsthand how she feels. You know, if she doesn't, um, die." His voice cracks, and he takes a swig of his bottled water.

"It's all so damn . . . sad," Nadia says. It's a small, common word but it's the only one that fits. Fucking Daniel. His work destroying multiple generations of lives will forever remain legendary, even if only a select few know the extent of the damage.

"Mom always had a hot temper. I've seen her get depressed a lot too. But I never thought she'd try to kill herself." He sniffs. "I feel like I pushed her. I shouldn't have said those things."

"Don't do that," Wyatt interjects. He's been very quiet since they got here. "She wouldn't want you to carry that burden." He sips at his vending machine coffee. It's probably his sixth cup of the night.

Jake nods. "I never thought she'd kill someone else, either."

"Pressure forces people into a lot of unlikely shapes," Wyatt replies. Nadia would bet he's tossed that line at a lot of his therapy clients over the years.

"I think I can forgive her, though," Jake says. "If she pulls through this, that's the first thing I'm going to tell her. It's going to be hard, but I can't leave her now."

"Forgiveness is definitely a process," Wyatt says. "Don't feel bad if it doesn't come to you right away."

Jake looks at him. "I don't expect you to forgive me. If Phoebe and I hadn't . . . she'd still be alive."

Wyatt shakes his head. "We can pass this buck around all day, kid. I played my own part in it."

Nadia is relieved to hear him acknowledge something that's been on her mind, particularly since Vicki grabbed that gun. Whether he meant to, Wyatt helped push the woman to the brink. Recalling the sheer forcefulness of his words makes Nadia uneasy. Then again, she's not so innocent herself. She thinks of her own attempt at blackmail, a detail that feels like another snowflake in a blizzard of circumstance at this point.

"My mom made a choice," Jake says with a sigh. "I guess we all made our choices."

"Yes. A lot of shitty ones," Nadia mutters.

A middle-aged man in scrubs, presumably a doctor, walks into the waiting room, accompanied by Ron, who looks especially grim.

They wave Jake over. "I have a bad feeling," he says, getting up. "Thank you for sitting with me, though."

Nadia and Wyatt watch him go. He seems to be shrinking back down into a small child with every step. As the surgeon speaks, Ron puts his arm around his son's sagging shoulders and they both bow their heads. Nadia doesn't need to hear the words to know Vicki didn't make it.

THEY'RE STANDING AT the curb in front of the house, a small suitcase for each of them at their feet. Only the necessities. They can buy whatever else they need when they get there. While she's planning to add a considerable amount of black to Phoebe's new wardrobe, she'll also make sure to keep a bit of pink in there too.

They aren't saying much. Part of it is exhaustion, but mostly she thinks it's nerves. They're taking a big step right now, jumping into the wider unknown, but after returning from the hospital and milling around aimlessly for the next couple of days, waiting for the relief that this was all over to finally come, they realized they had no choice. The house would never be right. The walls held too many reminders of what happened inside them, and the view across the street was sullied too. So they got to work making the sorts of arrangements people make when they're going on a vacation of indefinite length. Cutting the power, emptying the fridge, covering the furniture, stopping the mail.

But the most important of those arrangements is about to commence as they watch the truck with the flatbed trailer pull slowly up the driveway, toward the open garage door. The driver was informed ahead of time about the precious cargo he would be picking up, but when he steps out of the cab and gets a full look at the Ferrari, his mouth still falls open in awe, and he wipes his brow.

"Now, that is a sight to behold," he says. "You mind if I take a picture?"

Wyatt shrugs. "It's not ours anymore, but I won't tell if you don't."

It didn't take long for Nadia to source a private collector for the car, especially given its rarity and the fame and notoriety of its original owner. A big part of her would still love nothing more than to firebomb it with a Molotov cocktail or drive it into Lake Michigan, just out of pure spite, but she and Wyatt agreed there were more immediate needs for the kinds of proceeds a sale would bring. Most of it will be going toward starting a fund for any of Daniel Noble's accusers who need legal resources and mental health support. The move is likely to make a few waves once it goes public, but Nadia, in total Phoebe fashion, plans to shun the press if they come calling.

A small but generous portion of the sale will also be going to the Napiers. It took a lot of convincing for Ron, who wanted even less to do with the Noble money now than before, but Nadia finally got through to him by reminding him that Vicki only wanted to help her mother, and that the money was coming from selling off Daniel's most prized possession to a complete stranger, something the man would have hated. When Nadia spoke to Jake on the phone this morning, he seemed quietly optimistic. "Dad and I were thinking of going overseas."

She thought of Ron's medical malpractice issues and hoped he might decide to leave the profession behind for good now that money would be less of a concern. "So definitely no Stanford, then?"

"That feels like someone else's dream."

She wouldn't argue with that. "Just try to do something good with your life."

"I will. As long as you do something good with hers."

"I promise."

As the driver makes all the necessary connections to secure the car to the trailer, Wyatt says, "We should probably learn some Italian on the flight. There are some good phone apps for that kind of stuff now."

"Three words should cover most of my needs over there: 'pizza,' 'gelato,' and 'espresso.'"

"Amen to that."

The question she's been wanting to ask has been sitting in her mouth all day, growing larger and more restless. Time to spit it out. "Do you plan on staying in Rome long?"

"What are you really asking me?"

God, why is this so hard? Part of it is she's never learned how to properly navigate any relationship, especially ones that have any hope of being romantic. The other part is the tiny seedling of doubt still nestled firmly in the back of her mind that she's been unable to identify since the showdown in the Napiers' dining room. "In the beginning, we talked about leaving, moving on separately once things were squared away or we trusted each other. I just wondered if that's what you had in mind still."

She can feel his eyes on her and forces herself to glance up at him. He's smiling. "I was kind of hoping you'd want to stick around a little longer," he says.

She shrugs. "I mean, if that's what you want."

"What do you want?"

"I want to take it one day at a time," she says. "Maybe even just one moment at a time." *I want to make sure I'm right to trust you—to trust this.*

"I like that," he says. "I wanted to show you something, by the way." He pulls out his phone, opens the folder containing the photos, and deletes the ones that had nearly caused them a lot of trouble. "I think it's past time to get rid of those. What do you think?"

She gives him a wide grin. "Actually beat you to it already."

He lets out a relieved sigh. "Well, that's good to know." He slowly bends down to kiss her. It's the first time they've done that since before they walked to the house across the cul-de-sac. That bit of itchy doubt recedes as a new warmth floods in. Maybe this is when things start feeling better. She'll have to wait and see.

After signing the necessary documents for the tow truck driver, they watch the truck slowly drive back up the street, looking a little like a turtle with an exotic shell. "You want to get the Uber or should I?" Wyatt asks.

She's pulling out her phone when she sees another car turn onto their street, this one a late-model Ford sedan that just screams "cop." The cue-ball head of the driver confirms her suspicions, and a boulder turns over in her gut. "Shit."

"At least he's alone. That's probably a point in our favor," Wyatt says, though he's failed to scrub the worry completely out of his voice.

Detective Kelly parks at the base of the driveway, gets out, and ambles toward them. He looks friendly, but that's just part of his getup, like the tactical vest and the cargo pants. "Good morning, Detective," Nadia says, happy with the warm ease of her greeting.

He nods. "Mrs. Miller. Mr. Miller. Headed somewhere, by the looks of it?"

"We decided a little decompression was in order," Wyatt says. "Given what happened the other night."

Kelly throws a long glance at the Napier house, which already looks a little haunted with its darkened, empty windows. "Yeah, a hell of a sad thing. I've seen my share of suicides over the years, and they don't get any easier."

"Yes. I've lost a few clients in my therapy practice the same way. Her husband and son have a long road ahead of them."

Kelly nods and turns back to them. "That they do."

No one speaks for a bit, and Nadia has to fight not to shift her feet or do anything else to show her nerves. "Is this what your visit's about?" she asks.

"Oh no. Not much to investigate there, really. It was an obvious self-inflicted wound. She'd recently purchased the gun. Medical history noted some treatment for depression and anxiety. That's that."

"Gotcha," Nadia says. Which means Kelly is very likely here on a previous matter. And she's picking up that speculative vibe from him again, like he's trying to compare her features to those of the girl he's looking for. Though she's been happy to slip back into some of her old garments lately, she's grateful she selected a white blouse and black Gucci blazer from Phoebe's wardrobe today. Anything to help throw off the scent.

"Actually, I'm still on the Bachmann case, and I'm here because

I had something I wanted to run by you. It will only take a second. I know you're on your way somewhere."

This is the part where she wants to tell him she didn't have any answers for him before, so what makes him think she'll have any now, but it's just that kind of skittishness he's hoping to see. So she says, "Yeah, no problem. Anything we can do to help."

He pulls out his phone again and starts tapping the screen. "We've uncovered some pictures from Bachmann's email you might find interesting." He holds up the phone to show them the picture of a very familiar blue car. One that should still be resting under some brush on a remote Indiana farm. Nadia's mouth goes dry. "As you might be able to see, that's your house in the background. And that car? It belongs to our suspect. You can even see a silhouette, presumably hers, behind the wheel. Do you recall seeing this car parked on the street here at any point in the last month or two?"

She and Wyatt both peer closely at the picture, knowing exactly what they're seeing. "I think I've seen that car around, yeah," Wyatt says. "I see a few Executive Courier vehicles a week coming and going."

"Same," Nadia adds.

Kelly's expression is unreadable. "I was able to verify Miss Pavlica was not affiliated in any way with Executive Courier Services, so for whatever reason, she was disguising herself."

"I wonder why," Wyatt remarks.

"How often would you say you saw this car on your street?"

She shrugs. "I couldn't say. It's one of those things where you see a delivery vehicle and your brain basically forgets it."

Wyatt concurs.

Kelly shakes his head and puts away his phone. "It's just funny to me. I'm looking for a girl who is, and I know I said this before, the scariest spitting image of you that you'll find anywhere, and it turns out I find a picture of her parked out in front of your house. Not once, mind you. This Bachmann character took pictures of her over several days. It's like she had specific business on this street."

She isn't sure what more to say that would convince him of her ignorance. Nadia knows what obsession looks like, and Detective Kelly is at the start of one. If he continues down this rabbit hole, will it lead him to the truth? She doesn't think so now, but she's sure there are possibilities she hasn't yet considered, and she'll probably be working them out in her head as she crosses the Atlantic Ocean a few hours from now.

"I do wish we could be more help, Detective," Wyatt says.

He doesn't take his eyes off Nadia. "She'll turn up eventually. They usually do. And I bet she'll have a really interesting story to tell."

"I don't doubt it," she says.

Kelly wishes them farewell and walks back to his car. Nadia doesn't breathe again until it turns the corner and is out of her sight. Once it's gone, Nadia takes a deep breath and a last look around the neighborhood. Phoebe Miller doesn't live here anymore.

CHAPTER 26

Three months later

SHE SITS UP in the bed of their rented Ibiza flat to the sound of the ocean and Wyatt's light snores. She's shivering and filmed in sweat, but this isn't a sickness or fever setting in. Ever since they left the tarmac at O'Hare, Nadia has been waiting for the tight knot of unease in her stomach to slowly unwind. But the more miles they've put between themselves and Lake Forest, the more restless she's become. At first, she chalked it up to the dramatic change of lifestyle. But at last the source of her recurring little itch has revealed itself in the form of a dream, and it's more terrifying than any nightmare, because she already lived it once. She's relived it almost every night since it happened: the evening of Vicki's suicide.

A few of the details always change in the dream world. Sometimes they're in Phoebe's dining room instead, with that odd glass monstrosity of a chandelier casting sickly prisms everywhere. Sometimes Nadia stops Vicki from grabbing the gun. Sometimes it's Nadia or Ron who winds up getting shot instead.

But some details are static. Vicki lining up the picture frames on the table just so. *A visual aide, if you will.* Jake's face when he learns Phoebe had been stabbed. *That's why you ran me out of there!* Ron bowing his head when he tells Jake he's free to leave. *I won't stop you, son.* And Wyatt, at the peak of his impassioned plea for Vicki to accept the real truth of Phoebe's demise. *I loved her. I stared into her lifeless eyes and told her so.*

I stared into her lifeless eyes.

Her lifeless eyes.

There's the snag.

A question occurs to her, turning her blood to cold jelly: *But how could he have done that?* She's reminded of the voice that had slithered into her mind the night at the farm when they buried Phoebe, when she'd briefly lost contact with Wyatt and wondered if he might be lying in wait to finish her off.

The scales fall from Nadia's eyes and she sees the truth at last. Wyatt couldn't have looked into Phoebe's lifeless eyes, because Nadia had closed them herself, before he showed up. The lids almost didn't want to come down. She'd struggled with it, but they stayed closed. The memory of that sensation has never left her. He might have looked into Phoebe's lifeless *face*, but most definitely not her eyes. That cool voice returns: *Unless he'd found Phoebe before Nadia had, and turned an accident into a murder.*

Gently she gets out of their bed, desperate not to wake him. She needs space to think, to process. She throws on some clothes and heads out of the flat down to the beach. It's not unusual that she'd go for a morning stroll, so he won't come looking for her—she'll have some time to formulate a plan.

Once she's safe on the sand, the waves lapping at her toes, she turns her attention to what she knows. Now that she has some distance from her dream, she feels less certain. Perhaps Wyatt added that detail about Phoebe's eyes for extra theatrics, to really punish Vicki. But then other questions start rolling in. Like why was Vicki so up-front about everything but stabbing Phoebe? It was the one detail on which she would not budge. Wyatt said she was lying in order to make herself look better in Jake's eyes, and that made some sense. But Vicki had already gone a long way toward destroying her standing with her son, so why stop there?

And Wyatt worked so hard to manipulate Jake and Ron into believing it too. He'd taken control of the confrontation and beaten Vicki down, pulling all the right emotional strings to push her until she felt she had no other choice but to grab that gun.

But wait just wait a goddamn minute. Her more pragmatic self chimes in this time, the same self that always reminds her to take things one mess at a time. *Before you really start believing this, consider the logistics.* Wyatt left the house after his fight with Phoebe, railing at Nadia as he went. She sped away after he threatened to call the police, and went for a drive to clear her head and consider her next options. By the time she decided to turn back, almost two hours had passed. That was plenty of time for the confrontation with Vicki to occur that resulted in Phoebe's fall, and for Wyatt to also return home.

Nadia can so clearly now see Wyatt kneeling over his struggling wife and having another of the dark and tantalizing thoughts he'd morosely confessed he'd had when he shattered the coffee mug. After succumbing to that thought and staring into Phoebe's lifeless eyes, he probably wasn't sure what to do about the body, though he probably stared into those lifeless eyes for a bit. Overwhelmed with the enormity of what he'd just done, he left again to formulate a plan. Perhaps part of that plan was to make several phone calls to his dead wife to set up an alibi—right around the time Nadia showed back up and made her grisly discovery.

The snowball keeps growing as it rolls down the hill. Wyatt had an opportunity to plant the knife in Jake's room the night Ron stitched up his hand. Nadia had thought he was going to snoop around, and she'd been right. Snooping for a place to shift the second most incriminating piece of evidence. The idea that Vicki had hidden the knife in her son's room never quite sat right with Nadia, no matter how many ways she tried to make it fit.

Then, of course, Nadia helped him get rid of the biggest piece of incriminating evidence, Phoebe's body, later that night. All to Wyatt's benefit.

But there's one burning question that Nadia can't answer: *Why?* What would have pushed him to such a decision? Something had to have happened during that fight that truly enraged him. But what could have set him off in such a way to make him come back after he'd already left? Maybe they continued to fight over the phone or via text? Another memory slams home. Nadia, checking Phoebe's emails and spotting one she'd sent to Wyatt with the subject line "Good-bye." When she mentioned the email to Wyatt, he took the phone and deleted the message.

Nadia can see Phoebe, fresh from her fight with her husband, dashing off a cruel missive to him before the rest of the morning's festivities commence. Wyatt reads it, maybe fifteen or twenty minutes later, and it sets him off all over again, enough to turn him back around toward home. She needs to find this message to know for sure, otherwise she has nothing but conjecture.

Back in their bedroom, she observes Wyatt's prone form beneath the light sheet. Slow, even breaths indicate he's still sleeping deeply. His phone is within easy reach. She even knows his passcode. He isn't as smart about hiding it as he thinks. Nadia would bet anything that message is still resting deep within his inbox. She can imagine him returning to it now and again as a way to water his dubious tree of rationalization. Though she can just as easily imagine Wyatt convincing himself that no matter what his intentions had been when he returned home that morning, he did her a mercy when he found her grievously injured.

Listening carefully for any movement or changes in his breathing pattern, she creeps over to the bedside, nabs the phone, and retreats to the bathroom to do her searching. His email is well organized, everything divided into various subfolders for work, social networks, newsletters, spam, and another one that piques her interest immediately: wife. She taps on that, and a long list of emails bearing Phoebe's address pop up before her, but she's interested in only the one at the very top, the last email Phoebe ever sent her husband. "Good-bye."

"Thank you for making it easy for me," she whispers. Steeling herself, Nadia opens it.

Wyatt,
I had a nicer letter planned for you, but after what happened this morning, I'm no longer feeling so charitable. I'm leaving you. In just a short while I'll be headed halfway across the

world with someone who on his worst day makes my blood pump harder than you did on your best one. Hope you find the baby breeder you've always dreamed of, with a taste for jazz and a much higher tolerance for mediocrity. If I had any advice to offer you in your next relationship, I'd say try not to nearly stab her. Trust me, it won't go over well.

—P

Nadia reads the letter at least half a dozen times, engraving it in her mind, feeling sicker with every passing second. Phoebe must have been referring to the incident with the broken mug. At least Wyatt had been honest about that part. It's probably the closest he'll ever get to an actual confession.

Before finishing with the phone, she forwards a copy of the message to herself, careful to erase the trail.

When she returns the phone to Wyatt's nightstand, she notices he's flipped onto his other side since she went into the bathroom, and one of his arms has strayed to her side of the bed, likely searching for her in his sleep like he often does. Thankfully he didn't wake up wondering where she'd gone. He won't find her back in the bed now, if ever.

She goes out onto the veranda overlooking the water, curls up on the chaise and begins considering her future. After an hour, despite her best efforts to remain awake, the waves create a strong enough lullaby and she sleeps again.

· · ·

T HIS IS THE first time I've thought of you in a while, but you were bound to haunt me today. It's our anniversary. I might have gone the whole day without realizing it if my phone hadn't reminded me this morning. I've removed the entry from my calendar so that next year, I might be able to let this date pass in blissful ignorance, because the memories I'm having now are more recent ones I'd rather go on forgetting.

I didn't think I would ever be able to lose sight of past events. I thought they would stay lit up in the forefront of my mind like a neon sign; but the longer I'm here, the more it all starts to feel like something I saw in a movie. It helps that Nadia and I don't talk about it. We seem to do best by staying anchored firmly in the present, though I find myself drifting a bit farther ahead, wondering what's next for us, if she might share a dream for a family life you didn't want.

I don't think she realizes the significance of this day, and I would feel awkward telling her. It's probably a good idea to keep it to myself, like the other things I still haven't worked up the nerve to confess. I've come close a few times. We'll be in the middle of a great conversation or taking in an incredible view together, and a thought gets into my head that she would understand why I did what I did. She would forgive me, because she's also taken a life, and because she's the kind of person who can look at a soul stripped nearly naked, revealing all its warts and scars, and barely flinch. That fearlessness is what I love most about her. She's the version of you that would have come to be if Daniel had been absent from your life, or if your two sisters had been there for one another from the beginning.

And that's why, as badly as I want to tell her what really happened that morning, to clear my conscience once and for all, I stop short. She's your sister, and even though she never knew you, she feels a bond. So much of this new journey of hers has been for you.

I also think of Vicki and how I led everyone to believe it was she who'd used that knife. That's the biggest rub of all, more unforgivable than all the rest. I'm not sure I can forgive myself, though I do know that the man who did these things is not the man I know, not the man standing here now a whole ocean away from a place he will gladly never see again.

You'd be furious to hear me say that what I did to Vicki was worse than what I did to you. Some days I succeed in convincing myself I was doing you a kindness, stopping the pain, ending the misery. But that opens another door—whose pain and misery was I ending, really? Because I was beyond fury when I stormed back into our house that day, so angry at you for destroying us. And I know deep down that's why I ended rather than saved you.

Some things are better off staying buried. Eventually they break down and become one with the earth again. Like you. Like that long internal scream I've been holding on to since the day I walked into the house and saw her standing there. It's barely more than a whisper now. Soon it'll be gone, and although it still hurts me a little to say this, and that I should be grateful for everything you left behind that made this new life possible for Nadia and me, I hope you will go with it.

EPILOGUE

THE SUN IS now high in the sky and the cold waves roll across her feet as she relishes the salty air and solitude for an all-too-brief moment, though she reminds herself that soon, it will be just her again. Wyatt is back at the table with Fernando and Mercedes, a couple they've been spending a lot of time with lately. They're young and beautiful and extremely rich, like everyone else in Ibiza. Nadia didn't think that could ever get boring, but she's now craving something more rustic. Not a farm—she will never be ready for another farm—but a place with more green and gray than blue and gold. A place where every third car isn't a Lamborghini. Scotland, maybe.

"Everything all right?" She doesn't flinch even a little at the sound of his voice. He doesn't scare her, even after what she discovered a week ago. She doesn't believe Wyatt would ever hurt her, despite what she's now all but certain he did to Phoebe.

"I'm fine," she says. "Just wanted a little air."

"Dessert's on its way."

"Thanks. I'll be back up soon."

He kisses her shoulder before returning to their table. Fernando and Mercedes are having an influence on him. They're affectionate in a way that should be obnoxious, but they somehow make it cute, and Mercedes just announced her first pregnancy over dinner, which put immediate stars in Wyatt's eyes. It's why Nadia had to step away.

She glances about a quarter mile up this beach to study a house that has fascinated her since their arrival in Ibiza. It's the concrete fortress of a dubious merchant who is likely a drug cartel member. The security is far beyond any she's attempted to skirt before. Electric fencing, cameras everywhere. And that's before you get to the human and canine guards. But she wonders, if she did make her way inside, what little trinket she would take. What dark secrets she might find. It isn't the first time she's had these thoughts about a house since setting out to see the world, but the more she detaches herself mentally from Wyatt's orbit, the more regularly those thoughts visit. So does the quiet but persistent voice reminding her that the curious little thief inside her never went away, and she won't be satisfied much longer in this narrow box Nadia has stuffed her into. She knows herself well enough to believe this would be true even if she were still ignorant about Wyatt's deeds. Her heart quickens as she imagines the collection of stuff she might amass on a solo backpacking adventure across Europe.

Don't let that feeling go again. The more you ignore it, the more numb you'll get.

After spending last week making tentative plans, though still feeling indecisive, their friends' pregnancy announcement—or more accurately, Wyatt's reaction to it—helped seal the deal. She pulls out her phone and loads her travel app. Five minutes later, she's booked a flight to Edinburgh leaving tomorrow morning. A single ticket, one way. The next thing she does is a bit more complicated in its reasoning, but equally as compelling as sneaking off to Scotland in the wee hours.

She opens a message draft she typed out a few days ago, mostly just to see how it would make her feel. The words made her a little woozy then, and they do now too, but there's something else under that. A heart-pounding rush she used to get before she broke into a haze, or when she decided to strike out for Lake Forest to meet her sister. Pure anticipation.

Callahan Farms in Monticello, IN. You'll find a blue car nearby. Also check the livestock pits. To that she adds Phoebe's final email to Wyatt, the location of the knife (she'd returned it to the block on the kitchen island), and one more very important detail: a certain picture she'd told Wyatt she'd deleted, but hadn't quite. She erased it from her phone, yes, but not from the email she'd backed it up to. Because as Wyatt so accurately said, nothing is safe in the digital age, especially with people like her around. He might have done the same, but it doesn't really matter now.

When she's satisfied with the message, she adds the recipient: Detective Bob Kelly. The farm is out of his jurisdiction, but she's sure he can make something happen. Her thumb hovering briefly over "send," she reminds herself that if she does this, she's doing the equivalent of lighting a match to the life she once tumbled into a pile of dead pigs to claim.

And can she really do this to Wyatt? They had each other's back, and it was starting to seem like there was something real between them. Then she remembers Vicki, and the way he pushed every button and pulled every lever to bring her to the brink. Jake too, for that matter. They both paid a price. Wyatt should too.

She sends the message. Her heart doesn't quicken even a little, as if she'd finally found peace at the precipice. Perhaps she'll also have to answer for her sins one day, but they'll have to work harder to catch her first.

If Nadia has learned anything about herself in the last year, it's that she's pretty good at replacing old lives with new ones. Her sister's was fun while it lasted, but it's time to give it back—minus a few dollars and souvenirs, of course. She's been siphoning off a little cash here and there for a rainy-day fund. It's currently stashed in a pair of boots in her closet. There should be enough time to add to that between now and when she fully slips into her next to-be-determined identity. Maybe she'll make a quick trip into town for a few groceries and a sizeable withdrawal.

She returns to the table, where Fernando has begun singing a Spanish serenade to the new mother-to-be. A tray of coffee and cookies sits in the middle of the table. Nadia has seen and admired this service set many times before. The little sugar spoon in particular is her favorite, with the beautiful jade inlay in the handle. She reaches for the dish and uses the spoon to add some sugar to her coffee.

Wyatt notices this and gives her a funny look. "You're taking sugar now?"

She shrugs. "Figured I'd try something different." When he turns back to watch Fernando's performance, and she's sure no one else will notice, Nadia slips the spoon into her pocket.

ACKNOWLEDGEMENTS

For as solitary a profession as writing is believed to be, it's impossible for one person to do all the work it takes to deliver a book to the hands of you wonderful readers. And you are the ones I would like to thank first, because without you, this book that so many incredible people helped midwife into the world would have nowhere to go.

I must thank my husband, Ken, who believed in me from the moment I told him way back in 2008 that I was ready to start writing stories again. Since then, he has given me the space, patience, and understanding it takes to live with someone whose mind is often consumed with the fictional lives of others. My kids, Nat and Elias, deserve many of those same props as well. Thank you for heroically dealing with your absentminded mom.

I would also like to thank the amazing staff at the Washington Township Starbucks, who eventually came to know me by name, thanks to the nice workspace and delicious espressos they provided when I was churning away on the revisions for this book. They had no idea what I was working on, but now they do.

Speaking of patience, my agent, Stephanie Rostan, deserves all the gold stars and more for bearing with me through the multiple drafts it took just to get this book ready for submission. She saw the diamond buried deep within a rough draft no one would recognize as the book you just read, and by some miracle, we managed to unearth that sucker so others could see it. And a shoutout must go to her lovely colleague Sarah Bedingfield, who came in with countless crucial assists and manuscript comments that made the diamond sparkle all the more. I can't be more grateful for all the people at Levine Greenberg Rostan for making this whirlwind of a book sale feel completely manageable and streamlined. That includes Beth Fisher for all her work on the foreign rights side and Jasmine Lake at UTA on the screen rights.

But I can't possibly talk about patience and diamonds without mentioning my jewel of a friend and my main beta reader for this project, April Gooding. She read every single draft (save for the final ones, because I wanted to keep some surprises for her) with an enthusiasm that kept me going through my most discouraged points, and a sharp eye that kept me on my toes. My support team also includes Tiffany Kelly (and her husband, Bill, an ex-cop who provided the namesake for a certain detective in this story!), who kept me smiling and looking ahead during the long road of revisions and publication. And I cannot forget the tireless love and support from my parents, John and Lisa McWilliam. They taught me more than a little something about the importance of a good work ethic, and they always gave me room and encouragement to let my dark imagination unfurl itself.

I would like to thank Aja Pollock for her gimlet eye with the copyediting, and for reminding me how much I've forgotten about grammar since my school years. Thanks also must go to the incredible art department responsible for their stunning work on the jacket. Thank you also to the wonderful marketing teams at Putnam in the US and Sphere in the UK.

And finally, I must talk about the loveliest editorial dream team an author could ever hope for: Margo Lipschultz at Putnam and Viola Hayden at Sphere. From my very first phone conversation with each of them, I knew they were the ones who would be able to rocket *The Other Mrs. Miller* to the next level, and the way everything came together meant I had the immense privilege of working with them in tandem on this book. Watching these ladies enhance each other's strengths, bounce ideas back and forth, and become friends during the process has been more rewarding than I can say. I hope a day comes when I can be with both of them in the same room, though I'm not sure the world is ready for that much concentrated awesome in one place.

If you had a blast reading this book, these people deserve so much of the credit. If you didn't, or you found other errors, please send the blame my way. The people tasked with making me look good enough for the public are still human beings, and they were given a tough job. I cannot express enough how hard they worked, and how their belief in me inspired me to push myself to places as a writer I never thought I could go. I will never forget this experience.